Praise for Colleen Cambridge and the Phyllida Bright mystery series

"Two words describe this book: absolutely delicious. . . . A near-perfect traditional mystery." —*First Clue*

"What if Agatha Christie's housekeeper was the best detective of all? In this delightful book, she is! You will love watching Phyllida spot the clues the authorities miss when a dead body shows up in Agatha's library." —Victoria Thompson, *USA Today* bestselling author of *Murder on Wall Street*

"Cambridge weaves in just the right amount of historical detail and references to classic Christie novels while placing Phyllida and her intelligent sleuthing skills front and center. . . . Dame Agatha would be proud." —*Publishers Weekly*

"Cambridge balances *Downton Abbey*–style period charm with a tight plot that twists and turns right until the end, with utter believability. . . .The real-life historical players make only brief cameos, but Cambridge creates such a compelling cast of fictional characters that they are hardly missed. Reminiscent of Jessica Ellicott's Beryl and Edwina series, this novel will please readers with its historical world and a plot that would satisfy Poirot." —*Library Journal*

"Agatha Christie the person plays a very peripheral part in the proceedings, but Agatha Christie the writer haunts every page of this delightful book that both pays homage to the Queen of Crime, but also embroiders on her work with a fresh character and a fresh look at a part of her life. This is a wonderful series debut."
—*Mystery Scene*

"Finally it can be told: One of Agatha Christie's most popular novels was inspired by a murder at her (fictional) manor house solved by her (fictional) housekeeper. . . . Christie fans can expect a series." —*Kirkus Reviews*

"Charmingly told, with a full upstairs-downstairs cast of guests and servants. . . . Fans of Agatha Christie, historical fiction and fierce female leads are all sure to enjoy." —*Shelf Awareness*

"A good cozy to read with a cup of tea on the
—*New York Journal*

"Excellent." —*Mystery &*

Please turn the page

"Delicious fun—would a writer kill to be published?—and the locked-room mystery is a homage to the queen of crime herself."
—*Historical Novel Society*

"Phyllida Bright is the confident, shrewd, and eminently capable housekeeper for none other than the grand dame of mystery herself—Agatha Christie—and a great admirer of Christie's fictional detective Poirot, whose methods she seeks to emulate. Fans of Tessa Arlen and Jennifer Ashley will be delighted." —Anna Lee Huber, *USA Today* bestselling author of the Verity Kent mysteries

"Marple and Poirot have nothing on Agatha Christie's housekeeper, Phyllida Bright." —Alyssa Maxwell, author of A Lady & Lady's Maid mysteries and the Gilded Newport mysteries

"Phyllida Bright, housekeeper to Agatha Christie, has the crime-solving skills to rival her employer's famous detectives. . . . Utterly delightful." —Ashley Weaver, author of the Electra McDonnell mystery series

"It's such a pleasure when the first book in a new mystery series is well-crafted and I look forward to reading more of Phyllida Bright's adventures in detection." —*Criminal Element*

"It's obvious Cambridge had a blast writing the book, set in 1930s Devonshire, and her fun is infectious." —*Historical Novel Society*

"An entertaining whodunnit." —*Toronto.com*

"A British country-house mystery worthy of Dame Agatha herself!"
—Carol Schneck Varner, Schuler Books (Okemos, MI)

"Mrs. Bright is my new favorite amateur detective!" —Lori-Jo Scott, Island Bookstore (Kitty Hawk, NC)

"Great cozy mystery for fans of Agatha Christie and *Downton Abbey*. . . . I hope there is more to come, we need to learn Phyllida Bright's backstory, and where she learned to be such a badass."
—Vikki Bell, Broad Bay Café (Waldoboro, ME)

"A delightful murder mystery! *Murder at Mallowan Hall* felt like a combination of *Clue, Upstairs Downstairs,* and of course Agatha Christie." —Stefanie Lynn, The Kennett Bookhouse (Kennett Square, PA)

"A perfect read that calls for a cup of tea, a cozy blanket, and a warm fire." —Stephanie Skees, The Novel Neighbor (St. Louis, MO)

MURDER BY INVITATION ONLY

Kensington books by
Colleen Cambridge

The Phyllida Bright mystery series

Murder at Mallowan Hall

A Trace of Poison

Murder by Invitation Only

Murder Takes the Stage

An American in Paris mystery series

Mastering the Art of French Murder

A Murder Most French

A Fashionably French Murder

MURDER BY INVITATION ONLY

Colleen Cambridge

www.kensingtonbooks.com

KENSINGTON BOOKS are published by
Kensington Publishing Corp.
900 Third Avenue
New York, NY 10022

All Kensington titles, imprints, and distributed lines are available at special quantity discounts for bulk purchases for sales promotion, premiums, fund-raising, educational, or institutional use.

Special book excerpts or customized printings can also be created to fit specific needs. For details, write or phone the office of the Kensington Sales Manager: Kensington Publishing Corp., 900 Third Avenue, New York, NY 10022. Attn. Sales Department. Phone: 1-800-221-2647.

ISBN: 978-1-4967-4258-2 (ebook)

ISBN: 978-1-4967-4257-5

First Kensington Hardcover Printing: October 2023

First Kensington Trade Paperback Printing: October 2024

10 9 8 7 6 5 4 3 2 1

Printed in the United States of America

"You could get away with a great deal if you had enough audacity."

—A Murder Is Announced

CHAPTER 1

PHYLLIDA BRIGHT WAS DISPLEASED.

She leveled a stern look at the two young women who stood in front of her.

One of them was dripping wet from something that smelled exceedingly unpleasant.

The other was covered with soot and ash.

Both of them had the misfortune of being maids on her staff.

Neither were brave enough to look her in the eye, and in fact both seemed to be trembling in fear of her wrath.

As well they should, for the two of them were about to receive a *severe* talking-to . . . if Phyllida could keep from laughing. They did look ridiculous.

"Explain how this happened," Phyllida said once she gathered her composure. "Ginny, you first."

Ginny, the honey-haired parlormaid with a high-pitched voice, sniffled and pushed back a swath of hair that dripped in her face. Her normally pristine, starched uniform hung wet and awkwardly on her figure and her cap sagged over what had been a neat roll of hair.

"Only, I went out to empty the pail from the library fireplace and the next thing I know, *she* went and dumped a bucket of-of *slop* on me!" Her voice was teary but her eyes shot daggers at Molly, the kitchen maid who stood next to her.

"And therefore you found it necessary to retaliate by throwing a bucket of fireplace debris on her," Phyllida said in an arctic voice.

"No, ma'am, but it was an acci—"

"I didn't mean to, Mrs. Bright," said Molly earnestly, though her voice was also tight with tears. "She got in my way as I was pitching it out."

"I did not!" cried Ginny. "She pretended not to see me, but I know she did!"

"It was an accident, Mrs. Bright," Molly said, her voice breaking with emotion. "I swear it!" She had obviously attempted to wipe some of the ashes from her face but she'd only made it worse, as her cheeks and slender nose were smeared with soot. Her lace cap, still settled on a head of light brown hair, had created a sort of nest for a significant portion of the ash as well.

One good sneeze or bob of her head—or, heaven forbid, a curtsy—and more fireplace remains would be strewn all over. In fact, there was a trail of ash, not to mention dripping water, that had followed the two maids into Phyllida's sitting room—where they had no doubt been directed by Mr. Dobble.

Sent purposely, she was quite certain, for the butler at stately Mallowan Hall—home of Agatha Christie and her husband, Max Mallowan—loathed chintz and lace. Thus, Phyllida was under no illusion that it had been an "accident" that Mr. Dobble had sent the dirty, messy maids to her sitting room. Surely it was one of his not-so-subtle attempts to destroy—or at least damage—said chintz and lace.

And probably to disrupt Stilton and Rye, her cats, as well. Currently, Stilton was sitting gingerly on the back of Phyllida's favorite armchair. Rye, as per usual, was sneering at everyone from his perch on the top of a bookshelf filled with detective novels and reference books on gardening, housekeeping, fashion, and a myriad of other interesting subjects.

Molly went on, "Truly it was an accident, Mrs. Bright. And then she—"

"It was *not* an accident," shrieked Ginny, tears streaming from her eyes. "She did it on purpose! It's all because of—"

"I did *not*!" cried Molly, whipping her head around to glare at the other girl . . . and there it went: Her cap tipped sharply and released its fistful of ash. The soot flew everywhere.

Phyllida stepped back as the messy gray detritus scattered through the air . . . with a good portion of it drifting onto the floor, into the puddle of water dripping from Ginny.

"Out," Phyllida said, clenching her teeth to keep from laughing. *What a kerfuffle!* "Clean yourselves up *immediately* and then you will both return and put this room and the hallway to rights. You will not speak to anyone else, you will not dawdle, and you will return within ten minutes, starched and pressed and ready." She looked pointedly at the watch pinned to the starched white collar of her pale pink frock.

Ginny and Molly fled, unfortunately leaving more dripping and wafting in their respective wakes.

Phyllida looked at the mess in her normally cheery and pristine sitting room with its pink and yellow accents. There was ash everywhere, the place smelled from whatever liquid refuse had been in Molly's bucket, and now the water and the soot were making a lovely soupçon of sludge on the rug in front of her desk. She sighed, the last vestiges of humor evaporating.

She was going to murder Mr. Dobble. And from her time working in the home of Agatha Christie, along with being the detective writer's friend and confidante, Phyllida had many ideas of how to go about doing just that . . . creatively and painfully.

In fact, she could no doubt construct the perfect crime, should it come to that. Even her beloved Hercule Poirot, the finest of Agatha's detectives, wouldn't be able to solve a murder committed by Phyllida Bright.

But instead of giving in to her base urge to hunt down the butler and stab the man with a letter opener or strangle him with an apron string (poison was simply too benign an option in this situation), Phyllida once more collected herself. She was assisted in this tenuous battle for self-control by Stilton, the fluffy white cat with the grayish-blue streaks that had given her her name. Phyllida gathered the feline into her arms and buried her face in the soft fur for a moment.

It had been a very *trying* day. And it was only three o'clock.

Thank heavens the new vacuum machine hadn't arrived yet, or the household would be in even more of a tizzy.

"Yes," she murmured into the cat's neck, "I am very well aware that he did it on purpose."

Normally, Phyllida and Mr. Dobble got on well enough. They both had the same goal: running Mallowan Hall in such a way that made Mrs. Agatha and Mr. Max comfortable, pleased, and proud. Mr. Dobble was responsible for the footmen and the outdoor staff—the chauffeur, the gardener, and the man-of-all-work—and Phyllida's domain was the house, including the maids and kitchen. Normally, they managed their respective tasks without conflict.

But every so often, she and the butler did not see eye to eye. Only this morning the two of them had had a bit of a set-to regarding whether the massive walnut grandfather clock should be moved in order to wash the wallpaper behind it.

Phyllida insisted it be moved. How on earth could one expect to *clean* the area well enough without getting behind it or under it?

But Mr. Dobble, who was usually as exacting as she was about thoroughness, did not see fit to allow his footmen, Stanley and Freddie, to take the time to move the monstrosity.

Phyllida and the butler had had quite a seething discussion about it—fortunately, in the privacy of his pantry—and then, in a rather sharp about-face, Mr. Dobble threw up his hands. He suggested that the clock not only be moved, but be completely *re*moved from its location and either sold or destroyed with an axe he offered to provide . . . a solution which was not only ridiculous and uncharacteristic, but supremely unhelpful.

At that point, Phyllida had prudently removed herself from the butler's pantry in favor of a bracing cup of Earl Grey. It was either that or raise her voice, something she rarely allowed herself to do . . . even when messy, dripping maids invaded her sitting room on the orders of Harvey Dobble.

Instead, she'd sipped said tea—which, sadly, was devoid of the rye whisky she favored—then rang for Elton.

Elton was Mr. Max's valet, but he was rarely kept very busy in that role, and instead was more often conscripted to assist with other household activities. In fact, Mr. Max and Mrs. Agatha were in London at the moment, and Elton had been left behind simply because his master hadn't seen the need for him to accompany them. This was not a surprise, as Mr. Max was an archaeologist and quite used to doing for himself when on digs. The only reason Elton had joined the staff at Mallowan Hall was that Phyllida had recently proven him innocent of murder, whilst at the same time angering his previous boss, who sacked Elton in a fit of pique. Mr. Max had been kind enough to take him on, although Phyllida had thought more than once that a valet was superfluous for her employer.

Elton was more than happy to help move the grandfather clock, he told Phyllida eagerly when he arrived for her summons.

And that, she realized belatedly, was where she'd gone wrong.

If she'd just kept Elton out of the entire situation, neither Ginny nor Molly would have encountered him today . . . and then the two maids wouldn't have had their "accidental" mishaps. Phyllida was under no misapprehension about the cause of the incidents being simple clumsiness or inattention.

All of the maids had been mooning over the handsome and gentlemanly Elton and attempting to get his attention since he'd joined the household. And poor Stanley, the footman who'd been usurped from his throne as a favorite of the maids, now mooned about with a bewildered expression on his face. Fortunately, the two young men hadn't descended into the sort of feuding demonstrated by the maids—at least not yet.

Love—especially young love, and even more especially young infatuation—was one of the inevitable consequences in a household of younger staff members.

Phyllida released Stilton onto the cozy gold chair and its yellow and spring-green chintz pillow—which was untouched by the soot and slop, despite Dobble's attempts to the contrary. She could barely remember being that young and infatuated with a male person—and even when she had been, she would never have stooped to pouring slop or soot on a perceived rival.

She would have been much more subtle about it.

A trickle of long-tucked-away memories prompted a smile as she skirted the puddle of sludge that was seeping into the rug. Oh, she definitely would have been more subtle than tossing a bucket of ashes on someone.

As she came out of her small suite of rooms, Phyllida discerned the hurried footsteps pounding down the back stairs from the attic, where the maids had their rooms and wash basins. The green baize door, which separated the servants' passageways from the "public" area of the house, swung open and Molly and Ginny burst through.

Even as they did so, Phyllida saw Molly's elbow jam into Ginny's side, and Ginny's knee ram into the back of Molly's leg, sending the latter stumbling. Molly caught herself, and, with fire in her eyes, rushed to catch up with the other maid.

But what could have been a continued tussle ended as soon as Molly saw Phyllida. Her eyes went wide and she skidded to a halt, shoulders straight and hands coming to her middle. Ginny was nearly as quick at changing direction and intention, and thus Phyllida was faced with two panting but neatly dressed and coiffed young women.

After a good, long, pregnant silence—during which he suppressed an exasperated smile—she spoke. "I am disappointed in both of you, being senior maids and setting an example for the others. And over a *man.*

"Oh, don't think I don't know what precipitated your mishaps this afternoon," she went on when Ginny opened her mouth to protest. "Believe me when I say, men are simply not worth wasting such energy. Now, clean up the mess you have made."

With that, she turned neatly and walked away.

It was time to deal with Mr. Dobble.

But before Phyllida could make her way to the butler—who would likely be hiding out in his pantry, chortling over his master plan of destroying all occurrences of chintz and lace in the house—she was hailed by the first footman.

"Mrs. Bright," said Stanley, hurrying up to her. He was a good-looking lad, but before Elton's appearance on the scene, he'd taken serious advantage of that fact by flirting outrageously with the maids. Now, he'd become more subdued and, if Phyllida read things correctly, the footman was nursing a bruised heart due to Ginny's conspicuous interest in Elton. "This just came."

"Is it from the vacuum company?" she said, but then noticed the thick, expensive envelope. It was certainly not from Vac-Tric, which had been supposed to deliver a brand-new vacuum machine from London today.

"I don't think so, ma'am," Stanley said. "But I did hear from Mr. Wheatley that there's a bridge out between here and London, and it's stopped a lot of traffic. They think it might be another day before it's fixed up."

"I see. That likely explains the delay, then."

Stanley cleared his throat and shifted from one foot to the other.

Phyllida looked at him. "Is there something else, Stanley?"

"Erm . . . yes, ma'am. I-I just wanted to say that I would have been happy to help move the grandfather clock, ma'am. It's only, Mr. Dobble, he set me to polishing the tea- and coffee pots again."

"Of course, Stanley. I'm certain Mr. Dobble had his reasons." Which, of course, were to torment her.

"Thank you, ma'am," he said, then gave a little bow.

Nodding, Phyllida turned her attention to the thick, creamy envelope. She noted with surprise that there was no addressee on the exterior, only the words *Mallowan Hall.* A blue wax blob sealed it closed, but there was no discernible coat of arms or signet on the impression.

"How strange," she said, then called after the footman. "Stanley, who delivered it? Did they give an indication for whom it was intended?"

"No, ma'am," he replied, turning back. "They just brought it and went off before I could ask. They was on a bicycle."

"Very well," replied Phyllida. She examined the envelope more closely but found nothing that might give a clue as to who the message was from or to.

The problem of Mr. Dobble set aside for the moment, Phyllida dismissed Stanley and decided she could certainly justify opening the envelope. After all, when one delivers an unaddressed envelope, one ought to expect *anyone* to open it. If it was for Mrs. Agatha or Mr. Max she could ring them up in London and tell them about it.

There was a single card inside and it appeared to be an invitation. Phyllida's eyes widened when she read the words typed on it:

ANNOUNCEMENT

A Murder will Occur

Tonight

Beecham House

7 pm precisely

Regrets Only

CHAPTER 2

How extraordinary, thought Phyllida, rereading the strange invitation. She was immediately intrigued while also being horrified.

Was this some sort of game?

A warning?

Was this a clumsy—albeit creative—attempt by a journalist or other detective writer to gain Mrs. Agatha's attention?

Or was it a threat? And if so, who was being threatened?

And more importantly, for whom at Mallowan Hall was the invitation intended? Anyone in particular, or everyone?

Considering the fact that there'd been a number of murders in the last several months at Mallowan Hall and in the neighboring village, she could only hope that it *was* a game or a joke of some kind. And although Phyllida was a fanatic about detective novels, she also was acutely sensitive that murder and, indeed, any sort of death, was not a laughing matter or a topic of jokery.

Still thoughtful, she walked down the corridor to the telephone, and moments later, was placing a call to Mrs. Agatha and Mr. Max's London home. It was getting on to teatime, so presumably they would be in residence.

"Why, hello, Phyllida!" Agatha's cheery voice came over the line. "Is everything fine out there in Devonshire?"

Phyllida assured her friend and employer that everything was well in hand at Mallowan Hall, disheveled maids and their mishaps notwithstanding. Then she went on to tell Agatha about the anonymous invitation that had arrived.

"An announcement of a murder?" exclaimed Agatha. "Why, that's quite extraordinary, isn't it?"

As Phyllida had had exactly the same thought, she made concurring noises. "I can't quite determine whether it's a jest or some sort of game . . . or something more sinister."

"You're going to attend, of course," Agatha said, as if the matter was completely settled. When Phyllida began to protest, she overrode her firmly. "Well *someone* ought to go, and as Max and I are in London *and*, as you know, I am not at all interested in real-life murders—which, one certainly hopes there won't actually *be* one, but one never can tell in this day and age—you are arguably the most qualified person to attend a murder." She gave a short laugh. "After all, you're beginning to rival my snobby little Poirot when it comes to solving killings, aren't you?"

Since no one was about to notice, Phyllida couldn't help but preen just a little at the compliment. Being favorably compared to Hercule Poirot was the greatest of compliments.

Agatha's voice had changed to something more thoughtful as she mused further. "The announcement of a murder . . . how exceedingly intriguing, in a ghastly sort of way."

"One can hope it's not a real murder," Phyllida reminded her.

"Perhaps it's going to be one of those murder games," Agatha said. "Where everyone sits around the table and one person is the killer and he or she winks at people to 'kill' them, and one has to try and determine who the killer is."

"One can only hope that is the explanation," Phyllida replied, but she realized from her employer's distant tone that Agatha was no longer thinking only about the issue at hand.

"Imagine that. A murder being portended—or announced!—ahead of time . . . *A murder is announced* . . . why, that would be quite an intriguing title for a book, wouldn't it? Good heavens! Why didn't I think of it before?" Although the telephone line was scratchy, Phyllida could hear the sounds of Agatha scrabbling about for one of her ever-present notebooks. Despite the situation, she couldn't suppress a smile. Her employer found inspiration for her detective novels all over the place and from many day-to-day conversations.

"It would certainly attract attention—a title such as that," Phyllida said. She knew better than to interrupt Agatha when she was in the process of making notes.

"Yes, yes, I need to jot this down so I don't forget . . . a murder is announced ahead of time. Perhaps one could even take out a classified advertisement," she murmured. "That would cause quite the stir, wouldn't it? Especially if it were in a small village where everyone gets the paper."

"I should say," Phyllida agreed. She waited a few moments as Agatha made her notes.

"Very well. Yes. That's quite good. *Quite* intriguing," Agatha said, still sounding a bit distant. Then she seemed to gather herself. "Now, where were we? Oh, yes, the murder. You ought to go, Phyllida. In fact, I insist you attend. Only to find out what it's all about."

"The announcement gives the location as Beecham House," Phyllida said, relieved to have her friend's full attention once more. "Do you know the people there?"

"Beecham House . . . why, they're new, aren't they? They've just rented the place if I recall correctly. Can't summon the name . . . drat it, I've got too many suspects' names in my head already, and Max is out so I can't ask him. But surely you can find out more about them. I know how all the downstairs folk talk between houses," Agatha said with a chuckle. "One can only suppose your maids have spoken to *their* maids and have all of the gossip already."

Phyllida was inclined to agree. She would certainly be speaking to her staff shortly to find out what they knew about the new residents of Beecham House. "You and Mr. Max haven't met the people, then?"

"No, no, I don't believe so . . ." Agatha's voice trailed off. "Do you think they meant to invite us as a way of getting to know me?"

Agatha was the most famous person in the neighboring village of Listleigh and its environs. She was also extremely protective of her privacy, especially since her infamous eleven-day disappearance during the difficult separation from her first husband, Archie. Since then, she'd shied away from publicity and only did limited interviews with the press—a position Phyllida most certainly understood.

When one had mysterious or questionable events in one's past, one tended to seek anonymity . . . perhaps even by moving to the country and taking on a service job.

"I thought I would ring up some of the other houses nearby to see if they received a similar message," Phyllida replied, and wondered briefly if that was why Mr. Dobble was in such a fine fettle. Perhaps Mr. Billdop had elected to attend the murder instead of playing their weekly chess game. But she immediately dismissed that as unlikely. The regular chess game was as ensconced in his weekly schedule as Christmas on the twenty-fifth of December.

"Excellent plan. One hopes the announcement wasn't limited to the Mallowan household," Agatha said dryly.

"I should hope not," Phyllida replied. "I can't imagine what they will think when *I* arrive instead of the infamous Agatha Christie."

"Oh, it should be quite entertaining," Agatha said with a laugh. "I only wish I could be there. You will ring me tomorrow and tell me all about it, won't you?"

"Certainly," Phyllida replied. And it was at that moment that she realized she had less than three hours before she had to leave for the "murder," and there were a number of tasks she must accomplish before then.

So much for a quiet evening in her sitting room with a detective novel and her cats.

"You're going to a *what*?" Mr. Dobble said. He drew his tall, slender self up into an even more ramrod-straight figure. The shallow dent in the hairless scalp above his left ear seemed even more pronounced today. "Why, that's preposterous, Mrs. Bright. Surely you don't think—"

"Perhaps you would prefer to attend the gathering in my stead?" said Phyllida in an exceedingly sweet voice. "Oh, but I'd nearly forgotten . . . tonight is your chess night with the vicar. You're obviously otherwise engaged."

The look Mr. Dobble gave her was a cross between silently deadly and pained. "I will not be visiting with the vicar tonight," he said stiffly.

Phyllida managed to hide her surprise. There was obviously something amiss.

Nonetheless, she didn't reply to this pronouncement, but instead tucked the bit of information away in her mind. Perhaps that was the explanation for Mr. Dobble's unusually erratic and preposterous behavior earlier.

"At any rate, Mrs. Agatha requested I attend the—er—event at Beecham House," she went on. "Apparently they are new. Have you heard any information about them?"

Mr. Dobble seemed relieved by the change of subject. "Jeremy Trifle has been the butler there for many years. I understand the new people are merely leasing the place and have brought in some other staff."

"Do you have their names or any other information about the household?" Phyllida asked.

"I believe the name is Wokesley," replied Dobble, then his brows drew together in thought. "And perhaps he is some sort of theatrical person. Yes, I do believe that is what Mr. Trifle said. A theatrical sort of bloke . . . but something about sheep, too, if I'm remembering."

Theatrical? Well, that went along with the dramatic murder announcement. She couldn't figure the sheep element, however.

"Perhaps you could ring him to find out whether others were invited or whether it was only Mrs. Agatha and Mr. Max," she said, knowing full well that the invoking of their employers' names would deflate any argument he might wish to make. "Mrs. Agatha fears it is merely a way for them to meet her."

"I suppose I could do so," replied Mr. Dobble ungraciously.

"That will be most helpful. I will be leaving at six in order to arrive in plenty of time. I will of course require the motor," Phyllida informed him.

"Of course you will," he replied, his lips pursing as if he tasted something sour. "There is a bicycle available, Mrs. Bright. You might avail yourself of that mode of transport."

"Definitely not." Phyllida stood from where she'd brazenly taken an uninvited seat across from the desk.

"And what about that vacuum machine?" He looked down his nose at her.

Mr. Dobble was not at all in favor of any sort of device that might make the staff's tasks easier or more efficient. Perhaps that was why he'd been so determined to stymie her with the grandfather clock: His nose was out of joint over the excitement and trepidation of the vacuum machine's arrival. It was all the maids had been talking about for weeks—besides Elton.

"It has not arrived yet, as I'm certain you are well aware," she replied.

"Indeed . . . for I'm quite certain the sound of it would have disrupted every corner of the house." His expression was as sour as his words.

"Well, we shall certainly find out when it arrives, won't we?" Phyllida said brightly. "One more thing, Mr. Dobble. Should there be a messy incident between any of the staff in the future, it would be in the best interest of everyone involved not to send the individuals to my apartments in their state of dishevelment."

"Oh, dear," replied Mr. Dobble in a patently false tone of apology. "How could I have been so shortsighted? It must have been quite a disaster."

"Never fear," she replied. "Every bit of the chintz and lace in my parlor is still fully intact."

His expression soured, then eased. "That is excellent news." His gaze lifted, then hovered at a location above her eyes, holding a suspicious gleam. "Good heavens, Mrs. Bright. Surely that isn't a bit of soot in your hair . . . oh, dear. It certainly is. You best not shake your head, for it might get in your eyes."

Phyllida stilled and ferociously fought back the flush she knew was flooding her pale cheeks. Although she didn't have the freckles that often accompanied red hair, she did have light skin that was always in danger of exhibiting her emotions.

"Of course," she replied, then gestured casually toward her hair. "My point has clearly been made. Perhaps the next time, the instigators will find their way to your pantry instead." And with that pointed threat, she carried herself regally from the room.

She went directly to the nearest mirror and was horrified by the mess on her person. Somehow Molly had managed to transfer a good portion of ash to Phyllida's light and bright-colored hair. It was a unique hue of strawberryish-gold, leaning more toward the pink-red end of the spectrum. The color, as well as her newly fashionable chin-length style, was a cause of consternation to the butler, who believed every female ought to dress and coif as if she were Queen Victoria in mourning.

Since the queen was long dead and Phyllida didn't care a fig for Mr. Dobble's fashion opinions, she made it a point to keep her wavy hair arranged with sparkling combs or pins instead of covered by a cap, as the butler surely desired she would.

Unfortunately, he'd been correct in suggesting she shouldn't shake her head, for there was a peach-pit-sized clump of ash sitting precariously on a curl just over her left eyebrow. Muttering to herself, she gently disengaged the debris, grateful no one else had seen her in such a state of disarray. Especially Bradford, the chauffeur.

He would have had plenty to say about her dishevelment.

The thought of having to ride in the motor with him to Beecham House put quite a damper on the entire situation.

Phyllida rang over to the Rollingbrokes at Wilding House, and then to Miss Pankhurst, the grocer in town. Both households had received the same strange announcement in the same manner, and it appeared that the residents would be attending.

Satisfied that the announcement wasn't only a ruse to meet Agatha Christie, Phyllida returned to her apartments to find that Ginny and Molly had come and gone, and that everything was back in order, polished, swept, and mopped.

What to do about them and their rivalry was something else to which she'd have to attend, but for now she had plenty to do before leaving.

Someone knocked on the edge of the open door. "Mrs. Bright?"

"Come," she said, settling in her seat behind the desk.

It was Molly, and she carried a tray. Phyllida suspected it was an apology, for on the tray was not only a small pink teapot and matching cup of delicate china but an array of pastries, including something she hadn't seen in the kitchen earlier today: a strawberry cream scone. One of her favorites, as Mrs. Puffley, the cook, and everyone else well knew.

Also on the tray were two thumb-sized catnip biscuits.

It was definitely an apology.

"Thank you," she said briskly. "Set it there, if you please."

Phyllida took great care not to exhibit any favoritism among members of her staff, but she admitted privately that Molly was, in fact, one of her favorites. Normally, the young woman was attentive, neat, and efficient in her work, and she rarely gossiped. If one were to be honest, Ginny was also a favorite as well—for the same reasons. Which was why Phyllida was particularly annoyed by their rivalry.

"Yes, ma'am," Molly said with a brief curtsy. She did as directed and was about to take her leave when Phyllida stopped her.

"Molly, do you know anything about the new family up at Beecham House?"

A wave of relief swept the younger woman's face and her shoulders shifted down from where they'd crept up nearer her shoulders. "Aye—I mean to say, yes, ma'am."

"And . . . ?" Phyllida prodded when Molly hesitated.

"Well, Mrs. Bright, I hear they seem nice enough—though not as nice as Mrs. Agatha and Mr. Max. It's a man and his wife. No children—or at least, none there. Wokesley is the name."

"What do the staff think of them?" asked Phyllida as she added a more generous amount of sugar to her tea than was prudent. But it had been a very trying day, and she was about to attend some sort of murder, so a woman had to have some sort of sustenance.

"The housekeeper is come from London, and the maids are mostly from hereabouts," Molly replied. "Louise, who was at Gothing Hall, is there now—the parlormaid—and she says it's all fine and they're not so bad as masters and mistresses go. But she said how once the wife's brother was visiting and he got a little handsy, so she takes care not to be caught in the bedchambers changing sheets when he's about, though."

Phyllida's lips firmed. If there was one thing she didn't abide, it was a "handsy" man in the household. Or anywhere. Aside from that there was the question as to why the first parlormaid was changing sheets in the bedchambers. "Is there anything else you can remember?"

"No, ma'am. Not really. The housekeeper—well, she's all right, Louise says, though she's from an agency in London and don't seem to know a thing about country living. And the footman is too short to be in the job, but there he is anyway." Molly shrugged. Then her expression changed into one of wonderment and confusion. "Only, did you know that Opal wants to be a footman?"

Phyllida didn't pause from lifting the teacup to her lips, but her eyebrows rose in surprise. "Is that so?"

Opal Stamm was a relatively new addition to the household. She'd replaced Rebecca, the kitchen maid who'd been murdered in the orchard behind Mallowan Hall only a month ago. Opal was a sturdy, hardworking girl of fourteen with an earnest disposition. If Phyllida *were* inclined to have favorites, she would likely include Opal as another one of them, for the girl was impeccable when it came to getting her scullery tasks completed. As well, she was thoughtful and neatly groomed and had some semblance of a brain.

Molly was shaking her head over the strangeness of such a concept. "I told her, didn't I, that a girl can't be a footman, but she wouldn't listen. You'll have to talk to her, Mrs. Bright. She was looking at Freddie's livery in the laundry room, holding it up to herself because they're almost of a size, and I thought to myself, she'd be putting it on if I wasn't here to see her, she would."

"Very well, Molly. Thank you for all of that information. Surely you're needed in the kitchen by now." Phyllida gave her a knowing look. "Even though Mrs. Agatha and Mr. Max aren't here, dinner must still be prepared and served."

"Yes, Mrs. Bright." Molly gave a proper curtsy, then took her leave.

Phyllida shared the catnip treats with Stilton and Rye, the latter of whom deigned to make his way down from the bookshelf, and then she enjoyed her strawberry cream scone . . . all the while thinking about an announcement of murder.

Whether it portended a game or some sort of theatrical production, there was one thing for certain: People were bound to show up at Beecham House tonight.

"A murder is it, Mrs. Bright?" said Bradford as he navigated the Mallowans' Daimler sedan down the drive. It was a few minutes after six. "Seems right up your street."

Phyllida, who'd found herself sitting in the front seat instead of in the rear where she could pretend to ignore such banal commentary, decided to ignore him anyway. She would have climbed into the back initially, but Bradford had already had the front passenger door of the motor open for her when she came out.

She'd decided it would be far better not to argue or comment.

Aside from that, she often got queasy when riding down the narrow, curving roads of the countryside, and it was worse when she sat in the rear. She didn't want to arrive at Beecham House feeling under the weather.

But after a few moments of silence, Phyllida found it necessary to respond to his annoying and provocative comment. "I'm quite certain it's not meant to be a *real* murder. Surely it's simply one of those games. After all, who *announces* a murder in advance?"

"A madman," he murmured thoughtfully. "Or perhaps one

who is very cunning and smart. Either way, the ever-capable Mrs. Bright will be present on the scene to snoop—er, investigate."

"You may make your little jests, but I'm quite confident my investigative skills won't be called into practice tonight," Phyllida said.

After the most recent events at the Murder Fête—when two people had ended up poisoned and another stabbed, and Phyllida had identified the culprit—she'd quite given up denying her penchant for investigating to the likes of Bradford. It was simply a waste of breath.

"Poor Myrtle was quite in the doldrums when I told her she couldn't come tonight." He gave Phyllida a sideways glance. "But I explained that Mrs. Bright most definitely did not want to arrive at a murder covered in dog hair."

"Or with a snag in her stockings," Phyllida replied, frowning at the thought of the dog that was nothing more than an unruly mop of dark hair equipped with an insistent bark and slathering tongue. "I've had to replace an inordinate number of stockings since that canine has come on the scene." Not to mention the uncomfortable sensation of a wet tongue slurping at her shins through said silk stockings. She suppressed a shudder.

"Right. That's what I told her," Bradford said. "That Mrs. Bright simply wouldn't stand for it. But I did promise her she could ride along when I come to retrieve you. What time will that be, do you think, Mrs. Bright?"

She knew he kept saying her name in that ironic fashion in an attempt to get her goat. The fact that he refused to answer to "Mr. Bradford," which was only proper, only made it more pointed. "I am not quite certain how long this so-called murder will take," she replied lightly. "Perhaps you ought to simply wait in the event I need to make a hasty exit." More importantly, that would preclude him from returning to Mallowan Hall to retrieve the rambunctious Myrtle.

"A hasty exit?" Her attempt to put him off elicited a short chuckle and he shook his head. "Surely you don't want the likes of me simply loitering about whilst you're attending a murder, Mrs. Bright."

"You needn't *loiter*," she replied stiffly. "You could . . . well, polish up the motor or converse with the Wokesleys' chauffeur. If they have one."

He responded with another bark of laughter, but other than a mention of the vacuum machine's delayed arrival, remained blessedly silent for the remainder of the drive to Beecham House.

Phyllida had never been on the property before, but she had seen glimpses of the elegant white home from the road. There was a long drive shrouded by thick trees on each side, but the forest opened up into a large parking area near the residence.

The place wasn't nearly the grand estate that Mallowan Hall was, but nonetheless, Beecham House was a good-sized residence with three floors and many gables and dormers on the highest of them. Made from whitewashed brick rather than stone, the manor's front wall was covered with thick ivy that had been cut away from the rows of windows.

A stone walkway led to the three steps that led up to a generous covered entrance, and trim gardens studded with trees, bushes, and low terraces sprawled on either side of the path. There was ample space for the parking of motorcars, which was fortunate, for there were already five automobiles lined up in front of the house.

"It appears you're not the only one determined to attend the murder, Mrs. Bright," said Bradford as he wheeled the Daimler to a halt.

As Phyllida climbed out of the motor, she mulled her options. Should she attempt to enter through the front door, as a guest? Or should she go to the back servants' entrance and slip in that way?

Bradford seemed to read her mind. "What will it be, Mrs. Bright? Brazenly enter with the other guests, or slink around to the back where the butcher and the milkman come and go?"

"I never slink," she muttered, causing him to chuckle.

"The ability to slink could be an asset to a private detective," he said, closing the door behind her.

"Monsieur Poirot wouldn't be caught dead slinking." She just wished he'd go away and cease watching her. Phyllida loathed being indecisive, and even more, she loathed having a witness when she was.

At last she gathered her wits about herself and began to walk briskly to the front entrance in the wake of a man and woman who'd just climbed out of their motorcar. She was going to attend as a representative of the Mallowans, not as a housekeeper. She only hoped she wouldn't be turned away at the door—especially with Bradford as a witness.

But it wasn't as if the times were quite as strict nowadays in the separation between servants and the upper class. Those lines had blurred a bit since the war, especially with non-gentry like the Mallowans coming in and buying up old homes that required small armies of servants that the gentry could no longer afford. Of course, Phyllida's relationship with Agatha was unique—one of mutual regard, and much less employee and employer and more of friends assisting and supporting each other.

To Phyllida's relief, Bradford didn't attempt to follow her, or even to comment about her decision. She put the man firmly out of her mind as she approached the front door.

"Good evening," said the man who greeted her and the other two arrivals at the front door. He was presumably Mr. Trifle, the butler who was a friend of Mr. Dobble's. Before she left, Mr. Dobble had told Phyllida he'd spoken to Mr. Trifle but had been unable to glean any information about the "murder." Only that the butler had sounded frazzled and distracted.

"Welcome to Beecham House. We are delighted you could attend our little murder." Mr. Trifle laughed in a deep, bass tone that sounded a trifle eerie—and false—to her ears. He was older than Dobble, with thick white hair and bushy black brows that looked as if they were about to take wing.

"Thank you," Phyllida murmured, and found herself joining a small group of people in the foyer. The ceiling was high and the space was large enough to comfortably hold the dozen or so other attendees. There was a flight of stairs that began with three steps from the side of the foyer then angled sharply to the left and ascended along one wall, ending at a balcony that looked down over the foyer.

A large grandfather clock sat prominently in the space, reminding Phyllida of her altercation with Mr. Dobble earlier. However, this timepiece was even larger and more ornate than the one her butler had offered to take an axe to. The time was twenty minutes to seven.

Since no one had stepped forward to introduce themselves as the Wokesleys or other hosts of some sort, she looked around curiously.

Phyllida recognized several of the other guests, including Sir Paulson Rollingbroke, familiarly known as Sir Rolly, and his wife, Vera, who was an amateur detective writer and had been present at the Murder Fête last month. She had not won the writing contest, but she had also not been arrested for murder.

Miss Pankhurst, who owned the general store, was there, along with Bartholomew Sprite, the village chemist. They were studiously avoiding each other due to an ongoing rivalry for patrons. To Phyllida's pleasure, her friend Dr. John Bhatt was also present and she made her way to his side where he greeted her with a delighted smile.

"Phyllida! What a pleasant surprise to see you here," he said, taking her gloved hand and raising it to his lips for a brief kiss. John Bhatt's luxurious black mustache was nearly as stupendous as she imagined Poirot's would be, and the tips of its perfectly groomed and lightly waxed whiskers brushed over the light fabric of her glove. He and Phyllida had been meeting regularly in the café in the village of Listleigh, although their relationship hadn't progressed much further than a warm friendship . . . by her choice.

"This ought to be quite something. A murder being announced!" His English was excellent, though colored with the flavor of his native India.

"It is quite extraordinary," she replied with a smile.

A footman, who was barely the height of her shoulder, walked past with a tray of drinks. Phyllida accepted a martini studded with two olives and took a sip as she and Dr. Bhatt chatted quietly.

There was a low buzz of conversation from the others who were gathered in the foyer. It seemed as if everyone was waiting for something to happen.

And finally, moments later, it did.

A man and woman appeared on the balcony overlooking the foyer.

"Good evening!" boomed the man, making a dramatic gesture. The only thing missing was a cloak to swish about. "Welcome to Beecham House. I am Clifton Wokesley, and this is my lovely wife, Beatrice." He paused for a moment with a smile playing over his mouth as he waited for everyone to fall silent.

The pause gave Phyllida an opportunity to study the Wokesleys. He appeared to be in his forties, and wore a small, neatly trimmed blond mustache that matched a thick leonine head of hair. It was brushed back from his chiseled face and fell nearly to his shoulders. Bulky rings glinted on his hands—far too many of them in her estimation—and his demeanor made Phyllida think of a circus ringmaster: loud, brash, and excitable . . . and yet, one got the impression he was merely putting on a show. That, without the rings and the audience, he'd be a quiet, steady sort of fellow.

Although his abundance of hair and a protuberant nose kept him from being particularly handsome, Mr. Wokesley looked like the sort of man who was reveling in commanding the limelight.

In contrast, the woman next to him was as glamorous as any film star. Tall and willowy, she had screaming scarlet hair that Phyllida was certain had to have been tinted. She felt herself rather an expert on various shades and tints of red hair, having been born with such a unique hue of her own. But Mrs. Wokesley's vibrant ruby bob had certainly not come from nature.

Perhaps it was characteristic of the woman who'd choose such a loud color, for she seemed just as comfortable in the limelight as her husband, and he appeared quite willing to share it with her, for he took her gloved hand and drew her up next to him as he spoke.

"As I say, welcome to Beecham House. Take a moment to enjoy yourselves . . . for at precisely seven o'clock, *someone here will die.*"

And with that, he swept himself and Mrs. Wokesley off the balcony and out of sight.

CHAPTER 3

"GOOD HEAVENS," PHYLLIDA MURMURED, RESTRAINING HERSELF from rolling her eyes at the dramatics.

The chatter in the room rose with excitement as everyone turned to look at the large clock standing in the corner.

It was sixteen minutes before seven.

"Quite a unique way to introduce oneself to one's neighbors," said John, his excellent mustache twitching.

"Indeed." Phyllida was more certain than ever that this entire event was meant to be some sort of game or production.

They waited for the clock to strike seven, murmuring niceties and commenting on the crowd, the choice of cocktails, the décor, and so on.

Suddenly, a scream filled the air. The woman next to Phyllida jolted and clapped a startled hand to her chest, sloshing her martini. Everyone fell into an expectant silence punctuated by someone's low murmur. The group turned as one when a set of large double doors opened, just as the clock struck seven.

The room revealed by the opening doors was dark. Then suddenly, the lights came up—like a stage—and revealed a well-appointed drawing room with five people arranged in a sort of frozen tableau. A ripple of muted laughter and comments rumbled through the group when they saw the sixth person, lying facedown on the floor in the middle of the room.

A blade was protruding from the center of his back.

Phyllida heard Vera Rollingbroke whisper, "Such a *scream*!" as everyone edged closer.

No one, including Phyllida and apparently Mrs. Rollingbroke, believed it was a real dead body. In fact, Phyllida recognized the person mimicking a murder victim as Mr. Wokesley himself. His face was turned away, but she recognized his longish hair and the clothing he'd been wearing, not to mention the rings on his curled-up fingers.

As for who had screamed the alert . . . It could have been any of the five actors standing positioned in the parlor. Each held some object in hand and looked as if they'd been caught in a photograph in the midst of a cocktail party. Each also had a horrified expression on his or her face as they looked down on the "dead body."

"Good heavens!" cried one of the five, who happened to be a man. "He's dead!"

"Indeed," came a disembodied voice that Phyllida identified as Mr. Trifle. Everyone turned to see the butler standing on a small riser in the foyer. "Mr. Wendell Bowington was indeed dead, having been stabbed in his own parlor. But who could have done the deed?

"Was it his own brother, Dermott Bowington, jealous of his wealth and standing?"

The guests turned their attention back to the parlor when one of the five people in the tableau unfroze and postured about with a walking stick and a dark-colored drink. Apparently, he was meant to represent Dermott Bowington.

"Or could it have been Mr. Bowington's young and beautiful wife, Caterina, who'd recently been heard arguing with him?"

One of the two women, whom Phyllida easily recognized as Mrs. Wokesley of the faux red hair, unfroze and rose from the chair in which she was sitting. She had a pearly-white fan that she waved elegantly as she looked down upon her "dead husband" with wide, shocked eyes.

Mr. Trifle went on, introducing the other apparent suspects. "Mr. Bowington's former business partner, Oscar Charles, was also present and could have done the deed. There had been a falling-out between them and was only recently patched up . . . or was it?"

A second man, who was wearing an obviously faux mustache, became animated and lifted his glass to drink. He adjusted his pince-nez and looked around with a supercilious air, then settled back into stillness.

"And everyone knew that Mrs. Hilary Charles was not particularly fond of her husband's oldest friend."

Hilary Charles pretended to puff on a gasper in a long ivory cigarette holder as she looked down at the fake corpse with a sort of sneering expression.

"And, finally, Lionel MacGavity, Mrs. Bowington's long-lost brother who arrived at Bowington Manor on this very day. Could that be a coincidence?"

The actor playing Lionel MacGavity came to life and pretended to puff enthusiastically on his pipe, removing it as he pretended to take a closer look at the dead body.

Then he joined the others back in the tableau and became still as the narrator, Mr. Trifle, went on. "Who could have done such a ghastly deed? Honored guests, it is your task to find out. You have until the second ringing of the dinner gong to speak to the suspects, so don't waste any time. At the third gong, you will present your solution—if you have one. You may begin your investigations *now.*"

The sudden clashing of a dinner gong directly behind them made the spectators—even Phyllida, to her irritation—jolt.

Everyone laughed nervously, then burst into excited chatter. Even John Bhatt's eyes had lit up with enthusiasm as he surged forward with the others to interrogate the suspects as the play-actors moved into the foyer.

Phyllida, however, looked around with a cynical eye. This was a setup that could have come from any of Agatha's novels: the dead body, the manor house setting, stock characters who were the suspects—each of whom was conveniently in possession of a prop such as a pipe, a fan, a pince-nez, and so on, in order to help the guests (or, in Agatha's case, readers) keep them all straight.

Phyllida grudgingly admitted it was a clever way to do a Murder Game—far more interesting than sitting around a table winking at a person, or tapping one on the shoulder from behind to "kill" them. But, having had her share of experience investigating real crimes with actual dead bodies, she found herself decidedly unenthusiastic about a game.

Now that she'd ascertained what precisely had been meant by the murder announcement, she was surely free to leave and return to Mallowan Hall. It was still early enough that she could enjoy the latest novel she was reading—by a newcomer named Daphne du Maurier—and snuggle with Stilton and Rye, if the latter would permit. She might even have some real Stilton and rye as an evening snack.

And perhaps the vacuum cleaner had even been delivered in her absence, and she could amuse herself by poring over the directions. She certainly didn't want one of the maids—or, worse, Mr. Dobble—to be the first to unbox and try out the machine.

The other guests had plunged into their fake investigative processes by interviewing the suspects, but Mr. Wokesley, still playing the deceased Mr. Bowington, properly remained in his prone position on the floor in the parlor.

An attractive woman in a simple gray dress and an equally simple, restrained hairstyle was making her way through the small crowd with a tray of notepads, pencils, and even small toy magnifying glasses for the guests.

Thank heavens deerstalker hats weren't being distributed as well. That would have been far too trite. Phyllida applauded the practicality of providing notebooks and pencils, however. Nonetheless, she was still rather uninterested in clomping about with a dozen other folks, interviewing actors over a fake murder.

She was looking for Dr. Bhatt to say goodbye when the woman in gray carrying the tray approached her. "Are you possibly Mrs. Bright?" she asked a bit hesitantly. "From over to Mallowan Hall?"

Startled, Phyllida paused and smiled at the woman. "Yes, I am."

"It was your hair, you know, that clued me in. Anyhow, I am so pleased to meet you," the woman went on. She was in her early thirties with a pretty, fine-boned face devoid of any cosmetics other than a very pale pink lip color. Her dark blond hair was pulled back into a neat coil, but she'd arranged wisps in flat pin curls around her temples. She wore neither gloves nor any other sort of ornamentation except for a delicate gold chain around her neck and the telltale ring of keys hanging from her belt. "I mean to say, I'm Mrs. Treacle. The housekeeper here at Beecham House. I've heard all about you, Mrs. Bright."

Phyllida wasn't certain whether to be flattered or unsettled. "I see," she replied. Was the woman referring to Phyllida's expertise in managing a large staff at Mallowan Hall, or her still-developing investigative prowess?

"Oh, heavens, now I sound like a ninny," Mrs. Treacle said, looking embarrassed. The last few notebooks slid to one side of her tray as it tilted, and two pencils rolled off and onto the floor.

Phyllida crouched swiftly to pick them up and noticed that whilst Mrs. Treacle's sensible black shoes were perfectly buffed and shined, there was a smudge of something dark on one side, as if she'd stepped in something.

When Phyllida rose to replace the pencils on the tray, the other woman said, "I didn't mean to sound so—so, well, silly. It's only, I've never been to the country before, and I've so much to learn here at Beecham House, and the housemaid—her name is Louise—she says as how you're the bee's knees when it comes to—to all of it. Managing a country house."

Phyllida was more amazed than anything over this extraordinary speech, especially since she'd only become an expert on "country living" since taking the position at Mallowan Hall. "Indeed. Well, I am most flattered and would be happy to assist if you have any questions or problems that Mr. Trifle can't answer."

Phyllida winced internally. Mrs. Treacle and Mr. Trifle? She would find it difficult to work with a staff like that, for hearing the two names together would always make her yen for sweets—and she was certain she wouldn't be the only one. She hoped the cook's name wasn't something equally frothy, such as Truffle.

Mrs. Treacle gave her a conspiratorial look. "I don't know about you, Mrs. Bright, but I find that a butler knows even less about maids and housekeeping than a footman. At least in my experience."

Phyllida didn't bother to suppress a smile. She could relate to that sentiment, at least. "I can be reached at Mallowan Hall if you need to speak to me," she said, silently congratulating herself on resisting the urge to divulge, even to a peer, her frustrations with Mr. Dobble. That sort of disharmony was better kept within the household.

"Thank you so much. Why, only yesterday, I found myself cornered in the farmyard by a goat!" said Mrs. Treacle with a nervous laugh.

Considering the fact that, in her opinion, a housekeeper had no business being anywhere near a farmyard—goat or no goat—Phyllida was barely able to suppress her startled reaction to this pronouncement. Perhaps that was the explanation for the smudge on the woman's shoes—she'd been traipsing through a barnyard. Phyllida shuddered. And what on earth did the Wokesleys want with a goat? "That must have been quite an experience."

"It was nearly as frightening as when the chickens chased me off from checking for eggs."

Good heavens. This young woman clearly needed taking in hand if she was out pulling eggs instead of sending a kitchen maid to do it! But Phyllida held back, at least for the moment, the urge to lecture her counterpart on the dignity of the role of housekeeper.

At that moment, Phyllida caught sight of John Bhatt and threaded her way through the small crowd, which had spilled from the foyer into adjoining rooms such as another parlor, a music room, and a small library.

"It's quite clever, what they've done here," John said as she joined him. She noticed he'd written on several pages in his notebook and his dark eyes were bright and enthusiastic. "The Wokesleys. Each of the suspects are milling about talking to people, and some of them are even going down the hall so as to keep the interviews private. Don't want anyone else to know what they've found out, of course," he said with a chuckle, closing up his notebook and slipping it into his pocket. As Dr. Bhatt was also an aspiring crime novel writer, Phyllida found his competitiveness unsurprising.

"Quite. Do you have a suspect?" Phyllida asked.

"Oh, yes, of course. It's always the spouse, isn't it?" His dark eyes twinkled.

"And it's never the butler . . . except for one time in Mrs. Rinehart's book," she replied with a chuckle. "And she certainly heard about it from the critics, didn't she?"

They had a good laugh over that, then Phyllida explained she was going to take her leave.

John seemed disappointed, but he also didn't insist she stay. Most likely he didn't want the competition from the only *real* detective present.

Although the actual faux investigation held no interest to Phyllida, she waffled for a moment and wondered if perhaps she ought to stay, just to learn how everything had been worked out. She didn't believe for a moment that this game was a well-plotted mystery like those written by Agatha. The solution would likely be something ridiculous and convoluted instead of the obvious.

Before she could locate her wrap, she was forestalled by Miss Pankhurst.

"Oh, Mrs. Bright, it's simply not sporting that you're here too!" she cried in her gregarious manner. Her small, gray eyes danced with humor and Phyllida took no offense from her words. "Why, you'll put all of us to shame with your detecting skills."

Miss Pankhurst was what an unenlightened person might call a spinster. She was unmarried well into her fifties (a condition Phyllida thought to be quite sensible), and had been running the general store by herself since her father and mother passed away a decade earlier.

Willow-snap thin, Cecilia Pankhurst somehow had the energy to stock, pack, and manage all of the items offered in her store with only occasional help from a young neighbor boy. The only time Phyllida had ever seen a cross look on the grocer's face was when she encountered Mr. Sprite, the chemist and her rival and nemesis.

"Not to worry, Miss Pankhurst," Phyllida told her, glancing toward the parlor where Mr. Wokesley remained in his prone position. "I'm not doing any investigating today."

"Leaving it to the amateurs, then, are we?" Miss Pankhurst said.

"Quite," replied Phyllida as the footman came by, carrying a tray laden with cocktails. She hesitated, then relieved him of a martini, deciding she might stay a bit longer. Miss Pankhurst selected a short glass filled with something dark. Sherry, most likely. "How is your investigating going on?"

"I shall tell you my theory and you may correct me over what I've got wrong," said Miss Pankhurst eagerly as she began to thumb through far too many pages of tiny, crabbed notes. Phyllida felt a wave of remorse for asking the question. "I've spoken with three of the suspects thus far and I think one of them is lying."

"Suspects always lie," Phyllida told her.

"Oh. Oh, do they? Well, that makes things much easier then," said Miss Pankhurst, flipping madly though her notebook. The amount of writing on the pages left Phyllida feeling exhausted. "That woman with the long cigarette—she's got a look about her, don't she? The best friend's wife, she is. Only, I think she had it in for Mr. Bowington because he rejected her advances, is what I think," she went on. And on.

Unfortunately, Miss Pankhurst's logic was breathtakingly *il*logical. And her ability to present a theoretical case in any cohesive fashion was also severely lacking.

Phyllida could have spilled her drink as an escape tactic, but that would have ruined her frock, not to mention being the waste of a good martini.

"Mrs. Bright! Oh, pardon me, but will you look at this?" Vera Rollingbroke interrupted. "He was holding this in his left hand."

"Who was?" Phyllida asked, taking a crumpled scrap of paper from the other woman, who was quivering with excitement.

"Why, Mr. Bowington of course! Our dead body," replied Mrs. Rollingbroke, her eyes dancing. Instead of a hat, she had a sparkling blue and green comb in her sunny blond hair. Real jewels, Phyllida noted without an ounce of envy, that perfectly matched the brooch she wore pinned to the center of her silky bodice. "I know it *must* be a clue, but you're far better at determining that than I," Mrs. Rollingbroke went on. "I simply can't make heads or tails out of it."

"Right," replied Phyllida, declining to mention that Mrs. Rollingbroke was an aspiring crime novel writer, so she should be at least somewhat familiar with fictional clues and murders.

Instead she looked at the paper and the handwritten words neatly written thereon:

LIVE
ON

The scrap had clearly been torn away from the left side of some other sheet.

"What could it mean?" said Mrs. Rollingbroke, hovering over Phyllida and the scrap of paper with her magnifying glass.

Phyllida handed it back. "I believe it means the Bowingtons were planning to eat liver and onions in the near future."

"Oh!" Mrs. Rollingbroke's eyes went wide. "Why, that's—that's quite interesting. I don't think this is an actual *clue,* then, do you, Rolly?" she asked, looking at her doting husband. "Most likely a red herring."

"Don't know, Vera," he replied, patting her arm gently. "You're the detective writer, aren't you? Dash it, you fool me all the time with your stories, old bean."

His wife's cheeks turned rosy and she replied. "Oh, *Rolly,* you're so *frightfully* sweet." She sighed. "I suppose I'd best return this not-a-clue to the body then."

Phyllida decided this was the perfect time to slip away, when everyone was milling about and before the group was gathered to hear the solution. It would be less noticeable.

But she was just setting her empty martini glass on a table when someone screamed.

"He's *dead*!" It was Vera Rollingbroke, her eyes wide and hands covering her white cheeks as she stumbled away from Mr. Bowington/Mr. Wokesley. "He's *really dead*!"

Phyllida was already pushing her way to the parlor through the rest of the gawkers, whose expressions displayed varying degrees of excitement and confusion. Perhaps they thought this was part of the game.

"I-I was putting back the-the red herring c-clue and I r-realized . . ." Mrs. Rollingbroke swallowed hard. "His fingers were . . . strange. They didn't move. And—and he was . . . cool. Oh, *Rolly*." She turned her face into her husband's chest and began to weep softly, even as a shaking finger pointed to the man on the floor.

By now Phyllida had reached Mr. Wokesley's side. It took her one look to realize Mrs. Rollingbroke was correct: Clifton Wokesley was not acting.

He truly was dead.

CHAPTER 4

Phyllida saw no option other than to take charge. Certainly no one besides herself was equipped with the cool head or experience to handle a real-life murder, and the gawp-eyed onlookers confirmed this fact.

"Call the constabulary," she ordered when even the butler seemed unable to pull to his senses. "And no one is to leave." She looked at Mr. Trifle and made a firm gesture toward the front door. He hesitated—probably due to the inherent disinclination of a butler taking orders from a housekeeper—but nonetheless moved to stand next to the entrance.

John Bhatt, who was the only other person who seemed to have the wherewithal to react, was pushing his way through the silent cluster of party guests. He knelt next to Clifton Wokesley.

Beatrice Wokesley, sitting in the chair assigned to her character in the tableau, had given a soft wail. Now she was sobbing silently into a handkerchief. The fan that had been her prop had fallen, forgotten on the floor. On the table beside her was an untouched tea tray.

The other female actor stood next to Mrs. Wokesley and was patting her shoulder whilst gaping with unabashed curiosity and horror. She still held the long cigarette.

"Everyone step back, please." Phyllida didn't want anyone trouncing on clues, nor did she want people crowding in—and listening—as she got any relevant information from John.

Was it possible Clifton Wokesley had been dead this entire time? Since he'd taken his position on the floor as a dead body?

It was not only possible, but very likely. No one seemed to have gone near him once the "game" began—other than Vera Rollingbroke.

It would be even more clear once Dr. Bhatt gave an indication of how the man had died. Phyllida already knew it wasn't from a real knife being stabbed through his back; the prop knife had shifted to one side when she knelt to check Mr. Wokesley's pulse, confirming that it was a stage blade that had only rested on his back.

There seemed to be no obvious signs of injury.

Could he have been poisoned somehow?

"Attention," Phyllida called out. The room fell silent as guests and playactors turned to her. "Did anyone speak to or see any sign of movement from Mr. Wokesley once the Murder Game began? Since he took his place on the floor? *Anyone?*"

The room buzzed with various forms of negation.

"When was the last time any of you saw Mr. Wokesley alive—meaning, that you heard him speak or saw him breathe or move?" She directed her question to the five playactors, who'd taken their places in the tableau.

"I-I don't know. I s-suppose it was just before he made his announcement upstairs," said the actress with the long cigarette.

"We were all in the green room—er, the study—waiting to take our places on the stage," said the man with the pipe. "In here, I mean to say."

"Did you all come in here together?" Phyllida asked.

"No . . . everyone was in and out," he replied. "I-I forgot my pipe. We were all still getting ready. Costumes. Props." He shrugged.

"I came in and there he was—already on the floor," said the actor with the pince-nez. Fortunately, he'd removed the atrocity of his false mustache that could only have been a clumsy homage to Poirot. He must have been disappointed that the Mallowans hadn't arrived. "Was a bit surprised to see him already in place, but Clifton's a serious actor. W-was, I mean to say." He looked down at the inert figure. "This is terrible."

"No one was in the room when you entered, Mr. . . . ?" Phyllida said.

"Georges Brixton," he replied, pronouncing his familiar name in the French manner. He was a handsome man who seemed well aware of his good looks and lean figure. He'd removed his gloves, displaying his perfectly manicured hands and brows, but Phyllida wasn't inclined to trust any man with fingernails in better shape than her own. "Lights were down, of course. Only Cliff was here. Said something to him along the lines of, 'already on your marks, then, good for you,' but he didn't reply. Didn't think anything of it. Though he's never actually been onstage, Cliff thought of himself as a serious actor," he said, likely unaware he'd just repeated himself. "Was, I mean to say."

"Once you came in the room and saw him on the floor, did you leave again?" asked Phyllida.

"No, no, took my place as expected. Felt like he was putting me to shame, him already there with his prop in place. We were all running in a bit late, weren't we? Couldn't have known he was dead, could I? *Was* he dead?" Mr. Brixton's eyes widened and his shiny fingertips fluttered. "Good God . . . never say I might have been able to *save* him?" The pince-nez popped free and fell, dangling from a delicate chain.

"No," said Dr. Bhatt, rising from where he'd crouched next to Mr. Wokesley. "There would have been nothing anyone could have done to save him. His spinal cord was severed at the base of the skull from a single puncture wound. Death would have been nearly instant." Using a handkerchief, the doctor held up a very small, slender stiletto knife, smaller than even a letter opener. It was slick with blood.

Mrs. Wokesley gasped a horrified sob and struggled out of the chair and onto the floor next to her husband. "Cliffy! Oh, my darling Cliff!" She collapsed in a pool of sequin-studded fabric, gathering his inert body into her arms as she began to sob.

Phyllida's eyes stung at this raw display of emotion, and she blinked rapidly then returned to her interrogation. She would take a moment of silence and wishes of Godspeed for Clifton Wokesley later; now she must focus, for there was only so much time before the authorities arrived and put a stop to her investigative proceedings.

"The rest of you . . . did any of you come into the room prior to Mr. Brixton, when Mr. Wokesley was already in position on the floor?"

"I-I did," said the other woman. "Um . . . I'm Charity Forrte—that's Forrte with two Rs and an E on the end. I came in, then realized I'd left my prop—the cigarette, you know—in the study, so I left again. Cliff was already on the floor, but . . ." She swallowed and lifted a trembling hand to her mouth. "I don't know whether he was d-dead by then or not. I-I didn't speak to him. It was d-dark."

Phyllida estimated Miss Forrte to be in her late twenties. The woman had a curvaceous figure in a champagne-colored gown decorated with a subtle splash of red sequins and beads over the front of the shoulders and bodice. She had hazel eyes enhanced by extensive but tasteful makeup, and white-blond hair cropped so short it revealed a large portion of her ear lobes—and the huge ruby studs she wore thereon. Miss Forrte looked the sort who would be equally comfortable in an elite salon or a public dance hall and would wear the flashy rubies to either.

"What about you, sir?" Phyllida asked the man with the pipe.

"Oh, erm, right," he replied. On the short side and rather stocky, he was dressed in an aubergine paisley waistcoat that didn't quite work with his navy dinner jacket. "Hubert Dudley-Gore. Headmaster at Fitchler School for Boys. Erm, yes, right, I don't believe . . . well, perhaps I *did* come in before Brixton here . . . wasn't paying much attention because I'd decided my character would be holding a whisky, you see, and I went to fetch one. Took a while, you see. Wasn't certain how full to make it, you see—whether he'd been drinking it or had just gotten a new one. Erm . . . never been in a play before," he added with a smile that Phyllida found disarmingly bashful despite his fashion mishap.

"You aren't certain whether Mr. Wokesley was in his position on the floor, then," Phyllida said.

"I-I think I might have seen him, but I was so flustered about it all . . . It was dark coming in, you see, like a stage . . ." He shrugged. "I kept worrying I'd forget my lines and bollix it all up, you see."

"Quite." Phyllida looked at the third male actor. "And you, sir? Did you see Mr. Wokesley before Mr. Brixton was in the room?"

"Why are you asking all of these questions? Not a police detective, are you? Not even a member of the household, I daresay," he replied with the sort of bluster Phyllida found tiresome, for it was usually present in males who did their best to hide a lack of intelligence (and other failings) behind such bombastics. "Just a nosy woman aren't you? *I'll* not be answering any questions until the *real* authorities—"

"Oh, do shut up, Keller," snapped Mrs. Wokesley, looking up with a tear-streaked face. Phyllida automatically handed her a clean handkerchief, for she couldn't bear to see a woman with smeared lipstick and mascara. "She's only trying to help. Cliff's dead, and you needn't act so full of yourself." She wiped her face, doing more damage than rectification. "I'll answer the question, then. It's Mrs. Bright, isn't it? From up at Mallowan Hall."

"It is. Unfortunately, Mrs. Agatha and Mr. Max are in London and so couldn't attend your . . . er . . . gathering," Phyllida said. "She insisted I attend with her regrets."

"Of course. Cliff was so hoping to meet her, and now he—he nev . . . er will . . ." Mrs. Wokesley choked back a little sob, then eased her husband's shoulders to the ground. Using the chair in which she'd been sitting as leverage, she pulled carefully to her feet and squared her shoulders. "The self-righteous gentleman is Sir Keller Yardley. Did you come into the parlor before Georges was here?" she said, speaking to him. "*I* am asking the question now."

"Don't need to get all twisted up, there, Bea," Sir Keller replied. He was still holding his prop—the walking stick with a heavy silver knob—but he looked properly chastened now that his hostess had turned on him. His high cheekbones were tinged a bit pink. "Didn't know what for and whatsit." He gestured vaguely at Phyllida, as if her mere presence was enough of an excuse for his behavior. "Came in and Cliff was here, but he hadn't got into position yet. He was a bit giddy, you don't mind me saying, about the game, you know. Was playing with the stage knife."

"Did you help him put the stage knife into position?" Phyllida asked, realizing that someone other than Clifton Wokesley had to have positioned the prop on the actor's back once he took his place on the rug.

"No, no. Remembered I needed to refill my drink, so went back out. When I came back, the lights were out and he was on the floor with the knife in place. No one else was in here."

"Did you speak to him then? Do you know who positioned the knife?"

It was obvious from Sir Keller's expression that he abhorred being interrogated by a female—or perhaps by anyone—but he seemed to swallow his ire. "I did not and I don't know who positioned the knife."

Phyllida looked around at the group. "Who put the prop knife in place on Mr. Wokesley's back?"

All five of them looked at each other and shook their heads.

Phyllida frowned. One of them had to be lying, because someone had to have set the prop in position.

Why would they lie?

Possibly because whoever placed the stage knife onto Mr. Wokesley's back was the last person to see him alive . . . and very likely the person who'd killed him.

She could easily imagine it: *"All right, Cliff, get into position, there we go . . ." The person crouches or kneels next to him and positions the faux blade just below his shoulder blades . . . then once Mr. Wokesley is still and playing dead, the killer shoves the stiletto up into the back of his neck and skull. One sharp, purposeful thrust and it was over.*

It was very similar to the way Phyllida had seen Mrs. Puffley pith a writhing lobster. She suppressed a shudder and returned her attention to the body.

Mr. Wokesley's longish hair had obstructed the sight of the tiny hilt and the small amount of blood until Dr. Bhatt did his examination.

Before she was able to proceed with her interrogations, there was a commotion in the foyer.

The authorities had arrived.

Constable Greensticks trundled into the parlor, hat in hand. He was a short man with a pompous air and a mustache that put one in mind of a scrub brush. Phyllida had encountered him, along with Detective Inspector Cork, during the two murders she'd previously investigated. Despite his name, the constable—who appeared to be in his late thirties—couldn't be considered at all green in his job, although he hadn't impressed Phyllida with his investigative abilities.

When he saw her, his expression froze and his cheeks turned slightly pink. Phyllida suspected that was because she'd been seeing quite a lot of him as of late—not due to murder investigations or even anything related to crime, but due to the fact that he'd developed a fondness for Mrs. Puffley's scones. Any and all of them. Whether he was as fond of the cook herself was as yet undetermined.

"Good evening, Constable," she said.

"Oi, Mrs. Bright," he replied.

Phyllida was gratified that he hadn't added any sort of comment about the fact that she was present at yet another murder. She was certain she wouldn't receive the same courtesy from Inspector Cork, when and if he should make an appearance.

"Now, then, who's dead?" asked the constable in a carrying voice, causing Phyllida to wince over his lack of circumspection.

"Clifton Wokesley. He and his wife are the new tenants here at Beecham House. Dr. Bhatt has already done an examination and can give you details on cause of death," Phyllida said quietly. "But it was a single stab to the base of the skull."

"So it's *murder*?" Constable Greensticks said, now in an undertone and with wide eyes. "Oi! They didn't say *that* when they called. Only that someone died." He seemed far more polite and even accommodating toward Phyllida than in previous encounters, and she wondered if that was due to his attachment to Mrs. Puffley. Or her baked goods. He looked around. "Why are all these people here?"

"Why, they were invited to a murder."

"Another murder, is it, then, Mrs. Bright."

Bradford was clearly not asking a question but making a statement, and the dry edge to his tone seemed to somehow place the blame for such a tragedy at *her* feet.

The chauffeur had followed Constable Greensticks inside, but Phyllida couldn't fault him for his curiosity. She certainly would have done the same.

"Quite," she replied. It certainly wasn't a disadvantage to have the sturdy, broad-shouldered chauffeur on hand to assist with keeping the agitated guests from leaving. Every one of them would need to be spoken with or interviewed, and she certainly didn't want any of them slipping away before that could occur. She had very little confidence in the constable's ability to manage more than one task at a time, and at the moment, he seemed fully occupied with the presence of the body.

"How convenient—and, er, shall we say predictable?—that the indomitable Mrs. Bright happened to be present," Bradford went on in that same ironic tone.

"The word that comes to mind is 'fortuitous,'" she replied coolly. "After all, if it hadn't been for me, Constable Greensticks and Inspector Cork would still be chasing their tails over the Murder Fête deaths, and a killer would be walking free. Or, more likely, the wrong person would be in jail. If you recall, they did take a perfectly innocent person into custody until I set them straight."

"Right," said Bradford. She couldn't tell whether he was sincere or whether he was still teasing her. Before she could respond, he went on. "And there is quite a plethora of suspects. It should keep you busy for quite some time, weeding through them all and determining—what is it? Means, motive, and opportunity?"

She gave him a quelling look. "Whoever did away with Mr. Wokesley had to have access to the parlor *before* the doors opened. There was simply no opportunity for it to happen afterward. Thus, the number of individuals who might have done it is limited to the playactors, and possibly the servants, since all of the guests were confined to the foyer and hallway. It shouldn't take very long to determine who did the deed."

"Certainly not for someone as well equipped as you," Bradford replied with extreme gravity.

"Indeed." At that moment, Phyllida's attention lit on Vera Rollingbroke and her husband. They were sitting on a small bench near the staircase, huddled together. Mrs. Rollingbroke, who normally looked sleek and fashionable, seemed wilted and exhausted. "Excuse me, I should speak to Mrs. Rollingbroke," she said to Bradford, then made her way to the couple.

"Oh, Mrs. Bright, I simply *cannot* believe it," Mrs. Rollingbroke said in a low, rusty voice when Phyllida approached. She reached out and grabbed Phyllida's hand and clasped it tightly in her own. "Imagine . . . poor Mr. Wokesley, lying there *all that time* and not *one* of us knowing it!"

Phyllida nodded. She felt terribly awful about it too, but for the moment, she could not allow base emotions and regret to supersede investigative purposes. "I did want to speak to you about that, Mrs. Rollingbroke. You were the only person to approach the—er—Mr. Wokesley, were you not?"

"*I* didn't see anyone else going near him. But I thought, I just *thought,* that maybe a person ought to actually look at the body, even though it was supposed to be fake, for the game, you see. Everyone else was crowding around the suspects, interrogating them and trying to catch them in a lie, and after a while I thought I should just take a look. Like a real detective."

"Quite," replied Phyllida, realizing that Bradford had trailed after her and was listening. "Very logical. And when you went over to Mr. Wokesley, what happened? The first time, I mean to say. When you discovered the paper in his hand."

"Yes, of course, I just went over and was looking around—I didn't *move* him or anything," she said with a little shudder. "I knew—I mean to say, I *thought*—he was just pretending, and I didn't want to ruin things by making him laugh or move about or anything. But I did see a little bit of paper in his hand, and I thought it was probably a clue that no one else had noticed, and so I took it out of his fingers." She shuddered again. "I don't suppose . . . he must have already been . . . well . . . dead."

"It appears that way," Phyllida replied. She hadn't seen any of the guests or the five playactors go near the body—and even if they had, surely they wouldn't have dared stab Mr. Wokesley in the back of the neck in front of everyone, where anyone might have seen, or he might have cried out.

For this reason, she strongly believed Mr. Wokesley had already been dead when the drawing room doors opened and the lights came up. Still, she needed to know for certain.

"When you extracted the paper from his hand, what happened? Did his fingers move at all? Constrict or release, or do anything that you remember?"

"I daresay I might be misremembering now, Mrs. Bright, as a person does after discovering a dead body—such a *shock*—but I did think to myself that Mr. Wokesley must be an exceptional actor, for when I pulled the paper away, his fingers didn't move in the least. They were tight around it, and I"—here Mrs. Rollingbroke turned a little green, her nostrils flaring a bit—"uncurled his fingers to get it loose. I had to move them myself, and I thought, as I said, that he must be an exceptional actor, for he didn't react at all." She swallowed hard.

Phyllida nodded. "And when you went to return the paper? The, er, not-a-clue clue?"

"Right. I thought it was perhaps a bit unsporting of me to keep it, even if it was only a red herring—who has a list of food in their hand anyhow?—and I thought it best to return it for the next person. And when I tried to put it back in his fingers, I . . . well, I expected he would have took hold of it again, you see . . . and he didn't. And then I realized he felt . . . well, he felt cool and limp and . . . and *strange*. As if the life had gone . . . out of him." She choked back a sob and Sir Rolly gathered her up against his shoulder.

"There, there, old bean," he said, patting her and pressing a kiss to her head. "It's going to be all right now. You were the one who noticed, after all. If you hadn't, poor Wokesley might still be lying there with everyone walking about all around the chap."

"Indeed," Phyllida replied. "Thank you, Mrs. Rollingbroke. I'm certain you won't have to stay here much longer. I shall relate your information to the constable." She ignored the little snort from Bradford and walked past him toward the parlor.

"Mrs. Bright. *Oh*, Mrs. Bright, thank heavens you're still here!"

"Mrs. Treacle." Phyllida turned to greet the housekeeper as she emerged from the depths of the corridor. Mrs. Treacle was, quite literally, wringing her hands.

"Is Mr. Wokesley really dead? How? What happened? I've been in the kitchen—there was a *catastrophe*, with an entire cabinet of teapots going over, and the cook is absolutely useless, as she's only standing there shouting over it, and the scullion is just crying about it." Mrs. Treacle's face was flushed and a single wisp of hair had come loose from its moorings. Her finger twisted around a delicate gold necklace and now Phyllida could see a small flower pendant hanging from it instead of the cross she'd expected. "I simply don't know what to do."

"Well, you've come to the right person," Bradford, who'd followed her of course, said jovially. "Mrs. Bright is very well equipped to tell you—or anyone—precisely what to do in any given situation."

Phyllida didn't bother to acknowledge his ridiculous comment, nor to introduce him.

Instead, she fixed a stern expression on her face and replied to Mrs. Treacle. "The cook must cease her shouting and dramatics at once. Tell her this in no uncertain terms. There are guests waiting for refreshment, and the footman and the scullery maid can clean up the mess, as it's likely one or both of them were instrumental in its happening."

In Phyllida's vast experience this was usually the case. Footmen and maids were either flirting with each other, avoiding each other, or pretending to ignore the other, and that was how such mishaps occurred. "Erm . . . how many broken teapots are we speaking of?"

"Oh, a dozen, at least," Mrs. Treacle said, her voice creeping toward a wail. "I don't know if there is even one unbroken teapot left in this house. *How will I serve tea?*"

"Good heavens," Phyllida replied. That actually *was* a catastrophe.

Nonetheless, she decided not to ask how such a mishap could have occurred. Instead, she said, "I do believe I saw a fully intact teapot on the tray in the drawing room. Incidentally, who brought the tea tray into the drawing room?"

"Why . . . I did," replied the housekeeper, suddenly looking like a frightened rabbit.

"Oh, excellent," replied Phyllida, delighted to have another potential witness. "When did you do that? Who was in the room? Was Mr. Wokesley in his position on the floor at that point?"

"Why . . . I . . . no one was in the room. I only brought in the tray because Mrs. Wokesley would have expected it. No one was there at first, and I set it on the table, and then Mr. Wokesley came in." Mrs. Treacle's hands were wringing again. "It was after the gong, you see."

"You spoke to Mr. Wokesley?"

"Oh, yes," Mrs. Treacle replied. "He—he asked me to stab him in the back, he did. 'Mrs. Treacle,' he said, 'you couldn't stab me in the back, now, could you?' And I didn't know what to say! I was even a bit frightened, if I'm honest. And then he started laughing and showed me the fake knife, and how it worked." She shook her head. Then her eyes popped wide. "Is that . . . is that how he . . . *died?*" she said in a whisper.

"In a manner of speaking, yes," Phyllida replied. She was mildly surprised that the housekeeper seemed to be quite in the dark about what was going on here in the parlor of her own domain, but she supposed that a pile of twelve different types of broken crockery strewn over the kitchen floor could account for that failure.

"Did you assist Mr. Wokesley?" she asked.

"Did I—oh, yes, of course I did," replied Mrs. Treacle, her cheeks turning a little pink under Bradford's silent regard. "Why, Mr. Wokesley laid right down and I took up the knife. It felt awfully strange, but once I realized it wasn't real and wouldn't harm him, I found it wasn't so odd doing it after all. A bit exciting, to be honest. I felt like I was part of the play too. Like a director or whatnot."

Phyllida briskly dismissed this fanciful thought. "Quite. And once you positioned the faux knife, what did you do?"

"Why, I left the parlor. Oh, and I turned off the lights, as he said. He told me he wanted to . . . what was it . . . get to—no, get *in*to character."

"Did anyone else come in whilst you were—er—assisting Mr. Wokesley?"

"No, I don't believe so—wait. It was the man with the pipe—Mr. Dudley-Gore. He started to come in, but then he turned around and left straight away. And then I left and went to the kitchen."

"Oh, Phyllida, there you are."

She turned to see Dr. Bhatt. "Yes?"

"I thought you might like to know about the murder weapon," he said, gesturing toward the parlor.

"Yes, of course," she replied, and accompanied him back to the scene of the crime, leaving Bradford and Mrs. Treacle to discuss catastrophes and the fortuitousness of her own presence.

In the parlor, she found that Clifton Wokesley had been covered with a sheet and Mr. Trifle and the footman were preparing to assist in removing the body.

Phyllida looked at the diminutive footman and said, "There is a disaster in the kitchen that requires your attention. Now." Before Mr. Trifle could argue, the footman fled. Phyllida turned back to the foyer and said, "Bradford, your assistance in here would be appreciated."

"Of course, Mrs. Bright," said the chauffeur. He didn't need to be advised what was needed; one look at the situation and he went to work. That was the thing about Joshua Bradford that almost made him worthwhile to have around: He was quick-witted and speedy in action. Not to mention well-equipped to lift heavy objects.

Ignoring the affronted look Mr. Trifle was sending her way (Phyllida had plenty of experience ignoring affronted butlers), Phyllida glanced around the parlor. The five actors—who must now be considered suspects in the murder of Clifton Wokesley—were sitting quietly on the other side of the room, each drinking a cocktail of choice.

Assured that they were settled for the moment, Phyllida turned her attention to the murder weapon: a slender stiletto blade.

It was such a tiny thing. Wicked and small and dark with blood. Hardly as long as her middle finger, but deadly, deadly sharp. She shivered a little, and a wave of sorrow washed over her. A man's life had been taken, *wasted,* by this small and dainty knife. And unlike a bullet, which would be launched from a distance—or poison, which was also administered from a distance and often-times hours in advance, the lethal blade had been wielded by the killer's very hand. He or she must have been intimately close to the victim.

It seemed whoever had done the deed had wanted to *see* and *experience* the finality of death. Phyllida suppressed a shudder. Someone hadn't merely disliked Clifton Wokesley and wanted to get rid of him. It seemed they'd hated him so much they drove the blade into his body with their own hand as they were kneeling over him . . .

Perhaps like a lover.

Or a conquerer.

It must have taken great audacity to do such a thing when anyone could walk in at any moment and discover you.

Dr. Bhatt had wrapped the stiletto's acorn-sized hilt in a handkerchief before pulling it free, and the weapon now rested on the cloth on a table. Phyllida was struck by the surprisingly small amount of blood that was on the blade and its wrappings, considering the great damage that had been done.

Constable Greensticks was staring down at the knife, hands on his hips. He was clearly out of his element.

"You won't find any fingerprints on it," Phyllida said, breaking into whatever tangled thoughts might have been going through his mind.

The constable looked up in surprise. "Oi, what's that you say?"

"Everyone was wearing gloves," she told him. "There were only five people who had access to the drawing room, besides the servants, of course, and I am quite convinced they were the only ones to have the opportunity to kill Mr. Wokesley—and they were all wearing gloves as part of their costumes."

His face fell. "Right." He stared hard at the tiny lethal blade as if willing it to speak to him.

"But one ought to determine where and how the weapon was obtained," she said.

"Right," he replied, brightening a little.

"Erm . . . when is Inspector Cork expected to arrive?" Phyllida asked.

The constable made an annoyed sound. "Won't be here until tomorrow. Was in London up at Scotland Yard, he was."

"Ah. I see." Phyllida maintained a grave expression, but inside she was delighted. The inspector's delay would provide the opportunity to conduct her own investigation without it being derailed. "If I may?"

Without waiting for his response, she gathered up the cloth around the small knife.

"Do any of you recognize this?" she asked, approaching the five playactors.

Charity Forrte reared back and shuddered when she caught a glimpse of the knife.

"No," she said, turning her face away.

"Never saw it before," replied Georges Brixton, who'd posed himself in an armchair as if anticipating an artistic photographer to shoot an image of him. *Pensive Suspect,* Phyllida thought, *With Manicured Hands.*

"Awfully small, ain't it?" said Hubert Dudley-Gore of the Fitchler School for Boys and the Fear of Forgotten Lines. "To do all'at—erm—injury. No, I don't recognize it."

"I do," said Mrs. Wokesley tearfully. Phyllida was pleased to see that the smeared makeup had been wiped away. "I mean to say, it belonged over there." Mrs. Wokesley's hand shook a little as she pointed to a cabinet across the room.

"It was in the display," Phyllida said to herself, walking over to look at the cabinet. It was tucked in the corner, far from the double doors that opened into the room. "So anyone who spent any time in the drawing room might have seen it."

And none of the guests who'd arrived for the first time tonight and had no access to the drawing room would have known it existed. Nor, surely, would it have been noticed, stashed away in a shadowy corner of the room.

That was the final piece to convince her that Mr. Wokesley had been killed before the drawing room doors opened for the Murder Game. And that meant it had to have been one of the five actors who'd done the deed.

Having confirmed that deduction, Phyllida went to the fixture in question to examine it more closely.

It was a five-shelf corner cabinet with glass shelves and door. The door was currently closed but not locked, and there were a number of other decorative objects on display: china figurines, wood-carved statues and trays, an antique hand fan, vases, and a small velvet pillow where the little knife had likely rested.

Mildly disappointed, she closed the cabinet door. Each of the actors—with the exception of Sir Keller, who either hadn't wanted to or hadn't needed to respond, and Mrs. Wokesley—indicated they hadn't recognized the knife.

One of them had to be lying.

Unless, of course, Beatrice Wokesley had killed her husband.

CHAPTER 5

"OH, MRS. BRIGHT, ONLY I DON'T KNOW WHAT I WOULD HAVE done without you here!" said Mrs. Treacle when Phyllida came out of the parlor.

"Quite," Phyllida replied.

"Why, I went in there just like you said, and I told Mrs. Napoleon to stop her shouting and stomping and to get the refreshments ready for the guests, and do you know she did it?"

"Quite so." Phyllida avoided looking at Bradford, who was leaning laconically against the wall. Even though she wasn't looking at him, however, she could imagine the humor that was surely gleaming in his eyes.

"And Anthony, the footman—why he even came in and started cleaning it up without my telling him. He and Petunia, the scullery maid."

"Of course," said Phyllida.

"But . . . oh, Mrs. Bright, I just don't know how to *handle* all of this. All of these guests here and—and this happening." Her fingers twisted around her necklace again.

"Well, you certainly shan't go out pulling eggs from the coop again," Phyllida replied, refraining from glancing down at the other housekeeper's smudged shoe.

"No, no, of course not, but . . . oh, dear, would it be *too* much to ask you to—to stay and help out a bit? Advise me? Only for a short while?" Mrs. Treacle abandoned the gold chain to wring her hands instead. "It's only that I-I've never had a *murder* in my household before."

"Of course you haven't," Phyllida replied complacently. Inside, she was thrilled with the prospect of the opportunity to remain in the presence of the suspects for a bit longer. There was more work to be done to identify the culprit.

She had the weapon—the *means.*

She knew that each of the five actors had had the *opportunity* to stab Clifton Wokesley in the base of the skull, for she'd adjusted her imagined scene to account for the information she'd gleaned from Mrs. Treacle.

It would have been just as simple: Any of the five actors could have come into the room as he lay in his position on the rug. *"Oh, Cliff, look at you—already on your mark. But let me fix the knife . . . it's beginning to fall to the side. Can't have the murder weapon out of place, can we?"*

The person would crouch next to the unsuspecting and conveniently prone Clifton Wokesley, and in one vicious move they'd shove the little blade up into the hollow at the base of his skull.

Simple. Fast. Silent.

The only thing Phyllida didn't have—for any of the suspects—was a *motive.*

And that was what she would attend to next.

"I'll be most happy to deliver a tea tray to the constable whilst he is interviewing the suspects," she said, conveniently ignoring her previous dictum that housekeepers didn't fetch or serve. There were, of course, always exceptions. "Perhaps you'd like to set up in the study, Constable Greensticks?" She projected her voice toward said authority figure as he emerged from the parlor.

"Whatsit? Oh, aye, right. Interviews. Quite right. Yes, of course." The constable seemed pleased—if not relieved—by the suggestion. "But . . . all of them?" He gestured to the foyer, where the guests milled about and, Phyllida was satisfied to see, were being offered refreshes of their drinks. "Oi. There's an awful lot of people here."

"I'm certain the guests can be allowed to leave. None of them had access to this room to find and use the murder weapon, and I've already spoken to Mrs. Rollingbroke." Phyllida told him about her conversation with her. "The rest of them can be questioned tomorrow at the constabulary, I'm sure."

"Oi, right, then," said the constable. Thus fully instructed, he turned to the inhabitants of the parlor, speaking to the five playactors. "I'll meet with each of you in the study. One at a time, if you please. Mrs. Bright—er, I mean to say, *someone* will show you in as necessary."

Phyllida helped the constable settle himself in the study. It was a cozy but rather chilly room, and someone had built up the fire—something that had been done without her suggestion. Likely the forethought had come from Mr. Trifle, who seemed far more at ease in his role at Beecham House than the housekeeper. Of course, he'd been here for years, whereas Mrs. Treacle had not.

The room had a large and imposing desk behind which Phyllida suggested the constable take a seat. There was a pair of armchairs in front of it with a small table between them where she placed the tea tray that had been fetched by Louise, the housemaid. According to the maid's report, the catastrophe of the broken teapots was well in hand and there was not one, but two, intact vessels, including the one from the parlor. Tragedy had been averted. Tea would be served.

Still, one of Phyllida's first course corrections for Mrs. Treacle would be to advise her to obtain several more teapots. One simply couldn't manage with only two, especially with a houseful of guests.

Phyllida was about to open the study door to the first interviewee when Constable Greensticks cleared his throat, then spoke.

"Erm . . . what do you know about any of 'em, now, Mrs. Bright?"

She paused with her hand on the doorknob. "Not very much at all, unfortunately, Constable. The Wokesleys are new to Listleigh and Beecham House, and I don't know anything about the other actors besides their names and the roles they assumed in the play. I am certain, however, that your interviews will be quite instructive."

The constable cleared his throat again, quite vehemently. One might construe that he was a bit nervous, but Phyllida had no concerns about him getting the job done. After all, she would be here to guide him.

Beatrice Wokesley was the first person to be escorted into the study. Once again, Phyllida was struck by the unnaturalness of her ruby-red hair, which was still firmly pinned back on one side by a glittering hair comb. Her face was wan and pale, seeming to swim like that of a specter above the glittery choker she wore.

"I'm very sorry for your loss, Mrs. Wokesley," she said as she led the slender woman to one of the armchairs. "I know nothing can take away your shock and pain at the moment, but it's very important that you speak with the constable. Perhaps a cup of tea—with a splash of brandy?—might brace you up."

"Oh, that w-would be very good. Thank you, Mrs. Bright. It's so good of you to help out," Mrs. Wokesley said. Her eyes were red-rimmed and she clutched a handkerchief, but her voice was far less wobbly than it had been. "I s-still can't believe . . ." She caught herself on a sob.

"Now, if you could please tell Constable Greensticks about tonight's little—er—party game. And everyone who was in it." Phyllida poured tea and added a generous dollop of brandy along with three lumps of sugar to the woman's tea.

"R-right. Well, Cliff thought it would be a-amusing to introduce ourselves to the neighbors this way. He knew about Mrs. Agatha Christie living nearby, of course, and . . ." Here she gave an abashed laugh. "He *so* wanted to meet her, and he was *certain* that a M-Murder Party would entice her to come. You see, he's written a short play and he was hoping she'd look at it for him. He wanted to star in it . . ." She swallowed hard.

"Mrs. Mallowan would certainly have been here if she had not already been engaged in London," Phyllida told her kindly and quite possibly incorrectly. Mrs. Agatha was rather shy and tended to avoid gatherings of people she didn't know well. And she generally avoided looking at the work of unpublished writers.

"Cliff wrote the script for the Murder Game, and he invited

some of our f-friends to come and have a go of it. None of us—well, except for Georges—are actors, you see. It was just to be a bit of fun. Cliff's family has always been a patron of the arts—the woolen Wokesleys, you know—and he was quite determined to follow in his parents' and grandparents' footsteps and support the theater. He dreamed about being on the stage himself someday."

Phyllida nodded, allowing the rambling to continue without redirecting it. Beatrice Wokesley clearly needed to work up to the details of tonight before she was prepared to divulge them.

"The—er—woolen Wokesleys?" said the constable. He looked longingly at the bottle of brandy, but Phyllida had prudently placed it out of his reach. There would be time for that later; for the moment, he needed a clear head. Instead, she poured a cup of tea and gave it to him. Without sugar.

"Oh, yes, of course you know them—the wool factories in Yorkshire?" replied Mrs. Wokesley. "Of course, since the wool industry has begun to decline, they've divested into other businesses. Milling and the like. Still quite set up, however."

"Right, right," he said. "Those Wokesleys."

There was a pause as Mrs. Wokesley sipped her tea, her eyes widening when she tasted the heavy sweetness and cloying liquor. But she took a larger gulp and went on. "Cliff was so happy to be living in the country. He-he'd needed to get away from London since—since early this year, and when we finally did, he became a new man. We were only here for a fortnight before I saw the change in him. He'd had an awful time of it, you know, over the last months—the scandal and the tragedy and all—but at last my *dear, dear* Cliff was himself again.

"So when he devised having this—this murder game party as a way to introduce some friends to our new home and to meet our neighbors, you see why I couldn't say no. We invited a few friends to come p-play along. We never *imagined* something like this would h-happen. How *could* we?" Her voice broke and she muffled her sobs with the handkerchief.

Phyllida gave the woman a moment to compose herself, then

pressed on. "Tell me—er, the constable—about your friends. The ones who were here tonight. Did any of them have a reason to want your husband dead?"

"What? Why—of course not! Why would w-we have invited th-them . . . ? *Wait.* Do you mean to say you think one of them did it? Killed Cliff?" Mrs. Wokesley's voice became shrill. "Why, that's mad! None of them—*none* of them would have done such a thing!"

Phyllida merely looked at her, and after a moment she saw the denial fade from Beatrice Wokesley's face and horrified resignation settle there.

"But—but someone *had* to have done it, didn't they?" she said in a whisper. "One of *them* had to do it."

Phyllida gently lifted the hand with which Mrs. Wokesley was holding her teacup so that she would drink again.

"Let's begin with Georges Brixton," Phyllida said. "He's an actor, you say?"

"Y-yes. He's just got done with a small show—*Ever the Darkling World*—in the West End. It was on at Stages Theater, do you know it? Georges and Cliff met because the Wokesley family have always invested in the theater. And so, following in his father's footsteps, Cliff fancied being a sort of producer on *Darkling World.* And h-he always harbored the dream of being onstage himself someday. But the show didn't do as well as one hoped. Still, that was how he and Georges became close friends."

"Mr. Brixton played the role of Oscar Charles, the former businesss partner of Mr. Bowington—in the play, I mean," Phyllida said, remembering the way the pince-nez had popped from Georges Brixton's eye when he realized his friend had been dead even as he was speaking to him.

"Yes, that's correct."

"Did Mr. Wokesley and Mr. Brixton get along all right, even after the play didn't do well?" Phyllida asked. "Were there any hard feelings?"

"Oh, no. Cliff didn't hold Georges responsible for the play not catching on."

"And Mr. Brixton had no hard feelings against your husband for the failure of the play?" Phyllida asked.

"Oh." Mrs. Wokesley appeared startled at this suggestion. "Well, I suppose . . . there might have been a bit of a kerfuffle about it all. Georges was rather upset when the show closed after only a month when they'd planned for a six-month go. They did have a bit of a row about it—he claimed Cliff could have financed a longer run. And then Georges tried to convince him to financially back a different play to make up for the five months lost.

"Cliff declined and Georges was very unhappy about that. But it was just a minor disagreement. Certainly not enough that he would *kill* Cliff. And when we invited him to come up, why he was delighted. Surely he wouldn't have come if he'd been angry."

Unless he was *still angry and wanted revenge on Clifton Wokesley.*

Phyllida glanced at Constable Greensticks. She was pleased to see that he'd been writing in his notebook, similar to how he'd done when Inspector Cork was conducting interviews. She approved. It was best if he simply remained silent and allowed her to manage the interrogations.

"Very well. Now, what about Sir Keller?" Phyllida asked. She wasn't the least bit surprised when Mrs. Wokesley's pale face pinkened a bit in the cheeks.

"Sir Keller is a family friend—of my family, you see. I've known him for absolutely ever. He and Cliff didn't get on all that well, but it wasn't as if they loathed each other. You see . . ." Mrs. Wokesley took a large gulp of fortified tea. "Sir Keller and I were once engaged to be married."

Phyllida was not surprised to learn this bit of information. After all, she'd noticed the way Mrs. Wokesley spoke to Sir Keller—with great familiarity, particularly when she rebuked him—and also the way Sir Keller looked at her and the faint blush when she reproached him. There'd been something there.

"But it was a long time ago, when I was just eighteen. It was what our families wanted—only, after a time, Keller and I realized we didn't really suit. Thank heaven times have changed and families don't arrange those sorts of matches any longer! What a mess that would have been, Keller and me hitched up," she said with a little laugh, followed by another sip of tea.

"Whose idea was it to include Sir Keller in the murder game tonight?" asked Phyllida.

"Why, I do believe it was Cliff's," she replied. "He and I had several conversations about who might be good candidates to play the roles, and I'm certain Cliff was the one who suggested him. I thought it awfully sweet of him to think of that—after all, Keller and I are still very close friends."

Phyllida, of course, couldn't help but wonder how close. It was obvious that Mrs. Wokesley had very likely just come into a good-sized fortune, courtesy of the woolen Wokesleys and her murdered husband. Perhaps she wanted to marry Sir Keller after all . . . but only once she had a nice inheritance to bring along.

That was assuming Mrs. Wokesley was the heir. Something Phyllida would have to confirm, but not just yet.

"And then there is Charity Forrte," Phyllida said. "How does she figure into the group?"

"Charity was married to my brother," replied Mrs. Wokesley, who'd obviously been a Forrte before wedding Mr. Wokesley. "She's been rather at loose ends since their divorce. I don't see much of Ronald myself—he's an officer in the army, in Africa somewhere, I believe—but Charity and I had become quite close, and I thought it would be a kindness to invite her. Get her away from the city for a bit. She's always been a trifle too dramatic, and I had the idea she would enjoy the playacting."

"And she and Mr. Wokesley got on well?" said Phyllida.

"Well, they hardly knew each other, really. Cliff and I have only been married for two years, and Charity runs about with a different crowd. We didn't see much of each other whilst we were in London—she . . . well, as I said, she runs with a different sort of crowd. Rowdy and loud and that sort. But she's a good egg, and I suppose I had the thought that perhaps she and Keller might make a match of it."

That was interesting, Phyllida thought. Surely Beatrice Wokesley wouldn't attempt to matchmake her former sister-in-law with

Sir Keller if she had any sort of attachment to him. Unless she was lying.

"And did she and Sir Keller get on?" Phyllida asked.

"No," replied Mrs. Wokesley with a grimace. "Not as well as I'd hoped. I suppose I'm just not much of a matchmaker. I only wanted Charity and Keller to find happiness in the same way Cliff and I had done." Her eyes welled with sudden tears and she looked away. "I can't believe he's gone."

"Does Mr. Wokesley have any family that needs to be notified?" asked Phyllida, deciding now was the time to broach the subject of inheritance.

"There's only his mother and a sister, along with some distant cousins. I'll—I'll ring them. Tomorrow."

Phyllida nodded. "And the Wokesley fortune? Who stands to gain by your husband's death?"

Mrs. Wokesley blanched, then flushed. "Why . . . I suppose I do. I mean to say, Cliff's always said he's left most everything to me, after a generous portion to his mother and sister. And . . . and, oh yes, I believe there might be some bequests to a number of the arts foundations he supports."

"Such as the Stages Theater?"

"Most likely, certainly. Oh, and I think his school, too. Fitchler."

"Is that why Hubert Dudley-Gore is here? He's headmaster there, isn't he?" Phyllida said.

"Oh. Why, yes he is. He and Cliff were friends when they were at Fitchler together."

"And you believe your husband left a bequest to the school?"

"He talked about doing so, yes," replied Mrs. Wokesley. "You don't *really* think Cliff was killed over some pittance of money?"

"What is one person's pittance is another's fortune," replied Phyllida. "Men—and women—have killed for far less than what you or I might consider a fortune."

Mrs. Wokesley shook her head. "I simply can't believe it . . . of any of them."

Phyllida, who by now had taken a seat in the chair next to the widow, leaned slightly closer to her. "But one of them did, Mrs.

Wokesley. Your husband didn't stab himself. Someone in that parlor did it. If it wasn't one of them," she went on ruthlessly, "there's only one other person it could have been." She looked steadily at Mrs. Wokesley.

It took her a moment, but not as long as Phyllida might have expected. The woman jolted and put a hand to her chest. "Me? *Me?* Are you asking if *I* killed my husband? How could you *say* such a thing? No. *No,* I did not kill my Cliff." Bright red spots stained each of her cheeks and her eyes were filled with outrage.

Phyllida nodded. "The fact remains, then, that someone in that parlor did so. And if it wasn't you . . . If you had to say which of them is capable of murder, whom would you choose?"

"I . . . I don't know. I just don't know," replied Mrs. Wokesley, the color in her cheeks fading. "M-maybe . . . well, I don't know Hubert at all. Never met him until he came here. Or—or even Georges. I hardly know him either. M-maybe one of them could have done . . . ?" She lifted her tea and drank the rest in one long gulp. "Is there anything else?"

"Constable?" Phyllida said. "Did you have anything else?"

He jolted and looked up from where he'd been scratching notes. "Oh. Erm. No, no, thank you, Mrs. Wokesley."

Mrs. Wokesley rose and looked down at Phyllida with a regal air. "I do hope someday *you* don't have a person accusing you of killing *your* husband," she said in a shaky voice, then swept from the room.

Phyllida looked after her. *Oh, if you only knew.*

CHAPTER 6

PHYLLIDA PRUDENTLY TOOK A MUCH MORE UNOBTRUSIVE ROLE DURing the interview with Sir Keller.

Having already experienced his dislike of strong, capable women, she reasoned that Constable Greensticks, as clumsy as he might be, would be far more likely to extract pertinent information from Sir Keller than she.

Still, she remained in the study, doing the sorts of tasks Sir Keller would expect a woman—particularly a servant—to be doing: serving tea and brandy, fussing about with chair cushions and straightening knickknacks, drawing curtains, and generally remaining silent and retiring.

Sir Keller was a tall, lean man with thin, light brown hair. He wore a sparse, neat mustache and an air of impatience. His nose was long and slender and quite likely was the cause of his slightly nasal voice. Phyllida's impression of him was that he looked down upon everyone with whom he came in contact—and not only because of his height. He no longer carried his walking stick prop.

"Erm, yes, Sir Keller, thank you for meeting with me," said Constable Greensticks as the two men settled into their respective seats. "Er . . . I have a few questions for you." He glanced quickly at Phyllida, who gave him an encouraging nod.

She had, of course, provided him with a list of suggested questions whilst they were waiting for Sir Keller to be shown in. That in itself—the action of *being* shown in, rather than having a person shown in *to* him—seemed to propel Sir Keller into a foul mood at the outset.

"Frightfully inconvenient," he griped as he snatched up the bottle of brandy to splash more into his half-full glass. "Let's get on with it, then. I suppose you want to know who I think did away with old Clifton, do you?" He took a large gulp of spirits as Phyllida unobtrusively wiped up the splatters on the table.

"Well, I—certainly, your opinion would be very helpful, Sir Keller," said the constable.

"Well, it had to be that Brixton character, of course. The one with the Frenchie name," he scoffed.

"I see. And—er—why would you say that?"

Sir Keller gave Constable Greensticks a baleful look. "Well, it certainly wasn't Beatrice. And that other woman—whatever her name is—Chastity?—looks as if she'd be the sort to faint at the sight of blood—"

"Oi, guv, but there weren't all that much blood—"

"Devil take it—my point is," Sir Keller went on in that furious tone, "*she* couldn't have done it. Wouldn't be strong enough or have the fortitude, now would she? Got to have the strength and the determination to shove a blasted knife up inside a man's skull, now don't you? Not to mention the brains to—"

"Right, sir, but the doctor said it wouldn't take all that much strength—"

"I'm telling you, it was that Brixton chap. Don't even know why you're taking the time to talk to *me* about it—and upsetting Beatrice so. Understand you accused her of offing her own dashed husband!" Sir Keller's eyes blazed and Constable Greensticks sank down in his chair a little.

The constable glanced at Phyllida. "But *I* didn't accuse—"

"Sir Keller, might you like a bit more brandy?" Phyllida said smoothly before the constable could fully toss her to the wolf of Sir Keller. Not that she couldn't handle Sir Keller's ire, of course—heaven knew she'd faced down far worse than a blustering, irate, self-righteous gentleman. Injured and delirious soldiers. Snide and condescending physicians. Husbands.

"Of course I do. Dashed upsetting. All of this," he replied, shoving his hand with the glass rudely toward her.

"Quite right. I'm certain it was very upsetting for Mr. Wokesley, having a stiletto shoved into his skull," she said, pouring a generous glug of brandy into the vessel. She applauded herself for not sloshing even a drop on the odious man, but instead smiled warmly at him. "You must be a very good judge of character, Sir Keller—I mean, in order to identify the culprit so easily."

"Course I am. That Hornby Derby-Do, or whatever the chap's name is—the one from the boys' school? Thinks being a headmaster puts him in charge all the time," he scoffed. "The dashed man tried to tell *me* where to stand during the rehearsal for that bloody stupid play. What I mean to say is, the likes of him couldn't have done it either. Couldn't even remember his blasted lines, the rock-headed bloke. Certainly couldn't pull something off like that." Sir Keller tossed back the entire contents of his glass and thrust it toward Phyllida once again.

As she refilled his beverage—once again refraining from pouring a puddle into his lap—she reflected on his comments. Despite the frank delivery of his opinions, Sir Keller's characterization of the other playactors rang true . . . although perhaps they were slightly exaggerated. Phyllida knew firsthand that a woman like Charity Forrte might appear to be frail and shy, but in reality was more capable than a man who thought as highly of himself as Sir Keller did.

"Are we finished, then?" Sir Keller, with a full glass once again, began to rise. "Make an arrest so we can get on with it. Bea don't need to be upset any more than she already is." The angry lines on his face eased a trifle.

"I do have a few more questions," said Constable Greensticks, earning a glance of approval from Phyllida. "If you could take a seat, sir."

"Don't know what else there is to say," replied Sir Keller. He remained standing, and Phyllida was reminded how much more difficult the job of the authorities was when class played a role.

Even well into the twentieth century, the gentry often felt as if they needn't be bound by the requests or authority of the police. Until or unless they were arrested, those of the upper class often used their status as a way to avoid or outright ignore officials.

"Have a seat, please, Sir Keller, and I will finish this as quickly as I can," said the constable, surprising Phyllida with his temerity. Her respect for him—as minimal as it might be—edged up a notch. "This is a murder inquiry and that trumps any inconvenience you might have. And poor Mrs. Wokesley," he added.

Phyllida hid a pleased smile as she went across the study to adjust the curtains she'd previously drawn. She wholly approved of the policeman's tactic of the reminder of Mrs. Wokesley's difficulties. That, if nothing else, seemed a way to soften Sir Keller.

"Make it fast, then, will you. Need something a bit stronger than this," said Sir Keller, gesturing with his glass as he sank back into his chair.

"When did you arrive at Beecham House?" asked Constable Greensticks.

Phyllida knew it was important to determine when the guests arrived and whether they had spent time in the parlor prior to tonight. That information was crucial in order to identify who had the opportunity to notice the lethal stiletto on display in the cabinet.

She wasn't certain whether the killing had been premeditated or whether it had been a spur-of-the-moment exercise, and discovering that could help determine who'd planned the murder. She was certain Hercule Poirot, who always focused on the *psychology* of the murder, would approve of this approach.

"Arrived late yesterday evening," replied Sir Keller. "Missed dinner due to a flat tire on the road. Had to arrange for a ride instead. Everyone else was here before me. Brixton had plenty of time to make out his plan."

"Why do you think Mr. Wokesley asked you to be part of the—uh—the Murder Game?" Constable Greensticks asked, plunging on with his interrogation.

"Why . . ." Sir Keller seemed stymied for a moment. "How does that figure anyway? Asked me because he knew I could *do* it, of course."

"You and Mrs. Wokesley were previously engaged to be married." The constable continued to plow through his list of questions without the finesse Phyllida had hoped for. Still, he was, at least, asking them. "Wasn't it a bit awkward that you should be here?"

Sir Keller slammed his glass (now empty once more) onto the desk. Constable Greensticks lurched a bit in his seat. "Just what do you mean to imply by *that*?" Sir Keller demanded, half out of his chair again.

"Why, only that—"

Phyllida quickly intervened. "More brandy, Sir Keller? Surely you and Mr. Wokesley had no hard feelings between you over Mrs. Wokesley."

Sir Keller plunked back into his chair and held out his glass once more. "'Course not. Cliff and I were bosom friends. Only wanted the best for Bea."

"And she was quite happy with Mr. Wokesley, it appeared," said Phyllida, sloshing the last of the brandy into his glass. She would have to insist Mr. Trifle retrieve a fresh bottle if this were to continue. "Of course, appearances can be deceiving."

"Well, he certainly had the money," Sir Keller grumbled. "Kept her well enough, can't complain about that. But he wasn't... well, *ton,* as m'grandfather used to say. Didn't quite mix, you know. The woolen Wokesleys, they're called. Made their money in the *trades.*" Sir Keller gave a little shudder. "Mills and factories and the like. Shearing sheep."

Phyllida highly doubted that Mr. Wokesley had ever shorn a sheep in his life. Nor his father or grandfather. But she held her tongue and nodded at Constable Greensticks, who was looking forlornly at the empty brandy bottle. She read his mind: It was getting late and they had three more people to interview. They weren't getting very far with Sir Keller at the moment, so it was time to move on.

"Had you ever met any of the other playactors before tonight?" asked the policeman.

"No, no, of course not. How would I? I certainly don't run with *that* lot," snapped Sir Keller. "Only did it for Beatrice."

"Oh, it was she who invited you, then," said Phyllida. "It was given off that it was Mr. Wokesley who'd made the invitations."

"Don't know how it matters," said Sir Keller, rising with the finality of it being his time to exit.

Phyllida was agreeable to that as well. She was beginning to feel weariness all the way up to her eyebrows. She wondered if Bradford had given up and gone back to Mallowan Hall, or if he was lurking about.

"Cliff invited me, but of course Bea was delighted about it. Probably put the bug in his ear; told him I'd be perfect for the game, such as it was." Sir Keller picked up the brandy bottle, then dropped it back on the desk when he realized it was empty. "Be going off now. Mark my words, it was that Brixton fellow. Better nab him while you can."

His gait was a bit unsteady as he made his way out of the study without formally taking his leave. Phyllida saw no reason to stop him.

In truth, she was rather glad to be quit of the man. He reminded her far too much of Jamie.

Charity Forrte swept into the study, glittering from head to toe in her red and champagne gown and ruby earrings. She was a striking woman—helped by her white-blond hair, a full, pouty mouth, the scarlet gown, and sparkling gems—but her face was too sharp and pointed to be considered classically beautiful. Still, she was the type whom most men found attractive and interesting. She was carrying the long, elegant cigarette holder that had been her character's prop, leading Phyllida to believe that perhaps it wasn't only a prop after all.

"I simply can't believe it," Charity said, perching on the edge of her chair. Her eyes were wide and her lipstick had long been chewed off, leaving an irregular red rim around the edges of her mouth. Her pale blond hair had gone flat and wispy. "How could this have happened?"

She lit her cigarette in its long, ivory holder with a trembling hand. Tucking the lighter back into the tiny beaded bag she'd brought with her, she looked at the constable. "Right, then. Now what? Don't you have to ask me a bunch of questions to try and figure out if I did it?" She gave a strained laugh. "Just like the Murder Game—only now it's real."

Phyllida glanced at Constable Greensticks, who sat up a little straighter in his seat. "Erm, yes, Miss . . . er . . . ?"

"Charity Forrte—that's with two Rs and an E at the end. And it's Mrs.—or it was. I was married to Beatrice's brother. We divorced two years ago, not long after Bea and Cliff got hitched." She took a desperate drag on her cigarette. "Big wedding, that was. Fancy and expensive. Cliff has loads, you know. From his family. Guess that means Bea will come into it all." She looked around as if assessing precisely what Beatrice Wokesley would be inheriting.

"It's a bit strange, ain't it, that you would be invited to Mrs. Wokesley's house, you being divorced from her brother and all," said the constable.

"Not at all," Mrs. Forrte replied. "Bea and I are chums. Her brother is a bit of an arse, and she knows that as well as I do. Frankly, I don't miss Ronald in the least."

"Right," said the constable. He glanced at Phyllida.

"Would you like some tea, Mrs. Forrte?" she asked, and offered the new bottle of brandy Mr. Trifle had reluctantly retrieved. "And a bit of liquid strength?"

"Oh, that *would* be nice," replied Mrs. Forrte, watching as Phyllida poured tea and then added a generous splash of brandy. "I suppose you want to know if I killed Cliff."

"Did you?" the constable asked with a little smile beneath the brush of his mustache.

"Of course not," Mrs. Forrte replied with a sweep of her cigarette hand. Pungent smoke trailed behind it in an S curve. "Why on earth would I want to do away with Cliff Wokesley? I've only met him a few times."

"But you were at his wedding. What did you think of him?" said Constable Greensticks.

"Oh, well, he's like any other husband—he's an arse." Mrs. Forrte gave a laugh husky with smoke. "But Bea seems to like him well enough." Her face fell. "I do feel for her. She's quite devastated. It was an *awful* thing to happen—right there in front of us."

"Do you think that's what happened? That someone stabbed him whilst everyone was in the drawing room?" asked Phyllida.

"Well, I'm certain *I* don't know. But I wasn't paying attention. I was thinking about . . . about something else, and I was standing in the back of the drawing room mixing a drink, you know. The butler hadn't thought to come in, so I had to do for myself. But it *had* to have been done before we all came in, didn't it? The murder, I mean. Surely no one would have taken the chance . . . *right there!*"

"That is what we're attempting to determine," Phyllida replied, choosing the pronoun deliberately. "Did you see anyone speak to Mr. Wokesley after you came into the parlor for the last time? Anyone who went near him, perhaps bent to talk to him or to adjust the stage knife's position?"

"I-I don't remember. Maybe Sir Keller spoke to him. As I said, I wasn't paying attention. A martini was calling my name, and I've learned never to ignore that siren song." She gave a brittle laugh and dragged on her cigarette once more.

"A nice strong cocktail can certainly do wonders to bolster one's mood. Not unlike a bracing cup of tea," Phyllida said agreeably. She lifted a brow at the constable, silently encouraging him to continue.

"Can you think of any reason someone might want Clifton Wokesley dead? Did Mrs. Wokesley ever mention anything about her husband having problems with someone, or an argument or falling-out?" he said.

"That Mr. Dudley-Gore person seems a shady sort of character. Far too hearty and loud, if you ask me. Wouldn't want that lot teaching *my* boys if I had any—if you know what I mean," she replied. "More crass than class, you know."

"Other than your—er—impressions of Mr. Dudley-Gore, did you notice anything else that might help? How was Mr. Wokesley getting on with the other guests?" asked the constable.

"He seemed jovial as usual," Mrs. Forrte said. "Puts on a good show, I'll say. Always the amiable host . . . but I *did* hear something last night." Her eyes went wide as if she'd just remembered. "I didn't think much of it at all—you know how it is with men, sometimes they raise their voices over nothing. A horse race or when you overcall their bid in bridge. But . . ." She drew on her cigarette and narrowed her eyes as she seemed to look back at the memory. "I did hear Cliff and Georges Brixton. I'm certain it was him. Georges, I mean to say.

"They were in here, as a matter of fact," she went on, gesturing to the room at large. "I was walking past—it was just before we were about to rehearse for the silly little play tonight. Cliff had given everyone their storyline at tea and what they were supposed to say, and we were meant to study it up and then meet in the parlor to practice it. Actually have a *rehearsal.* Like we were on the West End or something," she scoffed. "I thought it was rather silly, but Bea indulged him. In fact, she was rather more excited about the whole Murder Game than I would have thought. She's normally more a serious sort. As I said, I found it rather ridiculous, but I went along with it."

"You heard someone in here with Mr. Wokesley?" Phyllida said, gently redirecting Mrs. Forrte back to her story.

"Yes, yes. I was trying to find the parlor and I got it all backwards. Even went through the servants' door—why they don't have it marked off in baize, I don't know. Anyone could have made that mistake. Quite mortifying, really, being turned around in the servants' hall.

"Then that woman, Mrs. something or other—I can't remember her name, but with the pincurls here?" She gestured to her forehead and temples. "She wasn't a *maid,* you know, which was why I was even more confused because I thought she might have been a guest here early—anyhow," she said, taking another drag on her cigarette, "she showed me the way to the drawing room and I passed by this room and I heard voices. It was definitely Cliff, and I'm certain it was Georges Brixton with him, as I said. He has a rather distinct voice—being on the stage and thinking of himself as quite the *actor*. Talks loud all the time, as if he's *projecting*—is that what they call it?—to an audience."

"You heard Mr. Brixton and Mr. Wokesley arguing?" asked Phyllida, once again trying to reroute the conversation. Why *were* witnesses and suspects so prone to going off on tangents?

"It sounded like an argument."

"Could you hear what they were saying?" said Constable Greensticks, his pencil poised and ready.

Mrs. Forrte settled back into her chair. "Hmm. Let me see if I can remember . . . It was something like . . . 'Dash it all, Cliff, I don't think it's quite the thing.' And then Cliff said, 'I don't give a bloody hell what you think, but that's how it is. Now if you don't—' and I didn't hear the next part because there was a loud noise—as if someone had banged their hand on the table. 'Not going to change my mind,' Cliff said. 'And if you don't like it, you can—' " Mrs. Forrte stopped abruptly. "I won't finish it, but he said something very uncouth. And then I heard the sounds of someone coming and so I started walking away." She drew on her cigarette. "That's what I remember. Do you think it's important?"

"Every little detail is important," replied Constable Greensticks as Phyllida noted that Charity Forrte had given herself away, at least after a fashion. She'd obviously stopped and lingered to eavesdrop, then when she heard someone approach, she made her escape so as not to get caught. This made Phyllida wonder whether Mrs. Forrte was listening for something in particular, or simply that she was nosy.

And how much of her "trying to remember" what she'd heard was real and what was exaggerated?

She glanced at the constable to silently suggest he let her proceed. "Thank you, Mrs. Forrte. I'm sure that was very helpful. I can't think of anything more we need to know, can you, Constable?"

When he opened his mouth to speak, she shot him a glare. He nodded and said, "No, no, Mrs. Bright, you're quite right. Thank you, Mrs. Forrte. You've been very helpful."

Phyllida walked to the door and opened it for the woman, then she paused and gave a wry little laugh. "Incidentally, Mrs. Forrte, I hope you don't mind my asking, but did you happen to notice that pretty little statuette in the drawing room? It was in that corner cabinet. It looked like an Egyptian figurine . . . but perhaps it was American Indian. I simply *adore* anything Egyptian," she added in a voice so sugary and uncharacteristic of her normal one that Constable Greensticks gaped at her.

Phyllida ignored him. "I was . . . well, I was hoping Mrs. Wokesley would allow me to take a closer look to see if it was. It reminded me of a little figure that my grandmother owned . . . I used to always admire it whenever I visited as a girl. Of course, I don't suppose I should even ask her now, but I thought perhaps you, being her friend, might . . ." She trailed off, mainly because she could no longer maintain the cloying, overly timid demeanor.

Plus she was afraid the constable would laugh and give it away.

"Statuette? Yes, I saw it," Mrs. Forrte drawled. "Ugly little thing if you ask me. I detest anything pink—it's simply just not enough." She preened a little in her crimson gown. "But Egyptian? Certainly not. It was most definitely Japanese. Not sure why Bea would have it in the cabinet, but there's no accounting for taste." She looked at Phyllida closely. "You say you wanted to look at it?"

"Only, it reminded me of my grandmother, that's all," Phyllida said, doing her best to appear embarrassed and babbling like Mrs. Treacle. "Never mind. It was a silly request. And I must have remembered it all wrong. I only saw it for a moment."

"Right," replied Mrs. Forrte. The shrewd look she gave her made Phyllida wonder whether she'd seen right through her act.

Charity Forrte might appear to be fluttery and superficial, but—as Phyllida had just demonstrated—looks and demeanor could be deceiving.

Hubert Dudley-Gore made his entrance to the study with a hearty laugh and an expansive gesture with the pipe he'd been holding for his prop. "So it's my turn, is it?"

He wasn't a tall or particularly imposing man, but his booming voice made up for that. He had an egg-shaped head, but his mustache was nowhere near as magnificent as Poirot's—it was thick and walnut-brown with far too much wax, which made it appear as slippery as his hair, which was parted off-center (purposely, Phyllida assumed, but one couldn't be certain) and combed back.

Clearly, Mr. Dudley-Gore was the sort who needed a wife or a valet to assist in his toilet, and since he was at Beecham House alone, there was presumably no wife. Nor a valet. Headmasters normally didn't have the funds to pay for extra servants, at any rate. She noted that he had removed the gloves he'd been wearing during the Murder Game, revealing two knobby rings, one on each hand, with square, chunky onyxes—inexpensive stones.

Despite his boisterousness, Phyllida discerned an underlying nervousness in Mr. Dudley-Gore as he made his way across the room with the same dramatic flair.

"If you could have a seat there, guv," said Constable Greensticks.

"Right," said the headmaster. "I suppose you'll be giving me the old inquisition now, won't you, then?" Again, his laugh was overly loud and long. "What did I see, where did I go, who do I think dunnit—"

Phyllida found it necessary to interrupt. "Would you care for some tea, Mr. Dudley-Gore?"

"Oh, er, I suppose I'd rather something a bit stronger, if I do say," he replied, casting a pointed look at the very popular bottle of brandy. "Rather shocking turn of events tonight."

Phyllida attended to his request, and as she settled the glass of spirits at his elbow, Constable Greensticks commenced with the questioning. "When was the last time you spoke with Mr. Wokesley?"

"Right, then. I'm not certain of the precise time, you know, but it was just before we were to gather in the parlor for the gong. Forgotten my lines at rehearsal, you see, and I asked Cliff what would happen if I ruined it all during the real game. You see"—now Mr. Dudley-Gore became as earnest as the schoolboys he mentored—"I've never been in a play before, and I got so nervous I forgot to say some of my lines when we were practicing.

Didn't know whether they contained pertinent clues or not, so I hunted Cliff up to ask him if it was important. And whether I should have a drink or not, too. Whether it fit my character, you see."

"What do you mean?" asked the constable, pausing with his pencil at half-mast.

"Why, giving our speech to the guests, you know, right? During the game?" the headmaster went on. "You see, each of our soliloquies had clues buried in them and in order for the Murder Game to go off, all of the guests would need to hear the clues—at least, if they asked the right questions. Fancy little game, what. *I* didn't even know who did it—none of us did—so I didn't know if mucking up my lines would ruin it all." He sighed. "I bollixed it up twice when I was practicing in my room. Terribly nervous, you know."

"I see," said Constable Greensticks. But he didn't quite sound as if he did.

"Do you mean to say you didn't know who was supposed to have killed Mr. Wokesley—er, I mean Mr. Wokesley *as* Mr. Bowington—in the Murder Game?" said Phyllida.

"No. The only person who knew was Cliff," replied Mr. Dudley-Gore. His eyes sparkled with boyish enthusiasm. "We were all five of us meant to act very suspicious and innocent at the same time, and only at the end would he reveal who the real killer was. Very amusing and suspenseful for all of us. Might even try the same sort of Murder Game for a fundraiser at the school. I could play the body! Then I'll have no lines." He laughed. "The whole thing was quite, quite clever, really. And very entertaining."

"But perhaps not so very entertaining for Mr. Wokesley," Phyllida said dryly.

"Oh, no, of course not," said the headmaster with an abashed expression. "Terrible thing to have happen. Absolutely terrible. And to top it off, we'll never know who really dunnit, now, will we? Offed Mr. Bowington, I mean to say."

"Erm . . . speaking of whodunnit, do you have any idea who might have wanted Clifton Wokesley dead?" asked the constable.

Mr. Dudley-Gore didn't hesitate. "That French fellow had something seemed a bit off with him. Don't know why he can't just be *George* like everyone else, but instead has to have that froggy way of saying his name. *Georges.* Don't trust a chap like that, you know. Brixton, I mean to say. Seemed pretty steamed about something."

"Steamed about what? Was he angry with Mr. Wokesley?" asked the constable.

"Don't know. Just glowered about a bit, you know, like in those horror films. Didn't find him very friendly at all," Mr. Dudley-Gore said.

"When you did speak to Mr. Wokesley for the last time—about your lines, was it?" Phyllida asked, firmly steering the conversation back to more relevant topics. "Was anyone else around in the parlor?"

"Oh, well. Hum. Let me think. Um . . ." He screwed up his face in a posture of contemplation. "Beatrice was there. She was talking to Charity Forrte—fascinating woman, might I add. Did you know she was actually *arrested*?" Mr. Dudley-Gore's eyes were wide with something like admiration.

"Arrested?" The constable sounded as if he were choking. Phyllida ignored the excited look he gave her. As she well knew, simply being arrested didn't necessarily make one a criminal.

"When was this?" she asked.

"Don't really know," said Mr. Dudley-Gore. His eyes still gleamed with interest. "Said she threatened to go on a *hunger strike*—just like those women who wanted the vote!"

"Good *heavens*," breathed the constable. His pencil listed to one side.

Phyllida—who was well aware of the brave and admirable suffragettes who'd gone on hunger strikes whilst attempting to get women the right to vote—managed to keep her expression neutral. Obviously, Charity Forrte had not been arrested (recently, anyway) for suffrage protests, as women who'd reached their majority had had the right to vote since 1928. It seemed to Phyllida that threatening to go on a hunger strike after being arrested was a slap in the face to those brave women who'd actually done so to their own physical and mental deficit. And since it seemed unlikely that Mr. Dudley-Gore followed women's history, she suspected he only knew about said hunger strikes because Mrs. Forrte had told him.

The fact that Charity Forrte had threatened such a tactic left a bad taste in Phyllida's mouth. Still, she remembered that shrewd look the woman had given her as she left the study. There was obviously more to the glittery, bubbly woman than appeared.

"Why was she arrested?" asked Constable Greensticks. Phyllida wasn't certain whether his breathlessness was due to the thought of such a beautiful woman being jailed, or because he was certain they'd found the culprit in the murder of Clifton Wokesley.

But he was doomed to disappointment, for Mr. Dudley-Gore shook his head. "Don't know. She didn't say. But it sounded ever so exciting—she said as how she was in the *bathtub* when the police came to arrest her!"

Phyllida decided that was enough of that and firmly quashed whatever imagery had popped into the constable's head. "Mr. Dudley-Gore, Mrs. Forrte's legal problems notwithstanding, perhaps we could spend a bit more time on what happened since you arrived here at Beecham House."

The constable flashed her a disappointed look—clearly he wanted to spend more time in his imagination—but he righted his pencil and turned his attention to their interviewee.

"Got here yesterday around teatime," said Mr. Dudley-Gore. "Wasn't quite what I'm used to—no sandwiches at all, and only two types of biscuit. Very dry, in fact."

"Who joined you?" asked Phyllida. She would have to speak to Mrs. Treacle about such a lackadaisical approach to tea. No sandwiches? Dry biscuits? Intolerable.

"Right. It was Cliff and Beatrice. Charity was there too, but she didn't stay long. Said she had a headache. That Brixton fellow too."

"And where was tea served?" Phyllida asked, thinking of the display cabinet with its stiletto knife and Japanese statuette (of course she'd known it was Japanese). If someone had noticed the statuette, they could very well have noticed the stiletto.

"Why, in the drawing room, of course," replied Mr. Dudley-Gore.

"Did you notice that pretty little statuette?" asked Phyllida. "With the pink robes?"

"Statuette?" He looked at her as if she'd grown a second head. "Not at all. A statuette? Y'mean like a doll? I didn't even walk over by the fireplace." He shook his head, frowning. "Was too busy wondering when the rest of the tea was going to arrive. Sadly, it never did."

"How do you know Mr. Wokesley?" asked the constable after Phyllida gave him an encouraging nod.

"Went to Fitchler together. Was years ago, of course, but once he learned I was headmaster at our old school, well, we renewed our acquaintance." He beamed, showing a spectacular number of teeth.

"How long ago did you renew your acquaintance?" asked Phyllida.

Mr. Dudley-Gore looked at her as if suddenly realizing she was there. "Why . . . who are you again?"

"Please answer the question," said the constable, surprising Phyllida.

"I—well, what is this? Some sort of inquisition?" Mr. Dudley-Gore's heartiness had undergone a swift and virulent change.

"It is a murder enquiry," said Constable Greensticks evenly. "I'll thank you to answer the question. When did you renew your acquaintance with Clifton Wokesley?"

"Erm . . . well, it must have been three, four months ago," replied Mr. Dudley-Gore.

"And he invited you here to Beecham House so soon after?" Phyllida said.

"Why not?" His eyes narrowed and a sheen of sweat popped out onto his smooth, brown forehead. "Old school mates. And Cliff was talking about a bequest to the school," he added as if he'd just remembered.

"Right, then. So now that he's dead, there will be some of the Wokesley money coming to good old Fitchler School for Boys, is that right, Mr. Dudley-Gore?" Constable Greensticks tilted his head as he looked at the headmaster.

"Right. Erm . . . I—er—I don't actually know." Mr. Dudley-Gore gave an uncomfortable chuckle. His ire had faded just as quickly as his bravado. "Was going to speak with him about it whilst I was here—part of the reason I wanted to do the Murder Game, you know."

"Are you saying you don't know whether Mr. Wokesley left any money to Fitchler?"

"That's correct. I believe he intended to do so, but I don't know whether it . . . er . . . actually happened. Suppose we'll find out, now, then, won't we?" Mr. Dudley-Gore's chuckle sounded even more forced this time.

When neither the constable nor Phyllida immediately spoke, the headmaster clamped his hand on the arm of the chair. "You don't think I killed Cliff for a bit of blunt for the school? Why, that's preposterous! And—and I didn't even have the opportunity! Beatrice was there when I was in the drawing room with Cliff. And—and that Charity woman."

"Now, now, Mr. Dudley-Gore, no one is accusing you of anything," Phyllida said. "You are saying that when you went into the drawing room before the Murder Game started, Mrs. Wokesley and Mrs. Forrte were already in there. What were they doing?"

"Why—I don't know. Standing at the back and talking female things, I suppose. I was too distracted and it was getting close to the gong. I was afraid I was going to forget my lines and I wasn't certain about the prop, you know. A full glass or half full, to go along with my pipe? Don't you understand? I was trying to get into *character.* I wasn't paying any attention to anyone else in the room."

"Was Mr. Wokesley in his position on the floor with the stage knife in place?" asked Phyllida.

"He—he wasn't lying down, but he was on the floor. He sat up when I started to talk to him."

"And then you left the room and Mrs. Wokesley and Mrs. Forrte were there with him?"

"Yes. No. I mean to say, no. They weren't. Erm . . . Charity walked out with me—said she wanted to freshen her lipstick or some other nonsense before the gong. And so did Beatrice—needed to fix her hair or something. Are we finished?" He rose so quickly he bumped his knee against the desk. Phyllida saw a flash of pain across his face, but it didn't slow him down.

"Y-yes, I suppose so. For now," said the constable without looking at Phyllida.

But she didn't disagree. She was rather looking forward to the fifth and final interview with Georges Brixton—the man whom everyone seemed to think could be a killer.

CHAPTER 7

"SO YOU THINK I DID IT?" GEORGES BRIXTON SAID AS HE SANK languidly into the chair.

Phyllida's first impression of him in the parlor had been colored by his sleek good looks and perfectly manicured hands—the latter of which, in her mind, did not belong on a man. Not that she preferred grease-stained fingers or ragged nails.

And now, buffed fingernails notwithstanding, Mr. Brixton's current display of aplomb only strengthened her misgivings. He seemed to have abandoned his false mustache and pince-nez props in favor of a glass of amber-colored spirits.

"Well, now, that remains to be seen, guv," said the constable, fidgeting with his pencil.

"You certainly had the opportunity, Mr. Brixton. Or do you prefer Monsieur Brixton?" Phyllida asked, silently offering him the bottle of brandy.

"Mister is acceptable." He downed the remainder of his drink, then nodded at the bottle of spirits. "We all had the opportunity."

"But by your own admission, you came into the parlor and found Mr. Wokesley on the floor. He was either already dead at that point, or you dispatched him yourself. We have only your word," Phyllida replied as she finished pouring his drink.

"I told you, I didn't know he was dead," Mr. Brixton said. "It was dark in there, you know. I spoke to him, he didn't answer, and quite honestly, I didn't think much of it. Cliff was taking the Murder Game very seriously. The man took everything related to theater and dramatics seriously."

"Yet not seriously enough to invest in a second play for you," Phyllida said. "We understand you and Mr. Wokesley had words last night—in this very room."

The glass in his hand hitched very slightly on its way to his lips, but Mr. Brixton smoothed out the movement and took his time sipping the brandy. "So someone heard us, did they? I don't suppose you'll tell me who it was. I do know wasn't Beatrice. She was upstairs having a lie-down. At least . . . as far as I know."

Phyllida merely smiled at him and said, "What were you arguing about, Mr. Brixton?" Even as she prodded him, she was acutely aware that at any moment he could refuse to answer her questions and even demand she be removed from the room. She had no authority here—only that which she could wrest from Constable Greensticks, who for some reason seemed perfectly willing to allow her to take the lead. Maybe he'd actually learned something during the last two cases in which she'd been involved.

"We were arguing about the play. Not the one in London—this one. The Murder Game. I told him he was a fool to make it so realistic. That someone was going to be angry about it. Not me of course," Mr. Brixton said with a flap of his hand.

Of course not, Phyllida thought. "Realistic? Surely you didn't believe someone would actually kill Mr. Wokesley."

"Don't be ridiculous. I mean to say, the play itself . . . well, it might have hit rather close to home for some of us. *I* didn't mind, personally, but there were others who certainly wouldn't want their secrets bandied about under the guise of a confounded murder game."

"So you're saying that somehow this Murder Game . . . wasn't entirely fictional?" Phyllida was intrigued.

"That's precisely what I'm saying. And I told him that. I told him it wasn't a good idea to mess around with revealing peoples' dirty secrets, skeletons in their closets, and all of that."

"Including your own," Phyllida said.

Mr. Brixton waved it off. "Everyone knew Cliff and I had had a row about the show. You'd do better to look more closely at the other characters—and I mean them literally as well as fictionally. Cliff had his own secrets, you know. You expose someone else's, they're going to do the same to you."

Phyllida nodded, but she wasn't quite ready to let him off the hook. "When you came into the drawing room to prepare for the beginning of the Murder Game, no one was in there except for Mr. Wokesley, is that correct?"

Mr. Brixton sighed the sigh of a terribly persecuted man. "Yes, that is what I have said. Multiple times now."

She ignored his dramatics. He was, after all, an actor. "Did you see anyone who *might* have been in there prior to you entering? Presumably you and the others entered and exited not through the double doors facing the foyer, but the side door? Was anyone in the vicinity?"

"That is correct. The door we all used led to the 'backstage' and 'green room' area—or so Cliff termed it. It opens into a small servants' hallway that runs between the drawing room and the library, and we used the library as our private backstage area. As I said, Cliff was very particular and serious about the *play*." Mr. Brixton's expression was wry. "I'm sorry to say, but I believe it was his play that got himself killed."

"Did you see anyone coming or going in the hallway before you went into the parlor for the last time?" Phyllida pressed.

"Not that I recall. Everyone was in and out of the library—the green room—quite a bit—getting drinks, freshening up. Couldn't keep track. Didn't think I'd *need* to. Why should I have done? Was supposed to be a *game*." The persecution had returned.

"Who was it you think wanted Mr. Wokesley dead?" asked the constable.

Mr. Brixton looked at Constable Greensticks as if just realizing he was there. "I certainly don't know," he snapped. "That's *your* job, ain't it?"

"But surely you must have some suspicions," Phyllida said soothingly. "After all, as an actor you must be used to character study."

Apparently, Mr. Brixton was more easily lulled by a flattering female than a male interrogator, for he settled back into his seat and took a casual sip from his drink. "Well, now, let me see. Sir Keller makes a person wonder if he's as well set up as he makes out. Claims he was late getting here from a flat tire and had to get a ride the rest of the way, but I heard the driver say he'd picked him up at the train station, not from a broken-down motor. Now why would he lie about that? Could be *he's* flat instead of the tire."

He paused, clearly for effect, then went on. "That headmaster fellow is a dashed clod-head. Making like we're all no better than his students, giving out direction and what for. Don't think he'd be smart enough to try for it in the parlor around everyone like that, but he's got motive, all right.

"Cliff was going to settle a big chunk on the school—and I can't imagine why he'd do that. He told me he *hated* Fitchler when he went there. And," Mr. Brixton said, his mouth twitching in a wry smile, "he claims—er, I mean to say, *claimed*—he didn't remember the fellow—what is his name anyhow? Danley? Darnley? No, Dudley-Something—the least bit."

Phyllida followed the choppy speech, but apparently Constable Greensticks needed clarification. "What was that? You say Mr. Wokesley didn't know Mr. Dudley-Gore?"

"I said he claimed he didn't remember him from school, but the headmaster chap put it about that they were old chums—he and his brother or someone, and Cliff," Mr. Brixton replied. "So ask yourself why Clifton Wokesley would be settling a pile on the school when he don't know the headmaster, and he hated it there." He gave Phyllida a sly look as he lifted one brow.

She had to give him credit: He was certainly doing his best to divert suspicion from himself.

"And I suppose you can think of a reason why Mrs. Forrte would have done the deed as well," she said.

"*I* don't know of anything off my head, but there must be something. Everyone else in that blasted Murder Game has a reason to knock off Cliff Wokesley—certainly she does too."

"What's Mrs. Wokesley's motive then?" said the constable. "Money, I suppose."

"He's got piles of it," was all Mr. Brixton said. He set down his glass. "Are we finished now?"

Constable Greensticks glanced at Phyllida then replied, "For now. You and the others will need to remain here until the inspector arrives tomorrow. *Please God,*" he said under his breath.

Phyllida chose not to take offense at his clear—and misguided—preference for the detective. Members of the male sex tended to stick together, mainly out of habit.

As Phyllida opened the door for Mr. Brixton, he paused and looked down at her. "What was your name again?"

"Mrs. Bright," she replied.

"Bright, you say?" He stroked his chin, still eyeing her as they stood in the doorway. "Have we met somewhere previously, Mrs. Bright?"

"Certainly not. I don't spend any time in London," she replied, quelling a small frisson of nerves.

He looked at her a moment longer, then made an ambiguous sound and murmured, "Good evening, then, Mrs. Bright. I hope you catch the killer."

It was nearly another hour before Phyllida finally sank into the passenger seat of the motorcar. Fortunately, Bradford hadn't returned to Mallowan Hall during the fracas of the murder investigation. She had no idea how he'd spent his time when she was interviewing suspects—although when she came out of the study with Mr. Brixton after his interview, she'd noticed Bradford deep in conversation with Mrs. Treacle.

That had irked her to no end. Mrs. Treacle had plenty of things to do with a murderer caviling about in her household; she certainly didn't have time to stand around gossiping with anyone.

"Bit of a rough one, there, hmm, Mrs. Bright?" said Bradford as he slid behind the steering wheel.

He'd opened the front passenger door for her before she could indicate she wanted to sit in the rear this time, where she could have closed her eyes to think whilst pretending not to hear him when he made snide comments about whatever took his fancy: her investigations—what he termed nosiness. The fact that dead bodies seemed to crop up when she was around (as if it was *her* fault). Her exacting standards—which he deemed persnickety.

"Murder is always rough," she replied and resisted the urge to take off her shoes (which she would have done without hesitation if she'd been in the back where he couldn't see). There was a price to pay for vanity and her feet were atoning for it now.

"No argument there."

When Bradford subsided into silence, Phyllida relaxed a trifle. Perhaps he was too tired to poke at her for once.

They rode down the dark, curving roads without speaking, and Phyllida felt her eyelids suddenly threatening to droop. She stubbornly fought to keep them open. Even though it was after midnight, she wasn't about to slump weakly in her seat.

She didn't *think* she snored, but if she did—which would have been purely a result of her awkward sitting position and nothing more—she knew she'd never hear the end of it. Besides, she wasn't tired so much as emotionally and mentally exhausted. It was quite taxing on the brain dealing with feuding maids, recalcitrant butlers, missing vacuum machines, and murder.

"So, Mrs. Bright . . . who's your prime suspect?" Bradford finally asked as he slowed at the crossroads south of the village. A turn to the west would take them to Mallowan Hall and the haven of her sitting room in less than a quarter of an hour.

Phyllida didn't even try to deny that she was investigating Clifton Wokesley's death. Bradford wouldn't believe her even if it was true, and they both knew she was the most capable person to be taking on the job anyhow.

"Not one in particular," she replied. "All five had the opportunity and they all, apparently, have motive."

"You've narrowed it down to the playactors, then," he said. "Those in the Murder Game."

She turned to look at him in the darkness. The only illumination was that spilling in front of them on the road from the motor's headlights, but she could make out the profile of his prominent nose and the dark, messy hair that never seemed to find itself in proximity to a comb or scissors. "No one else had access to the drawing room. It had to be one of them."

"Mrs. Treacle said the same thing," he told her, and Phyllida couldn't help but bristle a bit. As if that airy-fairy city woman had a clue about investigating murders when she couldn't even find a scullion to pull eggs for her!

"Mrs. Treacle clearly had an inordinate amount of time to stand about discussing such matters instead of seeing to her staff and guests. I had to ring thrice for fresh glasses and teacups during our interviews, and it took far too long for anyone to respond. Not to mention the fact that the surface of every piece of furniture in every room I entered was streaky." She couldn't quite suppress a sniff of distaste. "Honestly, if one doesn't know to train their maids to merely *dust* walnut whilst *polishing* every other sort of wood—with lemon oil being the best—then one has simply no business being in charge of a household staff."

Bradford made a noise that might have been a smothered chuckle, but she doubted he would have been so foolish as to laugh at her in her mood. The sound ended in a sort of cough and with him saying, "Nevertheless, she was quite in awe of you, Mrs. Bright. The Great Detective and Housekeeper Extraordinaire. She could hardly imagine how you could do both when either one of those roles is clearly beyond any other mortal woman."

Phyllida shot him a dark look. Too bloody bad he couldn't see her reaction. "Quite. Well, I'm delighted to hear that you were the recipient of someone's praise of myself and my abilities. Unfortunately, it was to the detriment of every household task under her purview, which is far more important in my estimation. And apparently tea was abysmal."

"Right," he replied in a suspiciously choked voice. He cleared his voice. "It seems that Elizabeth Treacle is in over her head at Beecham House."

Phyllida made a derisive sound of agreement, but otherwise held her tongue. Everyone had to learn from their mistakes. Some people simply learned faster than others.

And then there were those who never learned at all.

"She's rather a sad case, you know," Bradford went on. "No husband or children, and her only sister died in an accident. She could use the—er—guidance of someone like yourself."

Phyllida could hardly believe what she was hearing. "I'm not certain whether to be offended that you are suggesting it is my responsibility to assist Mrs. Treacle in a predicament into which she put herself, or gratified that you recognize my excellence and superiority."

She was also taken aback by how personal Mrs. Treacle's and Bradford's conversation had obviously been. Clearly, Elizabeth Treacle had given Bradford her entire life story instead of managing her maids and tending to her guests. And clearly she'd had plenty of time to stand around and gossip with the Mallowans' chauffeur.

"Quite right, Mrs. Bright," he said cheerfully, obviously enjoying the rhyme. "But regardless of which sentiment you decide to have a go, perhaps you might wish to offer your assistance to the woman. After all," he added smoothly, "it would give you more opportunity to investigate Mr. Wokesley's death."

Phyllida didn't respond. Of course she'd already thought of that very same point. But she simply didn't see how she could justify being away from Mallowan Hall for such a reason, especially with the imminent arrival of the Vac-Tric.

Inspector Cork was simply going to have to handle the investigation himself this time.

The question was whether he *could*.

Just then, the headlights revealed the entrance of the long, winding drive to Mallowan Hall, and Phyllida sighed with relief. Bradford navigated the motor smoothly onto the road, which was lined by an allée of elms and oaks after they passed through a massive gateway.

In the distance, she could see the large rectangular shape of the manor house she'd come to think of as her home—the first place she'd actually *felt* at home for a long while. Most of the windows were dark, but a dormered one at the top of the house indicated that some of the maids were just getting ready for bed.

"Long day was it then, Mrs. Bright?" Bradford said in a more even voice. If she didn't know better, she might have detected a bit of sympathy therein. "The disappointment of no vacuum machine delivery, and then the moving of the grandfather clock—which I understand didn't go as well as it could have done until the gallant Elton came to the rescue—and drenched maids dripping ash and soot in your sitting room, followed by a murder right beneath your watchful eye . . ."

"I didn't expect there to be a *murder*," she said wearily.

"A murder was announced in the invitation," he replied. "What precisely *did* you expect, Mrs. Bright?"

"Certainly not that," she said as the motor rumbled to a halt just outside the garage. "Definitely not that."

She paused as her fingers closed over the door latch, and turned to look at him. There was a bit more illumination though the headlights had gone dark, for an old-fashioned gas lamp lit a patch of ground between the garage and the back door of the house. "Despite what you might think, Mr. Bradford, I do not revel in the fact that horrible deaths seem to find me wherever I go."

With that, she shoved open the door and slipped out of the motor before he could come around and get in her way. Her shoes crunched sharply on the stones and dirt as she strode toward the three steps that led down to the kitchen door.

Even in her state of weariness and irritation, she noticed that before going to bed, Opal had swept the steps and dusted the lamp that shined outside the door. That young woman was a superior worker. Someday, she would make an excellent housekeeper.

Phyllida was just reaching for the door latch when she heard a noise from the shadows. It sounded like a whimper—but not, thank heaven, from the likes of Myrtle or any other four-legged, tailed, or fanged creature. It was definitely a human sort of whimpering, and now there was also sniffling.

She walked over to a shadowy shape huddled on a small bench that overlooked the herb garden.

"Oh! Mrs. Bright!" The shape jolted and unfolded itself from the bench into the form of a maid. She was still sniffling, but at least she had a handkerchief with which to attend to the drizzling.

"Ginny. What on earth are you doing out here at this time of night?"

"I . . . n-nothing, Mrs. Bright." The young woman's honey hair caught the lamplight, which gave her a sort of golden halo.

Phyllida stood, immovable in front of the young woman who was clearly not doing "nothing." She'd found that silence in combination with an impenetrable stance usually resulted in revelations and confessions—at least from parlormaids and footmen. Sadly, not from murderers, however.

"It's only . . . I don't know what to do." Ginny's normal first soprano voice was more of a tenor due to the scratch of emotion. "It's all a mess."

Phyllida sighed inwardly. It would clearly be a while before she could find peace and quiet in her apartment. She brushed a hand over the bench to clear it of any debris and sank down onto it. Then she patted the space next to her and said, "Sit."

Ginny stiffened and stepped back. "Oh, no, Mrs. Bright, I c-couldn't."

"It's late and I'm quite tired, for a man was murdered tonight. *Sit.*"

With a little gasp, the girl sat.

"Now tell me about it," Phyllida said, gentling her voice whilst still keeping it firm enough to discourage whimpering and whingeing.

"It's only . . . Molly and me, we used to be pals. And now alluva sudden, we're not." She scrubbed her nose with the handkerchief. "It ain't right, but I don't know how to fix it. I don't even know if I really want to. Molly, she . . . she just don't want to speak to me anymore. And today . . . well . . . she said something under her breath about me, and it wasn't nice, and I—I just . . ." She sighed miserably.

"It's over Elton, I expect," said Phyllida.

"I don't know, ma'am." Then Ginny moaned. "Yes, most probably. Only, I don't know how it happened. We both agreed when he first came here that neither of us would stand in the way of the other. We thought he'd be the one to pick, and neither of us would hold it against the other if he wanted to court them, right?"

Elton had joined the staff at Mallowan Hall after his unpleasant boss fired him during a house party. Had Phyllida realized what a disruption the handsome, deferent young man would have caused, she might not have facilitated him being hired on by Mr. Max.

But, to the young man's credit, it wasn't his fault the maids were all making cakes of themselves over him. In her observations, she'd never seen Elton indicate any sort of preference for any of them, but at the same time, always being the consummate gentleman. It was no wonder the girls were infatuated.

"But he hasn't singled out either of you, has he? And that makes each of you try to attract his attention even harder."

"No, Mrs. Bright. But that's not it at all. I'm not trying to attract his attention . . . well, not *really.*"

"Ginny," Phyllida said in her brook-no-argument tone, "I've seen it with my own eyes. You offer to sew on his button. Molly suggests Elton might wish to look at the moon when she has to take out the slop. You make certain you're in the laundry when Elton brings Mr. Max's ties to be freshened. Molly bribes Freddie to move over so she can sit next to Elton at dinner.

"And then there's Mary, who accidentally drops her basket of rags when Elton passes by the study so he has to stop and help her pick them up. And Bess and Lizzie are just as bad," she went on, naming the second parlormaid and two chambermaids. "It's as if every last one of you have dropped your brains in the well. Your brains *and* your self-respect," she went on firmly when Ginny made noises as if to protest.

The young woman subsided into silence. Then she heaved a sigh and sniffled. "I don't know what to do. I wish he'd never come here."

"What you *do,*" Phyllida said a trifle sharply, "is *nothing.* You cease attempting to draw his attention. You cease to compete with your friends. You cease to manufacture ways to cross paths with the man. You simply let it be. There is nothing more foolish than a woman throwing herself in the path of a man," she added. "Trust me, I have plenty of experience with the male sex and there is never a good reason to lose one's self-respect over them."

Ginny sniffled again. "You have?"

Phyllida set her jaw. "Yes."

"But . . . how? When? Are you speaking of—do you mean—*Mr. Bright*?" Ginny seemed eager to push aside her own problems to dive into the big question as to when or if her boss had ever been married.

Before Phyllida could decide how—or even whether—to respond, a dark blur bolted from out of nowhere, yapping and writhing and leaping. She stifled a gasp and barely managed to lift her feet away from the creature's path.

How on earth did such a wild, slathering beast manage to sneak up so quietly, and then explode into such chaos?

Good heavens. And now was Phyllida required to be grateful to Myrtle the Crazed Canine for rescuing her from having to address one of the few topics about which she refused to speak?

"Oh, Myrtle!" Ginny was giggling now as the excited dog attempted to climb onto her lap while barking at the top of her canine lungs. The creature was even trying to *lick her in the face*, an activity that made Phyllida bolt up from the bench in order to remove herself from the proximity of that lolling pink tongue and snuffling wet nose.

"Ginny, I suggest you put that beast down and take yourself off to bed. Morning will come early. And mind, I'll not have any of my maids acting as saboteurs to each other any longer—especially over a *man*. And good heavens—*do* wash your face and hands," she added with a shudder, imagining the maid resting her cheek on a pillow and sleeping atop dog slobber all night.

And where was Myrtle's master? Bradford was never far behind the wild beast. For all she knew, he'd taught the dog to purposely sneak up on her and then erupt into barking, wagging, licking, and leaping.

"Thank you, Mrs. Bright," said Ginny. Her cheek and the bridge of her nose glistened from the canines's ministrations, and Phyllida shuddered again. "Good night, Mrs. Bright."

"I suggest you make an effort to speak to Molly," Phyllida said. "I suspect most of the conflict between the two of you is unimportant and quite likely even nonexistent."

"Thank you, Mrs. Bright," she said and bent to give Myrtle one last pat on the head. "What a good girl," she said as the dog wriggled with delight.

Phyllida realized belatedly that with Ginny abandoning the scene, Myrtle would immediately transfer her attentions to herself. She did not want another ladder in her stockings and she certainly didn't want dog slobber on her hand, knee, or even her shoe, and so she hurried into the house on Ginny's heels.

As she ducked inside, she swore she heard a low masculine chuckle from the shadows.

CHAPTER 8

THE NEXT MORNING, PHYLLIDA WAS IN HER SITTING ROOM, DRESSED, coifed, and enjoying her morning tea and toast, when she heard the telephone ring in the hallway.

She pushed away from the desk, where she'd been preparing drafts to pay the suppliers, in between making notes about Mr. Wokesley's murder, and walked briskly to answer the call, hoping it would be news from the delinquent Vac-Tric delivery. Mr. Dobble was just emerging from his pantry when she lifted the receiver from its moorings.

"Mallowan Hall," she said.

"Phyllida! Do tell me *everything* that happened. You know I wasn't sleeping all night over it, and poor Max is quite grumpy this morning about me tossing and turning."

Phyllida had been planning to call Agatha when she was certain her employers were awake, so she was pleased that Agatha had beaten her to it.

Mr. Dobble hovered in the corridor, clearly intending to wrest the telephone receiver from her hand if the call had been for anyone else.

"It's Mrs. Agatha," she told Mr. Dobble, covering the mouthpiece with her hand. "She wants to know what happened last night."

Since Phyllida was feeling particularly generous this morning, she decided it was permissible for Mr. Dobble to listen in when she told Agatha what had gone on at Beecham House. After all, he would find out eventually. It was best if he got the actual information rather than gossip.

Aside from that, any sort of murder in the vicinity of Listleigh brought in hordes of press—and they always made their way to Agatha Christie's home, for some convoluted reason. It was best that Phyllida and Dobble both be prepared for such an eventuality, even though the Mallowans were not in residence and had had nothing to do with the murder.

So instead of waving him off or turning her back to him, she beckoned Mr. Dobble to come closer so he could listen. Despite her kind gesture, his expression remained tart-lemon-sour.

"Well?" Agatha was saying, her voice tinny over the line. "What was the murder announcement all about?"

Phyllida gave a brief explanation about the Wokesleys' Murder Game, ending with a dramatic telling of how the double doors had been thrown open to the drawing room to reveal a very real dead body on the floor.

"Good heavens!" Agatha's cheery voice dropped with horror. "I had no idea something so awful happened! Do forgive me for seeming so light and airy about it all. That must have been terrible. A terrible shock for everyone."

"Quite. But you had no way of knowing such a tragedy had happened. It certainly couldn't have been in the papers yet." Phyllida glanced over to see the same shock registering on the butler's face.

"No, of course not. Still, murder—even in games—is no laughing matter," Agatha said, still sounding subdued.

"Quite right," Phyllida replied. "It was very tragic, and such an odd way to do away with someone. To stab them in the back of the neck during such a public event when anyone could have walked in. That takes an inordinate amount of audacity."

Or lunacy.

"And how will they ever find out who did it with so many people there?" Agatha asked. "Why, from what you say, there must have been at least two dozen guests along with the playactors.

That's far too many suspects to be manageable. I try to stick with no more than seven at a time, and then I kill one or two of them off halfway through. But of course, this is real life and it certainly doesn't conform to fictional tenets."

"Quite," Phyllida said again, and explained how there were really only five people who'd had access to the parlor, as well as the servants.

"Oh, yes . . . the servants—who are always a font of information. Surely one of them saw or heard something. Yes, that is far more manageable. Five suspects. I must say again I am so very sorry about Mr. Wokesley's death. I'd never even met the man, but it's so tragic. Still, with the culprit narrowed down to five suspects, well, even Inspector Cork ought to be able to spot the perpetrator," Agatha said.

Phyllida made an ambiguous sound and caught Mr. Dobble's eye. He well knew how erroneously Inspector Cork had acted during the Murder Fête poisonings, arresting the wrong person and missing a shocking number of clues.

"But you'll assist him, won't you, Phyllie?" Agatha added. "Cork, I mean. Heaven knows he could use a woman's guidance."

While Phyllida heartily agreed, she wasn't quite ready to fully throw her hat in the ring as detective. After all, she did have a vacuum machine due to arrive at any moment and plenty of drama here at Mallowan Hall with which to contend. "I did guide Constable Greensticks in his conducting of the interviews since the inspector isn't able to arrive until sometime today."

"That was very smart of you, Phyllie," said Agatha. "And I'm certain they went quite well."

"They did. Poor Mrs. Wokesley seemed quite overset," Phyllida said, remembering the tragic expression on Beatrice Wokesley's face. "And the staff at Beecham House . . . well, quite honestly, I don't know how much assistance they'll be to the guests during this tragedy. Particularly the housekeeper. She seems rather inept."

"Why then, by all means you ought to go over to Beecham House and offer your support," Agatha said immediately. "It's the neighborly thing to do. After all, most households simply aren't well versed in what to do when a murder takes place. Unfortunately, you've had a bumper crop of experience in such matters, Phyllida."

"I don't wish to intrude, and there are so many things happening here at Mallowan Hall," Phyllida said. She was not being disingenuous. She was sincerely concerned about what state the house might be in once she returned from an extended visit to Beecham House.

For, despite her conversation with Ginny, Phyllida wasn't certain the maids would put aside their differences. And then there was the matter of Dobble and his loathing of chintz and lace, not to mention her cats.

Aside from all of that, she desperately wanted to be here when the vacuum cleaner was delivered. A rather unimportant reason in the grand scheme of things, but Phyllida had been the one to do all of the research on whether to get a Hoover or a Vac-Tric or some other machine. And she'd been the one to scrimp about in the household budget to find the room for such a purchase. She simply couldn't allow someone else to be the one to unbox and test it out.

"Oh, balderdash," said Agatha. "Dobble can handle things for half a day."

That was precisely what Phyllida was afraid of. Mr. Dobble would probably hide the bloody machine when it came if she wasn't there. She glanced at the butler, who was eyeing her balefully in return. Although he likely couldn't hear exactly what Agatha was saying, he could probably guess based on her responses.

But her boss and friend was asking her to make herself available . . .

"Perhaps I will make a brief visit," Phyllida said with a sigh. "I can at least apprise Inspector Cork—presuming he has arrived in Listleigh—of my observations and deductions."

"I think that is only fitting," Agatha replied warmly. "At the end of the day, the most important thing is for the perpetrator to be identified and arrested—regardless of who solves the case. Now what was the victim's name again? It struck a chord with me when you mentioned it."

"Clifton Wokesley, of the 'woolen Wokesleys.' He was married to the former Beatrice Forrte."

"Wokesley. Yes, that definitely sounds familiar to me . . . but I'm not certain how."

"He's been involved as a sponsor and investor in a theater in the West End," Phyllida replied, knowing that Agatha had her own contacts in the theatrical world of London. People were always wanting to produce her stories into films or plays.

"That could be where I've heard the name. I'll have to ask around and see whether anyone I know has any information on him. But I seem to recall something . . ." Agatha's voice trailed off. "Now what *was* it?"

"Mrs. Wokesley did mention something about her husband needing to get away to the country, and that he hadn't been himself since 'the scandal,' but she didn't elaborate and I didn't have the opportunity to pursue that line of questioning further," Phyllida said.

"A scandal?" Agatha sounded very curious and perhaps even a bit gleeful. "Why, how lucky it is that I'm here in London where I can do some investigating for you and try to find out. I can visit the newspaper archives and perhaps even speak to someone at Scotland Yard. They're always happy to help Agatha Christie. Perhaps I'll become your Captain Hastings, Madame Bright," she added teasingly.

"That would be most appreciated," Phyllida said. She could pass any relevant information on to Inspector Cork. "Perhaps you could also see if there are any interesting news articles or notices about some of the other suspects. Everyone has a secret," she said, thinking of Mr. Brixton's claim.

"I told Cliff it wasn't a good idea to mess around with revealing peoples' dirty secrets, skeletons in their closets . . ."

Everyone had secrets. But not every secret was worth killing over.

Yet someone's secret had been worth enough of a risk to shove a stiletto blade into the back of a man's skull.

"Why, Mrs. Bright, what brings you down here?" said Mrs. Puffley when Phyllida walked into the kitchen at half nine that morning. "Is the vacuum machine here yet?"

The cook at Mallowan Hall was in her middle forties and built like a steam engine. She had broad shoulders, muscular arms, and powerful hands—all the result of years of kneading, chopping, pounding, slicing, and butchering. Her wiry brown hair was mostly confined beneath a cap, and her perpetually flushed face sported a streak of flour across its chin.

The kitchen was a roomy space, and with three-quarters of it being underground, it remained at a relatively comfortable temperature even when the ovens were filled with breads, roasts, and pies, and numerous pots bubbled and steamed on the stove. There was a long worktable where Molly and Benita, the second kitchen maid, were hard at work. Opal, the lowest ranking maid in the entire household, was in the scullery washing eggs that Phyllida Bright, incidentally, did *not* have to pull from the hens' nests.

"Good morning, Mrs. Puffley," said Phyllida. "Unfortunately, the vacuum hasn't yet arrived, and there's been no message as to when it might. But I am going to make a brief visit back to Beecham House and I was hoping to take a basket of some of your biscuits or scones. I thought to add some rosemary jelly and currant jam as well. What do you have that might go with that?"

While Harriet Puffley lorded over the domain of the kitchen—the ovens, stoves, chopping block, steamer, fry pans, roasters, and mixing bowls—Phyllida reigned supreme in the distilling room, where preserves, infusions, and other household concoctions such as cleaning solutions were prepared under her watchful eye.

"Good morning, Benita," said Phyllida.

The junior kitchen maid looked up, giving Phyllida a shy smile before returning to her task of peeling potatoes. "Good morning, Mrs. Bright." She had recently been promoted from scullion to second kitchen maid and was still glowing from the welcome change. She was also not paying very close attention to the knife she was wielding, so Phyllida thought it best if she didn't distract her any further.

"Good morning, Molly," Phyllida said.

Molly looked up at Phyllida, a shadow crossing her face before she mustered a smile and murmured, "Good morning, Mrs. Bright." Then she ducked her head and returned to snipping the pile of green beans mounded next to her.

As usual, Molly was dressed neatly in her starched uniform, her hair scraped back into a tight knot so as to keep random tendrils from ending up in the soup or gravy. But her face had appeared haggard and Phyllida discerned a bit of redness in Molly's eyes when she returned her boss's greeting.

Clearly all was not well in Molly's world, but whether it was due to her feud with Ginny or some other reason was undetermined. After all, Mrs. Puffley had a tongue sharp as her butcher knife and wasn't afraid to flay with it a lazy or distracted maid.

"Why, I've got rosemary popovers—my secret recipe—and something new I've just tried out. Maize muffins. A spot of butter and some red jam or even honey with them would do the trick," said Mrs. Puffley. "Molly."

At the prompt, Molly moved to a cooling rack against one of the walls and retrieved a muffin tin.

"They smell delicious," Phyllida said, looking at the golden corn muffins, which were still warm. "That'll do the trick, Mrs. Puffley. Thank you.

"Molly, please pack up a basket with a dozen muffins, a small jar of currant jam, and a bit of Piero's honey," she said. "Put a sprig of chamomile in the honey, won't you?"

Piero was the man-of-all-work who came in one or two mornings a week to Mallowan Hall to repair items such as clocks or lamps, or to do similar sorts of tasks. He and his father managed beehives at home and Phyllida obtained most of the house's honey from them.

"Yes, mu'um," replied Molly, hurrying out of the room to retrieve the basket.

"Use one of the pressed blue napkins for the basket, mind; not the embroidered ones," she called after her. While Phyllida's intention was to demonstrate to Mrs. Treacle how a housekeeper could maintain control of her staff and efficiently run the household whilst a murder investigation was being conducted underfoot, she wasn't about to leave a piece of the Mallowans' best linens at Beecham House. The cheery blue calico would have to suffice.

"Very well then, now that you've cleaned me out of maize muffins, Mrs. Bright, I don't suppose you can tell me all about your latest murder," said Mrs. Puffley. She plopped a loin of pork onto the work table, making every utensil on the surface jump and clink.

"It's not *my* murder," Phyllida replied. "I only happened by chance to be present."

"'At's like I said—your murder," cackled the cook. "I suppose Barney'll be up here nattering on about it soon enough, but you couldn't tell me a bit now, could you?"

It took Phyllida an instant to realize Barney was none other than Constable Greensticks. Apparently, things had progressed between the cook and constable far more rapidly than she'd realized if she was referring to him by his familiar name.

But whether they were actually courting, or whether the policeman was merely taking advantage of free handouts from the kitchen, and Mrs. Puffley of a rapt audience for her stories and rantings, remained to be seen.

Deciding she was far too embroiled in other romantic conundrums relative to her household staff, Phyllida refrained from asking Mrs. Puffley about the nature of her relationship with Constable Greensticks. It really wasn't any of her business and she certainly didn't want to expend any energy thinking about it. Why, the constable had to be at least a decade younger than the cook! Not that Phyllida had any qualms about a younger man courting an older woman. Not in the least.

Since Mrs. Puffley was still watching her expectantly, Phyllida quickly explained what happened at Beecham House last night.

"Good heavens," Mrs. Puffley said as she deftly began to tie up the pork roast with string. "What an awful thing to have happened. Benita, the suet needs to be chopped. And that bacon. Fine as can be, mind you. And where is that Molly?"

"I'm here, mu'um," said Molly as she sailed in carrying the basket.

Phyllida took it from her and approved of the neatly packed food items. The maid had also tucked a small sprig of rosemary and a trio of Michaelmas daisies into the folds of the napkin. "Thank you, Molly," she said with a smile. "It looks lovely."

The tension eased from the maid's shoulders. "My pleasure, Mrs. Bright," she said with a little curtsy.

"Molly, chervil and parsley from the garden. Rosemary too, and don't dawdle," snapped Mrs. Puffley.

Molly, who was well used to the cook's abrupt manner and remained undisturbed by it, hurried from the kitchen, scissors in hand.

"I suppose I'd best be off," Phyllida said, sliding the basket onto her arm. "Although I suppose that means an encounter with Myrtle before I can wrangle Bradford behind the wheel of the motor."

"You can take my bicycle," Mrs. Puffley said, an offer that had Phyllida shuddering.

Phyllida Bright arrive at Beecham House with flat hair, out of breath, and perspiring? Never.

That was the one real drawback to living in the country: One couldn't walk or take the Underground or a trolley or omnibus. One had to rely on surly chauffeurs if one wanted to get somewhere.

"No thank you, Mrs. Puffley. I'll gird my loins and prepare for battle with the beast," Phyllida said.

Mrs. Puffley chuckled, shaking her head. "Dunno why you're always off complaining about that itsy-bitsy thing. She wouldn't hurt a flea!"

"That's because the beast's most likely *got* them," Phyllida retorted. *Itsy-bitsy?* Why, that creature had to be at least as big as an elephant!

Mrs. Puffley's laughter followed her out of the kitchen.

Phyllida checked the position of her hat in the small mirror on the way out of the back door. That was one small improvement she'd added shortly after arriving at Mallowan Hall—hanging a mirror there. Everyone ought to look their best before leaving the house, even if it was to cut herbs or scrounge for eggs.

Her pale blue hat—a woman's version of a trilby—with its single dancing feather of gray and black and a wide navy band, was in place. Her bright hair spilled out from beneath the chapeau's curled-up brim.

Phyllida had recently cut her hair to just below her chin, so she no longer had to fashion and pin it into a roll every morning. Instead, she used combs with sparkling beads and paste gems to hold the waves out of her face—and to ensure that Mr. Dobble had something else to frown and mutter about. Even more than chintz and an overabundance of lace, he detested anything about a housekeeper's attire that wasn't black, gray, or navy blue. And so Phyllida made certain to wear cornflower-blue or aubergine or spring-green frocks, some even with *patterns*! Today she'd chosen a light frock of butter-yellow rayon sprigged with tiny blue flowers and frilly cap sleeves.

Assured that her appearance was more than acceptable, Phyllida slipped outside. She discovered it had rained overnight, with the threat of more to come, and she took care to avoid walking in the damp grass so as not to ruin her shoes. There was a gravel path to the garage, and to her surprise she discovered that Bradford had already pulled the Daimler outside—whether in anticipation of her needing a ride, or for some other reason. It gleamed in the morning sun; perhaps he'd been waxing or buffing it or whatever one did with motorcars to keep their exteriors clean.

Phyllida hesitated, then approached the motor. The last thing she needed was an exuberant Myrtle dashing up with muddy paws to ruin her yellow frock. She frowned, looking around. There was no sign of life from either canine or master.

Amsi, the gardener, was across the way, almost to the stone wall that separated the main grounds from the apple orchard. He was trimming rosebushes, which reminded Phyllida that she wanted him to harvest some rosehips so she could supervise the making of jelly. However, she wasn't going to walk across the wet grass to tell him, so it could wait. Rosehips were plentiful and took a while to dry out.

She had taken two more steps toward the waiting motor when she heard a sound that sent a tremor of . . . well, not precisely terror, but severe concern. Accompanying that almost-terrifying noise of yapping was a dark blur, tearing out from the depths of the garage.

Phyllida swallowed a gasp and stumbled away as the beast bolted toward her. She prepared to be leapt upon.

But to her shock and surprise, Myrtle not only didn't launch herself at Phyllida's stocking-covered legs, but she came to a halt right in front of her. The creature's bum plopped to the ground and she looked up at Phyllida with dancing, beady dark eyes. Her black nose glistened and her dark pink tongue lolled from the side of her mouth as she panted happily.

"Quite," Phyllida replied to what was clearly a demand for acknowledgment and praise. "You are behaving in a shockingly ladylike fashion. I cannot imagine where you learned such genteel behavior." She looked around, expecting Bradford to make an appearance at any moment. "Regardless, it is quite an improvement on your previous manners. Excellent work."

Suddenly, Myrtle gave a little yip and bolted up to all fours. Phyllida automatically braced herself again, but the tangled mop turned and dashed toward her master, who'd just emerged from the side door of the garage.

"Why, good morning, Mrs. Bright," said Bradford—hatless and coatless as per usual—as he bent to pat the leaping, springing beast. It appeared he also slipped her some sort of edible treat. "I suppose you'll be wanting a ride up to Beecham House."

Phyllida did not care to be anticipated, but she certainly wasn't going to show it. Instead, she replied, "Quite right, Mr. Bradford."

He gave her a look that just stopped short of a roll of his eyes. Surely he was reacting to her use of his honorific "Mister," which she well knew he disliked. Thus, Phyllida only utilized the title when she was feeling particularly contrary. It was rather like the way he said her name—Mrs. Bright—in a sort of ironic tone.

"Very well, then, Mrs. Bright. She's all cleaned up and ready to go," he said, opening the front passenger door.

But before Phyllida could take even one step toward the gleaming Daimler, Myrtle leaped forward and launched herself into the motorcar, settling on the leather bench seat.

"Apparently Myrtle wants to ride along," Bradford said, giving Phyllida a cheeky grin.

Just what she wanted. A muddy dog climbing over her seat and possibly her lap, depositing hair, mud, and slobber all over her frock as well as in the basket of foodstuffs she was delivering.

"Perhaps she could stay here with Amsi," she said firmly.

"Did you hear that, old girl? *She* doesn't want you to ride along," Bradford said in a sad, crooning tone Phyllida had never heard before. "And with you saving her life less than a fortnight ago—and after you didn't even jump on her skirt!"

Myrtle seemed to comprehend her master's speech, and she bounded to the edge of the passenger seat, looking out at Phyllida with hopeful dark eyes as she panted hotly.

"She didn't save my life," Phyllida replied tartly. "You didn't actually save my life," she said again, this time to the dog. "You only assisted me extricating myself without ruining my frock." It was true. Phyllida had been perfectly safe after that incident with the motorcar when she was investigating the deaths at the Murder Fête. She didn't know why Bradford continued to state otherwise.

"And she saved yet another frock today by not jumping on you," Bradford reminded her. "Not to mention your silk stockings." He glanced toward her calves. "And a fine pair they're protecting too, aren't they, Myrtle?"

Phyllida was mortified when she felt her cheeks heat. Good *heavens.* What had gotten into the man? And what on earth had gotten into *her*? Blushing over a silly comment like that.

Not that she was blushing, truly. It was more of an irritated flush, she told herself firmly . . . whilst holding her breath in order for the telltale color in her cheeks to subside.

"There's mud all over the seat now." She pointed.

Bradford looked over and sighed. "And so there is. Myrtle, you've just ruined your chances of riding along, now, haven't you?" He scooped up the mop, then deposited her onto the ground, following that with a smooth hand gesture. Phyllida tensed again, preparing for the inevitable, but Myrtle merely sat and panted as Bradford cleaned off the seat.

When all muddy residue was gone and he was finished drying the bench, he gestured for Phyllida to climb in. "Your chariot, madam."

Now it was her turn to roll her eyes, but she did it so he couldn't see. There was no need to encourage such behavior.

Moments later, with Myrtle happily distracted by assisting Amsi—who didn't mind slathering or barking, but drew the line at digging—in the rose garden, Bradford navigated the Daimler down the drive. He was, of course, still sans hat and coat, although he had pulled on a handsome pair of brown leather driving gloves.

"Hoping to arrive before Inspector Cork, are you, Mrs. Bright?"

"I have no idea what time the inspector is expected to arrive, and even if I did, it would have no bearing on my bereavement visit to the Wokesley home," she said loftily.

"Right," he said, almost sounding sincere.

Phyllida remained steadfastly silent for the remainder of the ride, and to her surprise, Bradford did as well. When she'd first met him, he'd been reticent and relatively quiet. And very grumpy.

That might possibly have been because she'd half accused him of being a killer.

But over the last weeks, she'd been exposed to a more verbose version of Bradford—usually comments or digs at her expense. Sometimes with his own (usually misguided) theories about murder.

"There's no sign of the inspector's motor," said Bradford as he drove them up the drive at Beecham House. "Perhaps he's been delayed. You might be required to take over the investigation, Mrs. Bright."

She gave him a look. "And I suppose you'd like that, as it would remove me from the vicinity of Mallowan Hall for an extended period of time." Without waiting for a response or for his assistance, she opened the door and climbed out.

"When shall I come for you, then, Mrs. Bright?" he said, having remained in the motor and ducking to look at her through the passenger window. "Or do you prefer to ring?"

She noticed he didn't deny her supposition. "No . . . I shan't be long. An hour should suffice. Well, perhaps two," she added, thinking of Mrs. Treacle's capabilities—or, more accurately, lack thereof.

"Very well, then, Mrs. Bright." He gave a short little toot of the horn, then drove away.

Once again Phyllida was left with the decision: knock at the front door of Beecham House, or take herself around to the servants' entrance.

In the end, she went around to the servants' entrance. It wasn't that she didn't expect to be admitted should she approach the front door. It was that she thought it would be prudent to keep her visit under wraps from the guests—who were also the suspects—for the time being.

Although she'd interviewed the five playactors, Phyllida had not had the opportunity to speak to the staff about what had happened. As she well knew, the downstairs people saw and heard *everything*. And they liked to gossip.

Surely there was more information to be gleaned from questioning Mr. Trifle, Mrs. Treacle, the footman, and the housemaid. Perhaps even the cook—whose name thankfully wasn't Truffle but an equally confection-like Napoleon—would know something.

With this in mind, Phyllida followed the brick walkway around to the back of Beecham House.

She noted the chicken coop with its fenced-in yard and gave a little shudder over the idea of a housekeeper shoving her hand beneath a hen in order to remove an egg. She observed a small outbuilding that had probably once been a stable but, like many barns nowadays, had been converted to a motorcar garage. The small herb garden located just outside the kitchen door garnered her approval, but she noticed that the basil was going to flower, and that the mint had gone leggy and was threatening to overtake the chervil. She tsked over that and started toward the back door, also noting the lack of any barking, yapping, bounding, or slathering canine—although there was a goat tied to a tree.

She was just about to reach for the bell handle when someone screamed.

CHAPTER 9

THE SCREAM CAME FROM INSIDE THE HOUSE. PHYLLIDA DIDN'T WAIT to ring the bell; she yanked open the servants' door and rushed in.

She found herself in a narrow, windowless corridor that obviously led to the kitchen, scullery, and servants' dining hall. The screaming had not abated, and she was able to follow the sound of the high-pitched shrieking that even Ginny wouldn't be able to match.

It was coming from a small room, which turned out to be the larder.

Phyllida stumbled to a halt at the open door.

Mrs. Treacle stopped screaming when she saw Phyllida. The housekeeper from London was standing on a stool and had obviously been in the process of attempting to wedge herself onto one of the shelves.

"What on earth is happening?" Phyllida asked.

"It's—it's *there*!" Mrs. Treacle pointed toward the corner with a shaking finger. "Over there!"

"What is it?" Phyllida said, taking a small step backward.

She had no desire to have a mouse or vole dart over her shiny black patent leather Mary Janes. Still, she didn't quite comprehend Mrs. Treacle's abject terror of a small rodent. They certainly had mice and voles in London. Incidentally, these sorts of events were precisely why Phyllida had allowed Stilton and Rye to take up residence in her apartment, and had engaged them to patrol

Mallowan Hall. This sort of disruption would never occur if Beecham House had a good mouser or two.

"G-get a broom," cried Mrs. Treacle. She was half sobbing with what seemed to be terror, and she was still trying in vain to crowd herself onto a waist-high shelf of canned beans. She was slender enough to have a chance at it, though Phyllida wasn't confident the shelf would hold the extra weight. "Get it out of here! *Please.*"

And then Phyllida saw *it.*

It was not a mouse. Not even any sort of rodent.

It was a snake.

A big, silvery-brown adder with creepy red eyes.

It was huddled in the corner of the larder, coiled up with its head swaying gently as it appeared to look around.

Phyllida's heart surged into her throat and she took another step back. Mice, spiders, bats—even rats—were relatively commonplace invaders here in the country. She was quite experienced in dealing with those sorts of interlopers.

But a snake was a *very* different situation.

Phyllida didn't like mice or rats or bats in her house. And she loathed spiders with all those crawly legs and messy webs that cropped up in every corner, every day and had to be eradicated. But snakes elicited an entirely different emotion from her: fear.

Phyllida Bright was definitely afraid of snakes. Especially big silvery ones like the adder. Especially venomous snakes—like the one curled up in the corner, watching her with its murderous red eyes.

"Where's the dratted footman?" she asked, keeping one eye on the snake whilst looking for a broom or bucket or even a cloth. Anything that could help contain or capture the snake.

"I-I don't know," Mrs. Treacle said, still well off the floor.

"The maids? The cook? *Anyone?*" So far the snake hadn't moved but Phyllida didn't trust it.

"I-I think Mrs. Napoleon went to the b-butcher. And the-the maids are cleaning upstairs," Mrs. Treacle replied, her eyes fixed on the snake in the corner. "What are you going to do?"

Phyllida had no idea what she was going to do. She *wanted* to turn around and go back outside and let Mrs. Treacle or Mr. Trifle deal with the adder in the pantry. But Phyllida Bright did not admit defeat, and she certainly didn't admit fear.

And so she knew it fell to her to somehow rescue Mrs. Treacle from being treed—or more accurately, shelved—by a snake.

She eased back out of the larder, her attention darting between the snake and her environs, searching for something that would help. Then she saw it: a good-sized washtub, sitting on the floor outside the scullery.

Spewing out a long, silent breath, Phyllida took up the washtub. Its metal handles creaked and squeaked in their hinges, adding to the unpleasant atmosphere.

Gritting her teeth and figuratively girding her loins, Phyllida edged back into the larder. Mrs. Treacle was still levered between the chair and the shelf, with one foot on each surface.

Phyllida wasn't certain whether she was relieved or disappointed that the adder hadn't moved. It was still coiled and at the ready in its corner. She lifted the washtub, turning it upside down, and took two careful steps toward the snake. Her knees were shaking and her palms were sweaty. She couldn't remember the last time she'd been in such a state.

The snake was still as stone, but its eyes burned red. Phyllida's heart thudded hard in her chest. The washtub creaked in her grip.

She took another step closer and realized she was having difficulty swallowing, for her heart had surged up into her throat.

Her intention was to sort of toss and drop the washtub over the snake, trapping it like one would capture a spider beneath an upside-down tankard. However, there was a large chance of failure and Phyllida was mostly worried about what would happen if she missed the snake and it lunged or slithered or zapped at her.

Just as she drew closer, her attention landed on a tablecloth that was folded (and out of place in the larder, but she wasn't about to quibble). Moving slowly and carefully, one eye still on the snake, Phyllida set the washtub down and picked up the tablecloth.

Without allowing herself to think too much about what she was doing, she eased the tablecloth open, then flung it over the snake in a lightning move. Before the cloth had even fluttered to the floor, she had the washtub in hand and leaped toward the corner, dropping the upside-down tub over the writhing tablecloth.

It landed with a loud clang almost precisely where she'd intended. Everything was still.

Phyllida exhaled shakily and eyed the washtub. For all she knew, the snake was strong and violent enough to flip and flop itself out from beneath its metal prison.

But nothing happened. There was a quiet rustling and she could see the parts of the tablecloth that protruded from beneath the tub moving slightly as the snake fought to free itself, but the wash basin remained stable. Just to be certain, she put a ten-pound sack of flour on top.

"All right then," she said briskly, brushing her damp, shaking hands together. "Very well. Now to get a footman in here to remove the culprit safely to the garden. Mrs. Treacle, you may come down now."

"Are you qu-quite certain?"

"Of course I'm certain," Phyllida replied. Now that everything was well in hand, her heart had settled back into place and her knees were strong and steady. And her patience for terror-stricken city housekeepers was at an end.

"Thank you so much, Mrs. B-Bright," said Mrs. Treacle as she lowered herself to the floor. "Heaven knows how long I would have been trapped here if you hadn't come along."

"Quite," replied Phyllida. She refrained from mentioning the fact that there was never a good reason for the kitchen and scullery to be empty of cook, maids, or any other staff—especially when there was a houseful of guests, and even more especially when there was a murderer lurking about.

At the thought, Phyllida stilled. A prickle went down her spine as she turned to look at the flour-topped washtub, under which lurked a venomous snake that had somehow made its way into the house.

Had that occurrence been an accident, or had it been something more sinister?

"How did it get in here?" she said, more to herself than Mrs. Treacle because she didn't expect the housekeeper would have any sort of reasonable answer.

"I-I don't know," replied Mrs. Treacle predictably. "I came in here to get a jar of pickled beets and there it was. It's—it's poisonous, isn't it?"

"I believe the adder is in fact venomous," Phyllida replied calmly.

"What if I'd been *bitten*?" cried Mrs. Treacle, clapping a hand to her chest and gathering up her necklace around a finger. "I could have *died*!" Then her eyes widened. "Is it possible . . . do you think someone *put* it there? To-to kill me?"

"That is an excellent question, and one to which I've already set my mind. Whether its venom is enough to be fatal to a person is another question.

"However, the prevailing concern—if the snake's invasion was indeed purposeful—is whether you were the intended victim. After all, who could have known you'd be down here alone, not to mention being the only person to go into the larder at this time?" She fixed Mrs. Treacle with a look. "It's not at all usual—or permissible—that the kitchen should be abandoned to only the housekeeper."

Despite her tear-streaked face, Mrs. Treacle was still neat as a pin. Her dark blond hair was fashioned into a roll along the nape of her neck, and she had those tiny spit-curls neatly placed around her hairline. Mr. Dobble would have approved of her pale gray cotton dress, unadorned but for white lace collar and cuffs. She was an attractive and relatively young woman to be in such a position. Phyllida suspected she could be more than an entire decade younger than she—and clearly unaccustomed to such responsibility as running a large household (though not as large as Mallowan Hall) in the country.

Thus, Phyllida felt it was her duty to mentor the younger woman in her role.

"Right. Of course," Mrs. Treacle said uncertainly. "I simply—I only—well, there was another mishap upstairs and I had to send all of the maids and footmen to attend to it—broken glass and silver polish everywhere—"

"Another mishap? Like the teapot catastrophe?" Phyllida wasn't entirely successful in keeping the frustration from her voice. "I fear your staff must be entirely made up of bumbling clowns, Mrs. Treacle."

The woman's pretty face flushed a little. "Of course I will speak to them. Only, I think everyone is rather—upended with what happened to Mr. Wokesley last night."

"Quite right," Phyllida replied in a milder voice. She privately censured herself for being so brusque toward the younger, less-experienced housekeeper. The poor thing was clearly trying her best, and she likely only needed a firm hand to guide her.

At that moment, a heavy clomping down the hallway indicated the arrival of the footman.

"Oh, Anthony," said Mrs. Treacle—but only after darting a look at Phyllida as if to determine whether she meant to speak, "there is a—a snake under the washtub in the corner of the larder. Please dispose of it immediately."

"Wot? Wot kinda snake izzit?" Anthony's eyes lit up. "You want me to bash its head in, mum?"

"Certainly not," snapped Phyllida, who saw no reason to harm an innocent reptile. Whether its presence was an accident or an act of malice, it didn't matter. The slimy thing didn't belong inside and would be far happier slithering through the grass *far, far* from the house. "That would make an entirely unnecessary mess."

And aside from the mess of bashed-in snake brains, there was also the distinct possibility that the footman would cause yet another "catastrophe" or "mishap" in carrying out such a task.

"Yes, mum," said Anthony, giving a little bow.

"Now," said Phyllida, turning her attention to Mrs. Treacle. "I believe it's time for us to have a chat."

Mrs. Treacle blanched, her eyes going wide as the color drained from her face. "Of-of course."

Amused by the woman's apparent consternation, Phyllida took up the basket she'd brought and subsequently set aside during the adder debacle. "Lead the way to your sitting room or office, if you will, Mrs. Treacle. And may I suggest that you get one of your kitchen maids back down here posthaste. Where is the scullion? The guests will surely be wanting their tea and coffee—and perhaps even some breakfast?—any time now." She looked pointedly at the watch she had pinned to her dress. It was nearly ten o'clock.

"Quite right," replied Mrs. Treacle, whose healthy color had returned to her face.

Phyllida took careful observations of the environment of Beecham House as she followed Mrs. Treacle up three steps to a small corridor that led to her apartments, and, presumably, the butler's pantry and bedroom as well. What she saw didn't raise her ire relative to the condition of the house, but she did lift a brow at the loose metal carpet-rod on one of the steps.

"It's so good of you to come, Mrs. Bright," said Mrs. Treacle as she gestured into a small room with a single window curtained in yellow and brown calico. Pleasant enough, but not nearly as inviting as Phyllida's office at Mallowan Hall. "I don't suppose I've said that yet, with all of the excitement over the snake." She shuddered.

"Quite," replied Phyllida, taking a seat in an armchair near the small desk.

She was mildly surprised that the surface of the desk was neatly organized, with one stack of paper, a cup filled with pencils and ink pens, the framed photograph of a young woman holding a baby, and a small vase of daisies. A ledger, closed, was next to the stack of papers.

"Should I ring for tea?" Mrs. Treacle said.

"Oh, no, not at all," said Phyllida—mainly because she suspected it was a losing proposition, as the kitchen was empty of anyone to put on a kettle, not to mention actually deliver the beverage. And then there was the lack of intact teapots . . .

"Right." Mrs. Treacle gave her a weak smile and sat in her seat on the other side of the desk. "What . . . er . . . what did you want to speak with me about?"

Phyllida attributed Mrs. Treacle's nerves and discomfiture to her lack of experience in managing murders as well as being subject to interrogation. She gave the woman a smile meant to ease her mind and said, "I wasn't able to speak with you or your staff last night about what happened—what they might have seen or noticed during the evening. Additionally, I'd like to take a look at Mr. Wokesley's study."

"Oh. Right. I see. I suppose I'd have to ask Mrs. Wokesley about that," said Mrs. Treacle slowly. "I'm not certain it would be permissible."

Phyllida gave her a measured look. "This is a murder investigation, Mrs. Treacle. Everything is permissible in order to prevent another death."

"Oh. I suppose you must be right, then. And Mrs. Wokesley . . . I think she's still abed, anyway."

"Excellent." Phyllida rose and spoke briskly. "Now would be the perfect time for me to look around. And then perhaps I could speak to you and your staff afterward . . . assuming they've finished cleaning up the—er—catastrophe with the silver polish and the broken glass?"

"Oh. Right. Yes, of course," replied Mrs. Treacle, looking a bit dazed.

"I would appreciate it if you'd show me the way to Mr. Wokesley's study. I'd like to complete my observations before the constable returns with the inspector."

"Do you mean to say . . . you're going to be investigating the murder?" Mrs. Treacle came out from behind the desk. "I thought . . . well, I thought you were simply here to advise me and to . . . er . . . help put Beecham House to rights. I'm simply not cut out for managing a household with a murder in it." Her voice twinged into a sort of whine.

"And a murder*er*," Phyllida reminded her smoothly. "Don't forget that someone in this house killed Mr. Wokesley. And it's very possible he or she attempted to do the same to you this morning."

CHAPTER 10

Clifton Wokesley's private study, which was different from the library, where Phyllida and Constable Greensticks had conducted their interviews last evening, smelled of pipe tobacco and, faintly, of must.

It had recently been dusted, although the oak table and desk definitely needed proper polishing. To the credit of the household staff, however, there was a white milk-glass vase filled with fairly fresh roses, and the rug showed signs of a carpet sweeper having been recently employed. The curtains weren't dusty and the oil lamps (an old technology Phyllida did not miss at Mallowan Hall) appeared to have recently been dusted, so no ugly strings of greasy smoke clung to them.

Phyllida didn't know precisely what she was searching for, but she knew she needed to take the opportunity to snoop about before Inspector Cork arrived and upended everything by arresting the wrong person.

One thing in particular stuck in her mind—something that Mr. Brixton had said. He'd implied that there was some connection between the Murder Game characters and the actors who'd played them. She wanted to find a copy of the script or whatever notes Mr. Wokesley had made about the character roles so she could assess the veracity of Mr. Brixton's suggestion that there might be motives intertwined with the character roles.

Unfortunately, there were no notes nor scripts to be found either on or in the desk. In fact, the drawers were mostly empty except for some blank stationery embossed with BEECHAM HOUSE, DEVON, and a number of pencils, pens, erasers, and other similar office implements.

She had just closed the last drawer when the study door opened.

"Oh, excuse me, ma'am." The maid froze in the entrance. "I didn't know anyone was here. Is that you, Mrs. Bright?"

"Good morning, Louise," she replied. "Are you here to do the room?"

"No, ma'am, not yet. I was going to open the curtains is all. I already swept the rug. Only . . . Mrs. Treacle said you were wanting to speak to me." Louise came in and did a little curtsy. "Are *you* going to catch the killer, then, ma'am?"

Phyllida was aware of her reputation among the villagers of Listleigh, as well as that of the servants in and around the area. She'd become a sort of hero—though she strongly disliked the word; she'd only done what needed to be done to keep innocent persons from being incarcerated, or worse—to them, particularly the downstairs people. This phenomenon had been helped by her own staff at Mallowan Hall, who'd obviously indulged in quite a bit of gossiping, which apparently included singing her praises to all and sundry.

Thus, Phyllida ignored the question. Instead, she said, "Come through, then. Is there anything you can tell me about what happened last evening? I understand the actors were either in the drawing room or in the library and its adjacent hallway for most of the evening."

"Yes, ma'am. We were given strict orders that no one but the actors were to go into any of the rooms other than the entrance foyer or corridor during the game. Mr. Wokesley was very particular about it all. He said they needed their own room for waiting in—now was it a yellow one? Or a green one?"

This was nothing more than what Phyllida had already deduced. "Very well. And you and Anthony—were you serving any of the actors? Did you interact with any of them during the evening?"

"Why, no. We were mostly cleaning up the broken teapots," she replied, looking subdued. "There were ever so many of them. Anyhow, I did bring a tea tray out from the kitchen and put it on the side table between the library and the drawing room. Mrs. Treacle must have brought it into the drawing room for them, but Mr. Trifle said as how everyone only wanted martinis and Tommy Collinses and those sorts of things."

"When was the last time you saw Mr. Wokesley alive?"

"Oh. It was . . . well, I don't recall exactly, ma'am. There was a party going on with lots of people and it was very busy, you see. I think the last time I saw him was when he and that Mrs. Forrte were talking."

"And how were their demeanors at that time?" When Louise looked at her blankly, Phyllida clarified. "Did they seem relaxed or agitated or upset in any way?"

"Oh. No, ma'am, not as I could tell. But . . . I did notice Mrs. Forrte give him a—a sort of look when he turned away. It wasn't a very nice look, if you know what I mean, ma'am. Why, it was downright nasty."

Interesting. "Did you hear anything they were saying?"

"No, ma'am. If I did, I would tell you." She nodded vigorously and her short, springy black hair bobbed. "It was only about the play, I think. Where she was to stand and all. He did say something about a bracelet, I think."

"Very well, thank you. How were the other guests—I mean to say, the playactors who are staying here—getting along with Mr. Wokesley or each other?"

"I didn't hear or see anything strange," Louise said, clearly disappointed. "No one threatening to kill anyone, ma'am, or even being angry with each other. Everyone seemed in a fine mood when they arrived."

"Quite."

"But then . . ." Louise's round, freckled face screwed up as she frowned. "Well, it was when he—Mr. Wokesley, I mean to say—gave out the-the whatchu-callits—the scripts?—for the actors, well, some of them didn't look too happy about it."

"Do you know when Mr. Wokesley distributed the scripts?"

"It were yesterday at tea," said Louise. "Mrs. Treacle said as how there were papers all over the tables whilst she was trying to pour the tea, and she even spilt a little, she did, and she didn't mean to but they were everywhere."

"This was, presumably, before the mass destruction of the teapots," Phyllida said, mostly to herself.

"Ma'am?"

Phyllida shook her head. "So the playactors didn't receive their scripts until only a few hours before the other guests were to arrive."

"No, ma'am."

"Did you hear anyone say anything about the scripts?"

"No, ma'am. Only a little grumbling but I didn't know what about," Louise said, nodding vigorously. "That Mr. Dudley-Gore, he was right excited about it all, though. Mrs. Treacle, she might know more as she was there when they got their papers, you see."

"Very well. Thank you, Louise. If you think of anything else, or notice anything else, I would appreciate it if you would inform me."

The maid nodded again. She hesitated, then said, "Mrs. Bright . . . it *has* to be one of them, don't it? Who offed Mr. Wokesley?"

"Yes."

Louise's eyes grew wide and her cheeks drained of color. "I don't know if I want to keep working here if there's a killer about. Whatever will I tell my mam?"

"Nonsense," said Phyllida bracingly. "Someone had it in for Clifton Wokesley, that's true, but there's simply no reason the same person would want to do away with you or anyone else."

She went on. "They took a very big risk—and succeeded. Why would they risk themselves being caught by doing it again? Everyone is now on their guard. The perpetrator's best bet is to remain unnoticed."

Despite her brisk words, Phyllida knew there was, in fact, a very good reason for a killer to strike again: if he or she felt they were in danger of being exposed. "And therefore, if you notice or remember anything at all, even something small and insignificant, it's very important that you tell me—and only me—immediately, right then, Louise?"

"Oh, yes, ma'am. I wouldn't even tell those coppers. I'd be telling you." Louise's head bobbed earnestly. "I even know how to use the telephone."

"A very useful skill, to be sure. I do appreciate that, but Inspector Cork will be here to take over the investigation very soon."

"But he don't know how to do it as well as you do, Mrs. Bright," said Louise. "I know he don't. I heard all about it at the Murder Fête last month, how he arrested that poor, sweet *vicar*!"

"Nonetheless, Inspector Cork should be informed as well. I will, of course, tender my guidance and offer my deductions and observations, as necessary, to him and Constable Greensticks." Phyllida thought she was being extremely evenhanded in her handling of this situation. Unfortunately, Inspector Cork would never know of her deference toward him and his dubious skills.

"If you say so, ma'am." Louise remained unconvinced.

"I do. And . . . if I may offer you another bit of advice," Phyllida went on.

"Yes, ma'am." The maid's eyes shined with expectation.

"You must refrain from using any sort of polish on walnut furnishings. Only a feather duster—and one *very* lightly oiled on the feathers, mind—to collect the dust."

The expectation dimmed a little in Louise's gaze. "Oh. Yes, mum. I'll do that."

"You'll find your tasks much easier and more efficient if you utilize the proper tools and techniques," Phyllida told her.

Before Louise could respond, the shrill *brrring* of the telephone shattered the quiet.

Phyllida, having finished her exploration of Mr. Wokesley's study as well as her interview with Louise, saw no reason to remain in the room. She let herself out into the corridor just in time to see Mr. Trifle, the butler, answering the telephone.

"You've reached Beecham House," he intoned with pomposity that even Mr. Dobble would be hard-pressed to match.

Mr. Trifle listened, his bushy black eyebrows lifting like the

V-shaped wings of a gull. "I see. I shall indeed inform him upon his arrival. And . . . yes?" He glanced over and caught sight of Phyllida as the voice rattled on from the other end. "Oh. *Hrrmph.* Why, as it happens, I do believe she is." He raised his nose and managed to look down at her though he was several feet away. "Indeed. *Quite* so. Yes, of course, I will be certain to—er—pass along the message. Indeed. Good day, then, Inspector."

"Inspector?" Phyllida said as Mr. Trifle replaced the receiver. "Was that Inspector Cork? I presume he will be here shortly?"

Mr. Trifle, who seemed to have left the previous night's theatrics behind in favor of a far stiffer and more correct presentation, gave her a quelling look. "Mrs. Bright, that was Inspector Cork. He has advised me to deliver a message to Mrs. Wokesley that he has been unavoidably delayed due to a bridge being out on the road from London. He fears he will not arrive until late this evening."

"Good heavens," Phyllida said, utterly astonished by this news as well as galvanized by the possibilities it suggested.

"He has also instructed me to relay to the constable upon his arrival that he should take the lead on the investigation until he can get here."

"Why, of course that is—"

"*And* that, under no circumstance, is he to allow—erm, how did he put it?—'that interfering Bright woman' to, ahem, put her 'pointy nose anywhere near the investigation.'" Despite delivering such a rude message, Mr. Trifle didn't seem the least bit abashed by it.

"Is that so?" Phyllida replied. She might be interfering, but her nose was *not* pointy. It was long and pert and rather elegant.

"Indeed." Mr. Trifle seemed outright pleased by the contents of his message.

"It seems to me," Phyllida said, "that such a statement speaks more of Inspector Cork's lack of confidence in his own abilities—and that of his colleagues—than the presence of anyone else who might have an interest in bringing a murderer to justice. Such a delay in arriving—a full twenty-four hours after the horrific events!—is inexcusable when it comes to investigating a crime scene. Surely he could have sent someone else in his stead."

"I don't know, Mrs. Bright, but I do know he clearly stated that the likes of you should be nowhere near the crime scene," Mr. Trifle responded.

"I regret that it's far too late for that. Especially since I was present and witness to the discovery of the crime, as well as being the first capable person on the scene. Inspector Cork would be cutting off his blunt, pug, *freckled* nose to spite his face if he means to keep me away." Phyllida drew in a calming breath.

"I—"

"And furthermore, I—"

Phyllida was interrupted by the sound of someone rushing down the stairs. She and Mr. Trifle both turned to see Mrs. Wokesley thumping down in slippered feet. Her improbably ruby-red hair was wrapped in a black turban, and her flowing Chinese-style robe was the same unrelieved ink color, with only a bit of red embellishment near the wide cuffs. Her face was devoid of makeup and she wore no jewelry save a ring on her left hand.

"Who was that on the telephone, Trifle?" she said. As she drew closer, it became obvious she'd been crying. The tip of her nose was pink and her eyes were red. "When is the inspector going to arrive? I simply can't go on *not knowing* who did such a thing to my darling C-Clifton." Her voice broke at the end and she buried her nose and mouth in a handkerchief as Mr. Trifle explained the situation.

He finished with: "It's my understanding, ma'am, that the constable should be arriving any moment now, for the inspector indicated he'd been unable to reach him at the constabulary."

"But . . . you said *tonight*? The inspector isn't going to be here until tonight?" Mrs. Wokesley's eyes widened as fat teardrops spilled from them. "Why, that's . . . that's just not the thing. Not at all." Her voice quavered and her trembling hand dropped to her side. "M-my poor, poor Cliffy. I just don't know h-how this could have happened."

Phyllida decided it was time to intervene. "Mrs. Wokesley, perhaps you'd like to have a seat in the library, or the dining room? Mrs. Treacle could bring you a cup of tea, and we could add a dollop of spirits if you'd like something more bracing. And I can fill you in on the status of the investigation."

Mrs. Wokesley blinked, looking blankly at her. "Excuse me, but who are you?"

Phyllida was not the least bit put off by her question. The poor woman was in shock—or else she was an extremely fine actress who would be in the running for that American acting award with the gold statuette. "I am Phyllida Bright, and I assure you that the investigation is in full swing despite the delayed appearance of Inspector Cork, for it is in my capable hands. In fact, the inspector has consulted with me on two different cases in the last months. It would not be remiss of me to say that they wouldn't have been resolved without my assistance."

Still appearing bewildered, Mrs. Wokesley nonetheless allowed herself to be ushered into the library whilst Mr. Trifle stood staring after Phyllida with a rather fish-like expression. His twin V-shaped brows had gone completely flat.

Once she'd settled the new widow in the library in a comfortable high-backed chair near the fireplace—which, to Phyllida's dismay, was unlaid and unlit—she rang for tea.

Mrs. Treacle answered the summons, and Phyllida explained the situation—specifically, the need for tea and a bit of dry toast, and for a fire to be laid and lit—both for the comfort of her mistress. Phyllida refrained from pointing out that these needs should have already been anticipated, but she once more suggested that the guests would require a breakfast that hadn't seemed to be in any stage of preparation when she was in the kitchen.

"Yes, of course, Mrs. Bright," said the housekeeper. She appeared more startled by Phyllida's suggestions than ashamed at the lack of her own management skills. It was almost as if the woman had something else on her mind besides running a household full of guests.

"Now, Mrs. Wokesley, you'll have a soothing cup of tea in only a moment. Would you like the window opened for some fresh air?" Phyllida said.

"N-no. I'm feeling quite ch-chilled," said Mrs. Wokesley, briskly rubbing her arms beneath the black silk of her dressing gown. "It's so cold and dreary today. Is it going to rain again?"

At that moment, Anthony came into the library carrying a bundle of wood. Phyllida nodded in approval and gave him a smile.

"You'll be warmed up in a trice," she said to the widow as the footman set about lighting a fire. "Now, Mrs. Wokesley, I know that this is an unbearably difficult time for you, but I'd like to ask you some questions." Phyllida sat in the chair she'd placed next to Beatrice Wokesley, and even reached over to clasp the other woman's hand—which was slender, soft, and ice-cold.

"More questions?" Mrs. Wokesley asked dully.

"It would be very helpful in the investigation."

Suddenly, Mrs. Wokesley looked at her. The glaze fell away from her eyes and she seemed to focus on Phyllida for the first time. "It's you, isn't it? You're that detective—the one who lives with Mrs. Christie. Or, should I say, Mrs. Mallowan. You caught two killers, didn't you?"

"Three killers—and, yes, I was instrumental in the process," Phyllida replied modestly. "And I will do everything I can to find out who took your husband's life. And that's why I'd like to ask you some more questions."

"Yes, very well. I'll do anything to h-help." Mrs. Wokesley gulped back a sob. "What do you w-want to know?"

"Mr. Dudley-Gore and your husband were at Fitchler School for Boys together. Tell me about their relationship, if you please. I understand your husband meant to settle some sort of bequest on the school."

"Oh, yes. He might have done. I-I don't know. Cliff never talked to me about all of that sort of thing. Money, you know. It's simply so *vulgar.*"

"I see." Phyllida had her own opinions about a marriage where one partner was kept in the dark about finances and property. It certainly didn't border on vulgarity for one to know whether one's bills were going to be paid or whether one's spouse might give away a big chunk of funds on a whim. "I understand Mr. Wokesley and Mr. Dudley-Gore were quite good friends back in the day." She smiled. "It must have been nice for you to meet one of your husband's old chums."

"Oh. Right." Mrs. Wokesley blinked, then once again found her focus and looked at Phyllida. "The truth is, Cliff had never once mentioned Hubert until he told me he was going to be part of the Murder Game."

"I see. Did you get the impression that perhaps they weren't such close friends in school? Or simply that Mr. Wokesley never thought to mention Mr. Dudley-Gore?"

"I . . . to be honest, Mrs. Bright, I think they weren't such close friends at all. Not as close as Hubert likes to make out they were. I think"—she leaned forward and her voice dropped to a hush—"I mean to say, I *wondered* if perhaps he might have been exaggerating their acquaintance—Hubert, I mean—now that he's the headmaster. They're always trying to raise money, you know. Headmasters and headmistresses and the like. New roofs and updated dining halls and rowing team uniforms and all."

Phyllida nodded sagely. "Indeed. Did Mr. Wokesley happen to mention to you how he and Mr. Dudley-Gore became reacquainted with each other, now that Mr. Dudley-Gore is the headmaster at Fitchler?"

"I-I don't remember. I think Hubert sent him a letter or rang up."

"Renewing old acquaintances," Phyllida murmured, patting the woman's hand. "It must be very comforting for you to have your friends near during this tragedy. Sir Keller and Mrs. Forrte, I mean."

"Y-yes, yes it is," Mrs. Wokesley replied. "I hardly know Georges and I certainly never met Hubert until now. It *had* to be one of them, Mrs. Bright."

"We shall certainly find out," Phyllida promised soothingly.

"Keller would never do such a thing." There was a flash of emotion in her eyes. "I'm sure of it."

"Mrs. Forrte has had some problems with the law," Phyllida said. "Apparently she was arrested. Do you know what happened?"

"Arrested? Charity?" Mrs. Wokesley's eyes widened. "Why . . .

no, I don't know anything about it. It was probably some nonsense about—about shoplifting." Her expression changed to one of chagrin. "I mentioned that she runs with quite a different crowd, back in London you know, and there was a time when her lot used to dare each other to do silly things—like steal a bracelet whilst at a party or slip a watch into their pocket at a store. It was all harmless, *harmless* fun . . . and it certainly isn't akin to *murder.*"

"Of course not," Phyllida murmured.

"They returned the stolen items," Mrs. Wokesley went on, clearly trying to be convincing. "It was only a game."

"Of course," Phyllida replied, forbearing to mention that last night's event had been meant to be only a game as well.

By now, there was a cheery fire blazing on the hearth. The shadows cast by the flames danced over Mrs. Wokesley's drawn face, making it appear even more haggard.

Mrs. Treacle appeared, carrying a tray laden with tea service, cups, and a small silver cloche.

"Good morning, Mrs. Wokesley," she said, casting a glance at Phyllida. "I've brought you some tea and a bit of dry toast. Does that sound good to you?"

"Oh . . . I don't think I could eat anything right now," Mrs. Wokesley replied. "But some tea . . . yes, I do believe that would be all right."

"Very well then, ma'am," Mrs. Treacle said, then went about preparing the beverage with efficiency and grace.

"Mrs. Wokesley, forgive me for pressing you, but I do have another question," Phyllida said as the other housekeeper set the bone china cup in its saucer next to her mistress. When Mrs. Treacle gave her a questioning glance, Phyllida nodded in assent: Yes, she would like some tea as well.

"What is it?" replied Mrs. Wokesley in a tired voice.

Despite a pang of distaste, Phyllida knew she had no choice but to push for more information from the exhausted widow. "You mentioned yesterday that Mr. Wokesley hadn't been himself for a while, and that you were relieved to have gotten him to the country. That there'd been some sort of . . . event that had precipitated a change in his demeanor." Phyllida stopped short of saying "scandal," although that was the word Beatrice Wokesley had used last night. "What happened?"

"I don't know what it has to do with last night," Mrs. Wokesley said. She'd summoned enough energy to bristle.

"It may have nothing to do with it," replied Phyllida, catching Mrs. Treacle's eye as she placed a teacup in front of Phyllida. The housekeeper seemed unconcerned. Perhaps she was aware of what had happened. After all, servants knew everything—even newer ones.

Mrs. Wokesley sighed. "It happened almost a year ago," she said with great weariness. "There were a group of them in the motor in London one night, and Clifton was—well, it was his motor. He wasn't driving, but they hit a pedestrian—she ran right out in front of him! and—and she died. It was simply awful."

Phyllida nodded sympathetically. "He must have felt very bad about it."

"He *did*," Mrs. Wokesley replied, as if Phyllida had been expressing disbelief or doubt. "He was broken up about it for months. Simply wasn't the same. I-I tried to get him to attend the funeral for the poor soul, but he couldn't do it. He was so broken up."

"More tea, Mrs. Wokesley?" Mrs. Treacle cut in.

"No, no, I don't think I could even take a sip. Just take it away. Take it all away." Mrs. Wokesley slumped back in her chair, clutching her handkerchief. "It was bad enough what happened with the accident . . . but now this? I simply don't know how I can cope."

Phyllida exchanged glances with Mrs. Treacle, whose expression was benign and whose hands were steady as she gathered up the tea service.

"I'm terribly sorry for your loss, Mrs. Wokesley," Phyllida said.

Before she could go on, the sound of hurried footsteps approached.

"Oh, there you are, Bea," sang Charity Forrte as she swept into the room on a heavy cloud of perfume and cigarette smoke. "I've just left Sir Keller and the others scrambling about for breakfast in the dining room. You poor darling!" She surged to her former sister-in-law and enveloped her in an embrace. "Did you sleep at all last night?" she asked.

"Not very much, I'm afraid," replied Mrs. Wokesley.

"Would you like some tea, Mrs. Forrte?" asked Mrs. Treacle as Phyllida dodged the tea tray and started for the library door.

It was time to move on from interrogations to investigations.

CHAPTER 11

No one was present to see Phyllida slip from the study, dash along the short corridor, and hurry up the stairs to the first floor—a fact she'd been counting on, thanks to Mrs. Forrte's remarks regarding breakfast.

The butler and footman would be attending to serving the meal to the male guests, whilst the kitchen maid and cook (if Mrs. Napoleon had, in fact, returned from the butcher's; if not, Phyllida didn't care to contemplate the disaster that would be) should be ensconced in the kitchen. Louise would either be cleaning the parlor or some other ground floor room, or, more likely, would be on her way upstairs to see to the guests' bedchambers now that they'd been vacated.

At least, that was how it would have been if Phyllida was in charge.

Thus, once she reached the top of the stairs—which ran along the side of the foyer and ended at the balcony on which Mr. and Mrs. Wokesley had greeted their guests last evening—Phyllida paused for a moment. She stood in the deceased man's place and looked down to where she, Dr. Bhatt, Mrs. Rollingbroke and her husband Sir Rolly, and the other attendees had gathered for the game. Now, the foyer was empty and silent. Last night, it had been packed with loud and enthusiastic guests.

What had Clifton Wokesley been feeling at that moment, when he gazed down at the partygoers and announced the murder?

Excitement, most certainly.

Anticipation. Pleasure. Perhaps even pride over the future success of his game.

Had there been anything else? Any sort of apprehension or niggling?

"I told him it wasn't a good idea to mess around with revealing peoples' dirty secrets, skeletons in their closets, and all of that."

According to Georges Brixton, he'd warned Clifton Wokesley about making the Murder Game too realistic. Had Mr. Wokesley had any inkling he was in danger?

If so, he certainly hadn't given any indication of apprehension or fear. Phyllida's impression of him had been one of a man clearly in charge, certainly enjoying himself and, perhaps even laughing inside at his clever jest.

What about Beatrice Wokesley? What had she been thinking as she stood next to her husband and listened to him announce a murder? Had *she* had any idea her husband was in danger? That one of their friends was soon to be a killer?

Or had she stood there, proud and smiling and enthusiastic . . . all the while plotting to do away with him herself?

And the other playactors . . . who waited in what had been termed "the green room." Had the killer already been planning to do away with Mr. Wokesley as he lay on the floor, pretending to be dead . . . or had he or she seized a moment of opportunity?

Phyllida shook her head and stepped away from the edge of the balcony. She didn't have answers to those questions. Not yet, but she was certain she soon would.

If only she could solve the crime before Inspector Cork arrived and began to muck things up.

The corridor on the first floor was narrow and still lit by gas lamp sconces. Messy things, impossible to keep clean, and always accompanied by the faintest scent of gas and smoke. But they did the job, and Phyllida made her way down the hall with confidence.

Beecham House was far smaller than Mallowan Hall, so all of the guest rooms—four—along with the master bedchamber were situated on this floor. There were, she noted with approval, two bathrooms, one at each end of the hallway. Presumably there was a third one in the master apartments, where Mr. and Mrs. Wokesley slept.

Everything was silent up here, leading Phyllida to conclude that Louise hadn't yet found her way to this floor with her cleaning supplies. One maid for all of the bedchambers as well as the ground floor public areas was rather a stretch; surely it left the poor girl unable to keep up with the work of the extra guests. She wondered if Mrs. Treacle had had the foresight to bring in extra maids during the house party . . .

But the staffing at Beecham House was not Phyllida's concern. Murder was.

And so she discarded those thoughts and approached the nearest door. It was slightly ajar and Mrs. Forrte had said all the guests were downstairs and in search of breakfast, but Phyllida knocked anyway. When no one answered and it remained silent within, she gave the door a firm push. It swung open.

No one shrieked or shouted an alarm, so she stepped inside and closed the door firmly behind her.

It was immediately obvious that Mr. Dudley-Gore had been assigned to this room, for there was a sweater with a large F knitted into its front, along with a piece of stationery emblazoned with the Fitchler School for Boys' insignia. It was also clear that Louise had definitely not yet made her way to this bedchamber, which was a boon for Phyllida and her snooping. An unemptied trash bin could hold interesting information.

As Phyllida had already surmised by his haphazard fashion and anxiousness over stage props, Mr. Dudley-Gore was not a neat, calm, or organized individual. There were articles of clothing tossed everywhere, and not one item had been hung in the wardrobe. Instead, what wasn't on the floor spilled from a large, open trunk. The man could do with a good valet, but of course that wouldn't be likely on a headmaster's salary.

The bedside table held nothing of interest—a glass of water and a small box of matches from an establishment with abysmal spelling called Nite-Tyme. Phyllida wasn't concerned about her presence being noticed as she dug through the man's travel trunk; everything was a jumble already. She did, however, have to resist the urge to shake out an egregiously crumpled shirt. And the pair of mismatched socks on the floor made her wince.

Mr. Dudley-Gore possessed a small satchel that turned out to hold some paperwork and correspondence. Phyllida was unashamed as she opened it and thumbed through the papers. Bills, mostly, and a few letters presumably from parents. She skimmed one of the letters and was surprised to see that Mr. Dudley-Gore appeared to be well-liked—at least by this parent, the father of one Robert Crestler. The note was filled with effusive compliments—and, to her greater shock, the promise of a hefty donation to the school.

Quite interesting.

Phyllida read a second parental letter and was definitely astonished to find that *another* father was pleased with his son's schooling at Fitchler, and was also pledging a tidy sum as well. This document indicated that the school was in need of a new cricket pitch.

Thoughtful, Phyllida replaced the letters. Just as she was closing the satchel, she noticed another pocket containing a small, battered envelope. There was no writing on the exterior, so it had never been mailed. Inside, she found several equally battered photographs. One was a picture of two men in their twenties, and Phyllida immediately recognized a much younger Mr. Dudley-Gore. The other was clearly a close friend, as they had their arms slung around each other and they were mugging for the camera. She looked on the back and found the penciled words *Bertie and Stacey, Cornwall, 1923.*

Also in the envelope was a slightly newer photograph of a young woman. She had a round, pretty face, three charming dimples, and wildly curling hair. Her smile was infectious, even in the picture. Based on her clothing and hairstyle, Phyllida guessed the photograph had been taken within the last five years.

In a feminine hand on the back was scrawled: *H. My love always and forever, Rose.*

For some reason, Phyllida's eyes stung. Blinking with irritation, she tucked the photograph back into the envelope and replaced it in the satchel pocket.

She found nothing else of interest in Hubert Dudley-Gore's bedchamber. Even the trash bin was empty of items—because they were all on the floor next to it. A crumpled paper napkin with food residue, a tattered roadmap of Devon with coffee stains, and a bill of sale from a bakery in Wenville Heath.

Phyllida let herself out of the bedchamber and heard the sound of a door opening.

"Good morning, Louise," she said brightly as the maid stepped from what was presumably the servants' stairway into the corridor.

"Why, Mrs. Bright! What are you doing up here?" The words were hardly out of Louise's mouth before her eyes went wide and she fairly dashed down the hall, closing the distance between them as her carpet sweep and feather duster clunked in their pail. "You're invest'gatin', ain't you?" she said in a loud whisper.

"I was in search of a lavatory," Phyllida replied primly, but she allowed her eyes to dance with unspoken assent. "Which bedchamber will you begin with?"

"Um . . ." Louise glanced around then followed Phyllida's eyes to the room belonging to Mr. Dudley-Gore. "I think this one, ma'am? The—er—toilet is down that way," she added, then gave her a mischievous wink.

"Thank you very much," replied Phyllida. "Oh, and am I to understand that you're the only maid on hand to see to all of these chambers?"

"Oh, no, Mrs. Bright. There's Milly come in from town just for the house party. She'll be up here in a tick. She was just finishing up the front steps and sweeping the foyer."

"I see. Perhaps she might want to see to the bathrooms first," Phyllida suggested blandly.

"The bath—*oh!* Oh. Right. Yes, of course. I'll tell her that." Louise gave her a conspiratorial smile, but then it fell away. "I can't hardly believe it has to be one of *them,* don't it? We were talking about it all, you know, and, why, it *has* to be, don't it, Mrs. Bright?"

"It certainly seems that way. Did anyone notice anything out of sorts?" Phyllida asked. She hadn't had the opportunity to interview the rest of the staff. "That they mentioned? Anthony or the kitchen maid?"

"No, ma'am. Most of us were all cleaning up the teapots and such. Last night, you know. We still don't know how it all happened—a whole shelf broke and dumped everything *right over,* all next to the kitchen." Louise shook her head. "Glass and crockery everywhere."

"Quite tragic. Now, don't let me keep you from your work," Phyllida said, and walked to the next door on the hallway.

She didn't even look back as she opened it and slipped inside without knocking.

This was Charity Forrte's bedchamber. Phyllida was accosted by the residuals of too much perfume, and her eye was immediately drawn to the array of glittering objects on the dressing table. Whilst the room wasn't nearly as messy as Mr. Dudley-Gore's chamber, there were a few pairs of shoes on the floor and two frocks hanging over a chair. Mrs. Forrte—or, more likely Louise—had unpacked, and the clothing was hung in the wardrobe with a large steamer trunk sitting neatly closed next to it. The items Mrs. Forrte had chosen to discard were properly placed inside the trash bin.

On the bedside table was a jar of night cream and one of scented hand lotion. Phyllida examined the labels. Expensive. Next to them was a sleep mask and a pretty embroidered handkerchief.

The dressing table was covered with beautifying tools: lip color, nail varnish, mascara, kohl liner, brushes of all shapes and sizes, glittery combs, jewelry, and more face creams. There was a small tin box embossed with painted flowers and vines that captured Phyllida's attention, mainly because there was no label or printing on it.

She carefully pried it open to reveal the white powder she'd suspected might be inside. So Charity Forrte's crowd—apparently so different from that of Beatrice Wokesley's—was into cocaine. Or, at least, Mrs. Forrte was. But in Phyllida's experience, when a person indulged in such mood enhancers, they usually had a cluster of others about them who did as well.

She replaced the tin and turned her attention to the wardrobe and trunk. The frocks and gowns were glitzy and glittery and, once again, expensive. Phyllida couldn't help but wonder how a divorcée afforded top-of-the-line face creams and expensive clothing—not to mention cocaine.

The trunk was completely empty, but Phyllida wasn't fooled. She slid her hands around the fabric lining, feeling for anything that might be out of place or hidden, but to her surprise there was nothing tucked away. Apparently, Mrs. Forrte's secrets were all to be left out in the open instead of hidden.

Just then, there was a knock on the door. Phyllida straightened up and turned as it opened slowly. She had several excuses prepared.

"Mrs. Bright, can I come in now?"

It was Louise, her wide, enthusiastic dark eyes darting about the room as if to determine whether Phyllida had discovered anything. She seemed disappointed that there weren't any sort of clues lying about, such as a bloodstain, crumpled note, or footprints.

"Of course. I was just, er, finishing up looking for the lavatory," Phyllida replied.

"Oh, yes, of course, ma'am. Um . . . Milly is nearly finished with the bathroom on the east end. She'll be doing the other one next."

"Very well, thank you."

Sure enough, Phyllida had just stepped into the hall, leaving the door to Mrs. Forrte's room open whilst Louise cleaned, when a young woman clattered out of the bathroom at the far end of the hall. She was struggling with a mop, pail, and broom in one hand, and heaven knew what else in a large handled basket in the other.

"Oh, good day, Mrs. Bright," said Milly with a beaming smile.

Phyllida hid her surprise that the maid knew her name; either Louise had advised her of her presence or, as was happening more often, her reputation (aided by the unusual color of her hair) had preceded her. "Good day, Milly, is it?"

"Oh, yes, mum," replied the maid, clearly tickled that Phyllida knew her name. She straightened up and her mop and other accoutrements clattered again. "I'll just be getting on to the other bathroom, now, won't I, and you kin . . . er . . . do whatchoowill." She winked wildly.

"Quite." Phyllida gave her a smile and reached for the next doorknob.

As she passed by, Milly said in an earnest whisper, "You'll find who done this, Mrs. Bright. You find 'em, you do."

Good heavens. If Phyllida ever had to go undercover, she'd be advised to do it elsewhere than in Listleigh.

Sir Keller's room was neat as a pin, and it wasn't because Louise had been through and made it so. Phyllida surmised this because the trash bin hadn't been emptied (it was filled with paper napkins and tissues) and the bed was slightly rumpled. Aside from that, there were no telltale signs of a carpet sweep being run over the rug.

The thought reminded Phyllida of the imminent arrival of her much-anticipated Vac-Tric, and she wondered whether it had yet been safely delivered to Mallowan Hall. *Dobble had best keep his hands out of it,* she thought. It was a good thing she was the keeper of the household budget, for the butler would never have agreed to the nearly thirteen-pound expense.

Of course he wouldn't, for he'd never run a carpet sweep or used a carpet beater in his life, she was certain.

Phyllida came back to herself and thrust away those unnecessary and distracting thoughts, returning her attention to the bedchamber of Sir Keller.

Coats, shirts, and trousers were hung neatly and spaced regularly in the wardrobe. Shoes were lined up on the floor next to it. Ties were slung over one hanger, also spaced evenly. There was a limited array of men's grooming products on the dressing table: brush, comb, pomade, trimming scissors, and a subtle masculine cologne. To her surprise, Phyllida approved of all of it: not only the neatness and organization, but the quality of the brands and scents.

If he weren't such an arse, Sir Keller might be a man she could actually appreciate for his order and taste.

She thumbed through the hanging clothes, taking care to keep them neat and at their intervals. She felt each of the coat pockets and found obvious and inane objects like folded pound notes, matchbooks, handkerchiefs, and bills of sale.

It wasn't until she reached the pocket of a dark coat edged with the dust of travel that she plucked out a folded handwritten note that seemed far more interesting.

That proved to be the case, for when she opened it, she found a scrawling feminine hand that read: *I simply can't do it. B.*

B . . . for Beatrice?

Her nerves were humming, but Phyllida refolded the note and slipped it back into the breast pocket of the coat.

There were many possible answers to what she "couldn't" do—this "B" person, who was very possibly Beatrice Wokesley. And considering that her husband had just been killed, any number of those reasons could be provoking or ominous.

Thoughtful, Phyllida continued her search through Sir Keller's personal affects, but found nothing else that struck her . . . other than the profound organization that permeated the room. It was almost painful how neat and orderly every item of clothing was—from the folded socks (all matching, of course, unlike Mr. Dudley-Gore's) and the perfectly aligned clothing. And without a valet to attend to such matters . . .

Sir Keller was quite an interesting character. And, she suspected, he was deeply in love with Beatrice Wokesley.

Which gave him a fine motive to rid her of her husband.

And now, Phyllida had only two more bedchambers to investigate: that of Clifton and Beatrice Wokesley, and Georges Brixton.

It was in Mr. Brixton's room that Phyllida found the gun.

CHAPTER 12

PHYLLIDA LEFT THE PISTOL WHERE SHE FOUND IT: TUCKED UNDER THE neatly folded undershirts that Mr. Brixton had stacked in the bureau drawer.

The sight of the firearm had given her a start, bringing with it the sting of unwanted memories. It had been a while since she'd seen—or held—a Webley .455.

She shoved the drawer closed and finished her search of the chamber, but the gun was the only item of interest.

As she slipped out of the room, Phyllida considered all the reasons Georges Brixton might have brought a pistol to a house party.

Protection.

Aggression.

Habit.

Thoughtlessness.

She closed the door behind her, still mulling. If Mr. Brixton had brought the firearm intending to do away with Mr. Wokesley, what had made him use the stiletto instead? Easier? Quieter? *Bolder?*

Mr. Brixton had struck her as a man who liked being in the spotlight, and who enjoyed manipulating his audience. After all, wasn't that precisely what actors did—draw attention to themselves to demonstrate their skills? To play their audience? To fool them?

There were killers who wanted that same sort of attention and praise for their cunning. Even fame. Stabbing someone at the base of the skull when another person could walk into the room at any moment was certainly dramatic. And risky.

Whether it was Mr. Brixton who'd done the deed or someone else, whoever it was must have been either desperate enough to take the chance of being caught, or bold and brave enough to revel in the very perilousness and drama of such an act. Or both.

Phyllida started down the hall to the last bedchamber—that of the master and mistress of the house—but before she could slip inside, she heard the sounds of activity and arrival downstairs.

Drat. If that was Constable Greensticks, it would put a damper on her plans.

She hurried to the balcony's edge and looked down. To her surprise, the new arrival was Mr. Billdop, the vicar who was Mr. Dobble's weekly chess partner and very close friend.

Unfortunately, both Mr. Billdop and Mr. Trifle looked up at that moment and saw her, which required Phyllida to abandon her plan to search the Wokesleys' bedchamber—at least temporarily.

"Good morning, Mr. Billdop," she said, tripping lightly down the steps. She ignored Mr. Trifle, who, like any butler worth his salt, was surely fuming over the fact that she'd been abovestairs without his knowledge or permission.

"Why, Mrs. Bright," replied the vicar. He was a quiet, anxious man in his fifties with wispy hair and a dimpled chin that was precisely the shape of a fresh apricot. "What a surprise to see you here . . . er, perhaps not, heh? After all, you've quite a bit of experience with murders, now, haven't you? Heh, heh."

Mr. Billdop spoke from personal experience, as Phyllida had been instrumental in having him released from custody after Inspector Cork made a wrong move.

"Mrs. Mallowan asked me to pay a visit to offer her condolences," she replied, glancing at Mr. Trifle, then back at the vicar. "I suspect you are here to do the same."

"Of course. Although they were new here in Listleigh, the Wokesleys have become patrons of St. Thurston's. And one can always stand a visit from the clergy after such tragedies, no?" He looked at Mr. Trifle. "Is Mrs. Wokesley inclined to see me?"

"I'll ask her, sir." Mr. Trifle seemed reluctant to leave them alone, but he had no choice.

As he disappeared down the hall to the library, Phyllida—who'd not forgotten Mr. Dobble's strange and irritable mood of yesterday—said, "What a shame to miss your chess game last night. I do hope nothing is amiss."

"Oh, yes," replied the vicar. His cheeks flushed a bit pink. "Harvey—er, I mean to say, Mr. Dobble . . . well, er, it wasn't a good evening to play. My—er—an old friend is in town to visit."

"I'm certain Mr. Dobble understands that you wanted to spend some time with your friend," Phyllida replied smoothly.

"Oh, well, I . . . yes. Of course. He—he won't be here long." He gave her an unsteady smile and she sensed he had something else he wanted to say. But before he could do so, Mr. Trifle materialized.

"Mr. Billdop, Mrs. Wokesley would indeed like to see you. If you'll follow me." The butler looked down his nose at Phyllida as if prepared to insist she join them, or—which he clearly preferred—to leave the premises altogether. Regardless of which, Phyllida wasn't about to do either.

"I shall give your best to Mr. Dobble, Mr. Billdop," she said.

Phyllida was just about to start up the stairs once more, for it was a providential time to search the Wokesleys' bedchamber with Mrs. Wokesley being distracted by the vicar, when the knocker clunked at the front door.

Phyllida did not make a move to answer the door, even though she thought about it. Habits and responsibilities died hard, even when she was in someone else's domain. After all, *someone* had to do it.

But she needn't have worried, for an instant later, Anthony, the footman, appeared from the hall leading to the dining room. He had a smudge of some sort of foodstuff on his cuff and was carrying a serving spoon, which indicated that at least some sort of breakfast was being served.

Anthony answered the door to Constable Greensticks, who gave Phyllida a resigned look as he stepped inside.

"Oi, Mrs. Bright, did ye sleep over here last night, then?" He removed his hat and handed it to the footman, who disappeared down the hall with it, leaving them alone in the foyer.

"Very amusing, Constable," she replied with a little smile. He would have his little jests. "I understand Inspector Cork has been delayed yet again."

"It's that bloody bridge out in Maverville," he said in disgust, running a hand over his hair and causing it to spring every which way. "Bollixed everything up, it has. Right, then, but have ye solved the murder and captured our killer yet, Mrs. Bright?"

"Certainly not," she replied, lifting her nose a trifle. She refused to feel even a pang of remorse over what he might consider her lack of accomplishment.

The constable grunted in a most uncouth manner, but by now Phyllida had given up any expectation of polished manners from the man. "'Ave ye at least got a suspect or two, then, Mrs. Bright?"

She made her own noncommittal sound. Of course she had a suspect or two. In fact, she was leaning very heavily toward one individual in particular, but she certainly wasn't going to show her cards quite yet. After all, she still needed to wait for Mrs. Agatha to ring with the results of her research and investigations in London in order to know whether she was on the right path.

"I do think it's of paramount importance to obtain a copy of the original Murder Game script," she told him. "I was just about to take a look in Mr. Wokesley's bedroom to see if there was one about. I've already looked in his study," she added when the constable opened his mouth to speak.

He closed it and rubbed his mustache. "Right, then." He leaned slightly closer and dropped his voice. "Why would that be, Mrs. Bright? Of, er, Parliament importance?"

"I suspect there might be a clue to the motives of the five suspects within that script."

"Oi. If ye say so," he said, scratching his head. Phyllida eased back a bit, just in case. "Why'n't ye just ask for it, then, from Mrs. Wokesley?"

"Because," she said as she mounted the stairs, "then I wouldn't have the opportunity to poke around her bedchamber."

The Wokesleys' bedchamber was the largest and most spacious suite in the house, but it still paled in comparison to that of the Mallowans'. Still, Phyllida found the subdued blue and green chamber pleasant and well-appointed.

She'd been surprised to learn that Mrs. Wokesley didn't have a ladies' maid, but relied on assistance from either Mrs. Treacle or Louise. It certainly seemed that the Wokesleys could have afforded the cost of such a position—and that of a valet for the master of the house as well, but that lack was also a deficit in the household staff.

Phyllida wasted no time. She'd left the constable gawping at her, and she didn't know how long he'd allow her to poke around before putting a stop to it, or, more likely, mentioning her task to Mr. Trifle. Not that the constable seemed to mind her taking over, despite Inspector Cork's admonishments to the contrary.

As one might expect after last night's events, the bedchamber was in a sort of shambles. Female clothing was strewn everywhere, and there was evidence that Mrs. Wokesley had employed many tissues and handkerchiefs as she dealt with her shock and grief.

Phyllida considered such demonstrations a point in the favor of Mrs. Wokesley not being the murderer, although she certainly had read of killers who grieved the loss of the person whom they'd done away with. Love and hate were, she knew, extremely closeknit emotions.

And yet, a very cunning killer might also obstruct the plot a step further by displaying such signs of intense grief. Setting the stage, so to speak.

I simply can't do it. B.

The short message Phyllida had found in Sir Keller's coat pocket could certainly have been signed by Beatrice Wokesley . . .

and if she'd declined to kill her husband, perhaps Sir Keller had taken it upon himself to do the deed. If she could find something written in the woman's hand, it would be helpful in determining whether Mrs. Wokesley had penned the ambiguous note.

Her attention renewed by this additional purpose, Phyllida quickly rifled through bureau drawers and bedside tables. She was quickly rewarded by the discovery of Mrs. Wokesley's personal appointment diary, which rested innocently on her dressing table.

Although she didn't have the original to compare, Phyllida concluded that the sweeping, wide-spaced handwriting was very similar, most likely identical, to that in Sir Keller's note.

Interesting. Now she could only wonder what it was that Mrs. Wokesley "simply could not do."

The Wokesleys shared a bed—which suggested genuine attachment and intimacy—but each had their own dressing room with built-in wardrobes and dressing tables. There was also a small bathroom attached.

Nothing else stood out to Phyllida during the search. Despite an abundance of both masculine and feminine clothing, jewelry, and other accoutrements, the rooms were well maintained, relatively neat, and gave little indication of anything amiss. There were no illicit love letters tucked among Mrs. Wokesley's lingerie, no compromising photos hidden in pockets, no questionable bills of sale for jewelry or hotels among Mr. Wokesley's effects.

And there was no sign of the Murder Game script.

Phyllida sighed. Then, hearing the distinctive sounds of mop- and broom-clunking from outside the door, she straightened from the final drawer through which she'd been pawing.

She greeted Louise as the maid came in, but didn't dawdle to chat.

Phyllida's timing was excellent, for as she came down the stairs, the vicar was just taking his leave from the constable and Mr. Trifle. Mr. Billdop cast her a look, once again appearing as if he desperately wanted to speak to her, but in the end he only set his hat on his head and offered an oblique farewell.

Phyllida was perfectly content with that. She wasn't going to become embroiled in any other interpersonal issues involving staff members at Mallowan Hall. Managing hysterical and squabbling maids constituted enough dramatics for her taste, especially in combination with a murder investigation.

"Well, then, did ye find it?" said the constable when she reached the bottom of the stairs. He appeared oblivious to the supercilious butler and his expressive eyebrows.

"I did not," Phyllida replied, retaining a neutral expression even under the dark regard of Mr. Trifle. Then, in an instant, she decided to change her normal tactic of self-reliance and turned her attention full on to the butler. "The constable has been in search of the script for the Murder Game. Are you able to provide one for him?"

Mr. Trifle drew himself up, as butlers often did in order to make themselves appear larger and more formidable. It was a ploy that usually worked on maids and footmen—and even guests—but had no effect on Phyllida. "A copy of the Murder Game script? Why on earth would *he* be in need of that?" His emphasis on the pronoun clearly indicated his skepticism.

"The constable believes it might be instrumental to understanding a motive for the crime. Regardless, I don't believe he is required to explain any of his reasoning, Mr. Trifle," she said in a relatively mild voice.

The butler seemed prepared to argue further, but just then, Mrs. Treacle made her appearance.

"A copy of the Murder Game script, you say? Why, I recollect I saw one in the desk in the parlor. I believe it was Mr. Wokesley's, in fact. Shall I fetch it for you, Constable?"

"Yes, ma'am," replied the constable gravely.

Phyllida didn't spare the butler a glance, though she could feel him simmering. Butlers did not like to be shown up by housekeepers.

It was too dratted bad he couldn't be considered a suspect, for she would have liked to have taken him down a peg. For a person surely aware that one of his houseguests must be a murderer, he wasn't being very helpful.

Mrs. Treacle returned almost immediately to deliver the small sheaf of papers. Despite her impatience, Phyllida refrained from reaching for them herself. Instead, she turned to the younger housekeeper as Constable Greensticks took the script. "I trust everything is well under control after this morning's—er—reptile incident?"

"Reptile incident?" Mr. Trifle responded just as Phyllida had hoped.

"Indeed. Someone apparently allowed an adder to slither into the larder," Phyllida informed him. "Fortunately, the creature was safely confined and removed before he was able to distribute his venom."

"A venomous snake in the house?" Mr. Trifle's V-shaped brows arched up in each of their centers. "How on earth did such a thing happen, Mrs. Treacle?"

"It's certainly not *her* fault," Phyllida remonstrated him. "But it *is* concerning, considering someone was murdered last night and the killer is still at large."

"Oi, them adders ain't all that dangerous," said the constable with a little smile. "Ain't gonna kill anyone, anyhow. Though they might make ye a wee bit sick."

"Even so," Phyllida replied, relieved to hear this information. She hadn't known how poisonous the snake was. "The incident might bear some consideration. Perhaps the perpetrator wasn't aware that the snake wouldn't actually poison one to death."

"Good heavens," said Mr. Trifle, seeming for the first time to lose his air of superiority. "Are you suggesting someone allowed the snake into the house in an effort to off someone else?"

"I'm suggesting it should be considered a possibility," Phyllida replied. "After all, someone from London might not realize how dangerous the snake was—or wasn't. Or they might simply have wanted a distraction for some reason." She took the opportunity to slip the sheaf of script papers from the constable's loose grip whilst he, the butler, and the housekeeper discussed and exclaimed over the reptilian event.

"Oh, Mrs. Bright," said Mrs. Treacle, suddenly turning her attention to her. "I'd forgotten. I'd come to inform you that Mr. Bradford has arrived and is waiting to return you to Mallowan Hall." Were Mrs. Treacle's cheeks a trifle pinker at the mention of Bradford?

"Thank you," Phyllida replied, eyeing her closely. "I hope he hasn't been waiting long or keeping you from your business."

"Oh, no . . . well, he did have time to sit with me for a cup of coffee and a biscuit," Mrs. Treacle said. "He really is quite informed about mechanical things, you know."

Bradford's knowledge about mechanics held no interest for Phyllida. Her focus now was on the papers in her hand. And she certainly wasn't about to wonder how Mrs. Treacle had the time and opportunity to sit "for a cup of coffee and a biscuit" when there was a household to run, not to mention a murderer at large.

"Quite," was all Phyllida said, and before anyone could delay her any further, she took herself (and the Murder Game script) off to locate Bradford.

She found him sitting comfortably at the large worktable in Mrs. Napoleon's kitchen. He was coatless, hatless, and with a large mug of coffee and a plate bearing the remains of eggs, toast, and a thick slab of ham. He appeared to have made himself completely at home and had even rolled up the sleeves of his shirt.

As she and the cook hadn't been formally introduced, Phyllida commenced with that task and went on to congratulate her for managing to keep everyone in the household well fed during the entire uproar.

"Damned right," blazed Mrs. Napoleon, who had a blond halo of coarse, bristling hair. Fortunately, it was tied back by a bright red scarf that knotted at the top of her head. She had three chins—each of which waggled independently of the others—that also bristled with a smattering of blond hairs. "But that skinny little ninny they've got trying to run this place h'ain't been down *here* to say so."

Her brows, just as bristly and blond, drew together in deep puckers over her long nose as she jammed angry fists to her hips. "She bloody well forgot to place the order at the butcher's—*imagine that*"—she snorted—"and she don't even know where Mr. Tentley is, so I had to run meself over there on the bicycle and get it all."

"Good heavens," Phyllida said involuntarily. "That sounds quite disastrous."

"Damned right," Mrs. Napoleon said, slamming a meat tenderizer down onto the table so hard Bradford's plate jumped. "Can't even get her to set herself down and go over the menus and supplies list with me, can I? Not to mention the bills. Keeps losing 'em and rippin' 'em, and spillin' on 'em. She even spilt tea on the roast beef page in my new *Mrs. Beeton's*!" *Mrs. Beeton's Book of Household Management* was akin to the Bible when it came to running a household and kitchen. The latest version was nearly the size of an anvil.

"I don't know what they're teaching those young girls in service nowadays." Mrs. Napoleon's expression was dark enough that even Phyllida was inspired to take a step back. A small one, but a step nonetheless.

"Now, Mrs. N, surely you remember the early days of your youth, and in a new position," said Bradford soothingly. "Everyone makes mistakes. Why, even Mrs. Bright here has been known to misdiagnose a poison." He shot Phyllida a sidewise glance, then was intelligent enough to lift his mug so she wouldn't see him actually laugh.

Phyllida ignored his comment, which she knew was designed only to provoke. She had not misdiagnosed a poison during the Murder Fête affair, as he liked to put about. She had simply kept an open mind as to which one it was. After all, there *had* been two different types of poisons.

"And then there was the time she thought *I* was a murderer," Bradford went on, leading Mrs. Napoleon to stop her unwrapping of slabs of liver, mutton, and bacon and stare at Phyllida in bemused shock.

"What on *earth*—"

"Never mind that," Phyllida said impatiently. "Mrs. Napoleon, I'm so very sorry to have invaded your kitchen and interrupted your work. Bradford, if you've finished your meal, I'd like to return to Mallowan Hall as quickly as possible."

"Yes, of course, ma'am," he replied, giving her a mock salute as he pushed back his chair. "Mrs. N—er, Gertie, I mean—this was absolutely delicious," he said, grinning at Mrs. Napoleon as he forked up the last bite of apple dumpling. "I'm certain Mrs. Puffley would be honored to have the recipe someday, if you'd be willing to share."

"But if I do that, then you won't have an excuse to come by and chat about those new-fangled engines, now, will you?" replied the cook. She was absolutely *simpering* at the man!

Phyllida couldn't take it any longer. "*Mr. Bradford.*"

"Yes, ma'am," he said, swiftly rolling his sleeves back down as he nudged the chair back into place with his knee.

Phyllida had barely settled in the front seat of the Daimler when she began to scan the Murder Game script.

"What's that you have there, Mrs. Bright?" asked Bradford as he started the engine.

She explained briefly, then turned her attention back to the paperwork. But as soon as he began to navigate the motor down the curvy, forest-shrouded drive, she realized reading whilst riding would not agree with her stomach or head. Just like her beloved M. Poirot, she suffered from a *mal de mer*—but her sickness wasn't from the waves of the sea, but the curves and jolts of the road. She set the script down in her lap.

Bradford obviously took that as a sign to converse. "Well, Mrs. Bright, it sounds as if you've had a busy morning. Fighting off snakes, sneaking into presumably unoccupied bedchambers, and interrogating suspects. Have you identified the culprit?"

"Not yet." Somehow the admission didn't sting as much as she thought it might.

He made a tsking sound, but otherwise remained silent until they turned onto Rareacre Road. "Looks like some bad storms coming. Mrs. Napoleon said her hip was bothering her."

She looked out the window. England was gray more often than not, but today's gray was especially heavy and dark, sitting in the distance like a looming boulder. She sighed quietly to herself. "That won't help in getting the bridge in Maverville fixed."

"Right then. But that only means you'll have even more time to solve the crime before Inspector Cork can get here," he said in a surprisingly pleasant voice.

"Quite so. I suppose a person shouldn't look a gift horse in the mouth. But at this rate, the Vac-Tric is never going to arrive," she said crossly.

"Is that what's in the big crate?" He thumbed to the back of the Daimler. "Picked it up at the train station on my way to fetch you."

"You did?" She turned in her seat and looked at him in utter surprise and pleasure. "It's here?"

"Why, Mrs. Bright, I don't think I've ever seen you smile—at least, like that. It's surprisingly becoming," he added—simply, she knew, to ruin the compliment.

But Phyllida didn't care. She settled back into her seat, the smile still on her face.

"For someone who won't be actually using the machine, you seem very enthusiastic."

"Any device or tool that prompts efficiency and cleanliness is an asset to the entire household," she told him primly. "And of course, I'll be the first one to try it out. One can't have the maids conducting its inaugural run." She could hardly wait to get her hands on it. Thank heavens it hadn't arrived at the manor house, where Dobble might have infiltrated it first.

"Right." He drove in silence for a bit longer. "Are you aware that Stanley is thinking about giving his notice?"

"No, I am not," she replied. "But that is Mr. Dobble's problem and not mine."

"Right. But the problem seems to be stemming from your housemaids."

Phyllida bristled. "My housemaids? What on earth do they have to do with the head footman getting a new position?"

"Now, now, Mrs. Bright, you needn't go all huffy about it. I don't believe it's completely your fault they've been nattering at each other and nickering about like hissing cats. Although you could put a stop to it."

"Nickering? Cats don't nicker. Horses nicker."

He shot her a grin. "Indeed they do."

"And what do you mean you don't believe it's *completely* my fault? Of course it's not my fault—in any manner of speaking. It's all due to *Elton,* through no fault of *his* own, I'll admit. The maids are simply making cakes of themselves over him. And what Stanley has to do with it all is a mystery," she said grumpily.

"Right."

When Bradford didn't elaborate, Phyllida went on. "Why is Stanley going to leave?" Despite the fact that the footmen weren't her domain, anytime there was a staffing change, the entire household was disrupted. There would have to be interviews for a new head footman, likely sent from the agency in London unless someone local wanted to try for the position, followed by the training of the new one. All of that would take time.

"Why, he's in love with Ginny," replied Bradford. "Surely the great observer Mrs. Bright has noticed that."

"Oh, pish," she said, flapping her hand. "Men that age think they're in love with every skirt that flutters by or gives them a smile."

Bradford gave an ambiguous grunt and turned the motor onto the drive to Mallowan Hall.

"What does Stanley being in love with Ginny have to do with him finding a new position? It's utterly illogical for him to go away if he wants to court her. Not that I am promoting any sort of fraternization between staff members, but sadly, one cannot interfere with the natural course of things."

He glanced at her. "Of course not, Mrs. Bright. But Ginny doesn't appear to return his affections—at least, any longer. Now that Elton has come on the scene."

Phyllida pursed her lips and nodded. "Yes, I see your point. And, incidentally, Stanley's as well. But it's only a matter of time until Ginny realizes Elton is not the young man for her."

Bradford seemed surprised. "Ah. So you do realize." He gave her a strange look. "I thought you were oblivious to the problem."

"Realize? Me? *Oblivious?* That half the maids are throwing themselves at Elton? It's rather difficult to miss when they are showing up in my rooms dripping with ash and lye."

"Right. But you could easily—er—put a stop to it, if you were so inclined. If Elton were otherwise redirected, one might say."

Phyllida waved off his comment as the Daimler crunched to a halt behind Mallowan Hall. "It'll sort itself out, I'm certain, once Elton makes his choice. Which one hopes he does soon."

Bradford made a strange noise that sounded like a choking laugh. "I do believe he *has* made his choice, and therein lies the problem."

"Well, then it will certainly resolve itself soon enough. Besides, I've given Molly and Ginny a good talking-to and I expect to see a vast improvement in their behaviors. Now, if you'd be so kind as to bring the Vac-Tric into the house. As you might infer, I'm quite enthusiastic about uncrating it and testing it out."

Bradford gave her an inscrutable look and appeared as if he had something further to say, but she climbed out of the motor before he had the opportunity.

To her delight, it was only a few minutes later that Phyllida was gazing down with pleasure at the shiny cylinder of the Vac-Tric Deluxe, unboxed and ready to go. Its attachment of a long, rippled hose, finished with a broad attachment, not unlike the shape of a carpet sweeper, was in place. She'd read the instructions thrice, and the only thing left to do was plug it into an outlet and turn it on.

The housemaids—Ginny, Mary, Bess, and Lizzie—along with Freddie, the underfootman, were gawping in awe at the machine. Bradford had disappeared after removing the empty crate, but Stanley and Elton had also gathered in the doorway of the library—although there was a good amount of space between them, and

Stanley's expression was set and morose as it bounced between Ginny and Elton. Even Mr. Dobble hovered just outside of the room, presumably believing Phyllida was unaware of his presence. The only staff not interested in the new gadget were those in the kitchen, for they would likely never come in contact with it.

"Jesus, Mary, and Joseph," murmured Bess, one of the chambermaids, as she clutched the small crucifix she normally wore tucked beneath her uniform. "It's very large, ain't it, Mrs. Bright?"

"Much larger than a carpet sweep," said Mary worriedly. She often cleaned the front parlor and the study. As she was slender and diminutive, looking as if she'd blow away in a stiff wind, Phyllida could sympathize with her concern. It would be no small task to bring the heavy machine to and from the upper floors. The maids would have to work in pairs to do so, but that was permissible, as the efficiency of the device would make their work finished that much faster and easier.

"You want I should plug it in, Mrs. Bright?" said Freddie, leaning close enough that his reflection shined dully on the dark green cylinder. His eyes were lit with excitement.

"Yes, please."

As soon as Freddie fitted the prongs into the plug, Phyllida took up the hose's handle. "Shall I turn it on, then?" she asked, looking around at her audience.

"Yes, ma'am!" Freddie exclaimed.

"Saint Eligius, pray for us," whispered Bess.

Phyllida flipped the little metal switch. A loud roar filled the room and the hose jumped in her grip. Mary and Bess shrieked and reared back. Ginny clapped her hands to her ears, eyes goggling, cheeks pink with surprise.

For her part, Phyllida hadn't expected the noise to be *quite* so loud, and the rumbling vibration through the hose was rather intense. Still, she hid any sign of shock or surprise. Instead, she smiled complacently at her staff and began to run the rectangular-shaped attachment over the rug.

"*Gor* . . . look at that!" cried Freddie, pointing to the marks left on the carpet. He was fairly dancing with excitement. "It's really working!"

"It *is*!" Lizzie, Bess's counterpart as chambermaid, edged a trifle closer. "Do you feel any shocks, Mrs. Bright? Is it electrocuting you?"

"Of course not," Phyllida replied. "Would you like to try it?"

"N-no, ma'am, I-I think I'll watch a bit longer," replied Lizzie, gripping Bess's hand whilst Bess gripped her crucifix and silently moved her lips in continued appeals to Saint Eligius.

"Spill some ashes from the fireplace there, will you, Freddie?" Phyllida was required to raise her voice to be heard above the roar. The footman hastened to do as she asked. He scattered a much larger pile than she had intended on the rug, and Phyllida had a moment of regret, hoping she hadn't made a mistake.

But the Vac-Tric Deluxe did not disappoint. When Phyllida ran the attachment through the pile, it left a clean trail behind it.

"After only *one* run!" Ginny exclaimed, obviously thinking about how many times she'd have had to run the carpet sweep over such a pile for it all to come up. "It really does work!"

"Would you like to try it, Ginny?" said Phyllida. Her hand was feeling the effects of the constant rumbling vibration but she was jubilant. This was an incredible machine! Every household should have one.

"Oh, I don't know, ma'am . . ." The blond maid stepped back a little. She was still holding her hands over her ears, though somewhat more loosely.

"You ought to try it, Ginny," said Stanley with a bashful smile and his heart in his eyes. "It won't hurt you. It's only just loud."

Phyllida cast a glance at Mr. Dobble, who'd edged closer—probably unconsciously—to get a better look. His expression was unreadable. She could only imagine how irritated he was that his own footmen were ogling and goggling over a new device that had no part in their duties.

Ginny inched a little closer to Stanley, who'd conveniently moved just into the room near her. "Only, it's just so very *loud* and *big* and . . ."

"Motorcars and aeroplanes are loud too," Stanley told her gently. "And trains. You've been on a train."

"I suppose," Ginny replied. "All right, then. I'll—I'll try it." She glanced hopefully at Elton, but he wasn't looking at her. He was looking at Phyllida . . . and at that moment, Phyllida suddenly understood exactly what Bradford had been alluding to during their drive.

Elton was looking at *her*, Phyllida, in the same way Stanley was looking at Ginny.

Good heavens.

Elton jerked his eyes away, but the tips of his ears turned red and so did his cheeks—all of which confirmed Phyllida's startling conclusion.

Hiding her discomfiture, she turned her attention to Ginny. "Just take the hose at this part here, and push it about as if you were using a carpet sweep," she said, despite the fact that she'd been demonstrating this activity for several minutes.

Ginny glanced at the oblivious Elton once more, then Stanley—who was watching her with soft, liquid eyes—and braced herself. "All right." She reached for the hose and gave a little squeal as her fingers closed around it. But to her credit, she didn't drop or release it.

"It shakes," she said, moving it slowly over the rug in a straight path. "Along my arm. Mrs. Bright, are you sure this is safe?"

"Of course it's safe," replied Phyllida. "Do I appear injured?"

Just then, Mr. Dobble appeared fully in the doorway. "Mrs. Bright," he said in a carrying voice, "Mrs. Agatha is on the telephone line."

Phyllida hadn't even heard the ring of the telephone even though it was only down the hall, and she mentally marked that information down for future reference. The maids wouldn't hear the telephone or the door knocker if they were using the machine. They might not hear any of the summons bells either. Hmm. That could create problems.

"Thank you, Mr. Dobble." She looked around at the staff. "I want each of you to try it out. Lizzie, Bess, Mary—do you hear? Each one of you will be required to use it, and so you will try it out now."

"Yes, Mrs. Bright," they said in a chorus with varying degrees of terror and trepidation.

"I do hope no one breaks the bloody thing," muttered Mr. Dobble as Phyllida edged past him to take the telephone call. "Or sucks up their own feet."

She ignored him. There were more important things on her mind besides the curmudgeonly butler.

She was eager to learn what Mrs. Agatha had discovered.

CHAPTER 13

"I SHAN'T KEEP YOU LONG," SAID AGATHA OVER THE TELEPHONE line. She sounded particularly far away, possibly because of the thunderstorm that was just beginning to roll in. "Max is dragging me off to dinner with some archaeological fiends—it's all about doing the circuit to get funding for this year's dig, of course, and I don't mind at all—but I simply had to telephone first and tell you what I've learned."

"I hope some of it is about the motor accident in which Mr. Wokesley was involved," Phyllida said, pulling a notebook and pencil from the drawer of the table. There were always numerous notebooks and notepads stuffed in drawers about the house, usually for Mrs. Agatha's use. She had a habit of making notes on whatever handy packet of paper was nearby, so Phyllida made certain there were plenty of choices. "According to Mrs. Wokesley, it affected him quite deeply."

"In fact it is about that," Agatha replied, a note of surprise in her voice. "Apparently you've already been doing some sleuthing."

"I've only got the barest of details, so please tell me what you've discovered."

"Clifton Wokesley's motor was involved in an accident near the West End about nine months ago. There were two of them in the vehicle, and they'd just come out of a restaurant after one of those long dinners with pots and pots of wine and spirits. It was late and dark, but the weather was fine, so there was no reason the driver shouldn't have seen the young woman crossing the street.

"But he didn't," Phyllida said sadly.

"No. He didn't. And he was driving too fast. The woman was killed, and she left behind an orphaned child, as her husband died shortly after the war."

"Was Mr. Wokesley driving?"

"He wasn't, although it was his motorcar. It was a Mr. . . . hmm, where are my notes—oh, yes, here, right next to this list of clues for the idea I have about a murder that takes place during a bridge game—did I tell you about that, Phyllie? There's going to be a murder during a bridge game, it has to occur when someone is dummy. But I'll tell you about it another time." Agatha went on before Phyllida had the chance to reply. "Anyhow . . . a Mr. Eustace Brimley was the driver."

"I see." Phyllida was mildly surprised to learn that Mr. Wokesley hadn't been behind the wheel. From the way Mrs. Wokesley had spoken, she'd assumed he had been. But surely it was traumatic enough simply being in the motor to have caused him difficulty and the need to escape London. People reacted differently to tragic and horrific circumstances.

"But here's the more interesting bit," Agatha went on, glee in her voice. "One of your other suspects was also there that night."

Phyllida straightened up from writing notes. "Who was it?"

"George Brixton. No, it's *Georges.* The French pronunciation. I can't read my own handwriting at times," Agatha said with a laugh, "but I did underline the S at the end to remind me."

"Mr. Brixton was in the motor with Mr. Wokesley during the accident?"

"N . . . no . . . he wasn't in the motor. But he'd just walked out of the restaurant with Wokesley and Brimley, and he was a witness to the accident as they drove off. I was able to . . . er . . . access the police reports." Agatha sounded very pleased with herself, and a bit mysterious as well.

"That's very interesting," Phyllida said thoughtfully. Though she didn't know how or why it all would play into Mr. Wokesley's murder.

"It was quite a scandal with the heir to the 'woolen Wokesleys' being involved," Agatha went on. "Clifton Wokesley stopped going out completely for a while, although he did begin to socialize a bit after a few months passed. But then he and his wife left London."

"And he didn't attend the funeral," Phyllida said. "According to Mrs. Wokesley."

"He didn't? Well, I hope he at least settled some money on the poor orphan," she added flatly. "Even if he wasn't at fault, he *was* in the motor, and they'd all been imbibing. No one should have been driving."

"I don't know whether he did," Phyllida replied. "I wonder if there is a way to find out—besides asking Mrs. Wokesley."

"I shall give it my best shot. Good heavens! Was that thunder?"

"Yes," Phyllida said, glancing down the hall toward the foyer. The sky through the windows was dark as night. "There's quite a storm gathering right now. It looks to be a bad one."

"I'm sorry to hear that. I do hope the electricity doesn't go out. Now, would you like to hear what I learned about Charity Forrte?"

"I most certainly would," Phyllida said.

"There are rumors that she's a kleptomaniac. Hushed rumors, more of a gentle buzz . . . but people like to talk to detective writers, or so I've learned," Agatha said with a chuckle. "I suppose they think they might end up in a story someday."

"Calling oneself a kleptomaniac is an excellent way to excuse—and hide—outright thievery, don't you think?" Phyllida said, then she explained what Mrs. Wokesley had told her about Mrs. Forrte's "games" and "dares" of stealing valuable items. "She had a lot of expensive jewelry in her room—"

"In her room? Phyllida, never say you were snooping in her bedchamber!" Agatha sounded delighted.

"Of course I was snooping," Phyllida replied. "And she also had a tin of cocaine."

"Indeed! Well, that's no surprise. It seems she runs with that sort of crowd . . . from what I've been able to gather."

"You've certainly 'gathered' quite a bit of information in only a few hours," Phyllida said with a smile.

"As I said, a person is always happy to talk to a murder writer. There's something about the way their eyes light up when they get going, and everything just tumbles out. The clerk at the *Times* happens to be a big fan of Poirot, so she was quite forthcoming and helped me look through their archives."

"Were you able to learn anything about Sir Keller?"

"He's poor as a church mouse," Agatha said promptly. "Hardly has two beans to rub together. Puts on a good show, however. Was all set up to marry a woman named . . . hmm, let me see . . . ah, yes, a Miss Mabelle Sainsbury-Seale—what a *fantastic* name! I might just borrow it. Anyhow, Miss Sainsbury-Seale's got more than enough funds to keep a man like Sir Keller in luxury. But it seems the engagement fell through about six months ago."

"Who called it off?"

"She did. And Sir Keller did not take it well."

"Why did she call it off?"

"That is a bit of information I wasn't able to obtain . . . not yet anyhow. It's far more entertaining being an interrogator and investigator *without* having to be the one to put the pieces together," Agatha said. "It's like listing off a slew of clues and motives but not having to write the actual story." She sounded very satisfied with herself and Phyllida smiled.

"I feel like Poirot when Hastings or Japp deliver the information to him and he has to put it together," Phyllida said. "Only I haven't been able to marshal my little gray cells into order quite yet."

"I've no doubt you will, Phyllie. By the by, Dobble tells me the new vacuum machine has arrived. How is it?"

"It's quite impressive," Phyllida told her. "I believe it was a good investment."

"Excellent. All right, then, I must dash. Max is glowering and he doesn't do that often, and that means it's nearly time to leave. Oh . . . one more thing. If the storm gets very loud, you ought to go out and check on Bradford."

"Bradford? Why . . . of course." Phyllida frowned, then rang off the call as thunder crashed like a pyramid of tin cans collapsing. *"Go out and check on Bradford."* What on earth did Agatha mean by that?

She shook her head, filing away that bit of information.

Phyllida could hear the vacuum machine still running from down the corridor, but she declined to return to the library. The maids would have to learn how to use the vacuum without her assistance.

Instead, she nipped into her sitting room and closed the door. She needed a few moments to review Agatha's information and also to look over the Murder Game script.

Stilton was sitting in Phyllida's armchair, and she looked up with accusing blue eyes. She was clearly put out by the roar of the vacuum machine and, likely, the unpleasantries occurring outside. Rye was nowhere to be seen, so Phyllida suspected he was hiding under the sofa. He would give up one of his nine lives before admitting it, but he was terrified of thunderstorms.

"I know it's loud," Phyllida told Stilton, scooping the fluffy white feline into her arms. "But it won't be very long until it's over." She buried her face in Stilton's soft fur and rang down to the kitchen. She was in desperate need of a cup of tea.

Phyllida put her notes from Agatha aside and was just picking up the Murder Game script when there was a knock at the door.

"Come," she called.

"You rang, Mrs. Bright?" It was Opal, and, as usual, she was neatly dressed with her hair braided and pinned in a coronet around the crown of her head. She came in far enough to give Stilton a scratch under the chin, then waited patiently.

Phyllida smiled, appreciating the fact that of all her staff, Opal had been the only one not involved in any recent dramatics. If only the rest of them would be so circumspect. She asked for a tea tray and the girl went off eagerly to comply.

Peril at Beecham House was the title of Clifton Wokesley's Murder Game, and Phyllida frowned at the appallingly obvious homage to Agatha's brilliant *Peril at End House.* Nonetheless, she didn't allow the clumsiness to distract her from the process, and she began to read.

As scripts often did, it began with descriptions of the characters—in this case, accurately entitled *Suspects.* She found them very instructive, especially since Mr. Wokesley had identified the cast within the document.

The pages read:

> *Caterina Bowington* (Beatrice): *the wife of Mr. Bowington (victim). By all accounts, appears to have genuine affection for her husband. However, he is very wealthy and quite a few years older than she, and the couple has been heard arguing as of late.* Cherchez la femme, *one always says.*
>
> *Dermott Bowington* (Sir Keller): *younger brother of the victim. Jealous of his older brother's wealth and lofty position in society. Since his brother has no children, Dermott might inherit more than the family money if Mr. Bowington died . . .*

Phyllida paused here, her eyebrows lifting with surprise. Was the implication that Mr. Bowington the younger would inherit his elder brother's *wife* as well as the family wealth? If so, that was a very thinly disguised suggestion that Sir Keller still carried a torch for Mrs. Wokesley and would attempt to gain her affections—and hand—if her husband was taken out of the picture.

In light of the fact that Sir Keller's fiancée had recently ended their engagement—leaving him broke and with no prospects—it was uncomfortably close to reality. And a definite motive for both character and real-life person.

> *Oscar Charles* (Brixton): *Mr. Bowington's former business partner. They had a falling-out, but have recently reconciled. Nonetheless, Mr. Charles still has not forgiven Mr. Bowington*

for reneging on a business deal, for it has adversely affected his business reputation as well as his bank account.

Well, that was fairly accurate as well, Phyllida thought. Mr. Brixton had wanted funding from Mr. Wokesley for a new play, and he didn't get it. Had he come to Beecham House believing he would somehow change his mind? If so, why?

Hilary Charles (Charity): *wife of Mr. Charles, the business partner, she has several secrets of her own, including a fondness for pretty, expensive things she can no longer afford. She blames Mr. Bowington for her husband's business problems, and dislikes being around him for fear he will divulge her secrets to her husband.*

Hmm. Phyllida could see some connection between Charity Forrte and the character she was meant to be portraying—the allusion to her thievery and change of financial fortune—but aside from that, there didn't seem to be as much similarity. Unless she had some other secret that Mr. Bowington—and Mr. Wokesley—could reveal.

She was beginning to understand why Georges Brixton had warned his friend about the script.

Lionel MacGavity (Dudley-Gore)*: Caterina Bowington's long-lost brother, who's not been seen nor heard from in nearly thirty years. Is it only coincidence he shows up tonight, out of the blue? Is he really who he says he is? What does he want from the Bowingtons?*

Well, that was interesting. Phyllida's brows rose. The faint suspicion she'd had that Mr. Dudley-Gore might not have been as good a pal of Mr. Wokesley's blossomed into something larger and more solid. But even so, even if that was the case, there seemed to be no actual *motive* written into that character description.

The only motive she could derive from Mr. Dudley-Gore's presence at Beecham House—to obtain money for the school—gave him no reason to want Clifton Wokesley out of the way. In fact, with Mr. Wokesley gone, there was even less of a chance that the Fitchler School for Boys would get their new cricket pitch or dining hall kitchen.

And yet . . . he was the single cast member who didn't have a clear and obvious motive—both in the script and in real life. Which implied to Phyllida that she was missing something.

She moved on to read the beginning of the script.

ACT I
TIME: Late in the evening
PLACE: A drawing room in the Bowington residence, a large and remote country manor house in Devonshire

The doors are flung open to a well-appointed drawing room. Five people are arranged throughout the room and seem to be frozen in place. They were in the midst of a cocktail party, which has now been interrupted by a horrific discovery.

On the floor is Mr. Bowington. He is clearly dead. A knife protrudes from the center of his back. He appears otherwise undisturbed other than the cigar he holds in his right hand.

Phyllida stopped here and reread the beginning, frowning. There'd been no cigar in Mr. Bowington's hand when the Murder Game began. She went back and reviewed the descriptions of the characters, once again mulling over the seeming lack of (obvious) motive for Mr. Dudley-Gore.

"That simply makes no sense," she said aloud. She must be missing something.

"What doesn't, ma'am?" Opal had appeared in the doorway with the tea tray.

Phyllida gestured her in. "Thank you. And don't mind me . . . I was merely thinking over some of the motives of the guests at Beecham House last night."

She knew she didn't have to explain about the murder or her involvement in the investigation. Everyone at Mallowan Hall would be aware. It didn't matter how they knew; they knew.

A sudden flash of lightning blazed outside, followed by another horrific boom of cracking thunder. A gust of wind swept a sudden rush of rain against the window.

"That's a nasty storm, ma'am," Opal said, going to the window to look outside. "*Shew!* The apple trees is half bent over, Mrs. Bright!"

"Good heavens," Phyllida said. "Well, I'm relieved we're all here tucked away. I do hope no one is going out about in this." Especially Inspector Cork, on his way here from London.

Then she remembered what Agatha had said. *"If the storm gets very loud and violent, you ought to go out and check on Bradford."*

Phyllida did not want to think about that.

She didn't want to feel the need to check on Bradford regarding anything.

What on earth would he need her to check on him about anyway?

And she certainly did not want to take herself out into this horrific monster of a storm to the garage to that arrogant and snide man. Not to mention his mongrel of a canine, who would be even more sloppy and wet in a rainstorm.

But.

She was Phyllida Bright. She never shirked a duty and she rarely disregarded a request (unless it was from Mr. Dobble, and then she disregarded as many as she possibly could whilst still executing her duties in an exceptional manner).

If Agatha asked her specifically to do something, then Phyllida supposed she ought to do it—even if it would be unnecessary and, knowing Bradford, painful. She could hear him already: *Why on earth would you see a need to check on me, Mrs. Bright? You don't think I can handle a little thunderstorm? Did you expect to find me hiding under the bed?*

With a heartfelt and regretful sigh, she snatched up the teacup and took a big, fortifying gulp of the steaming Assam tea she'd recently begun to favor, thanks to Dr. Bhatt.

And with that to brace her for what was to come—she wasn't certain whether the worst would be fighting her way to the garage or facing Bradford and his superciliousness when he discovered she'd come to "check on" him—she rose from her chair.

"I must speak with Bradford," she told Opal—not because the scullion needed to know what the housekeeper was up to, but simply because the girl seemed so shocked that Phyllida was leaving the tea tray she'd just delivered. "Unfortunately, that means I must brave the storm."

"But, ma'am, perhaps you could simply ring him up," Opal said in a very logical and pragmatic suggestion.

"Indeed I could," Phyllida replied. She had thought of that, but Agatha had specifically said "go out and check on him." Since she saw no reason to give any further explanation, she merely smiled and gestured Opal to follow her out of the sitting room.

By the time Phyllida had located the pair of Wellies she only wore when absolutely necessary, along with a rain slicker and hat, she was feeling rather ridiculous. Who on earth would take their lives into their hands to traverse the yard from house to garage during this gargantuan storm?

But by this time, something was niggling in the back of her mind. Something prodded her, that Agatha wouldn't have asked her to do such a thing if it hadn't been important. It would take half a minute for her to dash from the back door to the garage. Yet, she still balked at going out there.

At the last minute, she stuffed the script into her pocket. At least she would have that as an excuse—weak and unnecessary as it was—when Bradford laughed at her for invading his domain.

She gave no explanation for her attire when she hurried down the stairs to the kitchen and larder and Mrs. Puffley caught sight of her from her worktable. She merely gave an abbreviated wave and went on her way.

However, when she got to the door, she paused. It was *wicked* out there. Utterly dark, and swirling, and nasty. A great streak of lightning split the sky into halves, making the world look eerily spotlit in the middle of a nightmare.

Phyllida took a great breath, ducked her head, and ran into the maelstrom.

CHAPTER 14

GEORGES BRIXTON NEVER FORGOT A FACE.

He expected this was due to the fact that he spent so much time studying mugs and their expressions on all sorts of people in order to learn how to mimic them for his work onstage.

Take that woman last night, with the unusual strawberry-gold hair and the pretty blue frock . . . he was certain he'd seen her before, somewhere. Quite a looker she was, for being a bit long in the tooth. But she might've made it onstage had she given it a try, with that hair and the eyes that looked over a bloke like she was trying to read inside his mind.

. . . Or decide how to do away with him if he crossed her.

Maybe the stage *was* where he knew her from. She'd've made a smashing Lady Macbeth with that cool demeanor and those intense eyes.

But try as he might, he couldn't place her. And she said as how she didn't spend any time in London anyway, so it must have been some time ago he knew her . . .

He shook his head, frowning as a rumble of thunder rolled in the distance. It bothered him when he couldn't place a mug. But it would come to him.

He took a sip from his drink, comfortable in this shadowy room tucked away in the back of the main floor at Beecham House, delighted to have some quiet time to himself. He'd first gone into Wokesley's study because he expected there'd be a stock of high-quality spirits within, and he hadn't been wrong. The twelve-year-old Scotch whiskey had been his choice and it was a good one. He'd brought the bottle with him to this out-of-the-way chamber that seemed to be a little-used sitting room. He'd ignored the lamp on the table next to him, hoping the dimness would deter anyone who might think to join him. Yet someone had stoked the fire even in here so it crackled pleasantly next to his chair, providing warmth against the damp in the air.

What a life of luxury Wokesley had lived. Rotten bastard.

Georges tossed back another gulp of the whiskey and hissed when its heat hit the back of his throat, mingling with the bitterness he nursed alongside his drink.

The others were occupied elsewhere—the women claimed to be resting before dinner, and then, presumably, they'd spend an hour doing whatever they did to their faces and hair to prepare for the meal. Bea certainly seemed broken up about the death of her husband, but once she realized the pots of money she now had, Georges knew she'd get over that fast enough.

He grimaced as he took a drink.

Dinner. What an ordeal that was going to be, everyone trying to make nice, all the while knowing the person across the table from you might have offed your host.

That bumbling chap from the school had gone out to watch the storm coming in, or so he'd claimed. The wind was coming up hard, though, and the thunder was rumbling and crashing closer now. But Georges didn't care if the man got drenched or blown to bits, or even zapped by lightning, so long as he didn't bother him. It was too dashed bad the constable had told them all not to leave Beecham House, or surely the headmaster would have been on his way back to the school by now.

That pompous nob Keller had been reading a book in the library—by another roaring fire—when Georges slipped by to raid the study of spirits. The bloke hadn't even looked up as he passed the doorway, a fact for which Georges was quite thankful. Last thing he wanted was having to make conversation with him. Especially since he didn't trust the man as far as he could throw him.

A streak of lightning flared outside the window, bathing the room in light for an instant, then going shadowy once more. Georges supposed he could ring for someone to bring a bit of tea. No one else had seemed interested in the meal, but he could eat. Dinner was hours away and the whiskey was going down very quickly.

He mused over his situation: stuck in a country house with a murderer. Just like something out of a detective novel. Maybe not a good idea to stay much longer.

Not that he was prepared to return to London anytime soon. The city didn't hold the same attraction as it used to, since that awful night with Wokesley and the others and the motor crash. He shuddered. He'd seen the vehicle mow into the poor woman, and heard the ugly thud as she rolled onto its hood then tumbled to the ground. Simply awful. He'd had nightmares for weeks.

Now that *Darkling World* had closed, he didn't have any new prospects or any reason to stay in London.

Thanks to Clifton Wokesley.

It was only right the bloke had invited him here to Beecham House. Georges hadn't even hesitated accepting the invitation, despite the silliness of the Murder Game concept.

But then, Wokesley had fancied himself an actor and a Great Patron of the Theater. The way he spoke about it was if it was a bleeding title, like the Duke of York or the Viscount of Somewhere Bloody Else.

Georges supposed if Wokesley wasn't rolling in it as much as he was, then *he'd* have been treading the boards, trying to make ends meet like Georges himself did.

So of course he'd decided to avail himself of Wokesley's hospitality when he got the invite. He thought he'd live on the man's beans in the lap of luxury for a while, and meanwhile work on him—Georges certainly had leverage now, didn't he?—along with his handsome wife, who clearly had all sorts of influence on the bloke—to finance another show.

When he'd learned Mrs. Agatha Christie lived nearby, Georges had been even more thrilled. Surely the woman had an old short story somewhere, which could be turned into a play—or better yet, a film!—and Georges would star in it. He'd been delighted when he learned Wokesley had actually invited her to the Murder Game, which was why he'd donned a false mustache and the pince-nez in order to evoke that finicky French detective of hers, with his little gray cells and order and method and so on.

And then everything had gone all wrong.

Damn it all, he'd *warned* the chap, hadn't he? He'd told him the Murder Game wasn't a good idea. Georges knew nothing good would come of it.

People didn't like their secrets being trotted out to the world—even if it wasn't obvious what the secret was. But anyone paying attention could have guessed how each of the players had been perfectly cast in their roles, with their own motives matching up to that of their characters. Georges didn't know any of the other playactors from Adam, and *he'd* figured it out for each of them.

But Wokesley hadn't listened to him, and now he was dead, and now there would be no new show. No Agatha Christie play starring Georges Brixton, who, incidentally, had an accomplished French accent and could grow a real pair of mustaches if need be. Perhaps he should start on that anyhow. After all, the new widow had loads of money now, and she seemed someone who could be easily influenced.

And with Mrs. Christie living so nearby . . . surely he could convince two women to do what he wanted. After all, they'd come out in the money on the other end too, wouldn't they?

Georges considered it and decided, on the other hand, that it would be a very good idea to stick around Beecham House for a while, even with a killer about . . . especially since there was a second person here whom he was certain he'd seen before . . . elsewhere . . . and in a place that didn't make sense.

But he couldn't quite remember it . . . couldn't recall exactly where he'd seen them before.

And so he poured himself another couple fingers of Wokesley's fine Scotch. He sipped thoughtfully as the thunderstorm approached, crashing and booming as if the heavens were having a party.

Or a war.

Where *had* he seen that person before? The out-of-place one?

He forgot about the idea of tea and poured another glass of whiskey. Dinner would come soon enough. Perhaps he'd even doze for a bit here by the fire and dream about where he'd seen that person before . . .

He must have done, for all at once, Georges startled awake.

The room was unlit but for the bit of glowing coals in the fireplace, but now it was shrouded in darkness. The world outside was like night as rain pelted the window and the wind stormed against the trees, glass, and bricks.

Thunder crashed loudly, eerily, and Georges realized that was what had wakened him.

No . . . it wasn't that. It was . . . he *had* been dreaming, and somehow he'd summoned them right here in front of him.

"Oh, I didn't see you there," he said, pulling himself up in the chair.

"You looked very comfortable. I didn't mean to disturb you."

He tried desperately to remember where and how he'd seen this person before, but his mind was befuddled with spirits and groggy with sleep.

"Where do I know you from?" he blurted out. "I'm sure I've seen you before."

"Oh, yes. I remembered you almost right away." The smile was . . . not right. There was something wrong about it . . .

Lightning blazed sharply outside the window, casting the person into full illumination . . .

Georges saw the flash of metal an instant too late.

There was an ugly, crashing roar of thunder, so loud it sounded as if the heavens had split . . . so loud no one heard the *pop* of the pistol.

CHAPTER 15

PHYLLIDA FUMBLED WITH THE SIDE DOOR OF THE GARAGE AND BURST through the opening just as another jagged bolt shot through the sky behind her.

"Good heavens," she gasped, slightly out of breath. She tossed aside the brolly she'd foolishly thought would provide some protection against the raging winds and pelting rain, and which was now pulled completely inside out. Oh, and there was hail too, she had discovered when it pattered onto her hat.

The interior of the garage was dark and silent but for the sound of gusting wind and rain. The Daimler sat in a shadowy lump in the center of a space large enough to house six vehicles if they were packed neatly. The building had been a stable at one point, but as the Mallowans didn't ride or hunt, it had quickly been converted to hold their motors and those of any houseguests who might visit.

Phyllida was mildly surprised to find the place quiet and dark. Even Myrtle seemed absent, and that was what bothered her most of all. Usually the beast materialized at the slightest provocation.

She stripped off her slicker and the hideous hat she'd donned to protect her head, but left the Wellies on her feet. Thus unencumbered but for the soft squishing and squeaking from the boots, she started toward the rear of the garage where she knew Bradford's workshop and apartment were located.

"Hello? Bradford?" she called out, then winced as she bumped into some metal thing that was in her path. That dratted jack was going to leave a bruise on her shin, and why would Bradford leave something like that in the middle of the walkway? Clearly, he had no sense of order.

There was no response to her calls. Was he even here? Perhaps she should have looked in the staff dining room to see whether he'd come inside for dinner already. Phyllida was annoyed with herself for not having thought of that, but she'd been in too much of a hurry to slip outside before anyone questioned her about where she was going.

It wasn't until she'd reached the workshop that she heard the quiet whine. It was so peculiar the hair on the back of Phyllida's neck lifted and she paused.

Then she heard it again. Was that Myrtle?

"Bradford?" she called. And then, greatly against her better judgment, she added, "Myrtle? Are you there? Come out, Myrtle!"

This invitation was rewarded with a short bark. But there was no sign of Myrtle or her master.

Phyllida, torn between mystification, concern, and irritation, continued through the workshop toward the small corridor that turned off to Bradford's apartments. She'd never had the occasion—or desire—to breach that area of the garage before now, but the sound of the bark had come from therein. Perhaps Myrtle was somehow stuck and her master was in the house, unaware of her predicament.

Not that Phyllida was overjoyed by the idea of being the beast's rescuer—she could only imagine how it would display its gratitude. She shuddered at the thought.

Still . . .

A sudden ripping, shredding thunder crack filled the air, making even Phyllida jump. She heard another whine followed by another bark, this time more urgent.

There was nothing for it but to venture on.

"Bradford? Myrtle?" she called again as she felt her way along the workshop's wall. It ended abruptly at an abbreviated hallway, and now she was rewarded by the soft glow of light spilling from around the corner.

It came from an ajar door. Phyllida's heart pounded and her

hands became a little clammy, for all at once she was apprehensive about what she might find. It could be anything from a trapped Myrtle, to a comatose or ill Bradford, to him being—well, she needn't think about any other options like bathing or sleeping that might reveal him in any sort of dishabille.

"Myrtle! Come out!" she called with a bit more force than she felt.

Another bark, closer now, and by then Phyllida had reached the open door. She knocked, but since it was open and she'd been calling, she didn't expect an answer.

She looked around the corner into Bradford's rooms.

The first thing she saw was a lamp in the corner, on, spreading that golden glow. It illuminated a neatly made bed.

On the bed was Bradford. He was sitting upright, his legs folded in front of him in a very strange position: knees bent at either side, ankles crossed, making a sort of pretzel-like position. His hands were resting palm-down on his knees. Myrtle sat in the valley in the middle of his lap.

When she saw Phyllida, Myrtle gave a little whine, then two short barks. This led Phyllida to believe, at first, that the canine was in some sort of pain or distress.

But when she stepped in further she saw that it wasn't Myrtle who was in distress. It was Bradford.

And in an instant, she understood something that she'd not allowed herself to even imagine; that she'd rejected without giving it any conscious thought: that the self-assured, arrogant, and cynical man seemed to be suffering from what people called shell shock.

It was an affliction with which Phyllida was only too familiar, having worked part of her time during the Great War as a nurse, sometimes at the front lines. She'd seen all forms of it—soldiers becoming terrified or frenzied or paralyzed at any loud or unexpected sounds. They often lost their sense of place and time, even a sense of themselves.

She'd been thrown across the room, piled upon, punched, even grabbed about her neck and torso like a hostage—all by soldiers struggling with their memories of the battlefield.

She'd simply never suspected Bradford of suffering from such a condition.

Some people called it being "nervous in the service." Others had labeled seriously afflicted troops as cowards.

Phyllida knew better. It had nothing to do with bravery or the lack thereof. It was all about the intertwining and imprinted memories and horrific experiences of artillery and explosions, the violence and terrible circumstances of war, all being brought sharply to mind.

She also knew to tread carefully. A man suffering from a shell shock experience could be violent and unpredictable. But he also needed assurance and stability.

Myrtle was clearly providing such comfort, and for that reason, Phyllida could appreciate the beast for the moment. The canine was also clearly worried for her master, who, so far, had made neither movement nor sound.

Phyllida took another cautious step into the room. She wasn't certain whether she should stay, but her dutiful self would not allow her to leave. Not yet.

"Bradford," she said quietly. Now that she'd stepped into the room, she could see that his fingers gripped his knees so tightly the trousers over them were wrinkled. His eyes were closed, rather than open and vacant as she'd often seen in a traumatized soldier.

And she realized his lips were moving. Was he praying?

Myrtle gave an insistent whine as if to ask why Phyllida wasn't *doing* anything.

"Bradford? Bradford!" she said a little more insistently. Still nothing. She gritted her teeth; she didn't want to reach out and touch him for fear of how he might react to the sudden sensation. Shell-shocked people were utterly unpredictable. "*Joshua!* Can you hear me?"

Apparently her use of his familiar name somehow penetrated to wherever he was. Bradford's eyes opened, and for a moment, all she saw was emptiness. A wave of apprehension and even fear rushed over her . . . and then the emptiness in his dark eyes faded into confusion, followed quickly by comprehension and clarity.

"Mrs. Bright, what in the blazes are you doing here?" His voice was normal: cool, even peremptory.

"I . . ." Words failed her. This was not at all the reaction she'd expected.

"Mrs. Bright?" He spoke normally, but his fingers still gripped his knees.

"The storm," she said, still fumbling for speech.

Understanding flooded his eyes, but apparently he wasn't about to make it easy for her. "It is rather loud and violent. Myrtle doesn't care for the noise or the flashes."

"Quite," she replied. "Mrs. Agatha suggested I might want to check on—er—Myrtle if the storm became extremely loud and violent."

His expression faltered, then he nodded brusquely. "Very well. Enough of the charade, then, Mrs. Bright. Yes, I suffer from shell shock. A mild case, to be sure, but at times loud storms like this can . . . be difficult."

Phyllida hid her surprise at his easy confession. "Understandable. I've seen far more acute cases."

"I'm certain you have."

"What were you doing? If I may ask. I'm curious . . . as I said, I've seen far worse cases. Were you praying?"

Perhaps it was because she spoke so gently that he answered without the prevarication to which she was accustomed. "It's called meditation. It's a practice to calm and clear one's mind. One repeats the same words over and over again as a way to block out the world around.

"It's helped, most particularly when I'm aware of an—er—impending problem, like a thunderstorm, and can do it before . . . er. Right. Your Dr. Bhatt suggested I try it. He also gave me this blend of tea to drink." He gestured to a cup on the table next to him, which Phyllida had not noticed. "It assists in calming one's . . . mood."

"May I?" she asked, gesturing to the cup.

He shrugged and she picked up the cup to sniff the dregs. "Cinnamon. Chamomile too, perhaps? What else?"

"Holy basil and lemon balm . . . and another herb from his homeland. Ashwa . . . something or other."

"I see." She set the cup down and took a step back. She noticed Myrtle seemed pleased with the progress made since Phyllida had entered the room, for she was panting whilst dividing her attention between the two humans. "Incidentally, he's not *my* Dr. Bhatt," she said firmly.

Bradford lifted a single brow, and that was when she knew they'd passed the danger point. He was himself again—which likely meant he would resort to snide and lofty remarks. "No?"

"No," she replied.

Lightning blazed outside the single window in the room. An answering rolling crack of thunder had Myrtle whining and ducking her head. Phyllida looked sharply at Bradford, but his gaze remained clear and his only discernible reaction was to stroke his shivering dog as she tried to burrow beneath his legs.

"As I said . . . Myrts doesn't like storms."

"Quite. Well," Phyllida said, "I suppose I should leave you to it." In fact, she'd suddenly become acutely aware of the fact that she was in Bradford's bedroom—not the first time she'd been with a man in his room, of course, and certainly not likely to be the last—but she found it a bit discomfiting.

"Right," Bradford replied. He swung his feet off the bed and stood, sending Phyllida backing up a few more steps in the small space . . . and then she felt foolish and irritated with herself. When on earth had Phyllida Bright become a shrinking violet?

Before either of them could speak, a shrill *brrrrinnnggg* filled the air, causing Phyllida to jolt. What on *earth* was wrong with her, being so jumpy?

He strode out of the room without a word, and she followed as the telephone in the workshop continued to ring.

"Bradford," he said, picking up the receiver. He listened for a moment, glanced at Phyllida, then said, "Yes, she's here."

Mystified, she took the telephone receiver. "Yes?"

"Mrs. Bright. There is an individual calling on the telephone line to the main house who wishes to speak with you," said Mr.

Dobble. He sounded terribly annoyed with the entire situation. "I shall disconnect herewith and ask the operator to send the call through to you . . ."

She wondered whether he was more annoyed that the telephone call was for her, or that he didn't know why she had gone to the garage. There were several reasons she wasn't about to enlighten him. "Thank you, Mr. Dobble," she said primly, and then pressed down on the telephone cradle to end the call. A moment later, the sharp *brrrrinnngggg* filled the air.

"This is Mrs. Bright," she said crisply into the receiver.

"Oh . . . oh, Mrs. Bright . . . can you come? *Oh, please?* It's—it's awful! Only it's Mr. Brixton . . . why he's *dead!* . . . and—and the extra maid has gone back home and she won't come back, and there's blood and ashes all over, and Mrs. Napoleon's threatening to quit! And Mrs. Treacle, why she's lying in bed with a cold cloth on her head because *she's* the one what found Mr. Brixton! All bloody and *all!*" Louise spewed this astonishing information in one long breath, answering any question Phyllida might have had before she could voice it.

"Good heavens," she said.

"Mrs. Bright, I'm *scared,* I am! Will you come?" By now, Louise's voice had traveled tight and high, and Phyllida could hear real fear.

She hesitated only a moment, then her strong sense of duty and proclivity for managing problems won out. "Yes, of course."

She replaced the receiver and looked at Bradford. "There's been another murder at Beecham House."

He didn't even hesitate. "How soon do we leave?"

Phyllida wasn't particularly delighted about driving through the wild storm in nothing but a flimsy metal motor with glass windows.

She was even less delighted about the panting, drooling creature that had wormed its way into the vehicle and now sat on its master's lap, bright-eyed and eager despite the raging storm on the other side of said flimsy metal and glass. It was almost as if the canny canine had been pretending to be afraid.

But even Phyllida couldn't abide leaving the beast alone in the garage when it was obviously terrified of the storm. And she certainly wasn't going to allow it to go into the house, even though Mrs. Puffley would have welcomed her with open arms. That would only open the door to future trespasses.

Besides, Stilton and Rye would never speak to her again.

So Phyllida squeezed herself as far away from Bradford and his copilot as possible, and prayed that they'd arrive at Beecham House without having a tree land on the roof of the motor. That would be quite inconvenient, not to mention potentially costly, as not only had Phyllida agreed to bring along the Vac-Tric, but she'd also conscripted Ginny to come with her. And Mr. Dobble had stirred the pot by suggesting that Elton could be spared, and that he ought to go along as well. Elton had been so shamelessly enthusiastic about this suggestion that Phyllida had had to avoid Bradford's eyes.

"It's the neighborly thing to do," the butler intoned far too gravely to be sincere. "Mrs. Agatha would suggest it herself if she were here. And you ought to take the vacuum machine with you as well, Mrs. Bright."

He probably hoped she'd forget it there. And he certainly knew what sort of problems between the maids that would occur with one of them being selected to accompany the handsome valet off-site.

But in the interest of time and practicality, Phyllida hadn't demurred. The vacuum machine was a new and exciting device, and it sounded as if Beecham House was in severe distress relative to housekeeping. Beyond that, she would certainly handle any dramatics that might ensue between the maids.

Besides, the morose expression on Stanley's face when Ginny fairly danced out of the house with Elton trailing behind, holding an umbrella over her head, could portend a disruption in the footman staff sooner than Mr. Dobble might like . . . and that was a problem with which he'd have to contend.

A flash of lightning cracked audibly just in front of the motor, and in the back seat, Ginny squeaked and dove toward Elton. But Phyllida was more concerned about their driver's state of mind than how her maid was manipulating herself into the young valet's arms.

She glanced over at Bradford from the corner of her eye, not wanting to fully turn and reveal that she was measuring his reaction. His profile was still and set, and it was too dark to discern how tightly he was gripping the steering wheel. She'd been surprised at how readily he'd suggested driving her to Beecham House; she'd thought he might insist on waiting until the storm was over. She would have offered to drive the motor herself, but she knew he'd have none of it.

The motor trundled steadily onward, slowly and carefully in the blowing rain, and—most telling of all—Myrtle seemed unconcerned.

Deceitful beastie! That unruly mop of a dog had surely been playing up its fears in order to get a ride in the motor. When it looked over at her, panting hotly, Phyllida was certain she saw the creature *grinning*.

Miraculously, they reached Beecham House unscathed. Elton leaped out of the Daimler before it had hardly come to a halt near the servants' entrance. He hurried over to Phyllida's door, opening it while holding up the brolly to protect her from the storm's assault.

"Be careful of the mud, Mrs. Bright," he said earnestly, helping her out of the vehicle—something she could certainly manage on her own and normally preferred to do—and then doing his best to block her from the wind and rain with his sturdy body. He was a strong young man and certainly very handsome, along with being solicitous. She could comprehend why the maids were competing for his attention. If she were younger (much younger) . . .

"You'll come back for Ginny, then, Elton," she told him firmly as he offered his arm to help her navigate through the puddles and mud.

"Oh, yes, ma'am," he said.

Once inside Beecham House, Phyllida extricated herself from the valet and turned her attention to the matter at hand.

Instead of being filled with activity and delicious smells, the kitchen was quiet and smelled of nothing but coffee and raw onions. Mrs. Napoleon was sitting at the worktable with a large baking dish filled with sliced onions, potatoes, carrots, and a mutton roast that hadn't yet seen the inside of an oven. She startled and gasped as Phyllida swept in. The scullery maid, Petunia, was drinking tea with shaking hands and wide eyes. There were streaks down her cheeks. Phyllida suspected if there weren't a furious storm raging outside, both kitchen workers would be long gone.

Catching sight of Phyllida, Louise, who'd been sitting at the same table, shoved her chair away and shot to her feet.

"Oh, Mrs. Bright, thank the Good Lord you've come! It's awful, it is. We don't know what to do—I mean about the murders—and Mrs. Treacle, why she's ever so upset she can't stop crying. She had to take to her bed."

"And where is Mr. Trifle?" said Phyllida.

"Why, Mr. T's just sitting in his pantry and drinking," said Louise, sniffling. "A lot."

"Quite. Well, I'm here now," she said to the cook and maids. "No one has any reason to hurt you, and I'm certain to soon identify the culprit now that he's made another mistake."

"A mistake?" Louise's eyes went wide. "What sort of mistake?"

"I haven't yet determined that," Phyllida replied briskly, "but I shall soon find out. Murderers *always* make mistakes. In the meanwhile, everyone must be fed so they can keep their strength up. It's time to demonstrate your English mettle, Mrs. Napoleon. And Bradford is here—see, he's coming in now. He'll sit with you right here in the kitchen and stand guard if you like."

Mrs. Napoleon's face lit up like sunshine over snow when Bradford strolled in, followed by Myrtle, of course. Despite Bradford being wet and dripping and the presence of the beast, the cook insisted he sit at the table, then pressed a cup of coffee on him, whilst promising a hearty meal coming up soon. She even stooped to croon at the four-legged mop and promised it a bone to gnaw on.

Phyllida shook her head, but held her tongue. It wasn't her

kitchen. "Now, Louise," she said, "if you will show me where Mr. Brixton is, and then I shall speak with Mrs. Treacle." She had no intention of involving herself with the butler, sotted or not. "I do hope no one has upset the crime scene."

Louise gave her a strange look. "Oh, Mrs. Bright, I didn't mean to, but when Mrs. Treacle screamed, I ran in with the ash bucket, and I saw him and I—well, I was so surprised I backed up and tripped over a stool . . . and the bucket went everywhere, all over the floor and sofa . . . It's a *disaster*!" She was sobbing in between her words. "And *someone killed Mr. Brixton!*"

Phyllida thrust a handkerchief in her direction. She'd learned it was best to have multiple handkerchiefs on hand when dealing with murder, for someone was always sobbing or wailing—or a bit of clean cloth might be needed to pick up or wrap up a clue.

"Is the constable still here?" she asked, gesturing to the doorway for Louise to lead her to the crime scene—or whatever part of it hadn't been blown to bits.

"He's talking to Mrs. Wokesley." Louise sniffled into the handkerchief as she trudged down the hall.

That, at least, was a positive development. That meant Constable Greensticks *wasn't* trampling all over the crime scene.

Louise had not exaggerated when she said the sitting room with Mr. Brixton was a disaster. Phyllida didn't think anyone could have made a worse mess of it if they'd tried—and having had Ginny and Molly in her sitting room, dripping wet and covered with soot, she was qualified to know.

Thank heaven she'd brought the Vac-Tric.

Once again, Phyllida was forced to put housekeeping tasks from her mind in favor of the crime scene.

Mr. Brixton had been shot—a fact Louise had neglected to mention during her speech. He was slumped in an armchair next to the fireplace where, it appeared, he'd been sipping a drink. Someone had put a bullet right in the center of his chest. His shirt was soaked with blood, and it had dripped down the front of him and into his lap and was mingling with some of the ashes that had been strewn all over. The heavy iron smell went right to Phyllida's nose—and her memory—sending her back, for a moment, to her work in the field hospital.

Whoever killed Georges Brixton must have walked right up to him and shot him at fairly close range. He might have been dozing in the chair and been unaware, or he might have known the person and had no reason to feel threatened. Either way, it was another risky proposition: firing a weapon in a house full of people . . . although the violent thunderstorm had likely obscured or camouflaged the sound.

"Did you hear the gunshot?" Phyllida asked.

"No, ma'am."

"And you said Mrs. Treacle discovered him?"

"Yes, ma'am. We all heard her scream, we did. I came running—I got here first—and th-there he was. And that's when I spilt the a-ash b-bucket." Louise's eyes welled with tears and she wiped them roughly with Phyllida's handkerchief. "I-I'm so sorry I ruined the crime scene."

"Never mind that, where was everyone prior to the discovery of Mr. Brixton?"

"I-I'm not sure, ma'am. I was cleaning in the parlor when I heard Mrs. Treacle cry out. Sir Keller had been in there—he was reading a book—but when I came in, he said to go ahead and do what I came for, and he got up and left straightaway. I don't know where he went after that."

"And Mrs. Wokesley and Mrs. Forrte?"

"They were resting upstairs, ma'am, far as I know. Me and Milly had already cleaned their rooms. And then they were going to dress for dinner, though I don't think Mrs. Wokesley cared much about that. Dinner or dressing. She's in a bad way."

"And what about Mr. Dudley-Gore?"

"Oh . . . why, I don't know for certain. I didn't see him."

"Very well. Thank you. I want to look in Mr. Brixton's room, but after that, I'd like to speak with Mrs. Treacle."

"Yes, ma'am." Louise looked around the small sitting room and heaved a great sigh. She looked miserable, as if she were about to burst into a gale of tears once more. "Mrs. Bright, me mam always said 'do your best job, don't never shirk at it, work hard, be polite, and someday you'll be a housekeeper or cook or even a ladies' maid, Louise' . . . but I just don't think she ever had something like this on. Murders and storms and all. I won't never get this room clean again . . . and poor Mr. Brixton! He was always so nice, for being a bit of a toff, you know. Not like that Sir Keller."

"Mr. Brixton certainly didn't deserve to have a bullet put in his heart," Phyllida said.

"He even talked to me sometimes. Like I was a real person, see? About what it was like in London, being an actor and all. It was ever so interesting, the way he talked about it. He liked to watch peoples' faces, he did, so he could learn how to act, you see. He copied them, see. He told me all of that . . . and now he's *dead*." Louise choked back a sob.

"Absolutely awful," Phyllida replied with feeling.

"He said as how he never forgets a face, Mrs. Bright. Imagine that. He told me as how he saw someone here that he *knew* he'd seen before, but he couldn't place them, see?"

Phyllida felt that little frisson of unease again. Mr. Brixton had said such a thing to her yesterday evening, asking if they'd ever met. "Did he say who it was?"

"No, he didn't go on about it much. Only that he knew them somewhere, and he'd remember it sometime. Or maybe he'd ask them, he said he might," Louise said, still sniffling.

"I see," Phyllida replied. "When did you—er—have this conversation with Mr. Brixton? About a familiar person he couldn't place?"

"Oh, it was just after tea—that was yesterday, you see. I was cleaning out the parlor to set up for the Murder Game, and he came in looking for something."

Phyllida's unease vanished. That had obviously been before she'd met Mr. Brixton, so he couldn't have been talking about her.

However . . . he had been talking about someone else. Someone that he'd seen somewhere before.

And now he was dead.

"He gave no indication at all about who it was? Man or woman or any sort of hint?" she asked.

"No, ma'am. Only that he wished he could remember who it was, and how they didn't act like they knew him at all."

"Very well," Phyllida said, hiding her frustration. If he'd given even more of a hint, he might still be alive.

Or it might have been the most innocent of situations and had nothing to do with his murder.

"Now, let us see to this . . . situation." She gestured to the room—the crime scene, and the disaster of the spilled ash bucket. When she informed Louise that she'd brought help—not to mention a vacuum machine—the poor girl nearly burst into tears again. This time they were happier tears, and she didn't need a new handkerchief.

Phyllida instructed the maid to close up the room for the time being and told her that the cleaning wouldn't begin until the body had been removed. Then she hurried off to dash upstairs.

When she got to Georges Brixton's room, she immediately pulled open the bureau drawer and dug beneath his undershirts.

The pistol was gone.

Grimly, Phyllida replaced the undershirts and turned just as a figure appeared in the open doorway.

"What are you doing?"

CHAPTER 16

It was Charity Forrte, and she wore an ugly, suspicious expression. She also had an unnatural light in her eyes which Phyllida suspected was due to the consumption of the contents of the tin on her dressing table.

"I was looking for the pistol that was in Mr. Brixton's drawer," Phyllida replied evenly.

The flare of shock in Mrs. Forrte's jittery eyes could have been attributed to a number of reasons. "A pistol?"

"Indeed. And it's now missing. One can surmise that its absence is related to Mr. Brixton's condition in the sitting room. Did you hear the gunshot?"

"No, of course not. What was Georges doing with a pistol?"

"We shall likely never know."

"But . . . whoever killed him still has the gun," Mrs. Forrte said suddenly, and she glanced nervously down the hallway behind her.

"Quite."

"Good heavens," she said, gripping the edge of the doorway. "Why, that's . . . that's . . ."

"Indeed." Phyllida decided it was the perfect opportunity to further question the woman whilst her guard was down. "Did Mr. Wokesley know about your—er—habit?"

"My *what*? I don't know what you're talking about." Her lips, long wiped free of cosmetics, shifted into a sneer. "You're awfully nosy, aren't you—whatever your name is."

"Mrs. Bright," Phyllida replied helpfully. "He knew about your cocaine habit, and he knew how you paid for it, didn't he?"

"I have no idea what you're talking about."

"You steal jewelry or other small but expensive valuables whenever possible—at shops, at peoples' homes, wherever. If you get caught, you make it out that it was a joke. Mr. Wokesley knew about it, didn't he? Did he threaten to tell someone? Mrs. Wokesley, perhaps?"

"I—I have a problem," Mrs. Forrte said. "I don't like to talk about it, but I-I can't help it."

"To which problem are you referring?" Phyllida asked. "The thievery or the cocaine?"

Mrs. Forrte's pretty face turned hard and angry. She stepped into the room and closed the door. "You don't know what you're talking about. Just like Clifton! He accused me of the same, you know, and he was just *wrong*. Just *wrong*!"

"You must have been very angry with Mr. Wokesley," Phyllida said, even as she looked around the room for something with which to defend herself should it become necessary. Mrs. Forrte's eyes were bright and hard and her breathing was fast and shallow. She was desperate and emotional, but Phyllida did not believe she was in possession of the revolver that had killed Mr. Brixton. Therefore, the fireplace poker should suffice as a deterrent, if necessary.

"I was! He had no right to spread lies about me. I don't *mean* it . . . I don't *mean* to do it. It just . . . happens."

"Taking the jewelry, you're speaking of. Did you steal something of Mrs. Wokesley's? A bracelet perhaps? Is that how he realized what was happening?" Phyllida positioned herself next to the fireplace poker but did not pick it up.

"No. It's not true! I *didn't* take it! I wouldn't take anything from Bea!" Tears glistened in her eyes, but the unnatural light in them still shined through. "Or-or I don't remember it if I did. And after what *he* did . . . well, he deserved everything he got!"

"Mr. Wokesley?"

"Of course!"

"What did Clifton Wokesley do to you?"

"To *me*? Nothing—except spread lies and half-truths. You don't think he actually let someone else drive his precious motor, do you? And to think everyone believed him. And then all the lies he's been telling about *me*! Why, the *police* even came to my flat and arrested me! All because of *him*. It took me plenty of money to sort out all the legal problems after that, and I told him so. I told him *he* should pay for all my solicitors—it's *slander* is what it was!"

"And when he wouldn't pay for your legal fees, you killed him," Phyllida suggested.

"Don't be absurd! Of course I didn't kill him. How would I ever get my money if I did?"

"You're friends with Beatrice Wokesley. Maybe you thought she'd be more likely to give you the money than her husband would, especially if she didn't know about your . . . problems."

"I didn't kill Clifton, you—whoever you are. What are you doing here anyway? Who *are* you?"

"I'm here to determine who killed Clifton Wokesley and Georges Brixton—and to make certain everyone in the household is fed, since it appears the housekeeper and butler are out of commission," Phyllida replied calmly. "And if you are truly innocent of murder, then you should be grateful for my expertise."

Mrs. Forrte didn't seem to know how to respond to that simple and accurate statement, so Phyllida took advantage of her consternation and decided it was time to make her exit.

She breezed past and let herself out of the room before Mrs. Forrte could react. She'd learned very little from their conversation, although Mrs. Forrte's insistence that Clifton Wokesley deserved what happened to him stuck in her mind.

Nonetheless, whilst Mrs. Forrte's shock and concern over the missing firearm seemed genuine, Phyllida wasn't quite ready to rule her out as a killer. The woman had as good a motive as any to do away with Mr. Wokesley, and Phyllida had already noted that she knew how to put on the act of an ingenue. She was also using cocaine, which could certainly affect her personality and mood.

Not only that, but Mrs. Forrte also seemed to be familiar enough with Mr. Brixton to refer to him by his first name, and to wonder what he was doing with a gun. How well had she known Georges Brixton? Enough to want to kill him?

Or had Mr. Brixton seen or heard something that put the murderer in danger of being discovered?

Louise's conversation with Mr. Brixton suggested that he had recognized or remembered someone here . . . someone who either wasn't who they seemed to be, or who had been in an unusual setting. If the same person had killed both Mr. Wokesley and Mr. Brixton—which Phyllida could not fathom it being otherwise—then it was very possible it was because he or she realized Mr. Brixton had recognized them. Thus wherever he'd seen or encountered the person before likely had a strong link to motive.

It was the only thing that made sense.

Phyllida hastened her way back to the kitchen. She could smell the roasting mutton and what was probably the beginning of gravy simmering on the stove. There was also the scent of something sweet and yeasty emanating from the second oven—very possibly peach cobbler.

Bradford, Elton, the scullery maid Petunia, and Mrs. Napoleon were all at the worktable. The two males were seated and had cups of coffee or tea. Each also had a small plate with sliced spice bread and a hunk of cheese. Petunia was standing whilst shelling peas and Mrs. Napoleon was moving between the table and the stove with the ease of long experience. Myrtle was curled up under Bradford's chair. She appeared to be sleeping comfortably.

When Phyllida entered the room, Elton stood, shoving back from the table so eagerly he nearly knocked over his chair, and Myrtle leaped to her feet, eyes as bright as Mrs. Forrte's had been, but for a different reason.

"Mrs. Bright, would you like to sit down?" Unabashed, Elton gestured to the seat he'd caught before it hit the ground, and pulled it away from the table for her. "Mrs. Napoleon has made some delicious spice bread."

Phyllida absolutely did not look at Bradford, though she was certain he was either rolling his eyes or, worse, trying not to laugh. She ignored Myrtle as well, though the beast was dancing in front of her as if expecting her to acknowledge its existence.

"Thank you, Elton, but no. I'd like to get a tea tray for Mrs. Treacle, Mrs. Napoleon, if I may."

"Of course, Mrs. Bright. Petunia, you may put those peas aside and prepare the tray for Mrs. Treacle."

"Something smells delicious," Phyllida said, of the mind that giving credit where credit was due was an excellent practice. "You've certainly been hard at work, Mrs. Napoleon. Is that mutton roast?"

"With parsnips, carrots, and potatoes," the cook replied with a pleased smile. "Mashed peas, sautéed liver and onions for later, and a bit of smoked fish paste as well. I've a fresh sliced rye for it, you see. Along with peach and blueberry cobbler."

"Brilliant," Phyllida said, already hoping for a serving of the cobbler with a cup of tea. She remembered she hadn't eaten since a single piece of toast this morning. Solving murders was certainly a way to cut down on calories.

"Here you are, Mrs. Bright." Petunia brought her a tray with a small teapot missing half of its spout and a large chip out of the base. "It's one of the old ones we found in the storage room. Most of the others broke last night, you see," she explained needlessly.

"Would you like me to carry that for you, Mrs. Bright?" asked Elton, who'd remained standing as any gentleman worth his salt ought to do. Bradford had hardly glanced up; he was enjoying his coffee and spice bread . . . and, most probably, also reveling in Phyllida's predicament. Myrtle had returned to her place beneath his chair, but she watched Phyllida with those beady dark eyes, plotting how and when to launch herself at Phyllida's stockings.

"If you would, Elton, thank you. And then you may assist Anthony to get fresh wood in all the rooms, along with ensuring the fires are kept going. I haven't seen Mr. Trifle, so I expect nothing has been done to that end. It's terribly damp, although it seems the storm has begun to wane a bit."

"Yes, ma'am," he said, taking up the tray without hesitation.

Phyllida remembered where Mrs. Treacle's sitting room was, and correctly surmised that her bedchamber was attached. She went through the sitting room and knocked on the connecting door.

A weak voice called, "Come in."

Phyllida took the tray from Elton and sent him off to keep busy.

She found Elizabeth Treacle in bed with a cloth over her forehead. "I've brought you some tea," Phyllida told her, looking around the room.

It was neat and simply furnished with few personal effects, as one would expect from an occupant who hadn't resided there very long. The lamp on the bedside table cast enough light to read by, but it didn't seem Mrs. Treacle had any books at hand. Instead, there was a small photo album and a personal diary nearby, along with a bud vase containing a single daisy. The doors of the small wardrobe were closed but a traveling trunk sat on the floor next to it, open, as if preparing to be utilized.

A large window set low in the wall provided an excellent view of the storm that had not abated as much as Phyllida had hoped.

"Oh, that's very kind of you, Mrs. Bright." Mrs. Treacle began to pull herself upright. "I didn't realize you'd—er—returned."

"Louise rang Mallowan Hall, quite upset," Phyllida told her, and carefully set the tea tray on the narrow bed next to the housekeeper. "She asked me to come since you—er . . ." She stopped short of saying "shirked your duties," but only just barely.

"Poor Mr. Brixton," said Mrs. Treacle in a weak voice. Her hand fluttered at her throat. "I . . . it was awful."

"I understand you found him," Phyllida said.

Mrs. Treacle nodded, then turned her attention to pouring a

cup of tea. "I see they've found another usable pot," she said with a weak smile.

"Fortunately. Please tell me about when you discovered Mr. Brixton," Phyllida said firmly.

"Oh. Yes. Right. I . . . well, I saw the door open to the sitting room and noticed someone sitting in the chair. It was rather dark, you know, and that room was hardly used, so I was a bit surprised to see someone in there. And then . . ." She swallowed, visibly bracing herself. "There was a bright flash of lightning and . . . and I saw him. Sitting in the chair. Th-there was blood . . . I screamed."

"Did you approach him?"

"N-no, no, of course not. I could see that he was dead." She closed her eyes and heaved a great sigh. "I've given my notice to Mrs. Wokesley. I simply can't stay here any longer, with killers stalking all of us as we sleep."

Phyllida ignored the dramatic portion of her speech. Beecham House might be better off if Mrs. Treacle did take her leave, and that pronouncement explained the open travel trunk. Mrs. Treacle was wasting no time.

Perhaps Louise could even be promoted to housekeeper; after all, it wasn't as if the house was as large and complicated to manage as Mallowan Hall. Despite her agitation, she seemed to have a solid head on her shoulders. "You saw Mr. Brixton from the doorway, and you could tell that he was dead? Or had you stepped inside?"

"Why . . . I was perhaps a step inside, of course. Why would that matter?"

"I'm attempting to determine whether anyone trampled over the crime scene," Phyllida explained.

"Oh. No, not at all. I—I couldn't bring myself to go any closer." Mrs. Treacle's trembling hand lingered at her throat as if searching for her necklace.

"Quite. And did you notice anything out of place?"

"Why, no, not really. It was dark, as I said, except for that flash of lightning. There'd been a fire in the fireplace and it had burned down to coals. I thought to send Anthony to see to it, and then . . . and then I saw Mr. Brixton. I cried out, of course, as *anyone* would do upon discovering a dead body"—Phyllida declined to correct her poor assumption—"and then Louise came running. *She* was the one who spilt the ash bucket everywhere," Mrs. Treacle said with a surprising bit of animosity. "And so if the crime scene, as you call it, has been trampled upon, it was due to her clumsiness."

"Quite so," Phyllida replied. "Did you hear the gunshot?"

"No. At least, I don't think so. There was so much thunder, you see, and I was in the kitchen and then in my sitting room for a time." Her hand settled back in her lap, fingers curled into her palm.

"When was the last time you saw Mr. Brixton?" It would be difficult to establish exactly what time the man had been killed unless someone had heard the gunshot. Someone had surely telephoned for John Bhatt, but it might take him some time to arrive and make his estimate on time of death. And even then it would be only an estimate.

"I . . . well, let me think. It must have been about half two. He was coming out of Mr. Wokesley's study, carrying a bottle of spirits. I didn't see where he went after that, but it wasn't upstairs."

"That's quite helpful." Phyllida had received the telephone call from Louise at about half four, so the body had likely been discovered at least five or ten minutes prior to that. So that was a relatively short window of time. "Do you know where the other guests and staff members were between half two and half four?"

"Sir Keller was in the parlor," Mrs. Treacle said promptly. "He was reading. Mrs. Wokesley told me she was going to rest in her room and she did not want to be bothered until dinner or unless the inspector arrived. Mrs. Forrte was in her bedroom as well . . ." She hesitated, frowning.

"Yes?" Phyllida encouraged her.

"I . . . don't know whether I should mention this, but I noticed something in Mrs. Forrte's room yesterday. Early in the day, after Louise and the other maid cleaned. I'd forgotten it until now."

"Go on."

"I-I'm sure it's nothing, but I was certain there was a bracelet that belonged to Mrs. Wokesley in Mrs. Forrte's jewelry case. At least, it looked it to me. I don't know much about gemstones and whatnot, of course, but I do help Mrs. Wokesley dress, and so of course I was familiar with her jewelry."

"Did you mention this to anyone? Before now?" Phyllida asked.

"I did ask Mrs. Wokesley whether she was missing her sapphire bracelet. She told me she hadn't noticed it gone, but I did check her case and it wasn't there. Mrs. Forrte must have heard me, for the next time I looked in her chamber—I felt the need to review the work done by the extra maid, you see—the bracelet I'd seen there was missing."

"Did you find the sapphire bracelet in Mrs. Wokesley's jewelry box after that, then?" Phyllida asked.

Mrs. Treacle nodded. "Yes, I did. It might have been a mistake. As I said, I don't know jewelry. I've never had any to speak of," she added with a wry smile.

"I see." Phyllida tucked that information away. Had Mr. Wokesley discovered that the bracelet was missing, and accused Mrs. Forrte? Perhaps he'd seen her returning it to his wife's chamber. Or perhaps Mrs. Treacle was mistaken and both women had similar sapphire bracelets. "And what about Mr. Dudley-Gore? Did you happen to see him this afternoon between half two and the time you discovered Mr. Brixton?"

"No, I don't know where Mr. Dudley-Gore was during that time."

"And the staff?"

"The staff?" Mrs. Treacle frowned, sloshing her tea.

"Yes, of course. Louise, Mr. Trifle, Anthony . . ."

"But . . . but surely you don't think any of the servants did such a thing?" Mrs. Treacle was now sitting bolt upright. "Why, that's . . . ridiculous. Where on earth would any of them get a gun?"

"Most likely it isn't relevant, but one must be thorough," Phyllida replied. "After all, we are now dealing with two deaths. I shan't allow a third to occur."

"Right. Yes, of course. Still . . . I can see no reason any of us would want Mr. Wokesley or Mr. Brixton dead."

"Even so, I should like to know where everyone was during that time period, Mrs. Treacle."

"Right. Well . . . Mr. Trifle was in his pantry when I was in my sitting room. I don't believe I heard him leave. Anthony was clearing up the last dishes from the dining room after luncheon, and then he was about to polish the silver for dinner—at least, I heard Mr. Trifle tell him to see to it. Louise and the extra maid from town—I simply can't remember her name—were finishing the bedchambers, and then were about to clean the ground floor sitting rooms."

"Did you see or hear anything unusual?"

"No . . . but I was in my sitting room looking over the menus, the laundry tally, and the supplies lists and menus. I might have given my notice, but I wasn't about to leave without finishing the preparation." She gave Phyllida an affronted look, as if Phyllida had suggested she might have shirked her duty.

"Very well. Thank you for all of your information. I'm quite sorry that you made such an unpleasant discovery."

"Indeed. I'm feeling rather ill again, just thinking about it," Mrs. Treacle said, leaning back against her pillow again and closing her eyes.

"Quite."

Phyllida took her leave.

Closing the door behind her, she hesitated. The butler's pantry was the next door down the hall. She really had no desire to interact with Mr. Trifle, but one was often required to make sacrifices for the sake of justice.

When she knocked on the door, a gruff voice from within bid her enter.

She found Mr. Trifle as Louise had described: sitting with a large, full bottle of beer next to him on the desk. She wouldn't have thought much of it if she hadn't seen the two *empty* bottles next to it, and the small amount remaining in the bottom of his glass.

"Mrs. *Bright,* is it?" he said in a bleary voice. "Come to tell us how the household should be run, what to cook for dinner, and how to catch a killer, have you?"

"It's quite unsettling, isn't it?" she said, because beneath his bravado she sensed a hint of fear, or at least disquiet. Which of course was quite understandable.

"Unsettling? *Unsettling?*" He slammed his hand on the desk, narrowly missing his glass. Everything on the surface jumped and clinked.

"Now, now, Mr. Trifle. Let's not break any bottles. It would be a waste of good beer, now, wouldn't it?"

"*Two* murders. I ought to give my notice, I ought. Could be anyone next, now, couldn't it? Should get out of here as soon as I can, shouldn't I? But been here at Beecham House fifteen years, I have, and ain't nowhere else to go." He stared unhappily into his glass.

"Nonsense," Phyllida told him briskly. "It's only a matter of time until the culprit is identified, then things will be back to normal. In fact, I've narrowed it down to two . . . or possibly three . . . of the suspects."

"You have? Well, who is it, then?"

"Now, Mr. Trifle, it would be a bit premature for me to name names at this point. However, there's really only a limited number of people who could have done both murders. Did you hear the gunshot?"

"Gunshot? No, no . . . I didn't hear anything." He held his head in his hands, elbows propped on the desk.

"Where were you between half two and half four?" she asked.

"I was here, of course. I went down to the cellar for a bit, get some wine for dinner. Brought up another bottle of whisky while I was at it. Not that anyone's going to eat after all this. But they'll drink. Mark my words . . . they'll drink."

Phyllida agreed that was likely the case. "Did you see any of the guests during that time period? I'm attempting to establish who might have had the opportunity to . . . er . . . accost Mr. Brixton in the sitting room."

"Erm . . ." Mr. Trifle lifted his head from the cradle of his hands and rubbed his perspiring forehead as he thought. "Saw Sir Keller in the drawing room, and then in the study. Sitting there with a book. Mrs. Wokesley was upstairs in her room, said she didn't want to be disturbed. Mrs. Forrte too. She was upstairs."

Phyllida suppressed a sigh. The same information everyone else she'd spoken to had given. It was clear none of the suspects had a good alibi during the time Mr. Brixton had been killed; everyone was alone with no one to vouch for them.

"What about Mr. Dudley-Gore?"

"Mr. . . . right. Uhm . . ." He rubbed his shiny forehead with even more alacrity, as if that would assist him in extricating the memory. For once, his expressive eyebrows were immobile. "Saw him outside. Standing under the portico, watching the rain. Barking mad to be out there in a storm like that, you know. Get knocked over by a tree limb, you could. Asked him if he wanted to come inside, and he said no . . . 'What to do, what to do,' is what he said. 'Came here, set things right, and now what?'" Mr. Trifle looked at Phyllida with confusion. "Whaddayou think he meant by that?"

"I'm certain I have no good idea," she replied.

"*Who* do you think done it, Mrs. Bright?"

She shook her head. "Who do *you* think did it, Mr. Trifle? You observed everyone far longer than I have done. Who would have the nerve and the bravado to kill two people when nearly anyone in the household could walk in and see them at any moment? Or who would be desperate enough to take the chance? Did you hear or see anything that might help?"

He shook his head, staring back down at his beer glass. "I've been thinking on it. They were all in the library together before the game started—called it the green room, for some dashed reason. I was in there too for a bit.

"Mrs. Forrte went out to freshen up, then came back. Sir Keller wanted a Scotch whiskey that was in the study, so he left to get that. Mr. Brixton—well, he couldn't have done it, could he, since he's dead now?"

Phyllida shook her head in negation. "Quite likely not."

"That Mr. Dudley-Gore, very excitable man, he is. Pacing, looking out the windows, back and forth . . . had to use the bathroom twice, he was so nervous."

"What about Mrs. Wokesley?"

"Why, she was gay and happy about it all. First time in a while, both of them were—the Wokesleys, I mean to say."

"What do you mean by that?"

"When they first came here, they just weren't happy people. Hardly wanted to do anything but sit in the library or parlor. Had no guests to speak of. Didn't go into Listleigh, or around to many of the ruins or sights."

"Do you know why?"

Mr. Trifle shook his head. "Summat about a motor crash. Someone died, back in London. But after a few weeks, maybe a month, they started easing up a bit, I suppose you'd say. Then they started planning the Murder Game and talking 'bout guests and parties and I could see as how they were easing up a bit, I suppose."

Phyllida nodded. That information confirmed what Mrs. Wokesley had told her. She remembered what Mrs. Forrte had said during her hysterical ranting. "Is it true Mr. Wokesley never let anyone else drive his motorcar?"

"Not even Mrs. Wokesley," said Mr. Trifle, nodding gravely.

"Do you think it's possible, knowing Mr. Wokesley as you surely did," she added solely to flatter the man, "whether someone else might have been driving his motor during the crash in London?"

"Don't know. Seems a bit off, wouldn't it?"

That was what Phyllida was beginning to wonder. Perhaps Mr. Wokesley had been driving in the car crash that killed the woman, and somehow that Eustace Brimley had taken responsibility for it. But she didn't see whether—or how—that would tie into someone wanting to do away with Mr. Wokesley. She decided to move on to another track of questioning before Mr. Trifle realized who was grilling him.

"Did you ever see Mrs. Wokesley interacting with Sir Keller?" she asked.

Mr. Trifle lifted his head and fixed her with eyes that had cleared significantly. "They were talking together in the corner yesterday, not long before the guests began to arrive for the Murder Game. Low voices . . . you know the kind. She seemed upset, and he was comforting her . . . or perhaps it was the other way round. Whatever it was, they were both . . . agitated. And seemed quite . . . comfortable together."

"I see. That's helpful. And Mrs. Forrte . . . did you see her interact with Mr. Wokesley at all?"

"She didn't like him. Not one bit. And he returned the favor. I heard him say something about 'shiny things' and 'make it right,' and she didn't like that. She looked at him as if . . ." He trailed off, then suddenly his entire demeanor changed.

He drew himself up and glared at Phyllida. She could almost see his brain—which had first been hampered by a good portion of beer and then slipped into the comfort of imparting his exclusive information—realize that *he* was the butler, and *she* was not, and that he certainly shouldn't be fraternizing with the likes of *her.*

The flow of information had lasted longer than she'd expected. Phyllida decided she'd learned all she was going to learn from him.

"Quite so," she said ambiguously, forestalling the rude comment he was surely about to make. "Thank you, Mr. Trifle. Oh, and by the by, I've asked the footman to build up the fires. Mrs. Napoleon has decided to stay on instead of leaving at first opportunity and she is roasting a bit of mutton, among other things, that will need to be served shortly. Unfortunately, Mrs. Treacle *has* given her notice and I believe she plans to leave on the morrow."

"Daft woman," he muttered, and Phyllida took no offense as she assumed he was speaking of Mrs. Treacle. "No great loss there."

Privately, she was inclined to agree, but gave no indication. Housekeepers and females, she reasoned, should stand united in front of butlers.

"Very well. Perhaps you shall bestir yourself to serve dinner, then, Mr. Trifle. I've already ensured there will be sufficient wood for all the fireplaces."

And with that gentle dig, she smiled and excused herself from the room.

It was time to find Mr. Dudley-Gore.

CHAPTER 17

PHYLLIDA WAS, FOR ONCE, SUPREMELY DELIGHTED TO ENCOUNTER Constable Greensticks as he was coming out of the library.

"Ah, Constable. There you are."

"Mrs. Bright." He didn't appear surprised to see her; perhaps he hadn't realized she'd even left and returned.

"Is there any news from Inspector Cork?" she asked, glancing toward the front door. The windows next to it were dark with impending night and the last of the storm, though the crashing and flashing seemed to have subsided. Still, it was raining heavily and the wind continued to buffet the trees and house.

"Oi, no, not at all," he replied. "I expect he'll get here as soon as he can."

"Excellent," Phyllida said, seeing no reason to hide her pleasure. "And Dr. Bhatt?" There was no coroner in Listleigh, so the doctor officially handled pronouncements and certificates of death.

"They've left a message at his surgery."

"Surely he'll arrive as soon as possible. In the meanwhile, I do believe it's time you and I spoke with Mr. Dudley-Gore."

"Oi, if you say so, Mrs. Bright," he replied. "What about, then?"

She had to admit, she preferred working with Constable Greensticks—who clearly had little to no interest in investigating killers—than his superior Inspector Cork.

She suspected the constable preferred to deal with simple

policing matters, such as trespassing sheep, broken windows, or unruly guests in the pub—rather than murders. After all, until recently, Listleigh had been nothing more than a quiet little town that offered occasional festivals, harbored some tourists, and experienced very little in the way of crime. He'd had it rather easy.

"We are going to speak with him about what he was doing yesterday during the storm, around the time Mr. Brixton was killed. He said something very curious and quite possibly incriminating to Mr. Trifle."

"Right, then, Mrs. Bright."

Moments later, the three of them were in Mr. Wokesley's study.

"Suppose you need to speak to all of us about that Brixton fellow then," said Mr. Dudley-Gore as he lowered himself into his armchair. "Ghastly thing, ain't it."

Phyllida eyed him closely. There were bags under his eyes, and his face seemed drawn. She decided to go for the jugular. "What did you mean when you said to Mr. Trifle that you came here to set things right and now what should you do?"

The color drained from his face, then rushed back in. "I don't know what you mean."

"I'm quite certain you do," Phyllida said firmly. "You were standing outside under the portico and you spoke to Mr. Trifle. What were you trying to set right by coming here?"

"I . . . nothing really," he replied. His hands were clenched in his lap. "I told you, I came in order to convince Cliff to-to settle some funds on Fitchler. Meant I needed to set it right—to get the-the blunt for a-a new school kitchen. And now he's gone, and it ain't going to happen."

Phyllida didn't believe him, but she moved on. "Mrs. Wokesley has suggested that you and her husband weren't all that close of pals during school—which is quite different from what you've indicated. In fact, she said Mr. Wokesley seemed to hardly remember you at all."

"Oh, well . . . we did rather run in different crowds," Mr. Dudley-Gore admitted. "He knew my cousin and another chap much better than me."

"What was the other chap's name?"

"Erm . . . don't really recall at the moment," replied the headmaster. "Been years, you know."

"Perhaps you recall your cousin's name." Phyllida gave him an icy stare and he squirmed.

"Right. Yes, of course. Benny it is—was, I mean to say. Benny Townley. Benny's been dead a while, you know. Ten years? Or is it eight?"

Phyllida hadn't known, of course. "And you don't recall the name of the other friend of his and Mr. Wokesley's?"

"If I think of it, I'll surely tell you." He looked longingly at Constable Greensticks, as if silently begging him to take over the questioning.

Phyllida did take a moment to appreciate her satisfaction and surprise at the continuing ease with which she'd been able to conduct her investigation. She knew it was only due to the constable's lack of desire and motivation to lead such a complicated task. It could also be due to his wish to be welcome in Mallowan Hall's kitchen. Either way, it didn't matter to her.

"Tell me about Rose," she said.

Mr. Dudley-Gore's eyes widened, then his entire expression sagged at the mention of the woman whose photograph Phyllida had discovered in his satchel. "H-how did you know about her?"

Well knowing the power of silence and expectant looks, Phyllida merely watched him.

At last, he heaved a sigh. "My wife. She died . . ." He dug into the pocket of his coat and withdrew a handkerchief, which he used to dab at eyes that had suddenly glistened.

"I'm very sorry," Phyllida said, remembering her own unexpectedly emotional response to seeing the photo signed *My love always and forever, Rose.* "Did she die recently?"

He nodded, seemingly unable to form words. At last he pushed them out. "Motor crash."

Inside, Phyllida sat bolt upright, though she didn't show any outward indication of her sudden interest. She kept her expression sober and spoke gently. "What happened?"

Mr. Dudley-Gore shook his head, blinking rapidly. He dabbed at his eyes, which were red and glistening although no tears were actually falling. "Motorcar . . . ran her down. Didn't even stop, the bastard." His words were choked, but he rallied and managed to continue. "She was . . . b-bicycling home from the m-market. Died t-two days later. In my arms."

"I'm very sorry," Phyllida said. She was sincere in her sympathy, but at the same time, her mind was mulling over the fact that two people involved in the Murder Game each had experienced motorcar crashes with two deaths. Could that be a coincidence?

From what Phyllida knew, it didn't seem as if the two vehicle crashes were the same or even related. But surely it must be more than coincidental.

"Did they find the person who did it?" she asked.

"No." Now his face turned dark and thunderous. "But if I ever find him, I'll kill him." He looked straight at Phyllida and the constable, fully cognizant of the situation and how his words sounded. "I mean it. I will. He took *everything* from me."

Phyllida swallowed. She believed him.

And in that moment, she also believed that the bumbling, easygoing headmaster could already have killed quite easily.

"What is it now?" Sir Keller demanded as he entered the library. When he saw Mrs. Wokesley sitting in a chair near the roaring fire, huddled beneath a blanket, he turned an even more furious glare on Phyllida and Constable Greensticks, who were also seated. "Will you never leave her be? Can't you see she's—she's . . . *Bea*?"

He went directly to her side and took her slender white hand, which Phyllida knew was cold to the touch. "Bea . . . don't worry. I'm going to get rid of them. You all need to *leave*." He swung toward them, his expression nearly as dark and thunderous as Mr. Dudley-Gore's had been. "Leave her alone, I tell you—"

"No, Keller," said Mrs. Wokesley in a surprisingly firm voice. "Don't you understand? They have to do this to—to find out who k-killed Cliff. And Georges. Sit with me, will you?" she said, tugging on his hand.

"Of course." Despite his quiet assent, the look Sir Keller shot at Phyllida and the constable was lethal. "Now, what is it you wanted to ask me about, Mrs. Bright?"

Phyllida had retrieved the note in Sir Keller's coat pocket from his bedchamber. Now she handed it over to Mrs. Wokesley and said, "Explain this, if you would."

Mrs. Wokesley looked at the note, then up at Phyllida. Her expression was one of bewilderment. "*'I can't do this. B.'* Where did you get this?"

"It was in Sir Keller's possession," Phyllida admitted—and braced herself for the storm to follow.

"*What?*" He did not disappoint, shooting to his feet and looming over everyone else. His patrician nose quivered with fury and his long fingers curled into fists. "How did you find this? Were you *snooping* about my room?" His eyes bulged in their sockets. "This is an invasion of privacy! How dare you!"

He might have continued ranting—or worse—if Constable Greensticks hadn't risen as well. Shorter but sturdier than the other man, the constable nonetheless stood his ground.

"Oi, there, have a seat, guv. This's a murder investigation, and there ain't no right to privacy in it. Someone's already offed two people, and we need to stop 'em before they do away with someone else."

Phyllida wasn't certain whether Sir Keller would have backed down if Mrs. Wokesley hadn't intervened again. "Keller, please. This is difficult enough as it is. They're right. We could all be in danger."

"Quite. Yes, dashed sorry, Bea. Don't mean to be adding to . . . right." He sank back into the chair next to her. "Let me see that."

He glanced at the note, then, frowning, looked up at the constable, then at Phyllida. "You say you found this in my possession? What do you mean by that? Where?"

"It was in your coat pocket," Phyllida said. "In the wardrobe in your bedchamber."

"I've never seen this before." Sir Keller tossed the paper toward them. It wafted a third of the distance then fluttered to the floor. "Bea?"

"I certainly wrote it—it's my handwriting," Mrs. Wokesley said, leaning forward to pick it up. "But it wasn't written to Keller."

"Can you remember where or when or in what circumstance you might have written those words?" Phyllida asked, holding out her hand for the note. With this new information, she needed to examine the paper more closely.

Agatha had written several stories where notes had been altered or pages had been strategically torn or even removed from letters in order to give off the wrong impression. If Mrs. Wokesley and Sir Keller were telling the truth—which Phyllida was inclined to believe—then someone had likely done their own strategic editing of a letter or note.

"Someone put it there," said Sir Keller nastily. "Probably *you.*" He was clearly speaking to Phyllida.

"That's nonsense," she replied, not at all cowed by his ridiculous statement or his masculine carrying on. "Why would I do such a thing? But I don't disagree—if you've never seen it and you didn't write it, then someone *did* plant it."

"But why on *earth* . . ." Mrs. Wokesley gripped Sir Keller's hand so tightly Phyllida could see his knuckles and fingers shifting. He didn't flicker an eyelash over it, and instead, patted her hand. "I just don't understand." She blinked rapidly and tears glistened on her lashes. "Isn't it bad enough that Clifton is dead? Now someone wants to make it look as if *I* did it?"

"Or me," Sir Keller said in a more modulated tone. "Or the two of us together."

Phyllida nodded. "Quite. If you didn't write that note to Sir Keller, Mrs. Wokesley, then that is the only explanation I can give. Perhaps you could look at it more closely and see whether it sparks any memories. In the meantime, I do need to ask about the nature of your relationship." When Sir Keller began to puff up again, she held up a hand and continued firmly. "If someone is attempting to falsify a motive for you, there must be *something* they know or have seen that would give it credence."

"We're old friends," Mrs. Wokesley told her. "Nothing more. Right, there, Keller?"

Phyllida saw it in his eyes—just as she'd seen it in Stanley's when he looked at Ginny, and in Elton's. But he said, "Right, there, old girl. Old chums, nothing more. If anyone believes otherwise, why they can—right." He rose and took both of her hands. "You should lie down, Bea. Won't you?"

"I-I suppose I will," she replied, standing unsteadily. "I don't really want dinner, you know."

"Of course not. We'll get you upstairs—"

"I'll ring for the maid," Phyllida interrupted, reaching for the bell. She glanced meaningfully at Constable Greensticks.

Fortunately, he picked up the signal. "Sir Keller, we have other questions for you. Have a seat, if you will, then."

Sir Keller gave them both a nasty look, but didn't argue.

Louise arrived almost immediately and escorted Mrs. Wokesley from the room.

"I should very much like to know who the bloody hell you think you are," said Sir Keller the moment the door closed behind them. He was, of course, speaking to Phyllida.

She merely shook her head and went on with her questioning. "I understand you were recently engaged to be married."

"You've certainly poked your nose into plenty of places, haven't you?" he said grimly. "I won't deny it. Mabelle—presumably you know her name—called it off and we parted amicably."

"I also understand that you're a bit lean on cash," Phyllida went on.

Sir Keller's fists clenched again. "As I said, you've poked everywhere. Yes. I'm a bit flat at the moment. What of it? I certainly didn't do away with Clifton to get his money—and his wife—if that's what you're thinking." His eyes burned. "I wouldn't do that to Beatrice. She loves—loved—him. I would *never* do that to her. Put her through this."

He rose. "I'm done speaking with you. You want to find the killer, you stop sniffing around me and Beatrice and start looking at that headmaster person. And Charity Forrte. There's plenty of rumors about her, you know."

Phyllida resisted the urge to point out that only last night Sir

Keller had vehemently insisted that Charity Forrte couldn't have killed Mr. Wokesley (too much blood, not enough strength) and had been quite certain Georges Brixton had done the deed.

"We are looking at everyone," Phyllida told Sir Keller.

"Look harder," he said, then stormed out of the room.

"Well, Mrs. Bright, how goes the investigation?"

Phyllida turned to see Bradford coming down the corridor. His hair looked damp and his shoes were wet as well. She didn't spare a thought as to why he was out of the kitchen and roaming the house; with a killer on the loose, it was a good thing to have the deterrent of a strong, intelligent man. And when she didn't see Myrtle on his heels, she breathed a mental sigh of relief.

"It's rather a mess, I'm afraid," she said more candidly than she'd meant to do. "I've just rung for a cup of tea and perhaps a slice of that spice bread. I was going to sit in the library and review my notes."

"You've made notes, then?"

"Well, not precisely. It's all stewing about in my head. But perhaps I ought to write it all down."

"Mind if I sit with you, then?"

Phyllida suspected his offer was mainly in order to irritate her—and possibly because there was, in fact, a killer about; not that she needed protection, but it was good practice not to be alone when a murderer was lurking in the vicinity—but she found she didn't mind. Truth be told, there had been times in previous cases where she'd discovered it beneficial to talk through her thoughts. Even with Bradford.

And this case was proving extremely confusing. Phyllida was beginning to wonder whether even she could solve the crime.

"Of course," she replied. "As long as Myrtle doesn't see fit to join us."

"She's happily gnawing on a beef bone Mrs. Napoleon was going to use for soup."

"Oh dear," Phyllida said, leading the way back into the library where she and the constable had spoken with Mrs. Wokesley and

Sir Keller a few moments earlier. "I hope Mrs. Napoleon isn't upset with her." Though Phyllida secretly hoped she was.

At least, not *too* upset.

The fire was roaring and two lamps were lit, making the space cozy and welcoming.

Bradford chuckled. "Not at all. Mrs. N gave it to her and decided she would make potato leek soup instead." He sobered as he waited for her to sit. "Mrs. Bright, there's something you ought to know."

"What is that?" She sank into the chair Mrs. Wokesley had been using next to the fire. It felt good. She hadn't realized how chilled she was.

"There's a large tree that's fallen across the drive. I don't see how to get past it—tonight, at least." That explained the damp hair and wet shoes. "It's too dark and the drive is narrow."

"You were outside in the storm?"

"We heard the lightning strike the tree, so I investigated. Unfortunately, no one is coming or going from Beecham House tonight, Mrs. Bright, even though the storm is nearly done."

She frowned. "Well, that's quite inconvenient. But there's nothing for it, I suppose. I expect Ginny can sleep with Louise. At any rate, that will give them time to finish cleaning up the sitting room where Mr. Brixton is currently resting in, hopefully, peace—after they've removed him, of course."

"Resting in peace? Not likely, that, being shot at close range."

She looked at him swiftly. "How did you know that?"

"You're not the only one who can investigate, Mrs. Bright."

Just then, the door opened and Petunia came in with the tea tray. Even from across the room, Phyllida could smell the spice bread. She stifled a moan of anticipation and waited silently but impatiently for the tray to be settled on the table next to her chair.

"Shall I get another cup, then, for Mr. Bradford?" Petunia asked, giving him a shy look.

"Yes, please do," Phyllida responded, ignoring the fact that the Mallowans' chauffeur seemed to have made yet another conquest with a kitchen staff member. As soon as the maid left, she turned back to him. "How close of range was Mr. Brixton shot? And how do you even know?"

"Very close. There is gunpowder residue on his shirt. Perhaps you didn't notice it, what with the blood," he said smoothly.

"It was rather dark in there," she said crossly. "And I didn't want to disrupt the crime scene—which you must have done if you got close enough to see powder residue." She glared at him as she looked at the cup of tea, which had already been poured then covered by a saucer to keep warm as, apparently, all of the intact teapots were in use elsewhere.

"I was very careful," he told her.

She gave an unladylike snort and lifted the teacup. It was impossible to suppress a sigh of relief when she sipped the bracing brew and its heat swept through her.

"The gun belonged to Georges Brixton," she said after a moment of enjoying a bit of spice bread. The piece was far too small to fully satisfy, but it would take off the edge of her hunger.

"Did it, now?" Bradford said, making a sound of interest. "Presumably it wasn't found at the scene."

She shook her head grimly. "Someone in this house still has it."

"Whoever it is has killed twice and could easily be prompted to do so again."

"Quite." She finished the last bit of bread and realized she hadn't offered any to Bradford. But he'd already been well fed by Mrs. Napoleon, she reasoned.

"Mrs. Bright," he said in a tone that made her look up.

"Yes?"

"Whoever it is has killed twice and could easily be prompted to do so again—"

"Yes, you already said—"

"—if someone were to continue to provoke them." He was looking at her with serious dark eyes. "Someone who likes to snoop around and demand answers and—"

"I don't demand answers—and of course I know you're speaking of me in your ridiculous roundabout way," she retorted.

"Regardless of how you obtain your answers, you certainly cannot deny snooping."

Phyllida sighed and was about to respond when the library door, which was partially ajar, opened wide. Petunia came in carrying a tray laden with dishes.

"Mrs. Napoleon said as how you ought to be eating," she said.

Phyllida smelled fresh rye bread and saw the tiny pots of butter and grainy mustard, along with two large hunks of cheddar and a slab of cold ham. And, to her immense delight, there was a generous portion of peach and blueberry cobbler. It was still steaming, and some kind soul had poured cream over the top of it. "Please thank her kindly for me."

Petunia gave a little curtsy, then left.

Phyllida gestured to the tray, indicating that Bradford should help himself if he desired. There were two sets of plates and flatware after all. Mrs. Napoleon certainly was taking her job seriously now that Phyllida had braced her up.

"No," she said, picking up the conversation where they'd left off, "I can't deny snooping. But I fail to see an alternative."

"You could allow the authorities to do the job," Bradford said, scooping up a healthy portion of the cobbler. "And potentially stay alive."

Phyllida snorted again. "And have them arrest the wrong person and let a killer go free? No."

He sighed. "I didn't think you'd listen to reason."

"It's perfectly *reasonable* for the most capable person to do the job, Bradford." She'd layered the bread with ham, cheese, and mustard, and at last bit into the first solid meal she'd had all day.

"Well, then, Inspector Bright, what have you learned? Who's your favorite suspect? No, no, let me guess . . . it's the loud and arrogant Sir Keller."

"He's certainly got a motive," she replied. "And a good one." Between ladylike bites of her sandwich, she explained about Sir Keller's relationship with Mrs. Wokesley.

"So the note was planted," Bradford said.

"Unless they were lying. And I don't think they were. I examined the note closely and I noticed the 'B' for the signature sign-off seemed to have been written with a slightly different shade of black ink, and it's almost crunched onto the page. Mrs. Wokesley's penmanship tends to have large spaces between the lines and words, and generous margins on either side of the prose. It's very possible that note came from a longer letter of some sort and someone added the 'B' to make it appear as if the single page was the entirety of the message."

Bradford nodded agreeably. "Shades of *End House*," he said, surprising Phyllida with his familiarity of Agatha's work.

"Speaking of lying . . ." She went on to describe her interactions with Mrs. Forrte, particularly in which the woman denied having taken the sapphire bracelet from Mrs. Wokesley.

"So you think Mr. Wokesley discovered Charity Forrte was stealing jewelry and other such things and she murdered him so he wouldn't expose her."

"It's one theory." She'd finished her sandwich and now wiped her fingers delicately on the napkin Mrs. Napoleon had provided. There was still a good portion of the cobbler left and she didn't hesitate to dive into it. The dessert was as heavenly as she'd anticipated.

"For a woman who doesn't eat often, you certainly enjoy your food." Bradford was lounging in his chair, legs out in front of him, ankles crossed, arms folded over his middle. He appeared utterly relaxed and at home as he toasted his wet boots in front of the fire.

The only thing missing from this cozy, domestic scene was a cat curled up on a cushion in front of the hearth.

Phyllida nearly choked on her tea. Domestic scene? Bradford? Where on *earth* had that thought come from?

"I haven't eaten but a piece of toast this morning," she replied.

"No need to get your hackles up, Mrs. Bright," he said with a shake of his head. "A person ought to eat, and they ought to enjoy their food when they do."

She sighed. Why in the world were they discussing her dining habits?

"The problem is, all of them have motive—except perhaps

Mr. Dudley-Gore—and they all had the opportunity to see the stiletto in the drawing room cabinet, and to use it. And the same holds true for Mr. Brixton: No one has an alibi during the time he was killed. And yet . . . nothing seems to fit. Nothing seems right." She frowned as she finished the last bit of cream-soaked cobbler. "And I feel as though I'm missing an important point about Mr. Dudley-Gore. There's something about him that seems wrong, but I can't put my finger on it. Surely it can't be a coincidence that his wife was killed in a motor crash and Mr. Wokesley was involved in one as well."

"There are an awful lot of motor crashes nowadays," Bradford said. "People drive too fast, and there's no regulation about it. There should be legal limits to speed posted everywhere. Until that changes, more people will be injured or killed."

"I don't disagree with that, but . . ." Her voice trailed off. She was *certain* she was missing something. Something someone had said, something she'd seen . . . something that niggled in the back of her mind. *Why* wouldn't her little gray cells behave and line up neatly?

"Wokesley'd been broken up about the motor crash he was in," Bradford said.

"How did you know that?"

"Mrs. Treacle was telling me about it. How when she first came here, he was moping and depressed and neither he nor Mrs. Wokesley wanted to do much of anything."

"I'm certain it was an awful experience, seeing a woman run down and killed. And Georges Brixton was there," Phyllida said, sitting up suddenly. "He was there. Not in the motor, but he saw the crash. Could that have something to do with why he was killed?"

"Who else was there besides Brixton and Wokesley?" asked Bradford.

"The driver's name was . . . oh dear, I did write it down but I left those notes from Mrs. Agatha at home. Eustace something, I believe." Then she paused. Eustace. Why was that sticking in her mind? She frowned and wished she'd thought to bring her notes.

"Mrs. Napoleon said Mr. Wokesley wasn't driving," Bradford said. "Although it was his motorcar."

Phyllida's head snapped up. "Charity Forrte was rambling on about that. I didn't have the opportunity to press her on it, but she did say something to the effect of . . . 'do you really think he'd let someone else drive his motor?' " She settled back in her chair, her mind flooding with thoughts and questions as if it had suddenly been undammed. "What if he *was* driving? And he ran down that woman—killed her? And someone else—this Eustace . . . Brimley! That's his name—what if Eustace Brimley took the rap for it?"

"Why would someone agree to do that?" Bradford asked. It was a reasonable question.

"I don't know. But it would be a good motive for murder, wouldn't it?"

Bradford made a noncommittal sound. "Perhaps . . . but why? If this Brimley bloke agreed to take the rap, why would he turn around and off Wokesley?"

"He changed his mind," Phyllida suggested. "Wanted revenge on Mr. Wokesley for setting him up."

"Besides, there's no Eustace Brimley here at Beecham House," Bradford pointed out. Also reasonably.

"No. At least, not that we *know* of," Phyllida replied.

"What are you suggesting? That Eustace Brimley is here and we don't know it?"

She glared at him. He knew precisely what she was suggesting. "Perhaps someone here isn't who he claims to be. Such as Mr. Dudley-Gore. Or—or even Sir Keller."

"Or Trifle."

"It can't be Mr. Trifle. He's been here at Beecham House for over a decade."

Bradford settled back in his chair and crossed his arms again. "Well, Mrs. Bright, it seems to me you're no closer to solving this murder than before."

She shook her head. "Yet, I'm close. I can feel it. I . . . have an idea. It's strange and I'm not sure about it, but . . . well, anyhow, I'm still wondering about that missing cigar."

"Missing cigar?" Bradford seemed intrigued.

"It was written in the script for the Murder Game that Mr. Wokesley—er, Mr. Bowington—was supposed to be found dead on the floor with a cigar in his hand. There was no cigar. But he was holding a scrap of paper."

Just then, the door to the library nudged open once more and Dr. Bhatt came in. He was soaked from the knees down, indicating that it was still raining and that he'd employed an umbrella.

"John," Phyllida said, rising. "You're here. How did you make it up the drive? There's a downed tree blocking the way."

"Left my motor there and walked," he said, making his way directly to the fire. "Drat the nasty, wet climate here. Bradford," he added by way of greeting.

"That's certainly dedication." Bradford rose from his seat. "I'll leave you two to your murder scene." He took the tray with him, indicating he was returning to the kitchen.

Phyllida gave Dr. Bhatt the pertinent information about Georges Brixton's death, and then turned him over to Mr. Trifle, who took him to the small storage room to where Mr. Brixton's body had been removed.

On her return, she found Louise and Ginny finishing their work in the drawing room. "You may see to the sitting room now," Phyllida told them. "Mr. Brixton has been removed. You'll certainly need the vacuum machine for that."

"Yes, ma'am," Ginny said with a decided lack of enthusiasm, which Phyllida ignored.

She wanted to speak to Mrs. Wokesley again.

CHAPTER 18

Phyllida found Mrs. Wokesley propped up in bed with a pile of pillows. There were two crumpled handkerchiefs on her side table, and she was clutching a third. A small glass of a dark brown liquid—whiskey or brandy—sat untouched next to her. The room smelled of grief and tears and stale perfume.

"I need to ask you about the motorcar crash," Phyllida said without preamble.

Mrs. Wokesley sniffled and nodded, gesturing with a limp hand for Phyllida to take a seat. They were alone in the room, which was constructive for Phyllida's purpose. If she was ever going to get the truth from Mrs. Wokesley, it was going to be here and now.

"What do you want to know?"

Phyllida saw no reason to beat around the bush. "Mr. Wokesley was driving when that woman was hit and killed, wasn't he?"

Mrs. Wokesley's expression froze, then crumbled. "It was awful. *So awful.* He simply couldn't get past what he'd done. My dear, poor Cliff! He was always such a sensitive man . . . and to have done such a ghastly thing . . . it nearly destroyed him, Mrs. Bright. He was so unhappy."

"I'm certain the young woman's family was equally unhappy," Phyllida said in a reproachful voice. "Not to mention the woman herself."

"Oh, yes, of course they were." Mrs. Wokesley's eyes filled with tears. "I don't mean to . . ." She shook her head silently.

"How did it happen? I mean to say, how did Mr. Wokesley convince Mr. Brimley to take the responsibility?"

"He—he told me that when the motor hit the woman, Eustace was thrown forward and bumped his head on the dash. He was s-sitting next to Cliff in the front. And Cliff—well, he didn't think. He-he just climbed over Eustace and shoved him toward the driver's seat. Eustace was confused, and he didn't realize what had happened."

Good heavens. Phyllida could hardly keep her appalled thoughts to herself, but she managed to do so. She could save the lambasting that was on the tip of her tongue for later—after she obtained all the information she needed.

"So Mr. Wokesley pushed Mr. Brimley into the driver's seat . . . and Mr. Brimley went along with it? Why would he do that?"

Mrs. Wokesley hesitated, staring down at her fingers twisting in the handkerchief. "Eustace owed Cliff money. Quite a bit of money. Cliff told him if he went along with it, he'd forgive the debt."

"And Mr. Brimley agreed and took the responsibility. And yet . . . clearly Mr. Wokesley felt an intense guilt over what happened to the woman. What was her name? Do you even know?"

"Of course I know. Daisy Longfellow. That was her name. We-we couldn't bring ourselves to go to the funeral services. It was simply too awful." Mrs. Wokesley also couldn't bring herself to meet Phyllida's eyes. "Georges went. He told me. I think he was trying to make us feel guilty. He was there, you know. Not in the motor, but just outside, when it happened. He saw it all."

"Do you think Mr. Brixton saw Mr. Wokesley change places with Mr. Brimley in the driver's seat?"

Mrs. Wokesley nodded, still staring at her hands. "He didn't say it outright, but he implied there was something about that motorcar crash that could cause a problem for Cliff. I-I think he came here in order to try and convince Cliff to fund another play. I think he was going to use that as—as leverage."

She looked up suddenly, her eyes fierce and hard and glinting with tears. "I know it sounds awful, Mrs. Bright. But I want you to know I begged Cliff to come clean. I told him he would feel better if he did, that he could make some sort of recompense and then he could begin to heal. I wanted him to set things right."

Phyllida declined to point out that Mrs. Wokesley could have done that herself without waiting for her husband's permission. "And he refused?"

"He did at first, but then I kept working on him," Mrs. Wokesley said. "I truly did. And I'd finally convinced him. I think that was what turned things around for Cliff and his moods. He was going to set things right. He was feeling better about things, and then he began to plan this Murder Game. He just wanted to do something fun before he—he confessed. Only, he never got the chance to come clean. Someone k-killed him first."

"Where's Mr. Brimley now? Did Mr. Wokesley tell him he planned to come clean?"

Now Mrs. Wokesley's eyes dropped to her lap once more. "Eustace jumped off a bridge five months after the motorcrash. About four months ago. He left a note that he couldn't live with what had happened."

Phyllida felt a rush of rage overtake her. It was all she could do not to take the woman by the shoulders and shake her, shout at her . . .

It was with great difficulty that she managed to keep the fury and venom from her voice. "And thus Mr. Wokesley caused the death of two innocent people."

"But don't you see," Mrs. Wokesley said earnestly, eyes glittering with tears, "Cliff was going to come forth and tell the truth—and he didn't *have* to do it, now that Eustace was gone! He was going to do the right thing! He was!" Her voice broke and Phyllida knew that even Beatrice Wokesley didn't believe her own words.

Disgusted and heartsick, Phyllida rose. Her hands were shaking and she hid them in the folds of her skirt. "Thank you for being truthful, Mrs. Wokesley," was all she managed to say as she stalked from the room, leaving the woman sobbing in her bed.

* * *

Ginny wasn't happy about the fact that Mrs. Bright had brought that horrendous vacuum machine along with them to Beecham House—mainly because her boss expected her to *use* it. And in the room where a *dead man* had been sitting.

Why, she expected a shock of electricity to zip down her arm and sizzle her the minute she took up the handle and turned it on. Even though such a thing hadn't happened when she used it at Mallowan Hall, it didn't mean it wasn't going to. You heard things about electrical accidents with telephones and vacuum machines and the like all the time! People *died*!

But she wasn't about to reveal her fears to the likes of Elton, who'd carried the heavy machine inside as if it were no heavier than a basket of linens. He certainly was strong. And ever so handsome. She only wished he'd show some interest in taking a walk with her, or even sitting next to her at dinner.

But he never did. The only good thing about *that* was he didn't seem interested in Molly either.

He didn't seem interested in any of the maids, really. She supposed that was all right with her.

Elton certainly wasn't like Stanley, who'd been a flirt since the moment Ginny arrived at Mallowan Hall. She'd been enamored with him for a while, but then Elton came on the scene and that was that. Stanley was old news and Elton was not.

Even so, Stanley had been kind of sweet helping her with the vacuum earlier today. And the last time she'd been out in the moonlight, he'd come out to make sure she wasn't cold or anything. Even offered her his coat.

Ginny glared at the stupid machine. She wished Bess had come to Beecham House too. Bess always had a saint to pray to for help about things—even when there'd been a murderer at Mallowan Hall. She'd even prayed while they were testing out the vacuum back at the house. Maybe that was why no one got electrocuted.

Ginny wished she could remember the name of the saint Lizzie had been praying to. Something like Eligin. Saint Elginius?

Did it matter if Ginny wasn't Catholic and she prayed? Would the saint listen to her?

And where was Louise? She was supposed to be helping her clean up this Murder Room, but Mrs. Treacle had rung for her—she was the housekeeper here, but Ginny hadn't heard very many nice things about her; she seemed a flutterbudget—and she'd had to go off and see to something else . . . leaving Ginny alone with this monstrosity of a machine.

She knew better than to make excuses or delay. Even though Mrs. Bright wasn't in charge here, she rather was, in a way. And when she told you to do something, you had best do it. And well.

With a sigh, Ginny picked up the electrical cord and eyed the outlet on the wall. If only Beecham House was one of the many large manors in England that *hadn't* been fitted with electricity, none of this would be happening. She could use a carpet sweeper like she normally did; though, she allowed, it would take a lot longer and she'd have to push a lot harder. But at least she wouldn't *die.*

Holding her breath, she carefully fit the plug into the outlet. Then she shrieked, for the machine *roared* to life immediately. Her heart shot into her throat and her belly dropped. She rushed over on jelly knees to turn off the switch on the vacuum.

Silence filled the room except for the pounding of her heart in her ears. With shaking hands, Ginny stared down at the large dark green cylinder of the stupid machine. Why had someone decided to invent such a thing?

She exhaled and looked around the room, trying to find something else that needed to be done. But she'd already dusted, and closed the drapes, and refreshed the flowers, neatened the pillows, swept the hearth and closed the fire grate . . .

There was the chair where the man had been found, shot dead. She shuddered. There was blood on the upholstery. Ginny didn't know whether Mrs. Bright would tell them how to get the blood out (she certainly had some experience in that), or whether they would simply remove the chair. Perhaps she ought to call Elton and that short footman Anthony to remove it. She smiled at the thought. She'd like to see Elton sling that chair up, one-handed, over his shoulder and carry it out . . .

She sighed again. Sadly, it wasn't her decision to order the chair removed. She had other things to do—mainly seeing to the thick coating of ashes all over the rug, right next to the Murder Chair. How on earth had Louise managed *that*? She couldn't have made a worse mess if she'd tried. It was almost as if she'd *thrown* the bucket down when she saw the dead bloke.

But there was nothing for it. The rug had to be cleaned, and soon, before Mrs. Bright came to check. Ginny didn't relish seeing a disappointed, disapproving look on her boss's face; she'd seen it plenty over the last two days. She liked her boss. A lot. She was fair and kind and friendly and even funny sometimes . . . unless you messed up. Then you got the steely-eyed look the staff called "Bright's Glare of Death," or "BGD."

Ginny licked her lips, then looked up at the ceiling and said, "Pray for me, Saint Eliginius—or whoever you are." Then she picked up the handle of the machine and, holding her breath, flipped the switch.

She didn't jump—at least, not as much—when the device roared to life and the attachment hose shuddered in her grip. And when she didn't die, she thought perhaps Saint Eliginius—or whoever it was—had heard her.

Gingerly, she began to push the rectangular base at the end of the hose attachment over the rug. It sure did work, leaving a clean swipe right through the mess of ashes. It was almost a miracle, really.

She amused herself by making a big X of cleanliness through the black pile, and then went through and crossed through the center of that. She'd make a star, wouldn't she? She was even getting used to the rumbling feeling of holding the hose. It made her skin itch a little, but not as much as it had before.

Ginny was nearly finished with the worst of the ash, right next to the Murder Chair, when all at once something *awful* happened.

The machine was working just fine, then all of a sudden it sounded like it was *breaking* from inside. There was a horrible clinking, clicking, shattering sound that ran up the hose and into the machine.

Ginny shrieked and dropped the hose before it could electrocute her, and she ran over to pull the plug from the wall (she *wasn't* going to touch the machine after that!).

She stared down at the now-silent monstrosity, her heart thudding and her knees weak.

Had she broken Mrs. Bright's new vacuum?

What was she going to *do*?

"Good heavens, Mrs. Bright, what is it?"

Bradford nearly stepped back as she stormed into the kitchen. He'd never seen her so furious—even when Myrtle jumped on her and put a ladder in her stockings. Mrs. Bright's eyes blazed and her fair skin was splotched red with what could only be fury. This wasn't annoyance. This was deep-seated anger.

"I simply—I cannot—" She flailed her arms about in an utterly uncharacteristic manner. "They're—they're—!" She pointed wordlessly upstairs as she audibly gritted her teeth.

Bradford might have been amused if he hadn't seen how incredibly irate and—sad? horrified? there was something else there in her expression—she was. Something had certainly set her off.

"This way, Mrs. Bright," he said, gesturing for her to join him out of the kitchen. Whatever had gotten her riled up likely didn't need to be shared among the gawking servants in Beecham House's kitchen.

For once she didn't argue. She stalked out of the kitchen, down the back hall past the pantry and scullery, and then, to his complete shock, *outside.*

The rain had mostly come to a halt, but it was still drizzling. When the normally persnickety housekeeper marched out into the wet, Bradford became seriously concerned for the daft woman.

"Mrs. Bright, what has happened?" Even Myrtle, who'd bolted to her feet upon Mrs. Bright's entrance, was only edging along at a short distance behind them with her ears back and her tail drooping, unwilling to step outside.

"I've learned what an absolutely horrible person Mr. Wokesley was," she said, ducking close to the house so she was beneath an eave. "It's quite wet out here," she said, annoyed.

Bradford smothered a smile. "It's been raining all day, Mrs. Bright."

"Indeed it has." She took a deep breath and seemed to calm herself, and then she went on to explain about what had actually happened during Mr. Wokesley's motorcar crash.

"So he forced another man—a friend of his, was it?—to take the blame?" It was no wonder there'd been murder in her eyes. If Clifton Wokesley were still alive, Bradford would have had a few things to say to him as well. He might even want to throttle the bloke . . . if Mrs. Bright didn't get to him first.

"He did. And the other man, the scapegoat, was Eustace Brimley. Wait . . . hold up . . . *Eustace.* Stacey would be a nickname for Eustace, wouldn't it?" she said, but he didn't think she was really talking to him. She seemed lost in thought. And not quite as angry now that she'd told him about it all.

"One would think so," Bradford replied, angling himself so as to block as much of the drizzle from her as possible without being obvious about it. Mrs. Bright was not the sort of woman who wanted to be protected by a man. Or anyone, for that matter.

Myrtle had sensibly stayed inside, and she watched them warily from the open doorway.

"Precisely. I need to speak with Mr. Dudley-Gore." With the same energy with which she'd stalked outside, she turned and marched back in through the door. The fact that she didn't dodge away from Myrtle's proximity indicated to Bradford that Mrs. Bright was still in quite a state of mind.

He wasn't certain whether he should follow her or not, but decided if she was going to confront Mr. Dudley-Gore—who could possibly be a killer—he should at least be nearby, whether she wanted protecting or not.

After all, if something happened to Mrs. Bright, who was Myrtle going to spend her time agitating?

CHAPTER 19

PHYLLIDA FOUND MR. DUDLEY-GORE SITTING ALONE IN THE LIBRARY—the chamber that had been used as the "green room" for the Murder Game. He had a glass next to him filled, as was often the case with a man sitting in a study or a library, with some amber liquid. He was also staring intently at his unlit pipe as if uncertain what to do with it.

He looked up when she strode in. "Why—er—Mrs. Bright, is it?" There was an air of hesitancy about him that suggested he knew why she'd come.

"You were friends with Eustace Brimley, weren't you?" she said, facing him with her hands on her hips.

He drew up his shoulders, and she could see the denial forming on his lips . . . and then he exhaled and deflated. "Yes."

"It was that photo of you with him that clued me in—it was labeled 'Bertie and Stacey.' Did you know him at Fitchler, or did you ever even attend the school?"

"Oh. Heh. Well, as it turns out, no . . . I never did attend Fitchler. But my cousin did—as I told you. Benny Townley. And he and Stacey were chums with Cliff, and so I'd met him a time or two."

"But you are the headmaster there."

"Of course." He seemed insulted she'd suggest he'd lie about such a thing.

"You never attended Fitchler, but you knew enough about it to lead Mr. Wokesley to believe you'd done so, and had even known him there. After all, it was a long time ago—he was only ten or eleven, you a bit younger. You somehow induced him to invite you here to Beecham House with a plan to get a bequest for the school . . . but that wasn't the only reason, was it?"

Mr. Dudley-Gore sank into himself even further, but he clamped his lips shut.

Phyllida sensed rather than heard movement in the doorway behind her. Bradford, most certainly. The man was infernally interfering.

"Oi . . . what's all this, Mrs. Bright?" And Constable Greensticks was with him. "Have you identified the culprit, then?"

"Mr. Dudley-Gore has just confessed to being at Beecham House under false pretenses, Constable," she said.

"What? No I ain't," he replied, half rising from his chair. "I'm headmaster, and I came hoping to raise some blunt from the Woolen Wokesley chap for his alma mater. That ain't a false pretense."

"You led him to believe you'd known him in the past. That's a false pretense. And," Phyllida said to the constable—and Bradford, who lurked in the doorway, "he was friends, and I venture to say, very *close* friends, with Mr. Eustace Brimley, the man who took the rap for Mr. Wokesley's motorcar accident."

"What, now?" Constable Greensticks scratched his head as if attempting to determine whether he should be springing into action and making an arrest.

Phyllida sighed. She couldn't expect everyone to be as quick-witted as she. "Nearly a year ago, Mr. Wokesley was involved in a motorcar crash in London where a young, widowed mother named Daisy Longfellow was run down and killed.

"When the authorities came on the scene, Mr. Eustace Brimley was behind the steering wheel and a bit out of sorts from a bump on the head . . . but it was Mr. Wokesley's motor. And by all accounts, Mr. Wokesley did not allow anyone but himself to drive his vehicle. It seems Mr. Wokesley had extorted Mr. Brimley into taking the rap for running down Daisy Longfellow in exchange for the forgiveness of a large sum of money he owed him—I mean to say, that Mr. Brimley owed Mr. Wokesley money."

"Oi. That's about the most terrible thing I ever heard," the constable said with great feeling.

"Indeed," Phyllida agreed. "Thus, I suspect Mr. Dudley-Gore came here also intending to get revenge for his friend—who, as I understand it, ended his own life by jumping off a bridge a few months ago. He must have been in a terrible condition," she added, looking at Mr. Dudley-Gore with unfeigned sympathy, "to resort to such a thing."

Surely it was this compassion that caused his reserve to dissolve. All at once, his face crumbled and he nodded as tears glistened in his eyes. "Stacey and I—we'd been pals since we were born. Grew up in the same village. Only reason I didn't go to Fitchler m'self was because me pop was a Harroway man and insisted I go there. But Stacey and Benny and Cliff, they were all pals there. And after, I was at Cambridge with Stacey and we were good friends. It was his sister's best friend I married—Rose—and Stacey was in my wedding and . . ." He shook his head. "It was me who encouraged him to go to Cliff for a loan. Wish I'd never done it, then he'd never have been in debt to the bastard. He made some bad investments in a ruby mine in Africa, and needed some blunt to help them through, here at home, because his business wasn't good the last few years. Architecture, it was."

"And when Mr. Wokesley gave him a way out of the debt, Mr. Brimley took it," Phyllida said.

"He regretted it almost right away. It was awful enough he'd seen the woman—the way she rolled up onto the hood of the motor and smashed into the windshield . . . blood everywhere . . ." He shuddered and dug a handkerchief out of his pocket with shaking hands.

"But to take the responsibility? He had nightmares about it . . . and everyone looked at him differently. Pointed fingers and whispered behind their hands. And he hadn't even done anything. Started drinking and turned into someone I didn't even know. And then . . . and then my Rosie died. Same way, almost, as that

Daisy girl . . . and it just about did Stacey in. And me too." He lifted a shaking hand to his face, dabbing at the tears now running unabashedly down his face.

"And so he couldn't take it anymore," Phyllida said, gently now. She sank into the chair opposite him, her heart filled with grief.

Mr. Dudley-Gore shook his head. "And so he . . . he ended it." He drew in a shuddering breath. "Wh-when he did that . . . I just . . . I just didn't care what happened after that. About anything. Rose was gone. Stacey was gone . . ."

"And so you killed Clifton Wokesley. The man who took everything from you."

"No," moaned Mr. Dudley-Gore. "No, I didn't. And that's the God's honest truth. I wish I *had* . . . don't you see? I wish I *had* done!

"At first, I thought maybe just getting a load of money from him would have been enough . . . but then I thought it wasn't *right* that he should live the way he did—in the clear, without anyone looking at him all dark and judgmental . . . without his reputation being destroyed . . . with the woman he loves! And I thought about getting rid of him. I thought about how I'd go about doing it. But I didn't. I didn't do it. I only wish I had," he added in a pained whisper.

And Phyllida believed him, drat it.

"So . . . er . . . what now, Mrs. Bright?" said the constable after a long moment of silence, broken only by Mr. Dudley-Gore's quiet sobs.

She rose and gave the constable a sad look. "That's your decision, Constable. I'm still in search of a killer."

Just then, Elton appeared in the doorway. "Mrs. Bright? There's . . . erm . . . a problem with the vacuum machine."

She blinked, then rearranged her thoughts from personal tragedies to household ones. "Yes, of course. I'll—I'll see to it."

She rose and started out of the chamber, using the moment to compose herself. Although she'd suspected much of it, Mr. Dudley-Gore's story had shaken her.

"Mrs. Bright?" Bradford's low voice caught her ear as she entered the hallway.

She paused. "Yes?"

He drew in a breath, then it seemed as if he changed what he'd meant to say. "Poor sot," he said, his face grave.

She nodded grimly, then went on, following Elton to the sitting room.

Therein she discovered Ginny, wearing a stricken expression, and Louise. They were both staring down at the vacuum cleaner as if they expected it to lunge at them at any moment.

"What seems to be the problem?" Phyllida asked, suddenly feeling extraordinarily weary and doing her best not to allow her emotions to affect her task.

"I-I'm sorry, Mrs. Bright," Ginny said. She was near tears. "I-I don't know what happened. Only, I was just using it to clean up the ashes and all at once it started making a horrible sound."

"What sort of sound?"

"Like a . . . clinking, clattering—like a *breaking* sound. I-I unplugged it right away, but when Elton turned it back on, the noise came again. Only, we-we didn't know what to do, so we sent for you."

"Very well," Phyllida replied. "Let's try it again and see what happens. You say you were using it and all was well and then suddenly it changed? Was the sound coming from the machine part? The motor?"

"N-no, ma'am, I think it was in the hose part. And then . . . I dunno, maybe it was in the machine part too. It all happened so fast, and it was so loud anyway . . ."

"Elton," Phyllida said, and he sprang into action.

The machine roared to life and Phyllida heard a strange metallic noise mingling with the normal sound of the motor . . . and then it went away, leaving only the roar of the machine.

"It stopped!" Ginny sounded both relieved and terrified—likely because that would mean she'd need to utilize the thing again.

"Indeed. But it sounded to me as if something might have been caught up inside it," Phyllida said. "As if it had scooped up something metallic."

It occurred to her all at once that perhaps whatever item had been vacuumed up was important to the crime scene.

"You want I should look inside, Mrs. Bright?" asked Elton.

"I think we ought to do so. Do you think you can find out how to open it?"

"Yes, ma'am, I'm certain I can." He seemed delighted with the prospect and hurried off to locate a screwdriver.

While they were waiting, Phyllida took the opportunity to check over the work Ginny had completed in the sitting room. "Nicely done," she told her. "How does the study look, then? And what about the drawing room?"

"I've just about finished in the drawing room, ma'am," Louise said, seeming not at all confused that Phyllida had taken charge instead of Mrs. Treacle.

"I finished the study before I came in here, ma'am," Ginny said.

Elton rushed back in, not the least bit out of breath, and was carrying a small toolbox. It took him only moments to open the vacuum machine. He donned a pair of gloves and began to carefully poke around inside.

"There's an awful lot of dust in here," he said, making a sort of sifting motion through the detritus. "Oh, hello—what's this, now?"

He withdrew his gloved hands, covered with dust and soot, and there was a long thread-like item. It took Phyllida only a moment to recognize it as a delicate gold chain, and to realize that surely had been the cause of the strange, clinking, clattering sound in the hose.

She pulled out one of her handkerchiefs and held it open for Elton to place the necklace on it. That was when she saw the pendant dangling from the chain.

She used the edge of the handkerchief to rub away the soot, revealing a small flower.

A daisy.

And then all at once her little gray cells marshaled themselves and fell into order.

The little idea she'd tucked away surged right to the front of her mind.

She understood everything.

CHAPTER 20

Phyllida paused at the door of Mrs. Treacle's sitting room and listened. Sure enough, there were sounds of movement inside.

Obviously, Mrs. Treacle was no longer indisposed in her bed.

She knocked.

"Yes? What is it?"

Phyllida opened the door without invitation and stepped inside. "It looks as if you're feeling better, Mrs. Treacle," she said.

"Oh. Well, yes, I am. I thought I'd best finish up in here since I'm-I'm going to be leaving tomorrow." Mrs. Treacle gave her a half smile. She was sitting at her desk and there were a few straggling papers on it. Phyllida's attention went to the vase of daisies she'd noticed earlier . . . and she remembered there'd also been a daisy on the table next to Mrs. Treacle's bed.

She saw the papers on the desk—supplies lists, menus, vendor bills.

Any lingering doubts she might have had vanished.

"I won't keep you long, then, Elizabeth," Phyllida said with a friendly smile as she moved toward the desk. "I hope you don't mind if I address you by your first name. After all, we've gotten to know each other rather well over the last day."

"Oh, no . . . no, of course I don't mind." The other woman seemed confused. "What—what can I do for you? I'm rather busy, you see . . ."

"I only wanted to return this." Phyllida held up the gold chain, letting it dangle from her fingers. She'd cleaned it off and now the daisy pendant swung gently, glinting in the lamplight.

"Oh . . . why, thank you. Where did you find it?" Elizabeth reached for it and Phyllida allowed it to drop into her palm. "I-I didn't even realize I'd lost it." She reached for her throat where it should have been resting.

"In the sitting room. Next to the chair where Mr. Brixton was shot and killed." Phyllida allowed those words, like the pendant, to dangle there for a moment. "You said you didn't go more than a step into the room . . . but this was found right next to the chair."

"Oh. Well, I was rather confused and shocked—I must have stepped in further than I realized." Elizabeth gave her a wan smile.

"One would rather expect to be confused and shocked . . . after shooting a man at close range," Phyllida said pleasantly.

"What—what are you talking about?" Elizabeth's face had gone white.

"Daisy was your sister, wasn't she? Daisy Longfellow? You must have been devastated when she was killed—so needlessly—by a driver who'd been drinking and not paying any attention. Anyone would understand the grieving sister, the angry sibling . . . the protective and vengeful auntie."

"I—I don't know what you're talking about—"

"Your poor niece. First to have lost her father, then her mother. Thank goodness she still had you, her mother's sister. But you were enraged by the man who killed your sister. Understandably so. You wanted revenge."

Elizabeth had ceased her protests, settling back into the chair at the desk, her hands gripping the edge of its surface.

"How did you find out Mr. Wokesley had really been driving? That it was really he who was at fault, that it was *he* who'd killed your sister?" Phyllida asked.

"She . . . Daisy was the light of my life since we were little," Elizabeth said. Her voice caught, but she pushed on. "I was so happy when she married Daniel, and even happier for her when Dilly came along. They were such a happy family . . . and then Daniel died. It wasn't anyone's fault; he was sick.

"But it *was* someone's fault when D-Daisy got run down—*run down* like she was some—some *rodent* that ran into the street! How can you not see a person? How can someone just *drive* into someone?" Tears filled her eyes but her voice remained hard. "It was awful. You have no idea how awful it was. Poor Dilly . . ."

"Eustace Brimley took responsibility for the accident," Phyllida said, listening for the sounds of Constable Greensticks and Bradford in the hall. She'd left the door slightly ajar so they could hear, but had insisted they remain there until she finished speaking to Mrs. Treacle. She didn't think the woman would be as forthcoming in their presence. "How did you know it wasn't him?"

"He told me," Elizabeth said flatly. "I-I was so angry about what happened, I wanted revenge. I wanted to *fix* it. It took me a while to track him down and find him . . . and when I did, he was a pathetic mess. Drunk all the time, hardly aware of who he was or where he was. His wife even left him. I thought about doing away with him—and I think he wouldn't have minded it after all—but then he said something one day."

"You were with him?"

"Oh, yes." She gave a bitter laugh. "I got a job serving at the pub he liked to frequent. Half the time, the pub owner or one of the others had to bring him home after he closed. I even helped him one night. But he talked—or, really, just slurred and rambled nonsense. And then one day he said something—something about 'I didn't even do it, you know? He made me say it, but I didn't do it.' "

Phyllida nodded. "And so you found out more details."

"It wasn't difficult. He was hardly aware most of the time, and if you kept bringing him drinks, well . . ." She scoffed and spread her hands.

Although she was on a different trail, a sudden thought struck Phyllida. "Did you know he was going to jump off the bridge?"

"I suggested it," Elizabeth said with a hard smile as she clutched at the edge of the desk again. "I told him the only way he'd find peace would be to end it all. He must have listened to me. And now you'll have to do the same."

Phyllida didn't realize what she meant until Elizabeth lifted her hand. There was an ugly, familiar flash of metal there.

It had been a long while since someone had pointed a gun at Phyllida.

And it had not ended well.

CHAPTER 21

"NOW, *PHYLLIDA*—I HOPE YOU DON'T MIND ME CALLING YOU that—get up very slowly and quietly and lock the door. Do it now." Elizabeth Treacle's voice was hard and cold, not to mention far more assertive than it had ever been.

What concerned Phyllida even more was the manner in which the other woman held the Webley: She was clearly not used to doing so, which made the situation even more dangerous.

Cursing herself for being outmaneuvered—at least for the moment—Phyllida stood and did as she was directed. She didn't think Bradford or the constable could have heard Elizabeth's command, for she'd dropped her voice and spoken quietly.

"Now move that chair in front of it—yes, there we go. Shove the back of it under the knob—right, then. You really are quite an intelligent woman. I was a little worried when I learned about your reputation, you know. Apparently, my fears were well-founded. I had only hoped to be gone before you put it all together."

"What next?" Phyllida asked, looking around the room for a potential weapon. Her eyes lit on the letter opener near a corner of the desk. She swiftly averted her gaze.

"I had planned to leave tomorrow morning, but then Dr. Bhatt arrived and things changed. And now that you're here, I've an even better option. This way, if you please, Mrs. Bright. Don't make any noises or sudden moves . . . my finger is on the trigger, and as you've learned, I certainly won't miss such a close target."

She gestured with the slightly wobbly pistol to the door that led into the adjoining bedroom. "In there."

Phyllida bumped into the desk on her way past it but her fingers missed the letter opener. *Blast.* She didn't dare attempt it again for fear Elizabeth would notice. Instead, she preceded her captor into the bedroom and trusted some other option would present itself.

"Very good," Elizabeth said. "Now, we're going to do the same in here—lock the door, and push that chest of drawers over a bit in front of it so it won't open. That won't keep anyone out for long, but it will slow them down. And by then, I'll be long gone."

Phyllida didn't miss the fact that Elizabeth had said "I," not "we."

"Very well," she said when Phyllida had finished blocking the bedroom door. "Now, out we go, my dear Mrs. Bright. No one will realize we've gone for quite some time, I'm certain."

She gestured to the large window, which was set so low in the wall that it would be easy to climb out. "Oh, and you can carry that for me." She gestured to the valise sitting on the bed. "I'll need both of my hands, of course." She gestured with the gun, as if her point wasn't obvious enough.

Phyllida took up the bag. It wasn't terribly heavy, but it was going to be inconvenient to carry. She considered the idea of swinging it at Elizabeth like a cricket bat, but decided it likely wouldn't have as much an effect as the firearm in the other woman's hand.

"Out we go," Elizabeth said, using the gun to gesture toward the window.

Beyond the glass, everything was dark and dreary. The sun had set and night was falling, shrouded by lingering storm clouds. The world was limned with the glaze of drizzle, making everything appear even more muted. There wasn't a single star visible.

Phyllida hoped she could use that fact to her advantage.

She tossed the valise through and had climbed halfway out, straddling the sill in a maneuver she hadn't executed for years, when Elizabeth gave her a hard shove that sent her tumbling through the opening. By the time Phyllida—furious and cursing internally—had picked herself up from the soaking, muddy ground, Elizabeth was standing there, pistol in hand: effectively nixing any chance she might have had to escape or attack.

Phyllida had to admit the other woman was not quite the dunderhead she'd thought she was. But the way she was gesturing about with the pistol indicated she wasn't as comfortable with it as one would like. That made her more nervous than anything.

"Let's go," Elizabeth said, prodding her with the gun barrel. "And don't forget my luggage, dear Phyllida. Mrs. Wokesley won't miss those jewels for a while. She's far too busy grieving for her murdering husband. And when she does, she'll blame it on Mrs. Forrte."

Irritated and frustrated—not to mention wet, muddy, and cold in her summery rayon frock—Phyllida slung the strap of the valise up over her shoulder and began to trudge in the direction Elizabeth indicated.

She regretted her choice of footwear almost immediately. Normally, her shoes—which were neither dowdy and low-heeled nor equipped with completely impractical heels but fell somewhere in between—were quite appropriate for daily wear, despite Mr. Dobble's disapproval. However, in this case, the patent leather and two-inch heels were utterly unsuitable for making her way over wet, slippery, uneven ground.

She wasn't certain whether she ought to worry more about turning an ankle or getting shot, and she contemplated the usefulness of faking the former.

Despite her unfamiliarity with the grounds of Beecham House, it wasn't long before Phyllida realized they were heading in the general direction of the main driveway whilst remaining in the shadows of shrubs, trees, and gardens—and out of sight from any windows.

For the first time, Phyllida wished there was a canine creature about who might announce their escape route. Unfortunately, Myrtle seemed to be safely ensconced inside.

Without a torch, she couldn't see much but the faint sheen of wet on shadowy shapes. She could certainly feel the ice-cold drops that splattered over her head, nose, and shoulders every time she brushed against a shrub or ducked beneath a tree branch. More than once, a twig caught in her hair and pulled, spilling an icy cascade of pooled water all over her like a private little rainstorm.

The air had chilled significantly, and it smelled of loamy soil and wet grass as well as the faint tinge of charred wood—likely from the tree that had been struck by lightning and fell across the drive—along with smoke from the fireplaces inside.

Phyllida's bare arms were becoming numb, and her legs were cold and soaking beneath her hem and stockings. She'd certainly been cold and uncomfortable in the past—more times than she cared to remember—but for some reason, tonight her bones seemed to chill far more quickly. Admittedly, she wasn't as young as she used to be.

"How did you manage to get assigned as housekeeper for the Wokesleys?" she asked, deciding that a distraction for both of them might prove useful. She, at least, could divide her attention between three things: navigating the dark, wet grass; seeking an opportunity for escape; and confirming some of the details of Mrs. Treacle's crimes. She hoped her captor wasn't quite as versatile.

"Wasn't hard at all," said Elizabeth. "Once I learned Wokesley was the real driver, I was able to find out all sorts of things about them. Servants talk, as you know," she said with an ironic laugh. "I found out what agency they were using to hire a housekeeper, and managed to bribe my way into taking the position from the woman they'd assigned. You'd be surprised what people do for money."

"Hardly," Phyllida said, shuddering as a gust of wind blew more rain and cold onto her. "How did Mr. and Mrs. Wokesley not connect you to Daisy Longfellow?"

"Why would they? Neither attended the funeral service, so they'd never seen me—although Georges Brixton did. I didn't know who he was at the time. If he hadn't been there, I wouldn't have had to kill him, you see."

"He recognized you?"

"Not at first. But I could tell I seemed familiar to him, because he kept looking at me like he wanted to say something. And when I came into the sitting room today to—well, you know—he was just on the verge of remembering. It was a good thing I'd already decided to—er—attend to that."

Phyllida noticed that Elizabeth sounded more than a little out of breath. *Keep her talking, keep her distracted.*

"What was your plan when you came to Beecham House?" Phyllida asked.

"Why, I was going to avenge my sister of course," Elizabeth replied. "What do you think?"

"You'd already decided you were going to kill Clifton Wokesley," Phyllida said. "You were going to come here to do away with him."

"He deserved it," Elizabeth said. "I wasn't certain how I was going to go about doing it, I just knew I would. I thought I'd get used to their routine first and wait. I knew the opportunity would present itself. And then the Murder Game came up and I knew that somehow I had to take advantage of it. It was just too perfect." Her breathing had become slightly more labored.

"No one would suspect the housekeeper," Phyllida said, irony in her own voice now. "Especially when there were so many other people who had motives and means."

"Right. I helped that along, of course." Elizabeth gave a breathless chuckle. "I thought I'd give the infamous Mrs. Bright something to work with."

"The note in Sir Keller's coat pocket—you planted it, taking it from a letter actually written by Mrs. Wokesley. And the supposed thievery of her sapphire bracelet by Charity Forrte. You arranged that as well."

"It was rather brilliant, I thought. Gave you plenty of red herrings—that's what they're called, right?—to chase about—"

"All the while pretending to be distressed and confused and naïve," Phyllida said.

"It worked, didn't it?"

"Not at all. After all, here we are," Phyllida replied.

"Yes. Here we are. Me with a gun and you carrying my bag like a good soldier."

"Surely you're not intending to walk all the way into Listleigh," Phyllida said, suppressing a shiver. Her fingers and toes had lost all feeling. Her ears hurt from being so cold.

"Not at all. See—there it is. The tree that's fallen and blocked the drive from anyone leaving? Just beyond it is Dr. Bhatt's motorcar. We'll be taking that. You *can* drive a motor, can't you, Mrs. Bright?"

"Of course I can drive a motor. But surely you don't have the key."

"That's why it was such an unexpected—what's the word? Something unexpected and happy?"

"Serendipity."

"Right—serendipity that Dr. Bhatt arrived tonight. He always leaves the key in the motor. I heard him tell Anthony the other day when he needed to move the vehicle. I was going to insist that he accompany me—Dr. Bhatt, I meant to say. I had planned to ring for him to bring me some powders for my headache, and then he would have been the one climbing out the window and carrying my bag . . . but I'm quite enjoying your company, Phyllida. You're far more entertaining—and intelligent—than that staid foreigner. Do you know he didn't even find it amusing when I was distributing the small magnifying glasses at the Murder Game? I was the one who suggested them to the Wokesleys, after all."

Phyllida said nothing. She was too busy thinking about what a pickle this was. Once they were in the motor, there was a largely reduced chance that she would exit it alive.

And even less of a chance that someone might be able to follow them. She was going to have to think of something quickly.

"All right, in we go, Mrs. Bright," said Elizabeth cheerfully as they reached John's tiny roadster. "It will be nice to get out of the rain, now, won't it?"

This might have been an opportunity for Phyllida to slip away, but Elizabeth insisted her captive climb in on the passenger side and then slide over to the steering wheel so that she could follow whilst keeping the gun trained on her, however wobbly it was.

Phyllida settled into the seat, placing the valise on the bench between them. It was a small vehicle, so the space was crowded. Her hope that Elizabeth was wrong and that John had not left the key in the motor tonight was unfounded.

Conscious of the firearm still trained on her, she fitted in the key and turned it, which unlocked the ignition so the engine could be started by pressing a button. At least she didn't have to stand out in the rain to crank it. The motor roared to life and a faint light illuminated the dashboard dials. It took her a moment to find the windshield wiper.

"Let's go," Elizabeth said impatiently, brandishing the pistol.

That gave Phyllida an idea. If the woman wanted her to drive fast, she could drive fast. Perhaps another tree would be down or she'd accidentally lose control of the motor and slide off the road.

"How did you figure it out, then, Mrs. Bright?" Elizabeth asked. She seemed a trifle more relaxed now that they were in the motor and out of the rain. Phyllida understood that sentiment. There would be no chance of anyone following them in a vehicle tonight, and wherever they were going, they'd have a great head start.

Again, she didn't like her odds of this journey ending with her alive. And so she focused on how to improve those odds.

"I knew someone had to have known about the stiletto knife, so it had to be someone who'd been in the drawing room before. Surely you'd seen it many times over the last few months you were here," she said, accelerating a bit more than was strictly prudent as they navigated down the driveway. But Phyllida had driven injured soldiers on and near battlefields at great speed and over rough terrain. This was hardly as difficult, though very nearly as deadly. And the rain splattering the windshield didn't help the visibility.

"Right. Of course. But how did you settle on me, exactly?"

Phyllida concentrated on driving: rather fast and then suddenly braking to go slower, jerking to the left then swerving to the right in order to avoid puddles and downed limbs. This was the sort of motion that normally made her insides churn and her head hurt, and she hoped Elizabeth was also prone to such an affliction. Fortunately, the jolting and twisting turns didn't bother Phyllida nearly as much when she was behind the wheel.

"It was several things," she said, leaning forward to peer out into the rainy night, then pressing on the accelerator to cause the motor to jump forward. "First, you actually had the best opportunity since you admitted being the one to position the stage knife. I confess, even though I thought of you immediately, I rejected the idea for quite a while. I simply couldn't see a motive."

"And because you were too busy suspecting the others," Elizabeth said happily.

"That is quite true," Phyllida admitted as she braked, then accelerated again as they turned onto the main road. She sped up and slowed down over and over so their forward progress was jerky and unpleasant. "But the more I thought about the fact that your entire staff had been cleaning up broken teapots during the time of the murder, the more I began to wonder whether you'd made *certain* they'd be busy. And out of the way."

Elizabeth chuckled. "It wasn't difficult. I loosened the upper shelf in the cabinet where all the teapots were. I knew someone would bump into the cabinet coming around the corner—they did all the time. It would only take a little nudge . . . With everyone cleaning up the mess of three shelves of teapots, and Mrs.

Napoleon screeching about it, there was only me to bring the tea tray to the drawing room.

"Once I got there, I wasn't certain how I was going to do it, but when I suggested to Mr. Wokesley that I could set the stage knife for him, he agreed readily. I removed the stiletto from the cabinet, then put the stage knife in place . . .

"I was talking to him as I stabbed him. I told him exactly why I was doing it . . . It was over in a moment. And then I turned off the lights and left the drawing room. No one would suspect the housekeeper. Why would they? And everyone knew what a fiend he was about the theater and playing his role—even if it was a dead man. No one thought anything of it when they came in and he didn't move or speak."

"What about the snake? Did you arrange that as well?"

Elizabeth gave a little shudder. "I took an opportunity. I saw the thing when I went out this morning. It was curled up in the tall grass right next to the bucket I needed, next to the door. Gave me quite a start. But I found a rake and used it to scoop it up and toss it inside. I didn't care where it went after that, it was simply having it in the house that was important. I wasn't certain what benefit it would give, but I decided any upset in the household would be helpful. And when you arrived on the scene, it was even better."

"Quite." Phyllida was still accelerating and braking, and swerving from side to side without appearing obvious about it.

"I was rather impressed by how quickly you trapped the snake, Phyllida. And, to be fair, I was not acting when I was climbing on the stool to get away from it. But you still didn't *truly* suspect me, did you?"

"I was beginning to wonder. When I suggested we speak in your sitting room, your reaction seemed to be one of fear and concern. That surprised me, and suggested you might have something to hide. And then when I spoke to Mrs. Napoleon and she was ranting on about you—losing menus and tearing shopping lists and being generally inept . . . I really began to question whether it was possible you were somehow involved.

"But it wasn't until we found your necklace caught up in the vacuum machine that I realized you must have been nearer to Mr. Brixton in the sitting room than you'd suggested."

"That didn't mean I'd killed him," said Elizabeth. Was her voice sounding a bit strained? She was gripping the dashboard with her free hand and when Phyllida took a chance and glanced over, she saw her captor staring straight out of the windshield—a remedy Phyllida often employed herself when trying to keep from becoming sick during a tumultuous drive.

She hoped that meant her plan was beginning to work.

"No, it didn't mean you'd killed him. But then everything else fell into place and it *did* fit. The daisies on your desk and by your bed—and on the pendant. That didn't click for me until I learned the name of the young woman who'd been killed . . . and then everything began to make sense." Phyllida was displeased with how close she'd come to completely missing identifying the culprit. If the necklace hadn't been sucked up by the vacuum machine, she might never have put the pieces together.

Apparently, her little gray cells needed a serious talking-to.

"The fact that you'd been the one to position the stage knife was, as I mentioned, cause for question. But it was the missing cigar, and the scrap of paper Mr. Wokesley was holding—which was clearly from a dinner menu—that clinched it for me . . . and the fact that the planted red herrings were simply too convenient to be real."

Phyllida swerved again and this time the tires slipped and slid, causing Phyllida's own heart to surge into her throat as something inside the motorcar clunked and shifted audibly. She didn't want to end up with the roadster crashed into a tree, for that could be counterproductive to her plan to exit the vehicle alive and unharmed.

"Slow down," Elizabeth snapped. Her voice sounded thready. "You're making me ill besides."

Excellent. Just as she'd hoped.

"I'm only trying to keep from getting stuck in the mud. And I can't see very well." Phyllida eased up on the speed as directed, but she did not cease with the jerky driving and swerving. One didn't have to be traveling quickly to feel the effects of *mal de mer*—or, in this case, *mal de route.*

Elizabeth must have seen the flash of light ahead of them at the same time Phyllida did, for suddenly she said, "Don't get any ideas," and poked at her with the pistol.

Twin circles of light, clearly a vehicle coming from the direction of Listleigh, drew closer on the road ahead of them. Phyllida knew at once who it was.

Inspector Cork had finally arrived at Beecham House . . . only a full day late.

CHAPTER 22

PHYLLIDA CONSIDERED IGNORING ELIZABETH'S WARNING AND EITHER driving straight on toward Inspector Cork's motor, or causing a crash in front of him that would induce him to stop.

But any sudden move could trigger her captor's finger on the loosely held gun, and they were in a very close space. Phyllida was a sitting duck.

Aside from that, even if she succeeded in stopping the other motorcar while managing not to be shot, Phyllida wasn't confident the inspector would be able to grasp the tenuousness of the situation quickly enough to keep Elizabeth from taking rash action. The woman might not be a dunderhead, but she was the one who had the pistol.

So instead, she gritted her teeth and drove straighter and slower—but no less jerkily—down the road, leaving plenty of room for the vehicles to pass each other.

She assumed that once Inspector Cork arrived at Beecham House, it would be obvious to everyone that he'd passed her and Mrs. Treacle in Dr. Bhatt's roadster on the way in. Presumably, they would come after them.

So now, instead of driving too fast, she decided to find a way to delay her own travels in hopes that eventually the inspector and constable would catch up to them.

There was only one road into Listleigh with only a single turnoff that led to a more remote area of farmland. Chances were

Elizabeth intended for them to continue into the village and beyond. It would be simple for the inspector and constable to surmise the direction of their travel.

Nonetheless, as they passed Inspector Cork's motor, Phyllida wished with all her might that he would somehow sense danger and force them to stop.

That was, she knew, a lofty hope—and one that was quashed when the other vehicle sped past without even slowing down.

"That was a smart decision," Elizabeth said, still staring out the front window.

Phyllida declined to comment. She was intent on finding a way to delay them—or, preferably, extricate herself—without getting shot in the process. An idea had begun to form in her mind, inspired in part by Mrs. Treacle's orders before they'd left her rooms. And along with that, she was still hearing the sounds of something in the vehicle moving and shifting during her erratic driving.

This was, after all, a motor belonging to a doctor. Perhaps there was something inside that might be useful. She carefully began to feel around near the floor between the door and her seat where she'd heard the clunking. It was the location a person might stow an umbrella to be handy for exiting the vehicle, but surely John had used his brolly when walking up to Beecham House.

But there *was* something there. Long, smooth, slender . . . it took her a moment to realize it was a cane or a walking stick.

Not precisely the sort of helpful tool she'd hoped for . . . although Phyllida didn't know what she had actually hoped for. A tranquilizer? Her own gun (not that she'd want to use it; but it could be an excellent deterrent)?

Still, a cane would be at least some sort of weapon, should she need one.

"Are we going to the train station, then?" she asked, partly to distract Elizabeth and partly for her own edification.

"The train station? Where I could be seen?" Elizabeth scoffed, but it sounded weak.

Phyllida shrugged. "Seems the speediest way out of the village, considering that the road from London has been causing delays for two days now."

Her captor seemed unwilling to discuss further, and Phyllida had to believe she was feeling the effects of her driving.

Now was the time to step it up and put her half-formed plan into motion.

She swerved right, then left, hitting the brake and then the accelerator rather more violently than she intended. She felt rather than saw Elizabeth tense up and her breathing become a groaning sort of panting. The fingers of her free hand were still gripping the dashboard, and Phyllida could see, from the corner of her eye, that the hand holding the revolver was sagging on the valise between them. The barrel was still pointing in her direction, but not as strongly.

Now was the time to make her move.

The curve in the road to the right, with the large and convenient tree on her left was just there . . .

Holding her breath, she swerved wildly around another puddle to the right and heard Elizabeth moan, then slammed the gearshift up a notch and jabbed her foot onto the accelerator. The car leaped forward, slipping a little in the mud.

Her captor made a strange gurgling sound with which Phyllida was quite familiar, and she groaned, "Slow down, I say. I—"

But it was too late. Phyllida had slammed on the brakes and turned the wheel just as they came to the curve.

Since she was turning the wheel toward the left, the roadster did not follow the curve to the right. Instead, it rolled off the road into the grass, narrowly missing—precisely as Phyllida had planned—hitting the large tree.

She slammed on the brake and opened the door, rolling out onto the ground and grabbing the cane as she did so.

This time, her fingers didn't fail her. They closed around the slender wood and, still on the boggy ground, she slammed the door shut.

The sounds of Elizabeth's irate shout, followed by the report of a gunshot, had Phyllida moving quickly. She jammed the cane beneath the door handle of the little roadster and stuck the other end into the soft ground, effectively blocking it closed.

Because of where she'd stopped the motorcar—very close to the tree—Elizabeth Treacle was now trapped inside the vehicle. She couldn't open either door far enough to climb out. Phyllida was, for the moment anyway, safe.

Another gunshot shattered the glass window above Phyllida's head; she was relieved she was near the motor on the ground and not within view—or gunshot range. But it wouldn't be long before Elizabeth had cleared away enough glass to climb through, so Phyllida wasn't about to delay.

She turned and began to run down the road back in the direction of Beecham House. Her knees were jelly and her entire body so chilled she wasn't certain her limbs would even move . . . but they did. She was more hobbling than walking when she heard the sounds of shrieking—and yet another gunshot—behind her.

Damn and blast! That woman was nearly as persistent as Phyllida was.

CHAPTER 23

ELTON'S SHOULDER WAS SORE AND BRUISED, AND HE HAD VERY LITtle to show for it. Frustration and fear surged through him as he rammed the door once more.

Blimey, the doors at Beecham House were heavy. Solid wood with heavy metal hinges. The thing barely creaked in its moorings.

If only Bradford would help him attempt to break down the door into Mrs. Treacle's sitting room, instead of rushing off somewhere else, Elton might have better luck.

He *knew* Mrs. Bright was in danger. They all did—him and Bradford and the constable. The door had been locked, and even once a key had been located and the lock turned, the door still wouldn't open. Something seemed to be jamming it in place.

What if she was inside, lying unconscious or injured—he wouldn't even consider the possibility that she might be dead—and no one could get to her to help?

At least no one had heard a gunshot.

He rammed the door as hard as he could once more, cursing Bradford for disappearing as soon as they realized something was wrong. The constable wasn't any better—he'd stayed and, at Elton's insistence, launched himself at the door with him a full two times before giving up.

Elton felt his eyes sting with frustrated tears. What was he going to do?

"Mrs. Bright!" he called for what seemed like the hundredth time, banging the door with a sore and bruised fist.

"They went out through the window," said a voice behind him. "They've gone."

Elton whirled to see Bradford, his face set, his eyes dark with an expression he'd never seen on the bloke's face. Made him want to take a step back, but he didn't. "What do you mean gone? She's all right? Mrs. Bright?"

"They took the doctor's motorcar," replied Bradford before turning to head back down the hall. He was soaking wet and his coat and shirt were dirty as well. His dog, also wet, gave a little yip before bounding along after him.

Elton didn't pause to appreciate the fact that the bloke had come to tell him his efforts were both futile and unnecessary. He ran down the hall after him. "We have to go after them!"

Bradford cast a cold look over his shoulder and kept going. "Brilliant idea."

"What are we going to do?"

"We're going to move that blasted fallen tree, so let's go." Bradford was four strides ahead of him and out the door before Elton could respond.

To his surprise, someone had induced—or possibly threatened—both of the remaining male guests, as well as Mr. Trifle, Anthony, and Dr. Bhatt, to slog out into the rainy night. He suspected Bradford had been the one to do that, and his admiration for the man ticked up a bit. Reluctantly.

Seeing that toff Sir Keller with rain dripping off his hat standing at the ready to roll the tree trunk out of the way was a miracle—even if he was whingeing in those genteel accents of his. That Mr. Dudley-whosits chap didn't look like he'd be much help, but he was there as well, wearing gloves and a hat that was too big, and appearing utterly at sea.

Bradford was clearly in charge, a fact that annoyed Elton. He wished *he'd* been the one to realize the two women had left through the window, and that *he'd* been the one to herd everyone outside—even that hoity-toity Sir Keller.

"All right, let's move this. Everyone get in your place. Count of three, we're rolling it this way," Bradford said with a gesture. "Just enough to get the motor past."

Elton took his place next to Mr. Trifle and hoped the old man wouldn't drop dead from the effort. Dr. Bhatt was on the other side of him.

"One . . . two . . . three . . . *PUSH!*"

The tree moved and Bradford kept shouting at them to "push." At last, when even Elton was running out of strength, Bradford shouted, "Rest."

Elton stood there panting, wet, and now dirty from tree bark. They'd made some progress, he saw, and there was only a bit more to go.

Eagerly, and with some desperation—they were almost there and time was wasting—he shouted, "Again! Let's do it again! Everyone! We've almost done it!"

"Right, then," said Bradford from the other end of the tree. "Count of three. One . . . two . . . three . . . *PUSH!*"

It was more difficult this time. Elton felt Mr. Trifle hardly moving next to him and suspected the man wasn't putting any effort into the task. The log was shifting, but it was taking too long. He was about to shout at the bloke to put his damned weight into it when someone cried out, "Look!"

Elton looked up and saw the light coming down the drive. "Is it them?" he cried, jumping back from the log.

"It's the inspector," grunted Bradford, giving one last mighty heave of the tree trunk. Elton dashed past him toward the headlights, uncaring for his own safety, and heard the chauffeur add, "About bloody time. Myrtle, let's go!"

By the time Inspector Cork climbed out of his motorcar, Elton and the constable were there to tell him everything. Bradford ignored them, sliding into the Daimler he'd driven from Mallowan Hall and starting it up.

"Where are you going?" Elton demanded, leaving the constable to finish filling in the inspector. "I'm coming with you."

"Then get in and quit nattering about it," Bradford snapped.

"You can't fit past the tr—" Elton's warning was choked off

when the Daimler leapt forward, skimming so close to the edge of the downed tree he almost heard it scrape. But it didn't.

Myrtle, the twenty-pound mass of damp, curling fur who'd somehow launched herself onto Elton's lap, panted and stared through the windshield, blocking his view, as the motor tore down the driveway. Elton glanced back to see two more headlights behind them—the constable and inspector were right on their tail.

"Hurry!" he said needlessly. He wanted to find Mrs. Bright first.

Bradford didn't deign to reply, but he drove as fast as Elton could have wished, all the while keeping control of the wheel around puddles, fallen branches, and bumps in the road. Even when the tires slipped and slid, he remained in control.

"There! What's that?" Elton cried when he saw movement in the darkness along the edge of the road. The headlights shined ahead, illuminating two figures. "It's them! Stop!" He was already fumbling with the door latch.

Bradford muttered something but slammed on the brakes. The motor's rear swung back and forth like a fish's tail in the mud.

Elton tumbled out the door, nearly taking a header into the mud. He caught himself in time and looked up to find Mrs. Bright and Mrs. Treacle standing at the side of the road.

Both women were wet and bedraggled, covered with mud and dirt. It appeared Mrs. Bright was holding a *gun* in her hand, training it expertly on the other housekeeper. Elton sighed inside. What a woman.

"Mrs. Bright!" Elton shouted, splattering through the mud toward them. "Mrs. Bright!" Then, overwhelmed with relief that she seemed whole and uninjured, he forgot himself and cried, "*Phyllida!*" as she turned in his direction.

The headlights clearly revealed the frosty, reproachful look she leveled at him, and Elton slapped to a halt. She was bedraggled and muddy and wet, shivering and utterly disheveled, and she still looked down at him like a queen.

"Mrs. Bright, I mean," he said.

She lifted a repressive eyebrow then turned away.

"*Gor*," he whispered to himself, suddenly even more enamored. She really was a hell of a woman.

CHAPTER 24

PHYLLIDA WAS SO COLD, NOT TO MENTION SORE AND ACHY, SHE COULD barely form words.

"Here," she said, carefully handing the pistol to Bradford while fighting to keep her teeth from chattering. "Do be careful. Th-there should be one bullet left."

She was only vaguely aware of the presence of the constable and inspector, who'd scrambled out of a second motorcar a moment ago.

"All right, then, Mrs. Bright?" said Bradford. The next thing she knew, something warm and heavy was settling around her shoulders. It was large and enveloping, and smelled of damp wool and mechanical grease. Bradford's coat, of course, and she was immensely grateful for it. She curled her fingers into its warmth and pulled it close around the front of her.

"Yes, of course," she replied, wobbly but unwilling to show it.

"Let's have a seat here, won't you, Mrs. Bright," Bradford said.

The next thing she knew, he was steering her toward the Daimler and then helping her into the passenger seat.

She sat gratefully, enjoying the sensation of security, warmth, and inactivity—and the absence of people peppering her with inane questions: *What happened, are you hurt, how did you get away, why are you wet/dirty/your hair such a mess, how did you get the gun . . .* and so on. She heard conversations happening around her, outside of the motorcar, and was grateful not to be required to participate. She ignored all of it, closing her eyes and enjoying the warmth slowly creeping over her body.

That is, until something heavy and fluffy landed in her lap.

Phyllida's eyes shot open and she stifled a gasp. She was face-to-face with Myrtle, who, for once, wasn't panting or barking or attempting to swipe its tongue over one of her extremities or *sniff* at her. Instead, the beast was merely looking at her, its head tilted to one side. If Phyllida didn't know better, she might have thought it had an expression of concern in those beady dark eyes.

She should shove the creature off her lap—she'd get hair all over her, not to mention the smell of dog, and she was in far too close proximity to those sharp teeth and lolling pink tongue—but the beast was delightfully *warm*, drat it. Warmer than Bradford's coat. Its welcome heat was seeping into Phyllida's middle and the tops of her legs, and before she quite realized what she was doing, she'd wrapped her arms around the fluffy monster.

Warmth. And . . . not precisely comfort, but something soothing. The creature heaved a sigh, and Phyllida braced herself for barking, licking, and whatever other nuisance the creature could demonstrate . . . but then Myrtle simply settled into a curled-up position on her lap, not unlike the way Stilton would circle herself onto a pillow.

When Phyllida heard voices approaching where she sat in the motor, she thought about pushing the dog off her lap . . . but she simply couldn't do it, damn the consequences.

"Mrs. Bright." Inspector Cork, a familiar sight with his freckled face, untrimmed mustache, and protruding eyes, stood at the open door next to her. He was younger than Constable Greensticks, but certainly more experienced in investigative procedures. "Is everything all right, then?"

"Quite so," she said, but with a little less crispness than usual. "Elizabeth Treacle killed Clifton Wokesley and Georges Brixton. And she abducted me as well. I trust you can handle it from here." She was proud of herself for not pointing out his tardiness in arriving at the investigation. It was, after all, most likely not his fault.

"Erm . . . yes, of course. But she claims you held her at gunpoint after striking her with a tree branch."

"Of course I did. However else was I to keep her under control? That was after she nearly blew my head off in the motorcar. And then she was flailing about, discharging it randomly whilst she was chasing me through the woods. That woman has very little concept of the proper grip on a firearm.

"And that reminds me, along with murder and abduction, she should also be charged with destruction of property, for she shot out the windows of Dr. Bhatt's roadster."

"I see," said Inspector Cork.

He might have insisted on continuing with his interrogation, but Bradford appeared at that moment. "I'm taking Mrs. Bright back to Mallowan Hall," he said, closing the door of the Daimler next to her. "If you need further information, Inspector, you can come up tomorrow. But it seems rather clear you've got your culprit there in the back of your motor."

Without waiting for a response, Bradford climbed into the driver's seat and started the engine. He was driving off down the road before Phyllida realized he'd left Elton behind.

She opened her mouth to tell him, then closed it. The valet's absence would make for a far more relaxing ride.

After a moment, she said, "Thank you."

"For what, exactly, are you thanking me, Mrs. Bright?" he asked. "I can think of any number of things—rescuing you after your foolish stunt, providing a coat—not to mention a dog—for warmth, leaving that lovestruck valet behind . . . good heavens, did he really call you Phyllida?"

Phyllida almost laughed, but she managed to hold it in, for the first part of his list penetrated her thoughts. "Foolish stunt? What precisely are you talking about? And you did *not* rescue me. I had things well in hand by the time you showed up. It did take you long enough to do so," she added tartly.

"I was referring to you allowing yourself to be abducted at gunpoint," he said. "A foolish stunt, insisting that you speak with Mrs. Treacle alone in her office and then being taken at gunpoint.

That was a grave miscalculation—something I would not have expected from the likes of you, Mrs. Bright."

"I certainly didn't expect her to have the pistol in her *desk*," Phyllida retorted. "Why would she have it *there*, when she was packing everything in her bedchamber—and when she'd taken to bed in there as well? I was fully aware that she was likely still in possession of Mr. Brixton's firearm, but I did not imagine she'd be shortsighted enough to keep it in her desk, where anyone might find it."

"As I said . . . it was a grave and unfortunate miscalculation on your part."

She ignored him, staring out the window. She was finally beginning to notice sensation in her toes, and it was almost painful, the prickling racing up and down her calves. Suddenly, she realized she was not only merely tolerating Myrtle on her lap, but had continued to hold and even gently stroke the beast on the top of its head. Clearly, being nearly frozen to death after traipsing through the woods had affected her judgment.

"Did you really hit her with a branch?" Bradford asked.

"I certainly did. The way she was flailing about with that pistol was dangerous, but since her grip was loose and clumsy, I knew it would be no difficulty to knock it out of her hand. Which is what I did.

"After escaping from the motor, I pretended to fall with a twisted ankle. And when she came close enough, I swung up and at her with the branch, surprising her and knocking the gun from her hand. She got off a shot just as the gun fell—I suspect there's a bullet in one of those oaks. And I daresay she'll have a bruise on her cheek and arm for a week or two."

"I see. Well, that was rather enterprising of you, Mrs. Bright."

"Oh, cease with the *Mrs. Bright* business. You might just as well call me Phyllida. Everyone else has done tonight," she said crossly.

He made a sound that might have been a laugh, but said nothing further until, "Whoever was driving your escape vehicle certainly seemed to be having a time of it."

"What do you mean?" she asked, patting Myrtle as the beast

shifted and rearranged herself on her lap. The creature was surprisingly soft, and she hadn't tried to lick Phyllida even once. The warmth and weight in her lap continued to be curiously comforting.

"The tracks all over the road. When I first saw them, I was under the impression someone had very little idea how to operate a motorcar." He glanced at her.

"*I* was driving, and I certainly know how to operate a motorcar," she said. "I was driving erratically in order to disorient my kidnapper."

"You might have hit a tree," he pointed out.

"Of course I wasn't going to hit a tree. In fact, I navigated the vehicle so it slid right up *next* to one, effectively trapping my kidnapper inside the motor." She went on to explain in detail how she'd turned the tables on Mrs. Treacle, blocking her in the motor and then dashing off when she began shooting about wildly. "Unfortunately, she managed to drag herself out of the window and follow me. Drat!" she said suddenly.

"Did you forget something, Mrs. Bright?"

"That's another charge Inspector Cork can bring against her—jewelry theft. She has some of Mrs. Wokesley's jewels in her valise in the motorcar."

"You can tell him all about it tomorrow," he said in a soothing voice. "That is, unless you've caught your death of a cold and are prostrate in bed."

"My death of a cold? Why, I've never been sick a day in my life," Phyllida said.

And then she sneezed.

CHAPTER 25

"Come now, Mrs. Bright. Doctor's orders," said Agatha Christie Mallowan with a smile. She set a steaming cup of something next to Phyllida. "We can't have our housekeeper and detective laid up for very long."

"I'm not laid up at all," Phyllida griped. "And you shouldn't be waiting on me."

She really didn't need all the commotion. She had a bit of a head cold—complete with sniffles and red-tipped nose, thanks to Elizabeth Treacle and her rainy-night abduction—but it was hardly anything to fuss over.

And *everyone* was fussing.

The maids kept coming by to re-tuck the blanket around her feet or shoulders, or to see if she wanted tea, toast, soup, or honey for her throat (which wasn't sore, only scratchy).

The footmen kept stoking up the fire so hot Phyllida was forced to shrug out of the blanket—and then had to suffer being re-tucked back in whenever one of the maids came in.

Elton had brought a bouquet of roses and dahlias under the guise of an offering from Amsi, but Phyllida suspected it had been his idea and not the gardener's. She'd chosen not to comment, but merely looked at him with a mild version of Bright's Glare of Death—or BGD, as, she was well aware, the staff referred to it.

Elton had fled the parlor, the tips of his ears tinged red.

Even Mr. Dobble had poked his bony nose into the room to inform her that Bradford had returned with the vacuum machine from Beecham House—which was really only an excuse to check on her.

Perhaps he was hoping she actually was on her deathbed.

All the commotion was mortifying. And annoying.

Agatha had arrived home with Mr. Max late this morning. She'd insisted Phyllida come out of her office—where she'd been perfectly fine, writing out check draughts and making up menus in between sneezes and sniffles—and sit in the front parlor near the fireplace, which immediately put her at the mercy of the over-attentive staff.

Agatha was the one who insisted her housekeeper and friend wrap herself in a warm blanket.

She also insisted Phyllida soak her bare feet in a tub of warm water whilst doing so, but Phyllida drew the line at that nonsense . . . though in exchange, she'd had to agree to drink whatever this concoction was that John Bhatt had prescribed.

"Drink it anyway," Agatha said, pulling up her own chair. "I need you to have your full strength and wits about you so you can fill me in on everything."

"You've heard most of it already. Surely Bradford told you all about it in on the ride from the train station," Phyllida said, doing her best not to sound sniffly and plugged up. Drat it. She hadn't lied when she told Bradford she'd never been sick a day in her life—and here she was.

It was too blasted bad she couldn't blame her stuffed-up nose and sneezes on Myrtle's proximity in the motorcar, but she hadn't been near the beast since last night and, if anything, things had gotten worse since then.

And to top it off, Stilton and Rye had refused to even look at her once they got a whiff of canine all over their mistress. She could only imagine what they were plotting for revenge.

"So it was the housekeeper—not the butler," Mr. Max said jovially, coming into the parlor. "Have you done one like that yet, Agatha? But more importantly, how *are* you feeling, Phyllida, dear?" He took a seat on the sofa next to his wife.

"I'm fine," Phyllida replied firmly, attempting once again to extricate herself from the cloying blanket.

"I haven't written it yet," Agatha replied to her husband, "but I do have a plan for a counterfeit butler to do the deed." She smiled wickedly. "No one at the dinner party recognizes him because they don't look at the person who serves them. But I've already done one with a housekeeper who doesn't actually exist."

Mr. Max raised his eyebrows and smiled. "Well, that ought to turn people on their heads. Perhaps even more than Roger Ackroyd." He looked at Phyllida. "I'm relieved you're uninjured. You could have come away with something much worse than a head cold, being trapped in a motorcar with a firearm and an angry woman."

"If you had seen the way she was flailing about with that pistol . . ." Phyllida allowed her voice to trail off because she thought she was going to sneeze, and she didn't want to give anyone any more ammunition for getting her feet soaking in a tub.

Imagine the staff seeing her with her *bare feet* in a steaming tub. Good heavens—the BGD would lose all of its effectiveness.

"Drink up, Phyllida," Agatha said, pushing the cup closer to her.

Phyllida picked it up and sniffed. "What is it?"

"Dr. Bhatt wrote it down—he knew you'd insist on knowing," said Agatha, sliding her glasses into place. "He would have come in to speak to you himself, but someone is having a baby out past Rareacre Road. Anyhow, it's hot water—or hot tea, he writes, would do as well—with honey, apple cider vinegar, lemon juice, capsicum, and ginger."

"Good heavens." Phyllida eyeballed the contents of the cup. She could smell the spiciness from a distance. It didn't appeal in the least. But she trusted Dr. Bhatt's remedies. After all, hadn't he helped Bradford with his shell shock?

She lifted the cup, took a sip, and her eyes went wide. It was hot, spicy—*very* spicy—pungent, and, yet, somehow soothing. She took another drink and it wasn't as shocking this time. In fact, it *almost* tasted good. And she could almost feel her sinuses clearing up again. The scratchiness in her throat eased.

She was just finishing the last of it when Bradford strolled in. It was rather unusual to see him in the parlor or even anywhere but outside or in the servants' dining room. He wasn't wearing a hat or gloves, but for once, he did have on a proper coat.

"Oh, there you are, Bradford," said Agatha, as if she'd been expecting him. "And Myrtle too! Why, hello there, young lady."

Phyllida sat bolt upright in her chair. *Myrtle was in the house?*

Bradford was looking at her with a barely concealed grin, for he was extremely aware of her consternation.

Mrs. Agatha and Mr. Max loved dogs, and Agatha had had her beloved Peter, a wire-haired terrier, for nearly ten years. He was likely curled up in his bed in her office—a habit Phyllida appreciated. One hardly knew when Peter was about. He didn't bark, lick, jump, or sniff.

The same could not be said for Myrtle.

Having received her due attention from Mrs. Agatha and Mr. Max, Myrtle trotted over to Phyllida.

They looked at each other: Myrtle with eager, beady black eyes, tongue safely tucked away, nose glistening with interest . . . and Phyllida down at it with her most intense glare of death.

She couldn't control a ripple of terror. If Stilton and Rye found out about this canine invasion, they'd *never* forgive her.

When Myrtle turned away, Phyllida was satisfied the beast had received her message. But instead of bounding off to get into trouble, the creature turned around like a watchwork and plopped itself down onto Phyllida's slippered feet.

A choked sound had her glaring at Bradford, but Agatha was smiling in approval, so Phyllida said nothing. Having the beast sitting on her feet was marginally better than soaking them in a tub, she reasoned.

"Now, then, as you said, Bradford filled us in on most of the story." Agatha looked over the rim of her own cup of tea, eyes dancing. "All of it made sense once you found the necklace and realized it was related to Daisy, Mrs. Treacle's sister, was it? But I still don't quite know what it was about the missing cigar that sent you down the correct path."

"Right, then. You see, the Murder Game script had a description of the dead body—Mr. Wokesley as Mr. Bowington—and he was supposed to be holding a cigar in his right hand.

"Not only did Mrs. Treacle not know about the cigar, to place it for the prop, she also lost a piece of paper from her pocket. Mrs. Napoleon—the cook—was always going on about how Mrs. Treacle kept losing supplies lists and menus, and tearing papers, and spilling things . . .

"I suspect what happened was that whilst she was kneeling next to Mr. Wokesley and stabbing him, during her exertions a paper was dislodged from her pocket. Mr. Wokesley struggled a bit—only for a moment, but it was enough that his fingers curled around the paper. When Mrs. Treacle finished her—her task, she must have seen the paper in his hand. She tore it away, likely not realizing there was a scrap still in his hand.

"Mrs. Rollingbroke is the one who found the paper. She thought it was part of the Murder Game, and brought it to me. I immediately recognized it as a scrap of a menu or shopping list—which was something only a servant or possibly the woman of the household might have on their person.

"That was curious, and for a time, I wondered if Mrs. Wokesley had found a way to murder her husband. Despite her show of grief—which I believed was genuine—I certainly suspected her. She had plenty of motive, and a possibly willing partner in Sir Keller."

"But it was Mrs. Treacle all along," said Agatha.

"Indeed. She'd waited for several months for the perfect opportunity. When it came, she acted with cool confidence and took a great risk. Unfortunately for her, I was on the scene—she must have had quite the bad moment when she realized I was in attendance. She made a point of introducing herself to me and coming across as a helpless, naïve city woman doing her best to run a household in the country. I very nearly fell for it," Phyllida said, studiously ignoring Bradford's raised eyebrows of skepticism. She ignored him. *He'd* certainly fallen for the helpless female routine.

"Well done again, Phyllida," Agatha said. "You and your exploits have certainly inspired me for a number of story ideas. Not to mention saved some lives, and brought some killers to justice."

"I certainly wouldn't have been able to do it without your investigative work in London," Phyllida replied.

"Speaking of London," Agatha said with a smile. "We're going to be going there for an extended stay. There's going to be a stage play of another one of my stories in the West End, for *Black Coffee* has been a decent success."

"That's *wonderful*," Phyllida said with great enthusiasm and pride. She knew that Agatha had wanted to be a playwright long before she started writing prose stories. "I'm so very happy for you."

"Indeed. And the even better news is that we are taking the household—or most of it—with us. Including you."

Phyllida froze. To London? "Oh, I see," she replied. "Why that's . . . that should be quite . . . interesting."

"Exactly," replied Agatha, beaming. "You'll need to heal up from that cold quickly now, so you can get everything together and decide who will be staying and who will be going."

Phyllida nodded mutely. The only thing that could make going to London worthwhile would be leaving Myrtle and Mr. Dobble at Mallowan Hall.

Surely she could find a way to make that happen.

After all, she *was* Phyllida Bright.

Dr. Bhatt's Most Excellent Cold Remedy

For use as soon as one begins to feel the symptoms of a head cold.

Mix the following with approximately 12 oz hot water or any sort of soothing hot tea:

- 1–2 tablespoons honey (preferably raw honey)
- 1 tablespoon apple cider vinegar
- 4–7 very thin slices of fresh ginger; it is not necessary to peel it. If you don't have fresh ginger on hand, ground ginger or galangal can be substituted at one half tablespoon
- 1 tablespoon lemon juice
- 1 teaspoon ground cayenne or capsicum; more if you can tolerate it

Drink as often as you like, preferably tucked up by a warm fire or under a cozy blanket with an excellent book to read. Mrs. Bright is also of the mind that a cat or two sitting on one's lap during this time is also extremely pleasant as well as being conducive to speedy recovery.

Read on for a special preview of the next Phyllida Bright whodunit from Colleen Cambridge . . .

MURDER TAKES THE STAGE

In this delightful historical mystery, Phyllida Bright—amateur sleuth and Agatha Christie's esteemed housekeeper—discovers a killer stalking the stages of London's illustrious theaters.

Housekeeper Phyllida Bright is quite in her element at Mallowan Hall, the charming English manor that she keeps in tip-top shape. By contrast, the bustling metropolis of London, where her famed employer Agatha Christie has temporarily relocated, leaves Phyllida a bit out of her depth. Not only must she grapple with a limited staff, but Phyllida also has to rein in a temperamental French cook who has the looks of Hercule Poirot, but none of the charm.

When a man named Archibald Allston is found dead in an armchair onstage at the Adelphia Theater, first impressions are that he died of natural causes. But the very next day, the unlucky actor playing Benvolio at the Belmont Theater is found with his head bashed in. And when a third victim turns up, this time with double-C initials, the fatal pattern is impossible to ignore.

With panic erupting among theater folk—a superstitious bunch at the best of times—Phyllida steps up to help with the investigation. The murderer's M.O. may be easy to read, but can Phyllida uncover the killer's identity before the final curtain falls on another victim?

"Yes, the clue—it is always the clue that attracts you, Hastings. Alas that [the killer] did not smoke the cigarette and leave the ash, and then step in it with a shoe that has nails of a curious pattern. No—he is not so obliging."

—Agatha Christie, *The ABC Murders*

CHAPTER 1

PHYLLIDA BRIGHT'S FEELINGS ABOUT LONDON WERE EXCEEDINGLY complicated.

On the one hand, a person couldn't deny that the city was exciting, energetic, eclectic, and enchanting (alliteration notwithstanding). One could buy anything, do anything, eat anything, and experience nearly anything one wished.

And Phyllida had done her share of all of that during previous residencies and visits. Her lips curved at the memory of a particular night at the Savoy.

Then the smile faded.

There were other not nearly so pleasant memories that accompanied her return to London, hence the mixed emotions with which she struggled. Phyllida didn't care for having such mixed emotions. It was much easier when things were straightforward. When she knew how she ought to feel and react.

But there was no help for it. She was here in London and, as was her nature, would make the best of it—all the while hoping to avoid disaster.

The ancient and yet shockingly modern city was a far cry from sleepy little Listleigh in Devon—although with the number of murders that had recently occurred in the small village where Phyllida managed the home of Agatha Christie and her husband, Max Mallowan, Phyllida began to wonder if the village might, in fact, be in competition for London on a murder-by-square-foot basis.

It was a shame, to be honest, that the vibrancy of the city and all of its civilized offerings were overshadowed by the fact that Phyllida did not want to be here.

In fact, probably the only person in the world who could have convinced her to return to London was Agatha, with whom Phyllida had been close friends since they worked in a hospital together at the beginning of the Great War. Phyllida's employment as housekeeper of Mallowan Hall suited both women perfectly, for a variety of excellent reasons.

But not only was Phyllida in London—against her better judgment—she was also currently crammed in the front of a Daimler with a panting, pricked-ear, *hot* bundle of wildly curling canine fur squashed on the seat between her leg and the motorcar's door.

She still wasn't quite certain how Myrtle had managed maneuvering herself into such an ungainly position, the impertinent little beast.

"All right there, Mrs. Bright?" said Bradford, the Mallowans' chauffeur and alleged master of Myrtle, the panting and—ugh!—*drooling* creature that had unconcernedly wedged itself next to Phyllida.

Phyllida's only response was to give Bradford a withering look. He knew quite well how she felt about that mop of fur—despite the fact that she and Myrtle had begun to come to an uneasy and reluctant truce.

Uneasy and reluctant on Phyllida's part, at least. Myrtle seemed delighted that she could insinuate herself into Phyllida's proximity whenever the latter was otherwise distracted by events such as nearly being squashed by a motorcar, being shot at by a crazed killer during a thunderstorm, or taking advantage of her debilitated condition when nursing a head cold.

"Right, then, Myrts, we're nearly there," said Bradford cheerily. He was actually wearing a cap today—of an unobjectionable blue tweed—along with an equally suitable coat and leather driving gloves. "Then you won't be so quashed up, now, will you? Can't be comfortable riding like that, can it?"

Phyllida resisted the urge to make a tart comment, for Bradford would certainly be delighted by such a reaction from her.

But his easy, almost crooning voice had an unexpected benefit, for Myrtle spun toward her master (Phyllida had noted more than once that it was questionable as to who was the master or mistress of whom in that relationship) and bounded across Phyllida's lap into that of Bradford's. Although the beast left a smattering of hair in its wake and faint paw impressions on her skirt, it nonetheless removed its warm, panting, drooling self from her proximity and, for that, Phyllida couldn't help but be appreciative.

"I'm not feeling very well, Mrs. Bright," came a weak voice from the back seat. "All this stopping and starting and turning and the motor's rumbling . . ."

Phyllida glanced at Bradford, then turned her attention to Molly, the head kitchen maid from Mallowan Hall, who was crammed in the rear with two other staff members from back home and two suitcases.

Fortunately none of the staff members in the rear were Mr. Dobble, the butler.

*Un*fortunately, Phyllida knew the butler had already arrived at the townhouse Agatha and Mr. Max were letting during this visit to London. Incidentally, contributing to her mixed feelings about returning to London were the unwanted presences of both Dobble and Myrtle. She had hoped to leave both of them back in Listleigh.

It was risky for Phyllida herself to turn to look toward the back of the motorcar, for she, too, occasionally suffered from what her beloved and gloriously mustachioed Hercule Poirot would have called *mal de motor* . . . sickness from riding in an automobile.

"We're nearly there, Molly, but if you need Mr. Bradford to stop so you can get some air, please say so. I'm certain he'd rather have a delay than clean up a mess in the back seat."

"Ohhh, Mrs. Bright, me too," moaned Opal, the scullery maid who'd recently come to work at Mallowan Hall. "I ain't never been in a motorcar this long before, mu—" The young girl stopped abruptly and swallowed hard. Her face appeared green from over the top of the battered suitcase in her lap.

That was not good. And they'd only been in the motor for the fifteen minutes it took to travel from the Paddington train station to Mayfair.

"We're turning onto the street now, ladies," said Bradford calmly. Phyllida noticed he'd taken the turn slowly and carefully and was easing the motor along as smoothly as possible.

She breathed a quiet sigh of relief. Although sitting in the front seat normally kept her from becoming ill, there had been an awful lot of stops and starts due to traffic and her own stomach had become quite aware of that, along with the incessant vibration of the vehicle. There had never been this much traffic in the city. And the construction! There were new buildings going up everywhere, and old ones being taken down, then replaced with more new ones. Phyllida had hardly recognized Fleet Street for all the changes.

Along with the construction was the even foggier, denser air than Phyllida remembered. Coal smoke poured from multiple chimneys on every block, motorcar exhaust streamed from tailpipes, and all of that was tucked down onto the streets by the thick fog that often shrouded London and had given the likes of Dickens, Stoker, and Conan Doyle the perfect setting for mysterious happenings.

"And here we are," said Bradford, stopping the Daimler in front of a charming brick townhouse across from a small, circular park. Said park was one of the reasons that had been cited during the discussion over whether Myrtle would travel to London. Phyllida had argued that the beast would have nowhere to gambol about, as was its wont, but Agatha had cheerily pointed out the proximity of the park—and the fact that her own wire-haired terrier, Peter, would also be joining them.

Agatha and Phyllida had many things in common, but a love (or lack thereof) for canines was not one of them.

The vehicle had barely come to a halt when Molly and Opal

were tumbling from the back seat, gulping for air that was only marginally fresher than inside the motor, being clogged with coal smoke and gasoline fumes as it was.

Before Phyllida had the chance to reach for her own door, Elton—the third staff member who'd traveled up on the train with them—was there, swinging it open with a flourish.

"Here we are, Mrs. Bright," he said, offering a hand to help her climb out.

"Thank you, Elton."

He blushed beneath his cap when her gloved hand touched his larger one.

She had never mentioned the occasion on which he'd forgotten himself in a moment of extreme emotion and inappropriately referred to her as "Phyllida," and she doubted she ever would. However, she did nothing to encourage his harmless but sometimes inconvenient infatuation with her.

Still, there were benefits to having one of the male servants, who were all under the purview of Mr. Dobble, being particularly attentive to her disposition. There were occasions when Phyllida found it necessary to circumvent—gently and unobtrusively, of course—the butler's idiosyncrasies.

Phyllida quickly and efficiently extricated her hand from Elton's grip and, ignoring Bradford's amused grin at her predicament, turned to appraise the home that would be her residence for the next several weeks.

Agatha and Mr. Max intended to purchase a residence in London, but they hadn't yet done so. Instead, they'd leased this four-story red brick townhome, known as Gantry House, in order to "try out" the neighborhood. They were in town and had brought part of their own staff while one of Agatha's plays was in the early stages of being produced in the West End.

Phyllida wasn't certain why it had been so important for *her* to come to London—Agatha had no need of her expertise when it came to dealing with the West End and all of its, quite literal, dramatics. And surely she could have hired a housekeeper from an agency in London—after all, Mr. Dobble would be there to guide and provide an excessive attention to detail.

But Phyllida supposed she'd been asked to come simply because Agatha preferred to have her own trustworthy staff around, particularly since she and Mr. Max might be doing occasional entertaining and because, like Phyllida, Agatha shied away from any publicity.

However, the townhouse on Matilda Street had no need of such an extensive staff as was in place at Mallowan Hall, so Phyllida and Mr. Dobble had been required to come to an agreement on which maids and footmen should come with.

Mrs. Puffley, the cook, had been left back in Listleigh to manage the skeleton staff, for the Mallowans had decided to engage a cook via the leasing agency whilst in London, and to keep on the single maid-of-all-work that was already at the house. Elton, who was officially Mr. Max's valet but who hardly ever performed those specific duties, had been elected to come to London due to his versatility in service and familiarity with the city.

For obvious reasons, Phyllida preferred to hire her own staff, and she was mildly apprehensive about a cook who was known as Monsieur Chardonnay. With this in mind, and comfortable in the fact that Elton and Bradford would see to the luggage as well as to Molly and Opal's welfare, Phyllida took herself around to the servants' entrance at the rear of the townhouse, where, she knew, she would find the kitchen.

The sooner she met this Monsieur Chardonnay, the better.

The passageway between the Mallowans' townhouse and its neighbor was hardly wide enough for a tow-cart to pass through without scraping the brick on either side. But in the back of the was a tiny, charming courtyard spilling with delphinium, daisies, dahlias, and more. A massive climbing rosebush burst with blood-red blooms, which cast a heady scent through the air. Phyllida noted with approval that a small ornate iron table with two matching chairs was situated beneath a graceful willow—which had been trimmed up to provide a cozy shaded nook beneath its curtain-like fronds—and that the flagstone walkways were swept free of leaves, sticks, and dirt.

The heavy back door—which, for obvious reasons, Phyllida preferred to use—was open to the fresh (such as it was) air, and as she approached the threshold, she was assailed by the delicious scent of roasting meat.

Given this cause for optimism, Phyllida opened the light screen that kept out unwanted critters and stepped into the house. She found herself in a tiny entrance that branched off into a handkerchief-sized scullery with a stone basin to the right and a minuscule pantry to the left. Straight ahead was a short corridor that ended at the kitchen.

Phyllida paused at the threshold of the kitchen, unnoticed by a maid, who was sitting at the table peeling boiled eggs. The only other occupant of the room was the cook, who was standing with his back to the doorway as he vigorously stirred something on the stove.

Her first impression was of a small but well-appointed room with a worktable that doubled as a compact dining table for the staff. She stepped inside and the maid looked up, then quickly rose to her feet.

"Ma'am," she said, giving a polite curtsy. Her voice was closer to that of a tenor than a soprano.

"Good morning," said Phyllida. "I'm Mrs. Bright, and I am the housekeeper while Mr. and Mrs. Mallowan are in residence."

The man turned from the stove and Phyllida nearly gasped aloud.

He was hardly any taller than she, with an egg-shaped head whose smoothly combed hair, which glistened slightly with pomade, had just begun to thin at the top. Beneath his immaculately white apron was a gently rounded stomach that, should he be viewed from the side, would give his figure the shape of a shallow half moon. His eyes were sharp and hazel-green, with thick, dark brows above them. But those brows—which were neatly trimmed—were nothing compared to the luxurious mustache that sat, perfectly combed, trimmed, waxed, and groomed, above a pair of frowning lips.

It was Hercule Poirot.

Phyllida blinked, then collected herself.

Of course it wasn't Hercule Poirot, but she had never seen a person who looked more like Agatha's famed detective than the chef, who was currently glowering at her.

"What ees thees?" he snapped in a very un-Poirot like way, but with a thick French accent. "Who do you say you are? Why are you in my kitchen?"

Phyllida pulled herself together (how mortifying to have been struck dumb at the man's appearance, however momentary it had been) and said smoothly, "I am Mrs. Bright, the housekeeper. As you come extremely highly-recommended" —that was an exaggeration, but she was not above using a bit of flattery to erase the sourness from his expression— "I am quite looking forward to working with you, Monsieur Chardonnay. Something smells delicious." She smiled and waited for him to plunge into a description of whatever mouthwatering dish he was making.

Instead, he made an irritated sound that might even have been a French curse word and turned sharply back to the stove.

Had Phyllida been a lesser sort of woman, she might have flushed with embarrassment or anger at such a set-down by a lower staff member—and in front of an even *lower* staff member. Instead, she kept her expression blank and lifted a brow at the maid, who, surprisingly, had seemed unconcerned by such a rude display.

"And what is your name?" she said to the maid, who'd remained standing.

"Billie, ma'am. If it pleases you, I mean to say."

Billie was the name Phyllida had been given for the maid-of-all-work, so that made perfect sense. And since neither she nor the Mallowans were in the habit of insisting the servants change their names in order to make it easier for them to remember, she nodded. "It is a pleasure to meet you, Billie."

Phyllida automatically scanned the young woman's appearance and found no fault. Billie's coarse, dark hair had been scraped back into a bun at the nape of her neck and she wore a proper lace coronet cap over a uniform of steel gray covered by an apron. She had a slender, bony figure and delicate features that seemed at odds with her low-register voice. She was taller than Phyllida—who wasn't all that tall herself—but it was notable, especially since her feet were as large as Elton's. Phyllida couldn't help but wonder if the poor girl tripped over them often.

"You will soon meet Molly and Opal, the kitchen maids I've brought with me from Mr. and Mrs. Mallowan's home in Devon. They will assist Monsieur Chardonnay, whilst you will assist Ginny with the public rooms on the first floor and the bedrooms above. It will only be Mr. and Mrs. Mallowan to stay, so the other bedchambers can be kept closed up." She watched the cook as she spoke, and noted the way his shoulders jerked, indicating that he'd heard—and was displeased.

That was too bad for him. He might resemble, at first glance, Hercule Poirot, but the cook certainly didn't possess any of the Belgian detective's civility. At least it appeared he could cook.

"Yes, ma'am," replied Billie with another curtsy. "I've met Ginny. And Mr. Dobble, ma'am."

Phyllida inclined her head. She had expected that, for Ginny and Dobble traveled from Devon earlier today via motorcar with Bradford (and Myrtle—which was why Phyllida had elected to take the train from Listleigh). The chauffeur had been back and forth from Paddington to pick up Agatha and Mr. Max, as well as Phyllida and the others.

Phyllida heard the sounds of the others from the motorcar approaching from the rear door. Ignoring Monsieur Chardonnay, she introduced the kitchen maids to Billie and asked her to show Molly and Opal to their quarters.

That left her alone in the kitchen with the cook. He had not turned from whatever he was doing at the stove, and Phyllida suspected that whatever it was, the task didn't require the unflagging devotion he demonstrated.

"I would like to see the menus you have planned for the next two days, Monsieur Chardonnay," she said briskly. "I'll be in the housekeeper's office in thirty minutes and will expect you to be prompt." She kept her voice friendly, but with that subtle edge that would have made any of her staff members sit up and take notice. "Molly and Opal will be here to take over any tasks in your absence."

She breezed from the kitchen without waiting for a response. A metallic clatter followed by a violent *thunk* followed her exit, and she stifled a smile.

Her working relationship with Monsieur Chardonnay was going to be quite stimulating.